PRAISE FOR *PLAYING SAINT*

"Bartels' debut novel is a page-turner from the very beginning. His excellent use of foreshadowing and his glimpses into the past create a story that readers can't put down. In the vein of Ted Dekker and Frank Peretti, Bartels weaves the supernatural into the natural in ways that are gripping and realistic, adding a shocking surprise that will leave readers stunned. ★★★★½"

> **—*RT BOOK REVIEWS***

"This is an exciting step forward for thrillers. *Playing Saint* grapples with complex themes as well as being richly suspenseful. Highly recommended."

> **—CLIFF GRAHAM**, BESTSELLING AUTHOR OF
> *DAY OF WAR* AND *SHADOW OF THE MOUNTAIN: EXODUS*

"A thought-provoking exploration into the power of faith and the reality of evil. Filled with memorable characters and tight writing, Playing Saint is an impressive debut from an author to watch."

> **—STEVEN JAMES**, BESTSELLING AUTHOR OF *PLACEBO*
> AND *THE QUEEN*

"Bartels holds readers' interest in this intrigue-filled thriller . . . Saint's character is particularly well developed as he changes from a self-absorbed TV personality into a true man of faith. This book will be enjoyed by those who love a mystery combined with supernatural elements."

> **—*LIBRARY JOURNAL***

PRAISE FOR *THE LAST CON*

"Bartels interweaves the story of an ex-grifter trying to go straight with the historic tale of a man and a group seeking ultimate power. I was quickly drawn in and kept turning pages."

—**RICHARD L. MABRY,** BESTSELLING AUTHOR OF *MIRACLE DRUG* AND *CODE BLUE*

"A tightly written page turner!"

—**CARRIE STUART PARK,** AWARD-WINNING AUTHOR OF *THE BONES WILL SPEAK* AND *A CRY FROM THE DUST*

"Rich in legend, deceit and thievery, along-side a story of family, grace and forgiveness. The struggle between doing what is right and doing what you want resonates. The characters are both lovable and frustrating, and always highly relatable. And of course, Bartels throws in a twist at the end that will leave readers stunned."

—*RT BOOK REVIEWS*

"With the same intense intrigue as *The DaVinci Code*, The Last Con is a novel that spans the globe and leaves the reader hungry for the next twist in the story. From Italy to Detroit and even France, Zachary Bartels' latest suspense includes artifacts, museums, security guards all wrapped up a puzzle that no one will see the answer to until it is far too late. Dig into Fletcher's story and get lost in the details of *The Last Con*."

—*CBA RETAILERS & RESOURCES*

"Zachary Bartels is the King of Snark, the Emperor of Twists, the Caesar of the Page-Turning Story. *The Last Con* had me neglecting housework, ignoring emails, and staying up well past my bedtime. I simply had to find out how the whole thing would play out. Life is short, reading time is precious. Still, *The Last Con* is a novel I plan to read again."

—**SUSIE FINKBEINER**, AUTHOR OF *A TRAIL OF CRUMBS* AND *A CUP OF DUST*

A Novel

ZACHARY BARTELS

GUT CHECK PRESS
Lansing, Michigan • Jackson, Tennessee

Clinch

Published by Gut Check Press,
P.O. Box 10003
Lansing, Michigan 48901
www.gutcheckpress.com

Published in association with KD Enterprises.

This content was first presented as part of an online digital audio program entitled "Clinch: A Podcast of Fiction and Not-Fiction." www.clinchpodcast.com Also available in ebook format.

Publisher's Note: This novel is a work of fiction. Names, places, and incidents are either products of the author's own imagination or used fictitiously. Any similarity between characters in this book and real people, living or dead, is purely coincidental.

For All the Listeners

of All my Podcasts

"'My father was a great man, of course,' says Christopher Branding. 'But he wasn't around a lot. Definitely practiced what he preached. I mean, ask my brother; the guy missed everything from T-ball games to my MBA graduation. I'm proud of him for all he accomplished, but, ya know . . . I would rather have had my dad around.'"

LaForest, Brent. "Prominent Author Leaves Mixed Legacy." *Christianity in View,* vol 31, no. 8.

Trenton Marsh was staring down the barrel of a gun.

He'd heard that expression countless times, and always assumed it was just that—a figure of speech. But at this angle, with the sun behind him, he could see clearly past the muzzle of the chrome-plated pistol, down the pipe, almost to the chamber where he knew a bullet was waiting at the head of a coiled spring for the order to end his life. Just the twitch of a finger and it would all be over.

The thought brought on a thick mental fatigue, dimming his vision around the edges, making his legs feel like Playdoh. But with it came a strange sense of control, as if this face-to-face encounter with his own impending death had somehow granted him the ability to slow time. Not that it was much help, since his own movements slowed with it.

Still, it gave him the illusion of a few extra seconds in which to weigh his options. He cranked his head and looked down at the thirty-foot drop waiting behind him, should he jump or catch a bullet. The roiling spray and subwoofer resonance of the water dared him to take his chances.

Trent had been coming up to Picture Falls Christian Camp each summer since he was six, but this was the closest look he'd gotten at the actual waterfall, having only admired it from a comfortable distance before. Down below, the crashing water continually filled a large round basin. Were he to take the plunge—even if he somehow avoided breaking both his legs—he'd bob around down there for a while in the churning waters, trying to make his way to where the basin emptied into the river. He'd be an easy target. Fish in a barrel. He'd heard that expression many times too. Always seemed like an odd phrase, until now.

He glanced down at the familiar weapon in his hands. It felt strangely heavy and clumsy. Between his submerged feet, the continual rivulet of blood rolled down from the injured man crumpled

1

in a heap a few yards upriver, his once-handsome face clamped down hard in a grotesque sock puppet of pain.

Trenton forced his eyes back to the man with the gun, completing the circle.

Oh, he realized. *He's talking to me.*

The man's crisp voice emerged from the ambient soundscape around them as time returned to normal.

"I'm serious, kid. Step away from the edge and give me what I asked for! I won't tell you again!"

For just an instant, uninvited and inconvenient, an image of Zoe's face flashed into Trenton's mind and he wondered if she was safe. Then it was gone, self-interest crowding it out. He looked back at the waterfall one more time, swallowing hard. There was no denying it: that was his only route of escape.

"Don't even think about it!" the man warned. "I've got a hair-trigger here. You jump and I'll put three bullets in you before gravity takes hold."

A thick scream of pain filled the air. And then there was more blood in the water. Lots more. It was a momentary distraction and, he was certain, the only chance he would get.

Trenton took a deep breath and made his move.

TEN DAYS EARLIER

CHAPTER ONE
"I PROMISE, IT WON'T KILL YOU."

"If your life is ordinary, you're not living like Jesus. *Ordinary* doesn't honor God or bring you closer to him. Only when you're teetering on the edge—in real danger of losing it all and radically trusting God alone to keep you from falling—are you trusting God at all."

—*Insane Faith: A Guide to Extreme Christianity for the Truly Faithful*
by Stephen Branding (Grand Rapids: Charter House, 2016), p. 104

It was a stupid idea; he could see that now. Jason had tried to warn him, but to be fair, Jason was not exactly an authority on the fairer sex and how to impress them. In fact, while he frequently claimed to be Trent's devoted "wingman," it often seemed more like he was out to sabotage his friend's love life, such as it was, for his own amusement.

Trenton drew back another arrow and let it fly toward the target. Bullseye. He smirked and glanced at Zoe, who was honed in on her phone and hadn't seen this third perfect shot. It was unlikely she'd seen any of them. So much for impressing her with his skill and precision.

It was Friday, the last full day of camp, and Trenton was feeling the urgency. He and Zoe had been doing this little dance all week, smiling at each other across the dining hall, flirty comments and raised eyebrows in the program center, pairing up for team-building activities. But time was almost up and Trenton had yet to make a decisive move. It had to happen today if he wanted to leave here with something substantial between the two of them—something he could build on. If he failed in this, he just knew she'd be wearing some jock's football jersey before school even started, leaving Trenton a fading memory.

Here at camp he had the advantage of forced close quarters, a limited pool of competing young bachelors, and chance after chance to make a lasting connection. Here it didn't matter that, while almost seventeen, Trenton lacked a car or even a driver's license. It didn't hurt him that he wasn't part of the popular crowd at school or in-demand with the ladies. It was a different world here. Just like travelers will fork over eighteen bucks for a turkey sandwich at the airport because, well, what choice do you have?, the rules were different at camp. And he'd squandered six precious days of airport pricing, waiting for his courage to kick in.

Zoe was interested in him; there was no doubt about that. She and her small entourage had spent the previous afternoon's free time with Trent and Jason, swimming in the camp's small inland lake. She looked amazing in her one-piece swimsuit, but Trenton was more than a bit self-conscious about his lack of muscle definition. His was, at most, a two-pack—if he counted the slight vertical indentation bifurcating his abdomen—and he'd seen her eyes wander to some of the more muscular campers as they splashed and swam.

That wouldn't do today. He needed to wow her. And so, not being much of an athlete and having no experience with older girls, he turned to the one activity at which he excelled: archery. He had been Wilderness Scouts state champion two years in a row. Trenton knew it was a dorky distinction, but he thought he could leverage it. Zoe's three minions had objected to the idea until she admitted it might be fun. Then they were suddenly game.

Stopping at the recreation building for equipment, they'd encountered a who's-who of the camp's misfits and outcasts, all collecting bows and arrows to try and kill the rest of the afternoon. Apparently the more socially awkward campers had finished their bracelets and keychains in the craft shop and were now, en masse, taking up Trent's sport. This was not a good sign.

"These are really good arrows," Trent said, pulling them from the center of the target, actually boring himself. "They used to have these crummy blunt-tipped practice arrows here," he continued, unable to stop himself from filling the silence, "but they replaced them last year. These fly a littler truer."

"Huh," Zoe answered, without looking up from her phone. Campers weren't supposed to have phones out of their cabins, but most of the permanent staff seemed to assume Zoe was a volunteer counselor, so no one challenged her.

Trent deflated a bit. This had played out better in his mind. By this point, he should be standing close behind Zoe, helping her with her stance and aim, able to take in the lavender smell of her hair. She'd giggle and defer to his knowledge of such a chivalrous art. Maybe there would be a joke or two about Cupid and his bow. Or not. Trent couldn't decide if that was clever or just stupid. It didn't matter now, though, as Zoe had failed to hit the target twice and then summarily given up.

"So, yeah," Trenton droned, bringing the arrows back to the line, "good arrows can mean the difference between hitting center ring and, like, the third or fourth ring."

Beyond her, Jason mouthed the word "Smooth," and gave him a sarcastic thumbs-up, which was oddly fitting as Jason had played bass in a garage band called Sarcastic Thumbs Up for the past couple years. Zoe snickered at something on her device's screen.

"Who are you texting?" Ashley asked. "That college guy?"

Zoe shook her head. "I'm reading an essay in the *New Yorker*."

Trenton felt a full-on panic setting in, like he was literally watching his chances with this girl fade away like the photo of Marty McFly. And this girl wasn't even a *girl*. She was a bona fide woman, reading thinky magazines on her phone, referencing foreign films and Indie bands, and in every way standing out from her fellow campers. Even the act of blowing Trent off while he tried so desperately to impress her somehow made her that much more attractive.

He was gawking at her again, taken aback anew by her beauty. She was petite, but not scrawny, with fair skin and hair the color of dark coffee, pulled up in a high bun. While the rest of the girls were dressed in shorts and T-shirts, Zoe wore a knee-length red dress that flared out at the bottom, fastened with a comically large belt. It looked to Trenton like the kind of dress an inventor would put on a Japanese robot, to make it look less like a robot. But somehow it worked perfectly on her. She'd have been at home in a fashion magazine, but somehow didn't seem out of place in the woods of Michigan's Upper Peninsula either.

Sensing his eyes boring into her, Zoe looked up from her phone. Trenton forced his mouth shut and the world's worst wingman let out a snicker. An awkward moment came and went, taking its time.

"This is lame," Trenton finally admitted.

"Ya think?" Ashley said, through a heavy sneer.

"Well, what do you guys want to do?"

"I'm going to change before dinner," announced Sadie, who had worn no fewer than fifteen different outfits over the course of the week.

"We'll come with you," Zoe said, offering a small conciliatory wave at Trenton. "Sorry, Trent. Sit by me at session?"

"Definitely."

The girls were gone in a matter of seconds, leaving a pile of bows and arrows behind—a vivid reminder that Cupid had yet to land a shot.

* * *

After a dinner of oddly wet chicken nuggets, doled out by the dozen from metal tubs, the teens were corralled into the program center for the evening's "session". Trent was still in the boys' washroom, double-checking his hair and delivering a pep-talk to the man in the mirror, when the large iron bell rang, announcing the start of session. He ran down to the old pine building and into the back of the auditorium, jostling past pool tables, his eyes scanning the crowd of eighty or so high school students and a dozen adult counselors.

He spied Zoe and then Jason, the two flanking a very inviting empty seat. Jason was fiddling with something on his lap while Zoe spoke in hushed tones with her friends. As Trenton slipped in between them, it occurred to him that, in all their time together as a group this week, he had not seen Zoe and Jason exchange more than a few words. In fact, it was hard to imagine them having an actual conversation. Zoe was so mature and sophisticated, something that challenged Trent to find his own serious side, to start accomplishing things that mattered.

Jason, on the other hand, acted pretty much like he had a few years ago when they were in middle school, never taking anything seriously, appealing to Trent's latent adolescent—the part of him that laughed at dirty limericks and fart jokes. Jason had supplied a running commentary of observations and punchlines through all of the week's sessions, providing all the more incentive for Trenton to distance himself from his friend by crowding the Zoe side of his chair.

A youth pastor with an acoustic guitar and a tenuous if over-confident grasp on the latest slang, called them all to their feet to "kick out the jams for Jesus." He howled through a few praise and worship songs, during which Jason made a show of clapping on the off-beat. Zoe closed her eyes and sang along with passion. Unable to carry a tune, Trenton mumbled the lyrics and tried to keep his eyes and mind off of her and on the Almighty, who was ostensibly receiving their words of devotion. After a few too many songs, they all sat down and Dean, the camp director, took the makeshift stage, planted beneath a row of oversized dayglo letters spelling out the words, "INSANE FAITH."

"Have a seat, have a seat," he said. The campers retrieved their Bibles from their chairs and settled in. Trenton found himself suddenly aware of his *Radical Teenz Study Bible*, well-loved and largely held together by packing tape. He knew it backwards and forwards and it had been an invaluable help to him over the years, especially through his mother's sickness and the months following her death. But it was a kids' item, emblazoned with bright colors and a zany font. To his right, Jason had the same Bible, albeit showing far less wear. They had received them as gifts from their church upon entering sixth grade. Glancing at Zoe's simple leather-bound volume, he made the decision to upgrade to something more grown-up upon arriving back home.

"Folks, this is our last night together," Dean said in a raspy half-whisper. "That's sad, but it's not, am I right?" No one seemed to know if he was right. "Now, before we get into the Word, I want to ask a new friend of mine to come up and share a little announcement. His name is Mike Van Buren and I'm ecstatic about what he's doing here at Picture Falls. You see, when I was about your age, we had this awesome program called Youth Leadership Boot Camp. It was a chance for the future leaders of the church to get some hands-on training, do some short-term missions projects, and get really serious about our faith. Goes perfectly with our theme this year." He gestured at the huge letters above his head.

"Sadly, that program bit the dust the year after I graduated high school and it's been lying dormant for . . . well, I won't tell you how many years." He laughed. No else did. "Anyway, Mike came to me a few weeks ago to ask about the prospect of re-launching Youth Leadership Boot Camp and I'm excited to say, we're doing it! Mike?"

An energetic man in his mid-thirties bounded onto the stage, somehow drawing a good deal of applause by his very presence. His red hair was close cropped and a couple of tattoos spilled out from under his UnderArmor shirt, onto his biceps.

"Thanks, Dean," he said. "Before I even get started, let me just say: I know this is last minute, but we didn't want to wait another whole year before relaunching this vital program. It's too important. So here's my spiel: If you want to leave *ordinary* behind and take your faith to the next level, I mean really crank it up, I want you to consider stepping up to the challenge. Your counselors are handing out some information right now. Read it and pray about it. If you want in, we're kicking this thing off with a three-day retreat right here at Picture Falls. It starts a week from Monday. Just ten days from now. Again, I know it's short notice. But who doesn't want more time up at camp? Anyway, I promise: it won't kill you. If you have any questions, I'll be back here tomorrow for the closing program. I'd love to talk to you and your parents about this."

"You guys, hold up," Jason called as they filed out of the program center. Trenton pretended not to hear him and picked up his pace, recognizing the tone and the look in his friend's eye, which betrayed mischief of some kind. Trenton was in no mood for it. He was on borrowed time.

"Guys," he said again. "Zoe."

She stopped and turned to face him. "Yes?"

He looked around furtively before saying, "We were thinking, let's all blow off campfire tonight and climb the Devil's Tail."

Trenton shot him a look. There was no *we* here. How obnoxious.

"The Devil's what?" Zoe asked.

Jason gaped. "You don't know about—?" He turned to Trenton. "Dude, she doesn't know about the Devil's Tail!"

"She just moved here from Vermont. It's her first time up here. Why would she know about it?"

Jason laughed. "Oh, you're gonna love it! It's this trail that starts behind the nurse's cabin and goes all the way up the hill, past the waterfall and then back around and comes out by the lake. Campers used to hike it all the time, but it's off-limits now."

"Is it dangerous or something?" Zoe asked.

"Not if you're with someone who knows the trail."

Trenton opened his mouth to shoot the idea down, but realized it was actually pretty solid. Campfire was a raucous communal time, capped with a short devotion and followed by a parade of tooth-brushing and lights out. Zoe had first reached over and interlaced her fingers with his at Wednesday's campfire and he liked that prospect, but it would certainly not permit any real one-on-one conversation.

"I don't know," Ashley said. "Hiking? That sounds kind of dreadful."

"Then don't come," Zoe said evenly, not even looking at her. "I think it sounds great. I'm going to go change. We can meet behind the nurse's cabin right after the bell rings."

"I'll change too," Sadie said.

* * *

"Dude, you are so *in*," Jason whispered as they waited in the darkness behind the nurse's cabin for the girls to arrive. "Seriously, she is so hot and so into you. You need to take her to the old camp!"

"Just shut up," Trenton chided.

"Camp Makeout. Do it!"

11

Camp Mukwa was a dilapidated Methodist camp, no longer used and, like the Devil's Tail, off limits to Picture Falls campers. It was known colloquially as Camp Makeout, as it was an infamous site for clandestine meetings among campers of the opposite sex.

"You scared?" Jason jeered, more accusation than question.

"No. I just— Why would I take her to the old camp?"

"What's the old camp?" Zoe asked, appearing silently and seemingly out of thin air, wearing a long black sweater and leggings.

"Whuh! You a ninja?" Jason exclaimed, trying to cover his embarrassment. "How long were you, um . . . "

Trenton shot him a lethal look. "The old Methodist camp. It's about a half mile beyond the boys' cabins in the woods. It's just sort of a quiet place people go to . . . talk. Are the others coming or is it just us?"

"They're right behind me."

As the six of them began their ascent of the Devil's Tail, Zoe took Trenton's hand, her quick steps making it difficult for him to keep up. Her three friends followed in a line, struggling to remain about a step and a half behind her, like royal attendants.

"Why did they designate this off-limits?" Zoe asked when Trenton suggested they stop to admire the view of the lake over the tree line. The view was okay, but what he really wanted was a few minutes of rest.

Jason answered from the back of the procession. "It's kind of our fault. Me and Trent."

"No it's not," Trenton said.

"Yes, it is. Let me tell the story."

"I really don't think they want to hear—"

"Oh, this sounds good," Ashley interjected. The others agreed, even Anna who rarely said anything.

"It's not even a story," Trenton warned.

"It's a legend," Jason assured, plopping down on a thick, bench-like root. "The very year they outlawed climbing this hill, Trent and I were hiking the Devil's Tail. You're going to find out soon that the way up is kind of steep, but the way down is nuts. And it's really sandy, so you have to sort of lurch from tree to tree to keep from tumbling down. But me and Trent were young and dumb back then and as we near the top, we start daring each other to run down. Being super-macho seventh graders ,we both decide to do it. Now, I'm faster than him, so—"

"Oh give me a break!"

"I totally am! Why else would I have been in front of you? But even though I'm faster, I was keeping it tight, ya know? Like I didn't want to get going too fast and hit a tree and die like that hippy singer guy. But Big T here, he wants to pass me, so he just starts running as fast as he can and he completely loses all control. And for some reason—and I've completely forgiven him for this—he comes up behind me and decides to stop himself by grabbing a hold of me!

"So he basically tackles me and I hit the ground, and we're going so fast that he basically starts riding me down the trail like a toboggan through the sand!"

The girls were all laughing, even Zoe. Trenton willed his friend to quit while they were ahead.

"And so the two of us are just flying down the trail. We must have gone more than halfway down before we finally hit a root or a rock or something and come to a stop. We're both crying like little kids. We're all cut up and bruised and dirty and everything. I mean, more me than him because I was directly on the ground, but we're both looking bad. And my hair's all full of his tears and snot."

"Okay, Jason," Trent said. "That's probably—"

"So anyway, we're both sobbing and all ripped up and bleeding when we come limping into camp. And everyone's like, 'Did you get attacked by a bear or what?' And we told them what happened. And the next year, on the very first day, they announced that no one was allowed to climb the trail without an adult chaperone."

Trenton fumed silently. Of all the stories he could tell, why choose one that painted him as a crying little boy?

Ashley floated over to Jason's side. "You poor thing," she said.

Jason milked it for all it was worth. Of course he could somehow come out on top even after that story. "It took a few years of therapy—

you know, physical, occupational, spiritual—but I eventually moved past it. I don't know about Trent though. Shell of a man, this guy."

Zoe began climbing again and they all followed suit. "You guys have been friends for a long time, then?" she said.

"All our lives," Jason answered, "since we were babies. Until this traitor left me."

"What do you mean?" Ashley asked, still stuck to his side.

"Let's just say Zoe's not the only one whose family moved far from home this summer."

"Far from home?" Trent objected. "The parsonage is like six blocks from your house."

"But you used to be *right next door*, man."

"What's a parsonage?" Sadie asked.

"It's a house, owned by a church, where the minister lives," Zoe said. "But I thought you said your dad was a police officer?"

"He's actually both," Trenton answered. "Kind of in process of transitioning from cop to pastor."

"That's a strange move. What brought that on?" She pulled herself up over a large root spilling across the path.

"*Insane Faith*, actually. My dad was in a study group that read it. Then he led another group in our house. Then he decided he had to give up his career and become a pastor. So now he's a seminary student and the chief of police and the pastor of the local church, all at the same time. I don't see him too much."

Zoe squeezed his hand. "Sorry."

They all climbed quietly for a while until Ashley broke the silence. "So, Jason, do you have a girlfriend?"

"You know, it's funny you should ask. Because I actually don't. Completely available over here."

"Interesting," she answered.

"Where do you call home, Ashley?" he asked.

"Cadillac."

"Huh. Not too far from us."

"What about you, Trenton?" Ashley asked.

"I'm from Clinch Rock."

"No, I mean do you have a girlfriend?"

Before he could answer, Jason said, "No girlfriend, but my boy has a stalker! Her name's Judith and she *looooves* him."

"She's not a stalker." Trenton wished his friend would trip and fall back down to the head of the trail. "She's just a friend."

"Don't believe it. And she's a little nuts. I mean, she's a good friend of mine and she's sort of cute in a weird, stalkery way, but don't cross her."

"What kind of name is Judith?" Sadie sneered. "Is she an old lady?"

"No, she's in our grade," Jason said, "but not from our planet. Zoe, you just moved to Clinch Rock, right? You'll probably run into her. She's the only girl on the wrestling team."

"Oh no," Ashley laughed. "Your stalker's a wrestler?"

"She doesn't wrestle anymore," Trenton mumbled.

"Right, right," Jason said, "she got kicked off for being too violent or something."

"Guys, can we please not talk about Judith? She's my friend and she's a good person and she's not a stalker."

Jason bit down a smile. "No, but she could totally—"

"Drop it," Zoe commanded. Jason obeyed.

They trudged on a bit further before Trenton held up a hand and whispered, "Stop a second. Listen."

"What is that?" Sadie asked.

"Picture Falls."

Zoe squinted into the darkness, looking for the source of the sound.

Trenton shook his head. "It's a ways up the slope. You can't see it. But in the daytime, it's gorgeous." She wrapped her hand around Trent's arm and leaned her head on his shoulder. He felt himself lift an inch off the ground and said, "There's another trail that branches off from here and goes up to the brink, but it's kind of overgrown. I've never hiked it."

They stood there, enjoying the sound for a couple minutes until Jason started *entertaining* again. Then they began their descent, down the steep and sandy second half of the Devil's Tail. Trent went first, from tree to tree, crisscrossing. Then Zoe came, landing in his arms each time. He had to admit, he owed Jason a big one for this idea.

In fact, he was thinking that this night could not possibly be going better as they left the trail and headed out onto the beach. That's when Zoe said, "You guys go on ahead. Trenton's going to show me the old camp."

CHAPTER TWO
"HUNGRY LIKE THE WOLF"

"If you're not taking risks, you're not living. If you're not living, you're dead. If you're dead, quit taking up space."

—*Insane Faith: A Guide to Extreme Christianity for the Truly Faithful* by Stephen Branding, p. xii

When he was a little boy, Trenton's mother had promised him that one day he'd meet a special young lady who would make him feel butterflies in his stomach. But as he walked toward the old camp, hand in hand with Zoe, it felt more like a rabid ferret. He knew that Zoe had lived in Europe for a year before moving to the ultra-progressive world of New England, where she had lived for another year before moving to the town where time stands still. She was older than him by at least two years and plenty worldly. All of this made Trent wonder about her motives in accompanying him to the old camp.

"What did you say they call this place?" she asked.

"Um, Camp Mukwa."

"Mukwa? What does that mean?"

"It's Ojibwa for 'bear.'"

"Fascinating." She shined the light of her phone around, illuminating the bare foundations of three buildings, complete with chimneys, and one mostly-intact edifice. "This reminds me of the lumber camp north of Clinch Rock."

"You've been to the lumber camp?" Trenton asked.

"We actually own it. My father and I are overseeing its restoration, along with some other properties in town. It's actually why we moved there. I should bring you out and show you our progress. It's actually pretty impressive."

"Sounds like a date. Or . . . you know . . . whatever."

"It's a date," she said, stepping close to him. He could feel her breath on his neck. "Trenton, I wanted us to have some time alone so I could make a proposition."

"Oh . . . kay."

She reached into the pocket of her sweater and withdrew a folded piece of paper. "Look, I'm really excited that you and I will be going to the same school this year. I know you're a junior so we probably won't have any classes together, but I'm hoping we'll see an awful lot of each other. How does that sound?"

"So good. Really great," Trent replied, chiding himself for coming off like a moron. He was concentrating so hard on hearing her over the pounding of his own heart that he had very little mental power left for talking.

"We've been so busy since the move that I haven't had a chance to meet anyone my own age. I'm glad I got to know you before school starts. But I want us to get to know each other even more deeply before then," she purred. "That's why I asked you to bring me out here."

"Look, Zoe, um . . . " She was unfolding the paper now, and handing it to him. In the moonlight he recognized the flyer they'd received at the evening session. "Youth Leadership Boot Camp."

"I've thought it over and I'm doing it," she said. "It'll look great on a college application and it should be a real growth experience. And if it allows me to spend some more time with you—time at camp, time on different service trips—well, all the better."

He stared at the paper for just a few seconds before declaring, "I'm absolutely in."

"That's good to hear."

Then he felt her lips on his, like a soft, wet snowflake in August, landing lightly and never melting.

* * *

Jason was alone in the cabin, sitting at the rustic table, nursing a bottled water, when Trenton returned. The grounds outside were thick with traffic to and from the washrooms, lights-out now fifteen minutes away, but Jason was going nowhere until he got what he was waiting for.

"Details, man," he demanded. "Now."

Trenton shook his head. "Sorry to disappoint you. I've got none to give."

Jason waved the words away dismissively. "Right, right, you're a gentlemen. You just tell me to stop when I get to the right base . . . " He started raising the fingers of his right hand slowly, one at a time. "No way," he said as they added up. "Seriously? Fifth base? What does that even *mean*?"

"It means stop being a jerk. She just wanted to talk." Trenton was finding himself a bit disgusted with his friend lately, with greater and greater frequency. He was perplexed by the way the guy could sit solemnly through Bible lessons and youth group meetings, flipping pages with everyone else and even scribbling notes, only to come out of left field with this kind of stuff.

"Yeah," Jason laughed. "Talk about what?"

"She's signing up for that Boot Camp thing and she wants me to do it too. She said she wants to get to know me better and this will give us all sorts of time."

"You're not doing it though."

"Actually, I am."

Jason took a swig of water and immediately sprayed it all over Trenton.

"Oh, come on man," Trenton complained. "Are you serious? Again with the spit-take? It's still not funny."

"Am *I* serious? You're the one who's planning to give up his very last week of summer vacation for a girl who just wants to *talk*! You need to have your head examined. We were going to do that three-day *Far Cry* marathon at my house! You promised!"

"We can still do it. Just later. Winter break."

"I can't believe you, Marsh. First you move away after we specifically promised each other we'd always be next-door neighbors, right up until we room together in college. Now you blow off important, established plans for—'

"Jason, she kissed me."

"She what now?"

"Kissed me. You were right. I'm in. I'd be a moron to screw this up. If you're really my wing man, you'll support me here." He hated encouraging his friend's hormonal preoccupations, but it was the only way to get the guy off his back.

Jason pursed his lips, thinking. "Well that puts a whole new paint job on things. Why didn't you tell me in the—"

The door swung open and slapped against the bare wood of the wall. "Trent, Jason. Where were you two during campfire?" Sean Tailor, one of their counsellors, entered the cabin and slipped onto the bench next to Trenton. "Care to explain yourselves?"

"Would you believe we were wrapped up in this super-theological discussion and we lost track of time?" Jason asked. "I promise: it won't happen again."

"Right," Sean said, "especially since this was the last night of camp." He smiled, knowingly. In his early twenties and quite down-to-earth, Sean was by a wide margin the more relatable of the cabin's two counsellors. Having graduated from Clinch Rock High the year before the boys entered, he had a certain cachet—a coolness they looked up to. "I don't suppose your *conversation* involved the four girls who were also AWOL."

Jason grinned. "Might have."

"Thought so." Sean chuckled. "No harm, no foul. But I tell you what: if either of you is considering signing up for YLBC, don't think you're going to get away with that kind of thing. Mike Van Buren will sniff you out, hunt you down. He's a nice guy, but he's strict. Trust me, I've gotten to know him a little bit. No sneaking off on his watch."

"Sorry," Trenton said. "It was a dumb idea."

Sean laughed. "Nah. We used to do that stuff all the time when I was a camper. They just started cracking down on it lately."

"I wonder what they used to do when Ed was a camper," Jason mused. "Drink moonshine and wax their handlebar mustaches? Listen to some music on the old phonograph?" Ed Piper was the cabin's other counselor, fifty years older than his counterpart and a good deal grumpier.

Sean shook his head, but the smile didn't fade. "Don't go there, man."

"Alright. But you know where I *did* go?" Jason said, his face lighting up. "The trash can. I accidentally kicked it over earlier today, and look what was way down at the bottom." Campers were now entering the cabin fairly steadily, while Jason reached into his hoodie pocket and produced a small round tin, which he pushed discreetly into the middle of the table. It bore the words "Blue Wolf Chewin' Tobacco," along with a crude logo.

Jason smiled, presenting the item. "We've all wondered what made that distinctive round imprint in the back pocket of Ed's jeans," Jason went on. "And I think we all had our suspicions. Now we know." He struggled to get the words out through his laughter. "*Chewin' tobacco*. Not chewing. Did you see that? *Chewin'!*"

"So what?" Trenton asked. "Pastor Pardee used to smoke cigars. Why is it so funny that Ed chews tobacco? He's an old guy. Old guys do that."

"You're kidding, right?" Jason held the tin up high for all to see. "*Blue Wolf?* This is literally the funniest thing I've ever seen. It's actually made of tin! Do you think he bought like a thousand of them in 1970?"

The door clacked open again and Ed ambled in, grumbling under his breath and smelling heavily of aftershave. Sean snatched the tin from Jason's hand and said sharply, "I'll throw this away for you, Jason." Rising to his feet, he added, "Why don't you do me a favor and grow up a little, huh?" He pocketed the tin and disappeared into the counselor's area.

"He's right, you know," Trenton said.

Jason frowned for a moment. "Yeah. I know. And I'm glad he took it away. I didn't need it." He bit his lip pensively and studied the table for a beat. "Because there were actually two in the trash!" He pulled another tin from the same pocket. "Ha! Look at the wolf! Isn't that great? Oh, man. I'm gonna miss Ed. Such a nice guy. All those long chats we had . . . like the time he told us to shut up because it was late. And the other time he told us to keep it down because it was rest period. Ah, the memories! Personality for days, this guy."

"He can hear you," Trent whispered, gesturing at the counselors' area of the cabin, partitioned off by a threadbare curtain.

"You think?" He turned back toward the counselor's bunks at the far end of the cabin. "Hey, Sean, Ed! You guys hungry?"

"It's late," Ed fairly barked. "Six minutes to lights out. Too late for snacks."

Jason looked around at his bunkmates. "But I'm hungry, Ed. I'm hungry like the wolf."

"You're what?"

"Hungry like the wolf. The Blue Wolf!" He buried his face in his arms on the tabletop, laughing.

The curtain opened and Ed appeared, dressed in red drop-seat long underwear. "What in the world are you saying?"

"Never mind," Jason called. "You look great by the way."

Ed ignored the comment. "We'll leave the lights on another ten minutes so you boys can read the Scriptures. Then I want to hear some snoring."

The curtain closed again and a smattering of laughter was heard around the cabin. Jason re-pocketed the tin and dropped his voice. "Anyway, back to the topic at hand. She's hot, she's rich, and she's way older. You, my friend, are blessed."

"She's not *way* older."

"But she is. Sara's in the same cabin with her and she said Zoe left her wallet on her bunk. And she got a look at her driver's license. Turns out your girl Zoe's 22!" He held his hand up for a high-five.

Trenton hooked his wrist and pulled it back down to the table. "She's not twenty-two."

"Look, Sara's no genius, but that's some pretty simple math. I heard Zoe spent a few years travelling the world with her father. That's why she's still in high school."

"One year travelling, not four. They don't let you attend high school in your twenties."

"Well, she *is* attending high school. Our high school. You play this right and you could be dating the oldest and hottest senior when school starts. And the richest."

"Why do you keep saying that?"

"Dude, she lives in the castle!"

"You mean the Cassel House."

"The Castle, the Castle House, whatever. It's a mansion—biggest house in town by far. I wonder what she drives."

Trenton just smiled. Jason may have been obnoxious and given to exaggeration, but he wasn't entirely wrong here. It had been the best night in memory.

At Ed's insistence, the lights went out and Trenton crawled into his sleeping bag, still smiling wide about the progress he'd made with Zoe tonight and the prospect of more time spent together—at home, at school, and through any number of trips and retreats. The smile weakened, however, as he thought about the chaos awaiting him at home.

An incredibly *old* new house, full of boxes, in need of so much work. A dad who was never home, rushing between school, church, and squad car, leaving Trent with a pile of new responsibilities, even as his own life was packed to the point of claustrophobia. And now he'd have to somehow squeeze in this Youth Leadership Boot Camp deal, and, if things kept on their present course, a new girlfriend. This week of camp had been a nice break from it all, but the break was over.

For some reason, as he drifted off to sleep, Trenton saw in his mind an image of himself, up there at the top of Picture Falls, trying to stand upright in the rushing water, while the current did its best to sweep him over.

CHAPTER THREE
"SUPERHERO EDITION"

"If you're going to spend time, money, and energy on travel, make it a mission trip! If you spend them at a restaurant, be sure you're discussing Christ with a nonbeliever or planning something insane for the Kingdom! We're not given 'time off' as disciples. Sick days are minimal and they don't roll over. And vacation days? Forget it! They simply do not exist."

—*Insane Faith: A Guide to Extreme Christianity for the Truly Faithful*
by Stephen Branding, p. 68

The next morning was a blur of goodbyes, suitcases, and church vans. The campers, along with the parents and church leaders who had come to retrieve them, packed themselves uncomfortably into the program center to sing the same songs and watch the same highlight video the teens had sung and watched the night before. There was wooing, as always. On the way out, they were all given an 8 x 10 glossy group picture to commemorate the week—along with a roster of each camper's name and address—and sent back out into the world.

Last year, Trenton had treasured the roster, because it contained Rachelle's address. She had been his "camp girlfriend" and they'd vowed to make it work through the year. He called her once and she sent him one letter. By October, they had seemingly forgotten each other. But this year would be different. Looking up from the roster, he saw Zoe approaching from her cabin, carrying a suitcase and sleeping bag, and smiled. This year, the girl was coming back to Clinch Rock and she didn't know anyone but Trenton. He jogged over to her.

"Let me take that for you," he said, relieving her of the luggage.

"Thanks." She pulled her purse back up to her shoulder. "Are your parents here to pick you up?"

"No, my dad's on duty today, so Jason's mom is giving me a ride." He followed Zoe behind the administration building to where three dozen cars were parked along the edge of the ball field.

"Why don't you ride with me?"

"Seriously?"

"Sure. It's a dreadfully long trip; I'd love someone to talk to. This is me." She pushed a button on her remote, popping the trunk of a newish Volvo. Trenton carefully deposited her suitcase, mentally high-fiving himself.

"Yeah," he said, trying to keep it cool. "Sounds like a good time. I'll tell Mrs. Dufresne."

As they emerged from the ball field, back into the gridlock of the main grounds, Trenton heard someone call his name and saw Sean Tailor approaching, along with Mike Van Buren, the energetic pitchman from the night before..

"Hey, I wanted you to get a chance to meet Mike one-on-one, since you mentioned you were signing up for YLBC."

Mike held out his hand and gave Trenton's an enthusiastic two-pump shake that hurt just a little bit. "Good to meet you, Trent. You're the first definite yes. I've got six maybes. This is gonna be so awesome."

"Zoe's in too," Trent said, gesturing to her.

"Great!" Even outdoors, his outdoor voice was overwhelming. He shook her hand as well, saying "Mike Van Buren, great to meet you."

"Trent's father is the new pastor down at Clinch Rock Community Church," Sean informed him.

"Really? That's awesome! Did you know that the first pastor there, a guy named Jeremiah Wolcott way back in the 1800s, was instrumental in getting this camp started? Him and this lumber baron, Benjamin Cassel. If it weren't for your church, we wouldn't even be standing here." He delivered the words with such intensity that Trenton didn't know quite how to respond.

"That's cool. Well, I guess we're heading out. Mike, I'll see you in about a week. Sean, see you around the Rock."

25

"Take care," Sean said, ignoring Trenton's proffered hand and going in for the bro hug. "It was good getting to know you a little better this week. Remember what I told you: *never give up unless you're giving up giving up.*"

"Sure thing," Trenton said. Sean's oft-repeated catch phrase made little sense, but he sold it with such confidence and enthusiasm that Trent couldn't help affirming it.

"*Trentuuuuhn,*" Mrs. Dufresne warbled from beside her minivan, some fifty feet away. Her voice carried over the din like a loon's call. "It's time to go."

"Crud. Jason must have already packed my stuff in her van already," he said to Zoe. "I'll go get it."

Mrs. Dufresne made a show of "getting a look at" Trenton, as if she hadn't seen him in years and invited him to "hop on in."

"Already called shotgun," Jason declared.

"Yeah, um, Mrs. Dufresne, I'm actually going to be riding back with a friend from Clinch Rock, so . . . " She stared at him, blankly. "So I'm just going to grab my stuff out of the back."

"Oh, no you're not, mister."

"Sorry?"

"I told your father I'd drive you home and the camp released you into *my* supervision, so no, you're not riding home with someone else. Do I even know this person?"

"No, but she's not an ax murderer. She's a camper."

Mrs. Dufresne clucked a couple of times. Actually clucked. "A girl? I don't think so, Trenton. Get in."

"Fine," he spat. He couldn't even look at her, with her stupid billowy pantsuit and fake-jewel-encrusted giant sunglasses. He turned and walked away.

"And where are you going now?"

"I have to tell Zoe I can't ride with her." He was searching for her when Ed bumped into him.

"Trenton," he said, holding out a meaty paw, "Enjoyed having you in my cabin."

26

"Thanks," Trenton mumbled, shaking his hand feebly. "It was good to meet you."

"If you ever need anything, my contact information is on the roster."

Not likely, Trenton thought.

* * *

Trenton was in a foul mood by the time he arrived home and he had plenty of time to relish it. The quickest way home from Picture Falls was by boat—a straight shot from Manistique on the shore of the Upper Peninsula, through Lake Michigan, to Pointe Fournier in the Lower Peninsula, followed by a forty-minute drive inland. All told, it took about two hours travel time, back when a retired friend from church made it his mission to provide water transportation for all the campers in the congregation. He was now in a nursing home, though, boatless, leaving Trenton to spend five and a half hours trapped in a land-bound vehicle, travelling in a wide half-circle, over the Mackinac Bridge. Five and a half hours with Zoe would have seemed like nothing. With Jason's mom, it was like three consecutive life sentences.

Giving Zoe the news that he couldn't share this ride with her had been beyond humiliating and her overly sympathetic response had made him feel like a little kid with a silly crush. Mrs. Dufresne had barraged them with questions about their week, loudly *uh-huhing* over their answers. Then Jason had insisted they stop for a late lunch at The Senora, a mediocre Mexican restaurant way out in the sticks. "Sure, the food sucks," he'd insisted, "but it's tradition." Trenton ate little.

When Mrs. Dufresne dropped him off, he grunted his thanks and grabbed his bags.

"Bye-bye Trenton," she called, backing out of the gravel driveway. Trenton cringed. Well, at least that was behind him.

He let himself into the parsonage, home for the past three weeks, and dumped his bags just inside the door, alongside a tower of boxes, all labeled with their eventual rooms of destination. The house was bigger than their old place, but far older and less comfortable. He grabbed a Coke from the fridge and watched a show on Netflix before lacing up his shoes to head into town.

Monday, he'd return to work. Today he just felt restless. Part of him wanted to call Zoe, but it was probably way too soon. He didn't want to appear over-eager. Didn't matter anyway, since he had given her his phone number and she had not offered hers in exchange.

As Trenton deposited an armload of empty cans in the recycling bin, he noticed the sink piled high with dirty dishes. His mother had kept an immaculate house, despite working full time. And since her death, Trent and his father had done a decent job of dividing the labor. But with the addition of a second job and classes, his father had begun neglecting the upkeep of the household, leaving Trenton with the sense that he was the parent, constantly cleaning up after a teenaged slob. He rolled up his sleeves and spent forty-five minutes bringing order back to the kitchen. How could one man dirty so many dishes in just seven days, while barely darkening the doors of the place? Dumping the last now-clean glass into the drying rack, Trenton headed out, not locking the door behind him.

The evening was cool and pleasant. Up until last month, Trenton had lived less than a block from downtown Clinch Rock, which was convenient as both Trent's school and the police station where his father worked were practically next door. Now they were a good mile away. It was a quick bike ride, but in light of today's humiliations, Trent was unwilling to hop on his Schwinn. What if Zoe happened to be downtown and saw him peddling around like a child? As he walked, he cursed his decision to forego driver's training the previous June in favor of a church trip to Guatemala. This summer had been even more jam-packed and now it only made sense to wait until he turned eighteen and just take the driver's test.

Fifteen minutes later, Trenton entered the police station, which felt far more like home than their current house did. He'd been coming here with his dad as long as he could remember and the sight and smell lifted his spirits just a bit. The building was old—original to the town—and very compact. Just inside the door, a high counter greeted visitors, beyond which were spread out six desks in three rows. Along the back wall were a set of lockers, two old fashioned jail cells (always empty), and his dad's closet of an office, marked with a small nameplate that read CHIEF ADAM MARSH.

"Officer Tango," Trenton said, nodding at the man behind the counter as he walked by.

"Whoa, hold up kid! Come back here."

Kid? Trenton stopped in his tracks and turned to face the lanky cop, one of the two new guys. "My name's Trenton," he said, "not kid. And I'm just popping in to say hi to my dad. You know, the chief of police?"

"Well, my names Officer Tyrell, not Tango. And you're not 'popping in' without signing in." He nudged a clipboard about an inch in Trent's direction.

"Never had to do that before."

The cop shrugged. "Things are changing. I think you know that."

Trenton began filling out his name and the time. His was the first on the sheet. "I could have sworn I heard someone call you—"

"Yeah, the guys call John and I 'Tango and Cash.' From that movie. But civilians can call me Officer Tyrell. And you are a civilian."

"Movie?"

"Before your time, I guess."

"Right. So is Cash his real name?"

"Yes."

"Wait. His name is John Cash?" Trenton laughed. "Like Johnny Cash?"

Officer Tyrell snatched the clipboard back and said, "Word to the wise, kid: don' t call him that."

"What's with Tango making me sign in? It's not like this is the Pentagon or something."

Chief Marsh looked up from the textbook in front of him. "Well, hello to you too, son. How was camp?" He wrapped an arm around Trenton and squeezed.

"Sorry. It was good. And it's nice to see you too. I just don't get him."

"You and me both. But Tango and Cash were Rich Barton's hires. I couldn't very well weigh in since I'm leaving the force. And the sign-in thing is Rich's idea too."

"Well, I'm not a fan."

"Neither am I, but I've been letting him take the reins more and more. Only makes sense; this will be his office in a couple months. Anyway, Tango and Cash worked together in Rochester Hills and they come very highly recommended. Rich says we were lucky to get them both." He closed the book, *Basics of Biblical Greek,* with a thud and leaned back in his chair. "So let's hear the highlights."

Trenton smiled. "Well . . . there was a girl."

"Ahh, the girl. Last year, you said the same thing."

"It's different this time. She lives in Clinch Rock."

"Really? Anyone I know? Maybe someone I've locked up?"

Trenton chuckled. "Shut up. She's new in town. Her name's Zoe Green."

"Brian Green's daughter?"

"I don't know. Who's that?"

"Also new in town, putting together that local history museum, spearheading this 'Reboot Clinch Rock' campaign with the mayor. Kind of a big shot."

"That sounds about right."

"Can't wait to meet her. But for now, I've got a ton to do. You alright having dinner on your own tonight? I have more studying, some paperwork to finish, and tomorrow's sermon isn't exactly what I'd call 'done' yet."

"No problem. Good to see you, Dad."

As he left the office, Trenton's phone vibrated . A text from Judith:

Free for dinner? Need to discuss something. Very important.

He felt a pang in his gut. He didn't know how, but he was sure: Judith had already found out about Zoe. This was not going to be fun.

* * *

Judith Morgan was the sole employee of Rerun, a shop owned and operated by Brook Yanich, the town's lone hippy. The sign above the door, stenciled onto a few slats of reclaimed barn wood, read "Rerun: Vintage, Retro, Clothing, Comics, Tchotchkes." It was the perfect job for Judith, in that it fueled her odd collections and unorthodox wardrobe, and was open unpredictable hours, based on when proprietor and clerk felt like showing up. Trent met her at the entrance.

"Trent!" She threw her arms around him and gave him a kiss on either cheek like a European woman in a movie.

"Hey, Judith." He grinned. There was no doubt he had missed her. They'd been best friends since the fourth grade and rarely spent long periods apart. She had even come along on vacation with the Marsh family a few times before Trenton's mom died.

"Well, what do you think?" she asked, indicating her T-shirt. It was old and worn and bore the faded words, "World's Greatest Grandpa" next to a caricature of a scowling old man. Beneath it she wore a long skirt and army boots. Her auburn hair was tied up in two little nubs on top of her head, reminding Trenton of a cartoon alien. The sun had coaxed out the pools of freckles on her nose and cheeks, as it did every summer.

"That's great," he said. "Looks like Ed, one of our counsellors. Dinner at the diner?"

"Of course."

They walked half a block to the White Tail Diner, a greasy spoon full of broken stools, faux wood paneling, and a surprisingly large number of mounted animal heads. They slipped into their favorite booth and ordered two breakfast skillets, their usual.

"Be right back," Judith said, scrambling over to the juke box and punching a few buttons, summoning the opening strains of a twenty-year-old Shania Twain song that they played ironically, but both secretly liked.

She slid back into the booth, chuckling. "So how was camp? Anything unusual happen?"

Trenton paused. Was this a leading question? A transition to discussing Zoe? Maybe not; Judith usually came to Picture Falls with him. She'd just missed the camp scholarship deadline this year.

"It was fun. We missed you, though."

"You're sweet." She took a drink of orange juice, swaying a bit to the music.

"So, you had something important you wanted to discuss?"

"Right. But it's kind of," she leaned in and said, "sensitive" in a hushed tone. "Like *your-ears-only* type stuff."

"Um, okay. I don't think anyone's listening in." He gestured at the empty booths and tables around them.

Judith reached into an old surplus bag and produced a colorful paperback book, placing it on the table between them.

"*Insane Faith: Superhero Edition,*" Trenton read aloud.

"Have you read this?" she asked.

"Yeah. I mean, no, not the 'superhero edition.' What does that even mean?"

"It's like the teen version or whatever. It's the only one they had at the library. Same stuff, just a little cheesier. But convicting. It really got me thinking."

"Seems to have that effect."

"Right. Your dad. Well, I get where he's coming from. Because I read this thing three times and I just kept getting more and more sure about what I'm supposed to be doing with my life."

"Which is—?"

She took a deep breath. "You know how—" She suddenly fell silent while their food arrived, watching their waitress suspiciously until she was a good twenty feet away. "You know how there are no Christian superheroes?"

"I know how there are no superheroes."

"I'm talking about like, remember Captain Bible? You had those DVDs when we were little and he was supposed to be like the Christian Batman? Remember how horrible that was?"

"Oh, right." Trenton felt his body relax. This wasn't about Zoe after all. He should have known; with Judith, almost everything was deemed super important and yours-eyes-only. "I always wondered about that," he said. "Why do they feel like there has to be a 'Christian version' of everything. Why can't Batman just be Batman?"

"Or at least make it good, right?" she said, emptying a third packet of grape jelly onto her toast.

"Right."

"Well, I'm going to be the one to do it, and do it right. I think this is the time and place for it."

"You're going to create a superhero?" Trent was not overly surprised. Judith had always been a bit of a comic book geek—increasingly since working at Rerun—and was artistic enough. The year before, she'd painted a huge mural on the wall of the art room at school, and it was definitely good. "That sounds fun."

"No. I'm going to *become* a hero."

"Huh?"

"Someone has to."

"Somebody has to . . . what?"

She tapped the cover of *Insane Faith: Superhero Edition*.

"You lost me, Judith."

She sighed. "I'm going to be Clinch Rock's masked hero. Or . . . heroine."

He laughed. "Of course you are."

"I told you: I know it sounds crazy."

Trenton sat back in the booth and studied her face. She certainly looked serious. But she couldn't be. Right? Trenton was speechless. Whenever he thought he'd come to terms with Judith's eccentricities, she cranked it up a notch. But this . . .

"Well?" she asked.

"That's insane, Judith."

She smiled. "I know."

"You're not serious."

"Like a global warming heart attack, dipped in a major oil spill."

"Let me see if I understand you here. You're planning to dress up in a costume and fight crime as a hero, in Clinch Rock." She nodded. "What crime? Nothing ever happens here!"

"I guess you haven't talked to your dad since you got back?"

"Actually, I just came from the station. Why?"

"He didn't tell you? While you were gone, some stuff went down. It was a wake-up call for Clinch Rock."

Trenton was skeptical. "Really. What exactly 'went down?'"

"For one thing, our store was broken into. "

"Sorry to hear that. What did they take?"

Judith shook her head. "That's just it. They didn't take anything, just knocked some holes in the wall, pulled up some floorboards. Isn't that weird?"

"I've heard of that. Did they pull out the copper?"

"Nope. Just opened up the floor and the walls, like they were looking for something."

"Could just be kids blowing off steam," Trenton said, mopping up the rest of his egg yolk with a piece of toast.

"Maybe. But then they broke into Sidebar as well. Smashed some bottles, knocked some more holes in the walls, and ripped up the carpet." Sidebar was Clinch Rock's poorly executed attempt at a themed watering hole, located in the lobby of the broken down former court house.

Trenton digested this. "That's weird, but it hardly amounts to a crime spree. Besides, how are you going to keep things like that from happening?"

Judith shrugged. "I'll patrol at night. My parents don't care where I go or when. May as well use that to my advantage."

"But why would this even enter your mind? You obviously don't have superpowers or unlimited funds and you aren't, like, a trained fighter or anything."

"Yes I am," she insisted. "A trained fighter."

"Oh, come on. I hardly think whoever's breaking into buildings and smashing them up with a sledgehammer is going to abide by the rules of high school wrestling."

Judith waved a hand dismissively. "Eighty percent of this stuff is just having the guts to do it, you know? All sorts of people have the right skills, but they don't have the strength of will. They don't have the Insane Faith."

Trenton studied the cover of the book before him. A muscular cartoon superhero stood beneath the title, fists pressed against his hips, cape billowing. "I think it's more a metaphor, Judith."

She scowled. "Don't talk to me like I'm stupid."

He knew she wasn't. In fact, she was a straight-A student. Absently flipping pages, he landing at a bookmark that bore the words "In the World, Not of It." Well, Judith had the second part down.

She opened her mouth to speak again, but stopped short when an older couple came into the diner and settled into the booth across from theirs.

"We'll talk more about this later," she said. "I better get back to the store."

"Okay. Just don't do anything crazy until we talk again."

She winked. "Wouldn't think of it. See you at church tomorrow." She gathered her things and disappeared out the door, leaving Trenton with the bill and a whole pile of questions.

CHAPTER FOUR
"SCUTTLEBUTT"

"Sleep is necessary—a necessary evil. Remember how Jesus flipped out on his disciples when he caught them sawing logs? A life of extreme faith is not about rest. It's about action!"

—Insane Faith: Superhero Edition
by Stephen Branding, p. 51

Adam Marsh sat at his desk trying to block out the knowledge that it would only be his desk for fifty-seven more days. He was also trying not to keep track of how many days.

He pushed the heels of his hands into his eye sockets and rubbed. What was he on, three and a half hours' sleep? The sight of his Greek textbook at the corner of his desk reminded him that tonight would be another late one.

"Afternoon, Chief Mash." Rich Barton walked in the door, in uniform.

"Chief Barton." When he created the position of Interim Co-Chief and promoted Barton, he had insisted that everyone in the department immediately begin referring to him as "chief." After all, best to get used to it now. The funny thing was, Adam was still not used to it himself and was increasingly sure he never would be.

"Sorry we have to do this on a Sunday," Rich said. "I know you're probably beat."

"No problem at all," Adam answered, knowing this would actually cause all sorts of problems. He had bowed out of Sunday lunch with a very influential parishioner to be here—lunch plans that were meant to smooth over an earlier gaffe. Oh, well. Crime knew no Sabbath. At least, not lately.

"Probably no point in driving," Barton said.

"Nah. And I could use the exercise." They went out the back, locking up behind them, and set off down the street.

"How are Tango and Cash fitting in?" Adam asked.

"Pretty good. They're still getting used to the pace around here. I mean, Rochester Hills isn't exactly *8 Mile*, but at least there was actual crime. I've almost been thankful for these incidents lately. I mean, not really, but it's helping ease the new guys into life in Clinch Rock." He was silent for a minute, huffing a little as he walked. "How do you think they're fitting in?"

"It'll take some time. They're the only officers this town has ever known who weren't born and raised here."

"Look, Chief, I hope I didn't overstep by—"

"No way. It's as much your department as it is mine. Maybe more so. If you think they're the right men, then I'm sure they are."

The two chiefs arrived at the old Town Hall, an impressive two-story wood structure. They walked up the steps, between the tall columns, and in the front door, where they were met by a nervous older man in a bowtie.

"Chief Marsh," he said. "Oh, thank heavens. I didn't touch anything, wanted to preserve the integrity of the crime scene."

"Appreciate it, Gill. Rich, you know Gill Krause, city treasurer."

"Yeah, we played the trombone together in marching band."

Gill led the policemen down a narrow hallway and into the main meeting room. "I stopped by today to pick up some paperwork and found it this way. It's an historic building. I just can't believe anyone would—" He trailed off.

There, scrawled across the far wall in green spray paint were the words "CRHS Rules!"

"Kids," Barton grumbled. "Clinch Rock High School." He turned to Adam. "Did you realize our sons were classmates with criminals?"

"That's not even the worst of it," Gill said, dabbing sweat from his brow with an enormous handkerchief. "Follow me."

The three of them entered an office. Sitting in the center of the floor was a massive old safe.

"They moved it from the closet in the corner," Gill offered.

"Yeah, we can see that," Barton said. The closet door, ripped from the frame, had been discarded against the wall and the hardwood floor had been scraped and scuffed along the safe's entire path.

"Did they try to open it?" Adam asked.

Barton ran his fingers along the seam of the door. "Not with a blow-torch, I don't think."

"Rich, fingerprints," Adam said.

"Oh right. Sorry. Anyway, these old safes are indestructible, so who knows what they did? They probably didn't think it through—just gave up when they couldn't pry it open. Kids these days. No *sticktuitiveness*."

"You really think *kids* dragged this thing seven feet? I guarantee it weighs more than a thousand pounds!"

Barton nodded. "You get four guys my Danny's size, they could move it. You should see the workouts Coach Fischer puts them through."

"I don't know," Adam said, following the trail back to the safe's original resting place. He shined a light into the closet. "Hey, Rich, look at this. A few of the floorboards are up. Subfloor too."

"Huh. Probably just pulled away when they dislodged the thing. Who knows how long that safe's been in that closet. I wouldn't doubt a hundred years. Probably stuck."

Adam shook his head. "I don't think so. Think about it: three break-ins, all of which have the floors at least partially pulled up. Seems like more than a coincidence. And the other two had holes in the walls."

"Any of that here?" Barton asked.

"Not that I noticed," Gill said.

Adam walked up to a large framed map of the town and carefully lifted it off the wall, revealing a jagged eight-inch hole in the plaster.

"Looks like a sledgehammer again." He surveyed the floor around them. "Only they must have cleaned up thoroughly." Checking the trashcan, he added, "Even took the plaster with them when they left."

"Huh," Barton said. "Maybe I should give these kids a little more credit."

"Or maybe they're not kids."

* * *

"I don't understand," Zoe said. "We're going to a skating rink, but we're not skating?"

"Welcome to Clinch Rock," Trenton said. His mood had recovered 100% from the evening before. After a long night of watching his phone not ring, he had prayed Zoe would show up at church. After all, she knew his father was the pastor and she seemed to be what they used to call *pious*.

She wasn't there, though, and he'd slumped into his pew in the back, sour and moping. But then, to his great delight (and the equally great displeasure of the old woman sitting behind him), Zoe had called halfway through the service. Trent had ducked out to talk to her. She was free this afternoon, she said, and wondered if anything was going on and if they could get together. He now sat comfortably in the passenger seat of her Volvo. It couldn't have worked out more perfectly.

"Yeah, Zoe, don't judge," Jason chided from the backseat. "They've got nachos *and* laser tag."

Okay, it could have worked out a little bit more perfectly.

Once inside, they settled into their usual table, back in the corner, behind the snack bar. They ordered a variety of junk food. The place was busy for a Sunday afternoon, middle schoolers thick on the skating floor and several tribes of older teens congregating around different tables.

Zoe took it all in with a sort of detached curiosity, as if she were observing some primitive South American village, untouched by modern man. "So there's one school in town and everyone in that school hangs out here?"

"Yep," Jason confirmed. "Except the stoners. They gather behind the building."

"Don't you have a coffee shop?"

Trenton shook his head, sadly. "Nope. We had one for a minute. It was called The Daily News Café. Instead of an Internet café, it was just a bunch of different newspapers people could read while they drank their coffee. Only they were all like a week old. It pretty much bombed."

"Was that downtown?"

"Yeah. It's empty now."

She smiled. "We'll have a coffee shop again before long. Trust me. You won't be able to find an empty storefront downtown."

"Hey, look who it is!" Jason called, rising from his seat.

Judith came in the door and made a beeline for their table. Jason ran to meet her.

"Judith!" he shouted. "How I missed you! Buy me a milkshake. I'm just kidding. Actually I'm not. Do it. Seriously."

"How many Red Bulls did you have today?" she asked.

"None. I found this new, cheaper energy drink at the Gas-N-Sip. It's called Wattage. I had three."

"Oh boy." Her eyes fell on Zoe. "Who's this?"

Trenton cleared his throat. "Judith, this is Zoe Green. Her family just moved to Clinch Rock a couple months ago."

Judith smiled. "Nice to meet you."

"We all met her at camp," Jason said, helpfully, then turned to Zoe. "You know, speaking of camp, a friend of mine told me she saw your driver's license. And this is crazy, but she said you might be, how you say, *twenty-two years old.*"

"Jason . . . " Trenton began.

"It's fine," Zoe said. "She saw my fake ID. I got it last year. I'm actually nineteen."

"But the thing with this ID," Jason persisted, "was that it had your name. I mean, I don't have a fake ID or anything," he fixed his eyes on Trenton and then Judith, "because I don't get into trouble. But the way I understand these things, they usually have a fake name."

"Jason, why don't you drop it, buddy?" Trenton said.

"No, it's okay." Zoe pulled her wallet from her purse and carefully removed two ID cards. "This is my real license. See? Nineteen. And this is the fake. I don't know why I even got it. My friends in Vermont were all doing it and I thought it would be fun."

The phony ID looked almost identical to the real one, except that it bore the name Zoe Frobisher and listed an apartment in Montpelier as her address.

Jason studied them silently for a minute. "You guys think I should get one of these?" he asked.

"No," they answered in unison.

His attention span maxed out, Jason's eyes skipped around the perimeter of the skating rink. "Oh, man. Everybody's here today. Judith, check it out: your two best friends." He pointed to a middle-aged man talking with a tall, brawny teenaged boy over by the pinball machines.

"Who are they?" Zoe asked.

"That's Dan Barton. Real gem. And the older guy's Coach Fischer. Kicked Judith off the wrestling team."

"He didn't kick me off; I quit."

"Not what I heard," Jason said. "There's scuttlebutt, Judith. *Scuttlebutt.*"

"I quit," she repeated, more adamantly. "He was putting me in exhibition rounds, even though I won all my challenges, just because I'm a woman. That's sexism. He's lucky I didn't file a complaint. I could have sued the school."

"Yeah, I don't like him either," Jason said, still gazing in the direction of the coach and the jock. "He was our gym teacher freshman year. What was that thing he was always yelling?"

"*No excuses, no delays,*" Trenton recited.

"Right. A chubby bald dude always carping about excuses and delays. Guy's like a top hat short of being that grumpy conductor from *Thomas the Tank Engine.*"

Judith laughed. "Okay, now I really am buying you a milkshake."

"I don't know," Zoe mused. "He's handsome in a way. Maybe a passing resemblance to Bruce Willis."

Judith snorted. "Not young, sexy Bruce Willis, though. More like older, waxen Bruce Willis, with his stubbled head and those vacant, beady eyes."

41

Zoe shrugged. "I guess." She put her hand on Judith's. "You know, I think it's really *neat* that you would go out for a sport that's so male-dominated. Good for you."

"Thanks. I was undefeated in my weight class. You know what my secret weapon was? I'm double-jointed. Watch this." She interlaced her fingers on the table in front of her and, without releasing them, brought her arms over her head and behind her back, then back down to the table.

"Wow, do that again." Dan Barton was towering over their table, leering.

"Shut up, Barton," Judith said.

"Such hostility. You know, the coach and I were just talking about—" He suddenly noticed Zoe. "Who have we here? You must be new." He held out his hand. "Dan Barton, varsity wrestling."

"Varsity jerkward," Trenton mumbled.

"What was that, Marsh?"

"Nothing, Dan. Why don't you just move along?"

"Maybe I don't feel like it." He turned his attention back to Zoe. "So rude; am I right? You know, I used to be like that too. I was actually a bit of a bully when I was younger. I'm not proud of it, but it's true. And Trent here used to always threaten me with his dad because he was the chief of police. Said if I didn't leave him alone, his dad would put me in jail. Funny thing: *my* dad's the chief of police now, too. And in not too long, Marsh, your dad is just going to be a civilian. Good thing I don't bully anymore, because nothing would be stopping me from kicking your butt." He let his eyes meet Trenton's, menacingly, for a moment, before the square-jawed smile returned.

Zoe leaned forward and locked eyes with the wrestler. "Let me ask you something, Dan: do you think any of us is impressed by this show of false machismo? Because we're not."

"Don't speak too soon, doll. I'm an acquired taste." He straightened up, seemingly about to leave, but then added, "Did the Bag Lady here tell you she used to be on the wrestling team? Coach had to kick her off because she couldn't control her temper. Hey, Judith, remember when you kept insisting that the sleeper hold was a real thing? That was hilarious. Coach Fischer's like, 'Judith, that's the WWE. It's phony wrestling,' and you were like, 'No, it's real.' So funny. Coach still brings that up at practice. *Don't forget to work on your sleeper hold, guys!"*

"It *is* real," Judith said. "YouTube it."

"Right, 'cause everything on YouTube's real. See you nerds later. Actually, I don't care if I see you three." He pointed at Zoe and said, "I'll see *you* later," and lumbered off.

Jason's face twisted up. "I cannot believe your dad chose that meathead's father to replace him."

"My dad just recommended him. The town council gave him the job. Anyway, Rich Barton's okay. It's not his fault his son is such a tool." He looked at his watch. "Guys, if we're going to make it to the soup kitchen, we need to leave in like twenty minutes. Last call for that milkshake."

Jason groaned. "I've already been to church once today. I bet God won't mind if I skip youth group."

"If you don't go to the service project, you can't go to the concert next week. Besides, Zoe's your ride, so you're kind of stuck with us."

"Fine. But I better not have to wash dishes. I've never washed a dish in my life."

* * *

"Do you think he's volunteering or is he actually here for dinner?" Jason was peering through the open door from the kitchen. "He sat down a while ago and talked to someone, but he hasn't eaten. Now he's just standing there, staring."

An hour into their shift in the kitchen, Jason had still not broken his record of never washing a dish.

"Who do you keep talking about?" Judith asked, pulling another large metal vat into the industrial sink.

"Ed," Jason said. "He was one of our counselors at camp. You know him. He's always reading the paper at the counter of the White Tail Diner on Saturday mornings. Clears his throat every two seconds. Drives me nuts."

"Oh, Mr. Piper.He's nice."

"Oh, yeah. A real sweetie, this guy."

Trenton pulled up his rubber gloves, which were a size too big and kept slipping down his arms. He took another mostly empty tray of garlic bread from a fellow volunteer and brought it over to the sink. The dining area was less than half full—maybe thirty-five or forty people, some of them kids, which really pulled at Trent's heart. And standing against the wall, surveying the operation, was Ed Piper. Trent wondered if he should go say hi to him. He looked lonely standing there, wearing the same old flannel shirt and jeans he was always wearing—not eating, not talking. Not doing anything, really.

Jason was still rattling on. "The guy brought chewing tobacco to church camp. Tells you everything you need to know."

"That *is* a little low-class," Zoe said, drying and stacking bowls, somehow both daintily and efficiently.

Judith stopped washing. "That's kind of a snobby thing to say."

"Oh, don't be so sensitive," Jason said. "It was called Blue Wolf Tobacco! You should have seen the logo on the tin. It's not just a picture of a wolf. Oh, no! It's a picture of a T-shirt, with a picture of a wolf on it!" He laughed and pounded the counter.

"Whatever," Judith said.

One of the adult volunteers poked her head into the kitchen and announced, "I need two of you to start collecting the salt and pepper shakers and condiments and any dirty dishes off the tables in the dining room."

"Trenton and I will do it," Zoe said. "Come on." She wheeled a metal cart through the door and over to the far end of the expansive room. A lot of the tables hadn't been used, so the work went quickly at first.

"Judith seems *nice*," she said, making perfect rows of each type of bottle on the cart. "I can see why you're so close."

Trent nodded. "She's a really kind person."

"Did you two ever date?"

Trenton laughed, hoping he wasn't overselling it. "No. It's platonic."

44

"Yeah, I can see why."

"What . . . What does that mean?"

"Oh, nothing bad. Just, you know, it makes sense that she was a wrestler. She's built like one. Thighs and hips. You know. Nothing bad."

Trenton had no response. Even while insulting someone in such a petty way, Zoe seemed somehow grownup and sophisticated, like she was hobnobbing over the tennis nets at a country club, rather than gossiping about a classmate while collecting squeeze-bottles of mustard. Trenton liked the way that felt. Like his life was bigger than it really was. Bigger than this town of 3,000 people.

And it didn't hurt when she asked, "Would you like to come over for dinner tomorrow night? My father is grilling lobster tails. They're to die for."

Trenton knocked a row of salt shakers off the cart. Had he just gone from hopeless crush to boyfriend to meeting Zoe's parents in the course of two days? "Yeah," he said. "Yeah, definitely."

"Wonderful. We eat at 6:30. You can come by about 6:15."

"It's a date," he said, beaming.

"For sure." She smiled. "And I'm sorry for what I said about Judith. That was small of me. She really does seem like a good person. I think I was just thrown by Jason's description of her. He made her sound completely crazy."

Trenton had a vision of Judith in mask and cape, swinging through the streets of Clinch Rock. "Yeah," he said, "you can't take anything Jason says at face value."

CHAPTER FIVE
"A LITTLE SUSPISH "

"People don't like it when I point this out, but the Last Supper was a working dinner."

—*Insane Faith: A Guide to Extreme Christianity for the Truly Faithful* by Stephen Branding, p. 179

Trenton got up Monday morning at 7:30 and stopped by the White Tail Diner for some breakfast before work. When the bill arrived, he noted with some annoyance that he'd just spent a full quarter of what he would earn that day. Second Life Home Store, where he had been working five days a week for most of the summer, was a nonprofit resale shop, taking donations of old-but-functioning appliances, unwanted furniture, and other home goods, and selling them at dirt-cheap prices to the public—ideally, that portion of the public unable to purchase new items for their homes. The same local parachurch organization that ran the soup kitchen (right next door) ran the Home Store.

The summer previous, Trenton had commuted 45 minutes a day with a friend of his dad's to paint lake houses in Ludington. It had been fun work and plenty lucrative. When he passed on the chance to do it again in order to lug and load two-ton appliances for peanuts per hour, it had seemed like a noble choice. His dad had been proud. But his muscles were always a little sore and he was continually annoyed that the vast majority of customers were middle class homeowners and contractors looking to save a few bucks. All the while, Trenton's own savings account wasn't looking much better off than when the summer began.

The first police cruiser arrived as Trenton was unlocking the store's large oak front door. It parked at the curb in front of the store and Jessie Finn stepped out of the car and headed for the entrance to the soup kitchen. He nodded curtly when Trent waved hello, and walked right by. Rumor had it that Jessie was none too happy with Rich Barton's pending promotion to chief, thinking himself a far better candidate, having been on the force longer than Rich and having volunteered for each and every overtime shift and detail during that time.

A moment later, a second police car pulled up, lights flashing but no siren, and Chief Marsh emerged, looking tired and somber. Trenton stepped out the door.

"Hey Dad," he called. "What's going on?"

The chief ambled over and took off his hat. "Soup kitchen was broken into during the night. Looks like the same people we've been dealing with."

"Seriously? We were just there last night, you know. The youth group."

"I know. You're all suspects," he joked, smiling weakly. "Anyway, I better get at it. Have a good day at work."

Trenton began wheeling some of the newer stoves and refrigerators out onto the sidewalk with a dolly, his manager's idea for drumming up business. But his mind was elsewhere and he wound up denting two of them. For some reason, the image of Ed Piper skulking around the soup kitchen kept coming to mind. He didn't seem to have been volunteering at the kitchen, nor had he eaten anything. Could it have been more than a coincidence that the building was broken into that very night? No one seemed to know much about Ed, other than it was his first year as a counselor at Picture Falls and that he got under Jason's skin. And his apparent penchant for a particular chewing tobacco.

Trenton's phone announced the arrival of a text message. His boss looked up at the sound. Trying to be sly, Trent slipped the phone from his pocket and checked the screen. Judith. Of course.

> Did you hear? Soup Kitchen broken into last night.

How could she know that so fast? Their town was small, but . . . Another text:

> Still not convinced?

Before Trent could reply, Sean Tailor entered the store and whacked him on the back. "Good to see you, camper," he all-but-shouted.

"Hey, man. What can I do for you today?" Sean worked for his father, a local contractor, and was a semi-regular at the store.

"Looking for a pedestal sink. You got any?"

"Sure. Follow me," Trent said, leading him to a back corner of the old building, where a variety of sinks and vanities were lined up like the skyline of a porcelain city. "Hey, Sean, you mind if I ask you something?"

"Not at all," he said, pawing through the goods.

"How well do you know Ed Piper?"

The young man paused and furrowed his brow. "Not too well. Kind of kept to himself. He snores a lot."

"But where did he come from? Does he live around here?'

Sean rubbed his stubbled jaw. "Seems like he said he just moved to the area. I'm thinking maybe that trailer park off 37? Why do you ask?"

"No reason."

Another text bleeped through from Judith. Probably sent from her family's trailer at the park off 37, Trenton thought.

> Need to talk later. Brainstorm who would want to do this.

* * *

"Clinch Rock Wrestling Sux!" The words were scrawled in the same bright green paint as yesterday's message. But Adam Marsh wasn't buying it. Whoever did this was clearly playing up the teenager angle, and yet the chief had found shiny new nail heads in a small corner of the kitchen floor and the same in a corner of the dining area. He figured the perps had carefully pried up the flooring, looked beneath, and then reattached it with a nail gun. Not exactly the behavior of kids blowing off steam. Not to mention they had avoided both Tango and Cash, who had patrolled all night—one in the car and one on foot.

He tried not to judge their police work. The Main Street business district was more than three quarters of a mile long with a number of side streets to cover as well. It wouldn't be too difficult to slip past two patrolmen. Still, maybe he should be the one to patrol tonight. As if he had the time.

Chief Marsh jotted a few notes in his pad. He was happy to have sole command of the crime scene, as Barton was busy elsewhere. Adam's co-chief had borrowed a drain pipe camera from a plumber friend and was snaking it through the opened floors and walls of the town hall and Side Bar, searching for any clues as to what the vandals may have been after. The vintage store, Rerun, never seemed to be open, so they were unable to follow up. It was a good idea, the camera. Adam wished he'd thought of it himself.

Jessie popped his head into the room. "Chief, they've got the security footage from last night cued up if you want to have a look at it."

"Thanks." Adam walked back to the small office and plopped down in a desk chair. He could tell almost immediately that the footage would be no help. The black and white picture was dark and incredibly grainy, showing a wide hallway, which he recognized as the main entrance. After a few seconds of no activity, he hit the fast forward button and told Jessie, "This may take a while. Why don't you head back to the station?"

"You got it, Chief."

Adam sank into the faux leather chair, feeling a wave of exhaustion wash over him. He'd been up studying the night before until about

3:00 AM and the office was on the dark side. Perhaps he should lay his head down on the counter and sneak in a quick power nap. No, that could be humiliating if someone walked in. On the other hand . . . The insistent buzz of a cell phone snagged him from his thoughts. He rummaged through his pants pockets and came out with the vibrating phone.

"This is Chief Marsh," he said.

"Hi Adam, it's Chet Bushman."

Adam grimaced. "Hey , Chet. How are you?"

"I'm good. But could you do me a favor and answer this line 'Pastor Marsh' instead of 'Chief Marsh?' That way there's no confusion."

"Sure thing, Chet. I just got a little turned around. I'm sort of in the middle of something." He chided himself for getting his two cell phones mixed up again, causing worlds to collide. This sort of thing was happening more frequently with each passing day.

"No problem. I guess they haven't gotten to that class in seminary yet. I know you're still new to all this." He chuckled, but in a spiteful way.

Adam swallowed back the words forming on his tongue and let out a polite chuckle myself. Bushman was one of five elders at Clinch Rock Community Church, making him Adam's boss in a very real way. The older man made it no secret that he had voted against hiring Adam as pastor, despite the enthusiastic recommendation of the retiring Dr. Pardee. He now seemed almost fixated on pointing out each and every one of Adam's pastoral shortcomings to anyone who would listen. Adam couldn't help but think that the two speeding tickets he'd giving him in the past year may have factored in to this.

"I just wanted to touch base about a couple of things," Chet said, with the tone of a father about to lecture his son on the importance of making curfew. "First off, don't forget about the board meeting next Tuesday."

"It's on my calendar."

"And I don't like bringing this up again, but you have yet to establish office hours. There are people who need to talk to their pastor. Not to mention shut-ins who have not been visited all summer."

Adam bit his tongue. "I'm doing my best, Chet. It'll be a lot easier in a couple months, when I'm no longer holding two full-time jobs, plus classes."

"You said that a couple months ago."

"I know. There are just a few loose ends I needed to tie up."

Chet sighed loudly. "Unfortunately, your congregation needs you now, not in eight weeks. Ruth Fletcher was at the emergency room last week with chest pains and Ruth Parker is having cataract surgery tomorrow."

The police chief was no longer listening. He was rewinding. In the blur of fast-forwarded footage, a dark figure had entered the frame and walked right up to the camera before the picture went black.

"Adam?"

"Uh, yeah, Chet. No problem. I'll talk to you later." He hung up. Stupid remote. He'd accidentally rewound right over the action and then some, bringing him back to the empty hallway. He pressed PLAY and waited for the intruder in real time.

The phone in his other pocket bleeped. He dug it out—a calendar reminder, "Shooting with Trenton, Wednesday @ 7:00 AM." Early morning archery had been a weekly summer tradition for father and son since Trenton was seven years old. This year, they had yet to make it out once in the midst of police, church, and school appointments. Regardless of how packed his schedule was, he would not cancel this time. He clicked CONFIRM.

A phone was ringing. Which?—this one. "Pastor Marsh," he said.

"Hi, pastor. It's April Somers." Adam cradled his aching head. Despite the pleasant-sounding name, April was continually bemoaning the state of everything—the church, her health, the country, that TV show where celebrities dance with ordinary people.

"What can I do for you, April?"

"I have three different swatches of fabric for the new curtains in the library," she said. "None of them really does it for me, but it's the best they had. Twenty years ago, fabric was cheaper, higher quality, and a lot more attractive. It's really a shame what's happened to the industry."

"Okay . . . ?"

"So when do you want to see them?"

"See what?"

"The swatches."

Adam felt like slamming his skull against the Formica. "I don't really think I need to see them, April. Whatever you decide will be just fine. I trust you."

"Well," she said, with a bit of a huff, "when Dr. Pardee was here, he always signed off on these things."

Still nothing was happening on the screen. He'd really overshot it with the rewinding.

"I'm afraid I just haven't got time, April. Thanks for the call."

There was a pause, during which he could almost hear her deciding who to call first to complain about how pastors today weren't nearly as good as they'd been forty years ago. And then she said, "Okay then. Goodbye."

Before he could even set the phone down on the counter, the other one began to buzz. He waffled a second before deciding on, "Chief Marsh."

"Pardon?"

"This is Adam Marsh."

"Hey Adam! This is Nick from Historical Theology class. Just calling to tell you that the study group tonight was moved back to 6:20, still at the library."

"I'm afraid I can't make it tonight."

"Sorry to hear that. Don't forget we've got a test tomorrow on the Ante-Nicene Fathers."

Adam felt a squeeze in his gut for just a moment at the thought of how unprepared he was for this test, but then the black-and-white man was back, right in Chief Marsh's face, and he mashed the pause button at just the right moment.

"You still there?" the man on the phone asked.

"Uh, yeah. I'll see you in class tomorrow, Nate," Adam said absently.

"It's Nick . . . See you."

Adam's eyes were locked onto the screen. He was looking at a frame of a man dressed all in black, including a black ski mask, reaching up with his left hand, in the process of yanking the cable out of the security camera. Even through the grain, Adam could see the man's droopy eyes, tinged with malice. They were unfamiliar. As he reached for the cable, the man's shirt rode up a bit on his belly, revealing the handle of a semiautomatic pistol.

Chief Marsh leaned back in the chair, still staring into the eyes of this unknown man who was violating the security of his little town, and made a decision. As much as he wanted the madness of the past few months to be over, he knew he couldn't lay down his badge until he caught whoever was doing this. No matter how long it took.

* * *

"Nice," Jason affirmed. "I don't think you can do better than that. Classic shirt-and-tie look—a little preppy, but not douchey. You look like Jeremy Renner."

"Thanks," Trenton said, inspecting himself in the mirror. It was a ritual that Jason would come over before Trenton went on a date, to give him advice, encouragement, and other input. Jason had been on exactly four dates himself, none of which had gone particularly well, but Trenton allowed the tradition to continue all the same.

"Actually, did I say Jeremy Renner? I meant Alfalfa. You know, from *The Little Rascals*?"

"Uh huh."

"Because of your hair. It's way too plastered down. What did you put in it?"

Trenton examined his hair up close. "Same stuff as always."

Jason shook his head. "See, that's your problem. You should have borrowed my product. Then you'd have some of this going on." He indicated his own hair which always seemed to defy gravity, sticking up all over the place in a display of calculated chaos.

"I'll have to make due, I guess."

They heard a knock coming from the back door, upstairs. "I'll get it," Jason said, mussing Trenton's hair. "You work on that." He paused, holding his hand up like a dead rodent. "Ugh." He wiped it on Trenton's bedspread on the way out the door. "Why is it so *sticky*?"

One thing Trenton loved about the new house was his bedroom, which was down in the basement and accessed through the garage, meaning he and his friends could come and go without passing through the main house. It had once been an apartment for missionaries home on furlough. Taking over this room, rather than one of two extra bedrooms on the second floor, had been a hard sell, but his dad had lacked the energy to keep arguing. It made Trenton feel quite grown-up, as if he lived in an apartment by himself. Of course, with his father rarely home during the past few months, he generally had the whole house to himself anyway, but that was beside the point. This was his bachelor pad and he knew exactly how he wanted it to look. If he could ever find the time to make it a reality.

"Oh Judith, it's you," he heard Jason call from the top of the stairs. "You're looking . . . bizarre."

"Is Trent home?" she asked.

"He is, but your timing is a little *suspish*."

"Huh?"

"Suspicious? He's getting ready for a date."

"I just need to talk to him for a second. It's important."

"It's a date with Zoe," Jason was saying. "From the other night. Or did you already know that?"

His hair more or less repaired, Trenton took the stairs two at a time, intent on ending this conversation before it got any more awkward.

"Hey, Trenton, look who's here," Jason said, "with something important to talk about. Right when your date with Zoe is about to start. Huge coincidence, am I right?"

"I just need a second," Judith said, looking at the wall between the two boys. "In private."

Jason snickered. "It's like that?"

"Shut up, Jason," Trenton said. "We can go inside." He unlocked the door to the main house and led her into the living room, where he plopped down on the couch and propped his feet up on a stack of moving boxes. "So what's up?"

Judith brought her foot up on the same box. She was wearing bright blue cowboy boots.

"What do you think?" she asked, beaming.

"Of what?"

"The boots! Someone brought them into the store today and I snatched them up."

"Um . . . " Trenton was at a total loss. *This* was somehow urgent enough to interrupt preparations for his first date with Zoe? He wondered if perhaps Jason had been on to something, albeit in an obnoxious way. Oh, well. At least she was off the superhero thing. "They're a little odd, but you pull them off."

"Right? And check these out. They came in with the remainder from an estate sale." She pulled two small white wings, about the size of an open hand, from her bag. Each had a shiny blue ribbon attached to it.

"What are they?"

"You wear them on your arms, like up here," she said, pointing to her bicep. "They look like regular porcelain, but they're actually aluminum oxide, so they won't break." She rapped one against the nearby coffee table. "I think these and the boots will set the tone for all of it."

"All of what?"

"My uniform," Judith said, as though it were the most obvious thing in the world.

Trenton groaned. Of course she wasn't on to something else. Judith was one of the most single-minded people he'd ever met. It would take a major blow for any sort of course correction to take place now that she'd set her sights on the superhero thing.

"Look, I've been thinking about this," Trenton said, "and I just don't see how it makes sense. I mean, even forgetting that superheroes don't exist—even in New York and Chicago—Clinch Rock is way too small of a town. Everyone knows everyone else. People would recognize you."

"That's what the costume is for. It has to be good, so when someone looks at me, they see the persona, not the person, you know?" She dug in her bag for a minute and came out with a sketch book, filled with ideas for superhero outfits. "It's hard putting it all together. I mean, in the movies, they just sort of draw it out and then suddenly they're wearing it in the next scene. But this is a big project in real life."

Trenton opened his mouth to speak, but thought better of it. There was a chance that Judith did not fully grasp the distinction between movies and reality, but he knew bringing that up would not be a smart move. She was so eccentric that it was occasionally hard to tell if she was just being odd or was indeed full-on crazy. Either way, reading a book about "insane faith" was probably not the best thing for someone with Judith's tendency toward extremes.

"I know I want it to be modest," she was saying. "In the comics, most of the female heroes' costumes are really slutty, which is totally demeaning."

Trenton flipped through the pages of the sketchbook. "The masks are really small."

"It's a domino mask. Lots of superheroes wear them."

"But it's only the size of, like, a pair of sunglasses. Anyone who recognized you with shades on would recognize you with this."

"The mask is only part of the whole thing," she objected. "I'll add a beauty mark or two with makeup, change the color of my eyes with contacts, maybe the color of my hair."

"What, you're going to dye your hair back and forth every night?"

She laughed. "Ever hear of a wig?"

Trenton tried to tally up in his mind how much this would all cost in both money and effort. At least that would delay her, hopefully long enough for her to move on to something else. It wouldn't be the first time Judith had jumped from one obsession to another without fully executing the first.

Then again, she had surprised him before with her tenacity and perseverance, not the least of which was joining the boys' wrestling team and competing for an entire season, her threats of a lawsuit enough to keep her on the team, but not enough to keep Coach Fischer from turning a blind eye to all sorts of hazing and mockery.

She'd also spent a weekend living in a shaft of the old boarded-up copper mine, on a dare. Then there was the previous summer, which she'd largely spent hopping onto trains as they passed through Clinch Rock, riding them to far away cities before hopping off and catching another back home. Somehow, reality just didn't seem to confine her like it did everyone else. Trenton's best hope was that, by the time she got all this stuff together, the break-ins would have stopped. After all, there were only so many buildings in downtown Clinch Rock.

"So . . . ?" she prompted.

"So what?"

"Which one do you like best?"

"I think they all look cool. In theory. You could make a great comic book with these."

She swatted the comment away with a wave of her hand. "I also need to decide on a weapon. I'm thinking something from the Bible, to go with the theme. Maybe a slingshot, like the one David used on Goliath. I've been working on my accuracy and I'm really good. I think I might be a natural."

"You mean a sling, right?" Trenton said. "The weapon in the Bible isn't a slingshot, like Dennis the Menace used."

She rolled her eyes. "I know."

"It's deadly, though. Look." He grabbed his backpack from the floor and pulled his *Radical Teenz Study Bible* from the front compartment, flipping the worn pages until he found the what he was looking for. "Look at this."

Judith sat down next to him and took in the drawing of the weapon. Trenton read out loud. "The biblical sling was comprised of two leather straps and a pouch from which the ammunition was fired. A good sling could carry its full force to the distance of 200 yards and skilled slingers could hit their mark from that distance. The Benjamites could sling a stone with enough accuracy to hit a target the width of a human hair. There are accounts in antiquity of lead ammunition being hurled with enough velocity to melt mid-flight from the friction of the air. Being hit by one of these was the equivalent of being shot with a musket ball!" Judith smiled.

"You could kill somebody with one of those!" Trenton said.

"I'm also considering the ox goad."

"What?! What is that?"

"I'm not entirely sure, but in the book of Judges, this guy named Shamgar took out a whole army of Philistines with one."

"Tell me this is all a joke," Trenton pleaded. "You're trolling me, right?"

Judith turned and looked him straight in the eyes. "Not even a little bit. I think God is calling me to rescue somebody."

Trenton looked around for someone to rescue him from this conversation. Unfortunately, he'd locked Jason out of the main house.

"You probably have to go, huh?" Judith said. "On your date?"

He checked his watch. "Yeah."

"Where are you taking her?"

"Nowhere. It's just dinner with Zoe and her parents at their place."

"You want to borrow the Iron Horse? You could show up at the Castle in style."

Trenton forced down a smile. "No thanks. I don't know if rolling up on your ancient scooter would score me any points with Zoe's family."

"It's not a scooter. It's a classic Honda 90. But you're right. Zoe wouldn't appreciate it. It's not snobby enough." She quickly packed up her things and hoisted her bag onto her shoulder. "Have fun on your date," she said. "I hope you're not too 'low-class' for them."

CHAPTER SIX
"ZEAL FOR THE PAST"

"Life should be an adventure. Never settle for less. If you've gone all-in, no-holds-barred, *cray-cray* for Jesus, there will never be a dull moment."

-Insane Faith: Superhero Edition
by Stephen Branding, p. 122

The Cassel House was well-known to everyone in Clinch Rock, although most mistakenly called it The Castle House, which made sense considering the two large turrets flanking the front of the edifice as well as its sheer imposing size. For most of Trenton's life, all of the windows had been boarded up with plywood and the grass had been mowed, at most, three times each summer. But as he approached the front door, the manicured lawn and beautifully restored windows—some of them leaded with colored glass—made it hard to even remember the place as it had looked abandoned.

The angry ferret was back in his stomach and seemed to have been downing shots of espresso during the short walk from the parsonage. Trenton took a deep breath and held it for a moment, standing at the front door. When he let it out, he envisioned his anxiety leaving with it, disappearing into the evening air. But he was still a wreck as he thumped the old knocker against the door.

A moment later, Zoe was standing before him, wearing a little black dress and a necklace of pearls. He opened his mouth to tell her how nice she looked, but only a small, halted squeak emerged, perhaps from the ferret down below. She laughed, her wide smile seeming to contain more teeth than the average mouth, although that made no sense, all perfectly white and straight.

"Come on in," she said, beckoning warmly. "My dad's in the parlor. He can't wait to meet you."

Trenton followed her through an ornate foyer and into a large, open room. There, Brian Green stood, waiting to greet him. He was a thin man with thick hair and a Van Dyke beard. He wore a vest over his shirt and tie, but no jacket. For some reason, Trenton had a hard time picturing him *not* wearing a vest.

He took a step forward and grasped Trenton's hand, giving it two firm pumps. "You must be the famous Mr. Marsh," he said. "I've heard much about you."

"It's great to meet you, sir."

"Call me Brian."

"Okay . . . Um, yeah. Brian." Trenton looked around the parlor as an awkward silence threatened to overtake the conversation before it even got started. There were two pieces of uncomfortable looking antique furniture a few steps from them, but otherwise, the room was bear. Nothing on the walls, which looked as though they had recently been repainted.

"It's a work in progress," Brian said, "but we can see it exactly as it will be. The colors, the art. She'll be restored just as she would have been in her hey-day during the 1890s." He walked over to a patch of new plaster and ran his hand over it. "You wouldn't believe the primitive wiring we replaced. It's a wonder the place never burned down."

A *ding* sounded from the kitchen and Brian excused himself to check on dinner.

"He likes you," Zoe said. "He can read people quickly. And I can read him."

Trenton smiled, a bit goofily. "Is your mother here too?"

Zoe's face fell a bit, though she tried to hide it. "My mother passed away. When I was eleven years old."

"Mine too," Trenton said. "When I was ten." She reached ever and took his hand.

After a moment, Trenton cleared his throat. "What's all this?" he asked, pointing to a folding table in the corner, covered in black and white photographs.

She led him over. "These are part of our collection. Photos from Clinch Rock's lumbering roots. What do you think?"

Trenton examined a picture of two dozen lumberjacks sitting on an enormous felled pine. They were broad-shouldered, tall men, but none of them as tall as the cross-section of the tree itself. "Whoa."

"Yeah, this whole area was covered in trees that size. But by the early twentieth century, it was all logged out. There are only a couple small preserves in the state where you can still find old growth pine forest. But who could blame them? Pine was like gold back then."

"I guess it paid for all this, right?"

"I think we're all ready here," came Brian's voice from another room. "Let's have a seat."

When dinner had been doled out—lobster tails, quinoa, and Brussel sprouts in olive oil and sea salt—Brian turned to his guest and asked, "Have you heard how much I paid for this house?"

"Uh, no. I mean, it's not—"

Brian laughed. "Forgive me. I'm having fun. I don't usually discuss money, but in this case it's just too good to keep to myself." He drew up his already perfect posture in the chair. "For the deed to this house, I paid . . . one dollar."

"Seriously?"

"It's a wonderful story. This magnificent place had been empty, falling apart for years. The property had reverted to the city, who couldn't seem to give it away, no matter how much they dropped the price. No one could afford to repair and maintain it. Eventually, they offered it to anyone who would pay off the back-taxes, which stood at about twenty thousand dollars. Still, no takers." He took a drink of his wine. "Then last year, they decided that this historic house had become an eyesore and had to either be restored or torn down. To that end, they forgave the back taxes and offered the place for a dollar to anyone who could show themselves capable of the restoration." Zoe beamed as she listened to her father. "And of course the town council was bowled over by our plans for the museum and all the rest."

Trenton stopped fighting with the lobster shell long enough to say, "Museum?"

Brian dabbed politely at his mouth with the cloth napkin. "Trenton, we aren't restoring this place for ourselves. This is the first step in a much larger revitalization plan for Clinch Rock as a whole. It's a long time overdue. My mother grew up here, you know. Not this house, of course, but one just down the road. She taught me to care about where we come from. To revere the past. That's something this town—most towns, really—has lost. We're going to give it back to them." He locked eyes across the table with Zoe and they both smiled. Trenton noticed that she too was drinking wine.

"Zoe tells me that you live in the church parsonage. I'll bet you didn't know that your home used to be the servants' quarters for this house."

"I . . . did not know that," Trenton said, suddenly feeling foolish and small, the servant to this man with the grand vision.

"It's true. All the houses in the two blocks between us were only erected about fifty years ago. Before that, it was one big estate and Mr. Cassel, a somewhat eccentric lumber baron, valued his privacy so much that he had separate servants' quarters built on the opposite edge of his property, inconvenient as it was for the help. That's why the house where you live is so much older than all the homes around it."

"Interesting," Trenton said.

Brian's face went sour. "I hate that word. *Interesting.* Find a better one."

"Um, okay. I mean, I'll—"

"Tell me, Trenton, do you even know why this town is here?"

"I . . . um . . . guess not."

"Don't feel bad," Brian offered, smiling again. "Most people don't. Clinch Rock was a mill town, founded in the 1890s. You know where the old mill is? Or what's left of it?"

"Behind the Sunoco, right?"

"That's right. They cut board there from the booming lumber industry. There were also two major lumber camps right nearby, both of them owned and operated by Mr. Cassel, as was the mill.

"But Benjamin Cassel was unlike other lumber barons. More like King Solomon. He came to the summit of riches and luxury and determined them to be worthless. Near the end of his life, he *found Jesus*, I suppose, and donated a large sum of money to expand the town church, where your father is parson, correct?"

"Yeah."

"Cassel was very close with Jeremiah Wolcott, the founding minister. And, having let his servants go, he donated the house where you now live to the church."

"Well, we appreciate that," Trenton laughed. "That's nice of him."

Brian gazed at him, stone-faced for a moment. "The story gets a lot less *nice* from there. It turns out that Cassel planned to do away with almost all of his worldly goods before he left this mortal coil. Specifically, he decided to give an enormous hoard of cash he'd been piling up—a majority of his entire fortune—to the church, to fund mission and humanitarian work among the local American Indians and the families of men who had worked in his camps. But when his bookkeeper, a mean old lumberjack whose knees and back could no longer take the toil, was asked to draw up the papers . . . well, he simply couldn't bear the thought of all that money just evaporating like that." Brian set down his silverware and leaned forward with exhilaration.

"One night, he cornered the lumber baron, right here in this house, and demanded that the money be given to him instead. Cassel refused. The confrontation came to blows and Cassel was killed in the bedlam. So the bookkeeper—his name was Wellick—crossed the grounds to your current home, dragged Reverend Wolcott out of bed in the middle of the night, brought him back here and demanded he give Cassel a Christian burial. You may have noticed the grave marker on your way in."

Trenton nodded. Every kid in town knew about the headstone, as it was the basis for many a ghost story involving the allegedly haunted Cassel House.

Brian continued, "And then Wellick did something that no one saw coming. He settled in here, made this *his* home, as if he had bought it fair and square. Can you imagine that? Taking over the house of the man you killed in cold blood?" Zoe shook her head, projecting awe more than disapproval.

"That is pretty crazy," Trenton said.

"Oh, that's not the end. Not even close. You see, it wasn't too long before Cassel's business partners in the Saginaw Valley caught wind of what had happened, and they sent hired thugs—an infamous group who called themselves the Crown Fire Boys—to put things right and locate the missing hoard of cash. These men were so hardened, even the lumberjacks feared them."

Brian slammed his palm against the long dining room table, causing Trenton to jump in his seat. "The men burst into the house, right through the same front door you entered tonight, and demanded the money. They searched every room, but could not locate it. And so they began to torture Wellick. They tied him to a chair and beat him, not far from where you are sitting. You can still see the evidence of it."

Trenton looked down, spotting a brownish stain in the wood floor about four feet from where he sat.

"It may have been the very chair you're sitting in. Fascinating, isn't it?" His eyes pulled down in affected sadness, but the corners of his mouth pulled up just a bit. Trenton glanced at Zoe, who was utterly transfixed by her father's retelling of these events.

"They did their worst," Brian continued, "But the old lumberjack wouldn't give it up, no matter what they tried. Do you see that bump in the wall behind you?"

Trenton looked. "Yeah."

"While they were cutting off Wellick's fingers, they thought they saw him glance at that wall and so they opened it up to have a look. It was never properly repaired." He leaned against the arm of his chair, studying the spot. "We're not going to fix that. It's part of the story of the house."

Trent's eyes skipped from the stained floor to the bulging wall and he suddenly thought of the recent break-ins, of floors and walls ripped open, the intruders looking for something. "Who have you told this story to?" he asked.

Brian smiled. "Whoever will listen. The week before last, I made a presentation to the entire town council. We're not looking for any funding from the city, but buy-in is important. And people respond to stories, especially this type of story. For millennia, few things have inspired the same level of interest as a hidden treasure. People will kill for it. Die for it."

"So no one ever found the money?"

"No. And Wellick died rather than give it up. Or perhaps he never had it to begin with. It's possible that Cassel never disclosed its location and the information died with him. Or—who knows?—maybe the Reverend got a hold of the cash even before Wellick made his move and it's hidden somewhere in your house. Since Wolcott died suddenly not long after all this, we'll probably never know."

Trenton laughed, trying to lighten the mood. "Don't tell my dad. He'll start tearing the place apart. From what he tells me, the church could definitely still use a hoard of cash."

Brian nodded, knowingly. "Money motivates people, perhaps more than anything else. There's even an account of the Rev. Wolcott coming here while the Crown Fire Boys tortured Wellick, trying to convince the man to give up the cash. Do you think your father would do that?"

"What?" Trenton looked from Brian to Zoe. "Of course not!"

Brian shrugged. "I'm sure he's a good man, but it takes money to run a lumber camp. Or a church. Or to turn a town like Clinch Rock around and make it what it once was. What it should have been. And you said yourself—the church is in need of some extra funds."

Zoe poked at him. "Stop being weird, Daddy."

Brian laughed. "I'm sorry, Trenton. You have to forgive my zeal. Sometimes I get so passionate about the history of a place, I forget myself in the present."

"Anyway," Zoe said, "Trenton's father is not just a pastor; he's the chief of police too. He'd have arrested the Crown Fire Boys on the spot."

"Of course," Brian said. "Zoe, would you mind clearing this and bringing in the dessert?"

"My pleasure."

When Zoe had disappeared into the kitchen, their plates all stacked precariously, Brian looked long and hard at his guest before saying, "I'm not stupid, Trenton."

"I . . . What? Did I say something?" He shifted uncomfortably in his seat, which seemed to be getting harder by the minute. He felt a bit as if he were the one tied to the chair, torture impending.

"I know you're looking for an excuse to spend some time with my daughter. And I can respect that. You seem like an upstanding young man, the son of a minister and a peace officer. A community leader. I've got nothing to worry about with you, do I?"

"No, sir."

"Good. Then here's your excuse: you help us with the museum and the rebranding of the town. The two of you do some busywork and some leg work together, and who knows? Maybe something special will develop."

Trenton nodded. "Thank you , sir," he said. He realized all at once the ferret in his belly was now fast asleep. Or maybe he'd vanished. Somehow in the midst of all the theft, torture, and avarice, he'd gotten the approval of Zoe's father, which he now saw was more important to her than he could have possibly anticipated. And not only that, but Brian had offered to create ongoing opportunities for the two of them to spend time together. With school starting just around the corner, this should have been the best news he could have possibly received.

Just then, Zoe reappeared, carrying three plates of peach cobbler, filling the room with the scent of baked sugar and butter. It was almost enough to distract him from the bloodstains on the floor and the gnawing feeling that his life was already over-full without the added responsibility of rebooting an entire town.

* * *

It was almost 11:30 by the time Trenton got home. After dinner, they'd returned to the parlor for coffee and more conversation, during which he had really taken to Brian Green. The man's intensity about the past was off-putting at first, but once Trenton got used to that, he found him charming and friendly. The three of them had talked about the challenges of such a large undertaking, as well as their ongoing project of restoring the old lumber camp and their future plans to purchase and restore the dilapidated saw mill. The whole thing left Trenton feeling very *up* and full of hope, as if anyone could accomplish anything if they just believed they could. Maybe that's what Sean Tailor meant by, *Never give up unless you're giving up giving up.* No, that still made no sense.

The light was still on in the living room, so he decided to drop in and say hi to his dad. They had spent maybe an hour together in the past two weeks, between camp and his dad's hectic schedule. And the fact that they now came and went through separate doors had only meant less face time for the Marsh men.

Even before slipping his key into the lock, Trenton knew something was wrong. "Dad?" he called, navigating his way past several stacks of boxes and into the living room. "You here, Dad?" No answer. Then a thump. And another.

It was coming from upstairs.

CHAPTER SEVEN
"LEG IRONS & WEIGHTS"

The disquiet in Trent's gut prompted him to tear open a nearby box marked "GARAGE – SPORTS EQUIP." Pawing frantically through the contents, he came out with a wooden baseball bat, which he held at the ready, quietly approaching the stairs.

More thumping and what sounded like someone talking in hushed tones. It was coming from his dad's room—no doubt about that. Despites his efforts to walk lightly, the old stairs creaked and complained with every step. He paused at the top of the staircase and listened. Should he call the police station? His arms felt heavy and he doubted if he could even swing the bat in his current state of mind.

Then he heard gasping. And grunting. Trenton slammed through the partially open door, weapon at the ready. No one. Wait, no. On the ground, against the wall, Chief Marsh was slumped, clutching his chest.

"Dad!" The bat clattered to the ground and Trenton was over the bed and at his side in a second. "What's wrong? Can you breathe?" His father's big hand grabbed him around the arm and squeezed.

"I'm calling 911." The grip tightened and Chief Marsh shook his head fervently. "Dad, you're having a heart attack or something! You need help."

"Not a heart attack," he managed to croak between gasps.

"How do you know?"

"Water." The grip loosened. "Please."

"Okay." Trenton ran to the bathroom and filled a plastic cup with water, sloshing half of it onto the floor as he returned to his father's side. "Here, let me help you." He tipped the cup and his dad took a long gulp of water. His breathing slowed a bit and he leaned his head back against the wall, eyes closed.

"How do you feel?"

"Better. I'll be okay"

"I still think we should call an ambulance."

Dad snapped to attention. "Absolutely not. All calls to central dispatch are relayed to the station. We'd have Barton at the front door in three minutes. Or Tango and Cash. They'd use it to hurry me out the door for good. I'm not ready for that."

Trenton plopped down next to him. "Maybe it's time, though, right? You're running yourself ragged. I mean, if that wasn't a heart attack, what was it?"

"It was a panic attack." He sighed. "It's not the first. Dr. Skinner taught me these breathing exercises to get through. It works. I'll be fine."

Trenton was unsure. "But if you're having panic attacks and you're on your way out of police work anyway, doesn't it kind of make sense to just call it quits now? You're spread way too thin. And now all these break-ins . . . "

"I've been running a police department for fourteen years without any issues from stress. Not an ulcer. Not a single sleepless night. We've had two armed robberies, half a dozen burglaries, an arson, and even a murder in that time. I think I can handle a few vandals. It's just all the other things piling up. But it's temporary. I can do anything if it's temporary." He forced a smile. "I promise, it'll be fine."

"Will you also promise me that you're done at the end of October? No more putting it off?"

Chief Marsh hesitated. "No. I can't promise that."

Trent clapped the cup down on the floor next to him, a little harder than he intended. "Will you at least take some personal time? A couple days at least?"

"I'm taking Friday off, remember? Even ditching class and a deacons' meeting. I'll have a nice drive down to Grand Rapids and spend the whole day kicking back at the Stephen Branding conference."

"That's not what I mean. From where I'm sitting, that guy's partially to blame. I mean, it was a good book and everything, but there's only so much one person can do."

Trent's dad sat up straight. "There's always more. It's just a matter of managing it. Priorities. Did you know Stephen Branding works 80 hours a week? He's optimized his sleep schedule so he only needs four hours a night and three twenty-minute naps throughout the day. "

Trenton had only heard about this maybe thirty times from his father. "Yeah? And how many panic attacks does he have?"

"Watch it, kid. I'm still your dad, even if I'm not around as much as I should be."

"I didn't mean it that way. I'm just worried."

"Don't be. Your old man's unbreakable." He smiled and gave Trenton's shoulder a reassuring squeeze "Are we still on for shooting Wednesday morning? And breakfast at the diner?"

"If you have the time."

"I wouldn't miss it for anything." He stood up and helped his son to his feet. "Seriously, don't worry about me. I'll be fine. Let's both get some sleep."

* * *

2:13 AM. Trenton sighed. His mind was churning and sleep was as far off as it had been two hours ago when his head hit the pillow. His usual routine of scrolling through Facebook on his phone only keyed him up all the more. The never-ending posts, the flurries of activity, only served to remind him of his father's psychic overload and added to his own. He turned off the phone, clearing the chaos from the screen and ordered his mind to do the same thing. No such luck. His internal remote was broken, such that every attempt to power down merely changed the channel from one set of worries to another.

There was Dad, of course, hopefully sleeping soundly upstairs, but more likely lying awake himself, fighting down concerns about church budgets, unsolved crimes, unpleasant career transitions, a teenage son he rarely saw, and graduate classes that were quite literally Greek to him. Or worse, what if he was in the throes of another panic attack? Or an actual heart attack, dismissing it as something less while his body gave way?

Trenton knew he had a tendency to worry too much when it came to his father's well-being. And he knew it was likely a result of losing his mom to a car accident years earlier. With only one parent left, it was only natural for Trent to fixate on the dangers of strapping on a gun each morning and responding to emergency calls. For that reason, he had been initially relieved by his father's plans to trade in the badge for a Bible. But now he wondered if the transition would ever really happen. And in the meantime, his dad seemed continually exhausted and distracted, just when he needed his wits about him most.

The remote clicked. And then there was Judith. Ever since grade school, Trenton had felt a responsibility to help her fit in and keep her from following through on some of her crazier ideas. What if she was out there right now, prowling the streets of Clinch Rock while Tango and Cash patrolled? If they crossed paths, naturally they would assume she was the culprit. Or what if she happened upon the real burglars? Sure, she was smart and tough, but she wasn't a superhero.

What he needed was something to distract her from her current fixation. She wouldn't give it up outright, but he might be able to redirect her energies elsewhere. He just had to tempt her with something more appealing. Something like a weird new band that played instruments made out of reclaimed coffins. Or maybe another new collection—antique Peruvian military insignia or something. But what exactly? Judith's varied interests seemed to follow no discernable pattern.

Trenton changed the channel again. *Think about Zoe.* A rush of puppy love and euphoria replaced the angst for a moment, followed by frazzled nerves and a low-level dread. Sure, things had gone well tonight, but he somehow knew it wouldn't last. Once she saw him at school— a tiny minnow even in their small pond—she'd forget him and move on. The fact that her father seemed to be pulling for him buoyed his spirits once again, but that support came with a price, and Trenton was hard-pressed to imagine himself with the time and energy it would take to make a real contribution to Brian Green's "Reboot Clinch Rock" campaign. The prospect of a girlfriend had been all upside at camp. But camp was insulated from real life.

Apart from work and school (which was only a week and a half away) he'd inherited a slew of new responsibilities over the past few months—and not just regular teenage duties like mowing the lawn, keeping the dog fed and walked, or taking out the trash. He also had to keep the laundry under control and even bring the payments for water, power, and gas down to the utility company, lest they be shut off. Not to mention that he'd become his own cook at least half the time. All of this had initially struck him as an exciting preview of adulthood, but it was getting old and left Trenton little time and energy for his own pursuits. Jason had been complaining all summer about how he missed the old Trenton, before he "went corporate," whatever that was supposed to mean.

And yet Trenton always found time for Judith. Why was his mind going back to her? Probably because it was just going in circles, he told himself, stir-crazy lying here in this bed. Forget it; there was no point in flopping back and forth, from one side to the other, keyed up as he was. He clicked on his light and sat up. The first thing he saw was the three tall stacks of boxes, a reminder that he had also promised his dad he'd take care of their unpacking before the summer was over, as well as a few small repairs around their new house. Progress was practically nil so far.

The next thing he saw was the *Insane Faith* tear-off desk calendar on his night stand—a gift from his father of course. Since it was technically tomorrow, he decided to just own it and ripped off a page, start fresh. Today's quote read, "Remember, Jesus said to store up your treasures in heaven. But you can go even further than that! Pile them high! Are you focusing on your life now, rather than on your life in heaven? Quit it! Stack up mountains of jewels for your crown! Then you'll see the stuff of this life for what it is: leg irons and weights, dragging you down."

Trenton knocked it off the nightstand and onto the ground. This was the sort of thinking that had convinced his father to dive into the pastorate, to move them from the only home he'd ever lived in—with all of its memories, including memories of his mom. Now Trenton had the distinct feeling that *he* was nothing more than a weight, dragging his father down. On the back of the calendar, he saw the words

"Superhero Edition" and the little caped cartoon, reminding him once again of Judith.

He decided he may as well be productive and climbed out of bed, pulling on some shorts and a T-shirt form a pile of clothes on the floor, and flipping on the overhead light. There were boxes to be unpacked, but that would require decision-making and organization and he was too tired for that. His eyes fell to the outer walls of the room, which were covered in an ugly knotty pine paneling. Before moving in, Trenton had received permission from the church board to remove the paneling and expose the fieldstone behind it. Maybe a little manual labor would usher him to the gates of dreamland.

It took about five minutes to locate the box with the prybar and hammer, and Trenton went to work with a vengeance, starting at the corner and working his way out. At first, the tongue-and-groove boards resisted his efforts, but soon, they were falling away as quickly as he could insert the bar behind them and twist his hips. The stone foundation, ancient and rustic, was exactly the look Trenton wanted.

He was about halfway down the longest wall when he encountered a particularly stubborn panel. It seemed to be nailed down to something. Careful to keep the noise to a minimum, Trenton picked up the hammer and began methodically knocking the bar in and prying it up. After a few repetitions, he could see behind the panel—not to the stone wall of the house's foundation, but to wood. He slowly convinced six more panels to release their hold and was amused to find that they were all attached to one expansive piece of lumber. He ran his hand along it. Not plywood or particle board, but solid wood. He thought of the pictures of giant trees, felled by lumberjacks more than a century ago. Two more slats came down before the stretch of wood ended and the block wall resumed.

Rooting through the box of tools, Trenton found a tape measure and stretched it out along the dimensions of this enormous cut of wood. Seven feet tall and nine feet wide. A sudden lightbulb came on, seeming to cast a warm glow in the midst of the sickly fluorescent bulbs of his bedroom. He would ask Judith to use this wood as the canvas for a mural, right here in his bedroom. She'd done a mural on the cinder block wall of the art room at school. It had taken her all semester, consuming evenings and even weekends. Yes, this had the potential to distract her from capes and costumes long enough for the whole thing to blow over. Besides, it could look cool.

Trenton smiled smugly at his own genius. It was perfect. In fact, it was the only thing that made sense. After all, he couldn't see how the wood had been mounted to the wall and, therefore, had no idea how to take it down—may as well incorporate it into the decor. Another thought crossed his mind. He could call Zoe tomorrow and tell her about this lumber-related discovery. She'd insist on coming down here to inspect it.

He'd have to clean up a little bit, but his pseudo-apartment definitely couldn't hurt his image. And she'd love to see this enormous piece of pine, probably cut at the saw mill she and her father planned to buy and restore.

Perhaps it was lack of sleep, along with the tales of conspiracy and lost treasures Brian Green had been spinning that night, but Trenton suddenly wondered what exactly might be concealed on the other side, and for how long. A treasure map on the back? A million dollars? Just a peek. He shoved the pry bar in as far as he could behind the board and pushed with all his might. No movement. A few blows from the hammer to knock it in further and he cranked on it again. There was a snapping sound and a deep creek and the whole thing pulled away a few inches.

The first thing Trenton noticed was the air—stale and old and wet, blowing in his face. He rubbed his eyes and peered into the void—yes, it was empty back there! Nothing but black. He grabbed his phone and thumbed on the flashlight app, directing the beam into the mysterious space behind the wall. It almost looked like there was another room back there, but he couldn't be sure. Killing the overhead lights, he again shined the beam into the void and waited for his eyes to adjust. His heart was now pounding in his chest and the sense of fatigue evaporated. It was a square recess, about six feet by eight. A secret room, built right into the foundation of the house and walled off many years ago.

And there was something in there—a bulky piece of furniture. A dresser maybe? Or a desk? There were definitely drawers—three of them. And Trenton was suddenly overwhelmed with an urgent need to know what they contained. He reinserted the pry bar, about to twist his hips one more time, but stopped short.

No. He wouldn't go in there. Not tonight. Despite how overwhelmingly intriguing it all was—no, *because* of how intriguing it was—he would save it for tomorrow. This was how he would get Judith off her superhero kick, even while satiating her apparent hunger for intrigue and adventure. Accessing the secret room, going through the contents of those drawers, finding the answers to when and why it was walled off to begin with. She would eat it up. They would do it together. Sure, it meant another item on his already crowded plate, but it would solve a problem and take a load off his mind.

Trenton grabbed his phone and shot Judith a text:

> Have to show you something. When do you get off work?

Ten seconds later, his phone chirped with a reply:

> 4 PM.

Clearly, she was also up at this hour. An image of a costumed Judith perched on the clock tower of the old town hall flashed into his mind. He pushed it out.

> Me too. Come over after?

> Sure.

> Great. C U then.

After indulging himself with one more brief look into the mysterious room, Trenton turned off the light and crawled into bed, immediately feeling a welcome heaviness to his eyes and mind. Somehow, despite the secrets walled off just ten feet away, he drifted off to sleep.

CHAPTER EIGHT
"C.F.B."

"You know where we get the word *breakfast*? From 'break the fast.' You've been fasting all night and now you need some fuel. It's functional. Don't sit down and get comfortable. Break your fast and get a move on. There's work to do."

—*Insane Faith: A Guide to Extreme Christianity for the Truly Faithful* by Stephen Branding, p. 82

Trenton awoke to the annoying chime of his ringtone. He swung his legs around the side of the bed and subjected his face to a violent rubbing. The glowing red numbers on his clock came into focus: 6:46—less than four hours' sleep. Against his better judgment, Trenton reached for the phone. If it was Jason, he'd kill him.

ZOE <3, the display read. *Zoe?* Instantly alert, he mashed it to his ear. "Hello?"

"Hi, Trenton? It's Zoe. I didn't wake you, did I?"

"Oh, no. No. I've been up since . . . like . . . a while." He suddenly got that "less than three" was a heart. She'd put her name into his phone after dinner the night before and this was the first he'd seen it. *Zoe heart*, she'd written.

"Oh, good," she said. "I was wondering if you might want to come over this morning and help me catalog some photographs and documents for the museum."

"Oh. I guess I—"

"It's not overly exciting work. In fact, it can be tedious. I only ask because my father thought you might be interested."

"Yeah," Trenton said, pouring on the enthusiasm a little too freely. "Absolutely! Sounds fun!"

"Are you free right now?"

"Sure! I'll be right over."

Trenton got ready in fast forward and practically ran the three blocks to the Cassel House, pausing at the last corner to catch his breath and check his watch. 7:05. He was supposed to be at work by nine, but he could probably get a good deal of "cataloging" in before then, whatever that meant. And, more importantly, score some vital points with Zoe.

She met him at the door before he could knock. Seven in the morning and she was completely put together—hair and makeup—and bounding with energy.

"Thanks for being willing to do this," she said. "I know it's probably too early and too boring."

"Happy to help," Trenton answered, following her past the small coat room and into the parlor, where her father was hefting a file box onto a stack of four identical boxes, next to another stack of three.

"Would you like some coffee?" Zoe asked. "Fresh-ground, French pressed."

"That would be great."

"Do you take anything in it?" she asked.

Trenton's brain locked up for a moment. What was the right answer here? He usually put about two parts coffee to one part cream and one part sugar, but that was juvenile and wouldn't fly here. Should he take it black to try and appear manly like the lumber jacks pictured all around him? Or with some overly specific instructions, like he imagined the lumber baron who built this house would have demanded everything? Okay, now it had been like five seconds and he just looked like he'd never had coffee before.

"Uh, one lump," he said.

"Great. Be right back," she said, disappearing through the swinging door to the kitchen.

Her father, having arranged the boxes just so, strode over and offered his hand.

"Good morning, Trenton."

Trent gave it a shake. "Good to see you again. Thanks again for dinner last night." Quieter, he added, "And thanks for the reference. I owe you one."

Brian shook his head, confused. "Reference?"

"Zoe said it was your idea, me helping. I appreciate the chance to spend some time with her."

"So you meant to say, 'Thank you for the referral.'"

"Oh, right. Sorry."

The older man smiled and poked him in the shoulder. "I'm teasing," he said. "You're most welcome." Trenton laughed, mostly at the pathetic attempt at informal banter. He could no more imagine Brian Green saying, "I'm messing with you," than he could imagine him without the vest and wire rim glasses. "By the way," Brian continued, "I hope I didn't come on too strong last night with the tales of the town's history. I know I have a tendency to overdo it."

"Not at all," Trent answered. "The stuff that happened here is fascinating."

"It sure is. And honestly, I wouldn't be surprised if you found something equally fascinating in your own house. All part of the original estate."

"Actually," Trenton said, ready to jump at the opportunity to secure his preferred-suitor status, then hesitated. For some reason, he felt as though he'd almost broken confidence. But with whom? "I was thinking the same thing," he finished.

"Well," Brian said, checking his watch, "I'm off to the county records office. I'll leave you two to your work."

Brian all-but-ran out the door, leaving Trenton alone in the familiar room, where he'd sat and talked with the Greens well into the night. There were some new additions to the parlor, however. Along with the stack of boxes, there was a six-foot-tall display, clearly the first of many planned for the eventual museum. It was a blown-up black and white photograph of two men, nearly life-size, standing side-by-side, neither one smiling. One was simple, wearing a plain suit and hat, while the other exuded sophistication and authority. A large block of text to the right of the men read, "Benjamin Cassel met the Reverend Jeremiah Wolcott in early February 1893. This would be a turning point for the lumber baron, who, battling depression and showing symptoms of what many now believe was ALS, sought redemption through Wolcott's ministry. The two men became close friends and, within a year, Cassel had funded an expansion of the nearby Clinch Rock Community Church, deeded his servants' quarters over to the congregation, and was preparing to donate the vast majority of his holdings to Wolcott's spiritual and humanitarian work. This would prove to be a fatal act of altruism for Cassel."

The entire display was encased in glass, within which was prominently mounted a yellowed envelope with the words "J. Wolcott" scrawled on the front in an unsteady hand and the corner of an old page peeking out the top.

Zoe re-entered the room, carrying two ornate coffee cups and coasters on a silver tray. Trenton took one and, at her invitation, perched himself on the edge of a Victorian settee. His tail bone flared a bit. His least favorite part of the previous night had been the sparsely-padded antique furniture. Zoe sat next to him and took a small sip of her coffee. Trenton followed suit.

Even with no cream and relatively little sugar, the coffee was smooth—not at all bitter. He looked up at Zoe, wearing a navy blue dress, bathed in sunlight, beaming in through the enormous windows and thought, *I could get used to this.* He'd taken on the role of bachelor-slob before his time, at ten years old when his mom had died, leaving the Marsh men to fend for themselves. But if Zoe wanted to civilize and refine him, he would put up no fight at all.

"I love it here," Zoe said with a contented sigh. "Vermont was home and it always will be in a way, but there's just something about this place. Like I've always belonged here, even before I laid eyes on it."

"You mean the town or this house?"

"Both." She then hesitated, pursing her lips in thought, and amended, "The house. I more mean the house itself. I love how it reveals a little something new every day. It talks and we listen, like getting to know a person."

Trenton just nodded and took another sip of coffee.

"Even the letters we'll be going through this morning—they were all up in the attic. Bundles of them, just waiting to be discovered." She set her cup down with a clink. "You know, we were so busy bending your ear about this place last night, we never even asked you: have you and your father found any surprises in the parsonage?"

Trenton so badly wanted to tell her about the false wall and the secret chamber, to say the words that would undoubtedly bring Zoe down to his bedroom right now, squeezing through that gap in the wall, thanking him profusely for sharing this incredible find. Together, they could go through the contents of the antique desk and then, together, bring it to her father, who would probably offer Trent a dowry or something right then and there.

But no. That was Judith's room. That's what was holding him back. It would take something big to get his friend off the superhero kick and something like this was not likely to come along again anytime soon.

"Not really," he answered. "I mean, my dad's the fourteenth pastor of the church and all fourteen have lived in that house. So I'm sure everything's been discovered."

She shrugged. "You never know."

"Yeah." He vowed to himself that if Judith didn't take the bait, he'd be calling Zoe first thing the next morning, with news of his big discovery.

"Did I see you admiring our exhibit?" she asked, rising gracefully from the settee and moving over to the display.

Trent placed his cup next to hers and walked up beside her, gazing at the photograph. "Yeah, it's great. Very professional looking. How many of these are there going to be?"

"Scads. There will be display cases and informational placards throughout the house. But this is the first one. And it's perfect that we're working on it together—since these men were such good friends and they lived where we live. Apparently, Cassel would visit the reverend so often, he wore a path between our house and yours. Too bad it's not still there." She leaned her head against his shoulder and caught his eye in their reflection, their faces hovering over the image of the two men. After a few, far too brief moments, she said, "I guess we should get to work," and broke the connection. She pulled the top file box from the shorter stack and removed the lid like an eager child opening a birthday present, then very delicately removed three thick file folders.

"These are all letters to Cassel," she said, with the tone of an expert on a PBS documentary. "I'll go through and find the ones from Jeremiah Wolcott and you peruse them. They're a little harder to read than you would expect, but you get used to it. What we need is the three most interest—" She stopped herself. "Rather, the three most *captivating* letters, which will give visitors a sense of the relationship between these two men. When we've got them, they'll go there." She pointed up to the display, at three rectangular outlines, where three pages could be mounted between the thick sheets of glass. "I don't want to sound weird or superstitious," she added, "but I'm really excited you'll be doing this. Since you live in his house, maybe you can get into head or . . . I don't know."

They returned to the dining room table and, at Zoe's insistence, Trenton put on a pair of white cotton gloves, to keep the oils of his hands from damaging the paper, she explained. It was slow-going at first, as Trent struggled to read the tilted cursive script of years gone by. But Zoe was right and, before long, he was reading quickly, one side of what seemed to be almost daily communication.

The earliest letters introduced the pastor and his church, giving a summary of Wolcott's work in the community, among the families in town, the lumberjacks in the camps, and the copper miners. These had a very formal tone, as Wolcott was writing to the man who owned all of these interests. But soon they became far more friendly as the pastor seemed to be answering spiritual questions, giving advice and encouragement regarding specific situations, and referencing long face-to-face conversations between the two.

Trenton guessed that these letters were exchanged by hand during their visits, meaning they had two plains of conversation going at all times—written and verbal. He couldn't help but think that Stephen Branding would approve of Wolcott, whose days were packed with service and prayer, leaving no time for a family, but somehow plenty for a millionaire friend who would soon become a millionaire patron.

Wolcott's words were gentle, but firm, communicating in no uncertain terms that the life of the playboy—parties, possessions, and power—led right down the broad road to hell. Somewhere around the twelfth or thirteenth letter, Cassel seemed to have had a religious conversion, and the tone of the letters became for less confrontational and more comforting, reassuring Cassel that he was now on the right path and would be rewarded. Trenton was locked in to this unfolding drama, knowing that it would end with the violent death of one man and the possible corruption of the other, if one believed the reports of Wolcott cooperating with the Crown Fire Boys as they tortured and killed the book keeper.

Before he knew it, there was a tall stack of letters on the table next to him—his discard pile—and five contenders for the coveted three spots in the display, which Zoe was now carefully reading. He pulled out his phone to check the time.

"Oh, crap!" he shouted.

Zoe looked up at him with distaste. "Excuse me?"

"Sorry. It's just. I'm twenty minutes late for work. I gotta go." He stood quickly, knocking the chair over backwards, onto the blood stains in the floorboards. "I gotta go," he repeated. "But don't do the rest of these without me, okay? I want to read them."

She nodded. "I wouldn't think of it."

* * *

Adam Marsh sat at the red light—the only one in town—and fumed. Another day, another break-in, this time at Lafever's Hardware. Although there had been no actual signs of forced entry. Perhaps the perp (or perps) had hidden in the restroom or behind the paint counter while old man Lafever locked up. Or maybe he had forgotten to lock up. Whatever the case, they'd pulled up some floor boards, cracked into the walls, and, for the first time, stolen the contents of the register, before slipping out unseen by Jessie Finn and Rich Barton, both of whom were patrolling through the night. Adam felt a wave of guilt at not having taken an overnight watch yet. He was in a foul mood and guilt was his favorite libation of late.

A friendly little beep from the car behind him stole him from his thoughts. The light was green. Waving out the window, he took a left, toward the station, wondering if he should even be driving, tired as he was. He wheeled around the side of the station and slammed on the brakes, grinding to a stop mere inches from another police cruiser. *Oh, yeah.* He had decided to begin sharing the RESERVED FOR CHIEF spot with Barton, and this was Barton's day. For some reason, this made his mood all the fouler.

All the spots taken, he parked a block away and jogged up the steps to the station entrance, stopping cold just inside the door. Sitting on a bench in the small makeshift lobby, just this side of the desk, were three men, all elders at Clinch Rock Community Church. Chet Bushman was clearly in charge, sitting tall, his ear hair swirling out, impossible not to look at. To his right sat Wally Summers, beleaguered husband of April Summers, and next to him was Scot Galt, owner and proprietor of Clinch Rock Grocery and a third generation Scottish Immigrant who always seemed to Adam like he might be on the verge of grabbing a battle ax and knocking off heads a la *Braveheart.*

"What'd they bring you guys in for?" Adam joked.

The men looked back at him, stone-faced. "We would like to meet with you in your office if we could," Chet said.

"Sure. Come on back."

"Hold on, gentlemen," Tango said from behind the desk. "All visitors have to sign in."

Adam could feel the blood pulsing in his temples. "Not today," he said, pushing the clipboard back at the officer.

Once in his office, Adam sat at his desk—a landfill of police reports, class notes, and Bible commentaries. Chet sat down opposite him and the other two men stood, one on either side of him like mob enforcers, both of them ignoring the other empty chair.

"There's no easy way to say this," Chet said. "We represent a majority of the elder board and we are very seriously considering removing you from the position of pastor."

Adam was surprised at how little he felt upon hearing this. He'd known Bushman was working against him, but now that he was making his move, Adam felt neither anger nor consternation.

"As I understand the bylaws," he answered, evenly, "only a two-thirds vote from the congregation can do that."

Chet smiled, just a bit. "That's usually the case, yes, but you'll remember we drew up a special contract for you. For the moment you're serving at the pleasure of the board."

"Or displeasure," Adam said.

Scot spoke up. "We don't want to go that route, Pastor. We just need to see you putting a little more into church and a little less into this job. Haven't you already hired a replacement here?"

Adam was suddenly aware of his gun on his hip in a way that unnerved him. He ignored the question and spoke directly to the ring leader. "Chet, I thought we already worked this out when we negotiated my pay." At Bushman's quiet insistence, the board had offered an arrangement in which their new pastor would only receive half his pastoral salary while he still served as chief of police, then after retiring, would receive three quarters until he finished his Master of Divinity, which was looking like it might take ten years at the present rate. He felt a cloud of poison anger expanding in his chest. How could they complain after he'd agreed to that?

Wally, the most reasonable of the three, put in, "We'd just like to see you adopt some office hours. And a schedule for visiting shut ins and nursing homes."

"We actually insist on it," Chet said. "When Dr. Pardee was pastor, he visited every shut-in each and every month and provided home communion quarterly. And he had open office hours every Monday morning."

"Well, I have classes Monday morning," Adam said, gesturing at the stack of textbooks. "Might I remind you that you were equally insistent that I take a full load of seminary classes?"

"We were thinking you could be available tomorrow morning."

The chief thought a moment and then nodded. "Fine."

Chet nodded too. "Okay then. I'd like you at the church by seven thirty. Dr. Pardee often had visits from parishioners before the went to work."

Adam sighed. "I'll be there. Is that all?"

"Just that. And visitation. Thanks for being flexible, Pastor." He stood and the three men filed out.

Only when he picked up his phone to enter the appointment did he see the conflict: *Wednesday Morning, 7AM: Shooting with Trenton.*

He looked at his watch: 3:40. Trent would be home from work in about half an hour. Maybe they could get in some archery now and grab dinner. The pile of textbooks reminded him of the test tomorrow morning. Third declension nouns. Oh well. This was more important. He grabbed his keys.

"I'm heading out," he called over his shoulder. Officer Tyrell didn't answer.

* * *

Trenton leaned against the counter to catch his breath. When he showed up half an hour late this morning, his boss—a 350 pound hulk named Todd—had ignored him for nearly ten minutes, like a child giving the silent treatment. Just when Trent had decided to go home and write the day off, Todd had assigned him a series of the most unpleasant tasks the old resale shop had to offer. Todd was gone now and this was Trenton's first chance to rest.

"Guess who's back," Sean bellowed, blasting in the door. "Your favorite camp counsellor and personal hero, Seeeeeeean Taaailor!" Sometimes, later in the afternoon, it seemed like Sean had been drinking. But it was hard to tell his usual brand of bombasm from mild inebriation.

"You look beat, man!" he practically yelled.

"Yeah, it's been a long day."

"Not to make you work or anything, but where you hiding the doorknobs around here? I need something kind of old."

Trenton led him over to the corner, where bins full of hinges, knobs, and other hardware were mounted on the wall.

Sean began inspecting each doorknob one at a time. He glanced up at Trent and asked, "You getting enough sleep, my man?"

"Not lately."

"Hey, you know I never give up, but you gotta slow down sometimes. Recharge." He reached up to the highest bin and selected a couple doorknobs for a closer look. Trenton felt suddenly alert. There on Sean's arm, amidst the sea of bad tattoos, something had grabbed his attention. A picture of a crown, over which was suspended a small flame and the letters C.F.B. Something about it was familiar, in a disconcerting way.

"What's that tattoo mean?" Trent asked. "CFB?"

Sean looked at his arm as if he didn't remember his own ink. "Oh yeah. My first tatt. High school. It stood for the Crown Fire Boys."

Trenton's pulse quickened. Why would his camp counselor have the name of the ruthless gang who had exacted justice for Benjamin Cassel's murder permanently etched into his forearm?

"But, what does it mean though?" he asked.

"It was this stupid group of guys I belonged to back in the day. We hung out together, had each other's backs."

"Like a gang?"

"Ha! No. Well, I guess, but not a real one. We didn't do anything exciting. Just drank behind the Gas 'n' Sip and used M-80s to blow things up. The only cool thing was, it was sort of handed down, passed on from class to class. Steve Parker's older brother tagged us. I'd be kind of bummed to find it wasn't still around."

"How far back did it go?"

Sean scratched the tattoo, as if to agitate the memory. "Pretty far I guess. Flynn's dad had the same tattoo. That's where we got the idea. He said the mayor was even a member in his day. I guess they were pretty serious about it back then. For us, it was just an excuse to blow off steam." He put back all but one doorknob. "This'll do. Ring me up?"

"Sure," Trenton said. For the first time in hours, he remembered the secret room and Judith and her conspiracy theories and all that was just waiting to be uncovered in a few short minutes. He looked at the tattoo again. Probably best if he didn't mention the mayor thing to Judith.

* * *

When Trenton arrived home, Judith and his dad were sitting on the front porch, laughing. They were tapping messages to one another in Morse code, a habit they had begun years before and which, from Trent's point of view, had long since lost all of its "cuteness."

It had begun when Trent was a Cub Scout and supposed to master the dots and dashes for a merit badge. His mother already knew it and tried to teach him, which proved futile. Both Dad and Judith (who was more or less a fixture at their home back then) had picked it up though, and ever since, tapping messages to each other had become their little thing. Whenever Trent objected, on the grounds that he felt left out, they simply reminded him that no one was stopping him from also learning Morse Code, maybe even picking up that overdue merit badge.

Seeing the two of them there, drinking lemonade and giggling at whatever she had just encoded, he felt a pang of jealousy. When was the last time his dad had made time for *him*? He made a show of walking around her motorbike to access the steps up to the porch.

"Hey guys," he said. "What's going on here?"

"Nothing," his dad said. "Just catching up. I feel like it's been forever since I've seen my Judy-bug."

"You don't have to work? Or study or anything?"

Dad cleared his throat. "Actually, uh, it turns out I've got to be at the church tomorrow morning, so I was wondering if maybe you wanted to shoot a few arrows now and then get some dinner?"

"Sorry. Judith and I have plans."

"It's something secret," she said, shrugging.

"She could come too. Be like old times."

Trent stonewalled. "Like I said, we've got plans. We can just reschedule for . . . whenever." As soon as the words left his mouth, Trenton felt horrible. Was he punishing his dad for having to break their plans even while he tried to make it right? His stomach turned a bit and he added, "How about Thursday? Do you have class"

"Yeah, 10:30."

"I work at nine. How about we shoot some bullseyes at about seven and then hit the diner."

"Okay," his dad said, but he couldn't hide his disappointment. He tapped a little message to Judith as she descended the porch. She nodded to him, and blew a kiss. The image of his father, sitting there all alone, shoulders slightly slumped, remained in Trenton's mind as he led Judith through the garage and down into his room.

"What did he just say?" he asked.

"He said you should learn Morse Code." This was always her response when Trenton requested a decipher.

As he plopped down on a bean bag chair, Trenton felt unexpectedly nervous. On the way home, he had decided to bring up the superhero thing one more time, poke some holes in it, and then ultimately sink it with the reveal of his secret room and its mysterious contents. But he was beginning to worry that there would be nothing of note in there. No, common sense told him you don't completely wall off a piece of furniture unless there's something in there you don't want found.

"How did your little date go last night?" Judith asked. If there was an edge to the question, it was subtle. Still, Trenton was determined not to linger on this subject.

"Fine. It was nice."

"Moving a little fast, aren't we? Meeting her parents already?"

Trent didn't answer.

"You think I care, don't you? Like I'm jealous or something? Because I'm not."

"I know," he said. "I see you're wearing the boots again."

"I have to break them in."

Trenton figured this was as good an opening as he would get. "So, how's it coming with the costume and the equipment?"

"Pretty good," she answered. "There are a few hard-to-get-ahold-of items and some pricey stuff. But I've got savings."

"Like what, for example?"

She screwed up her face in thought, an incredibly cute expression, which always made Trenton think *what-if?* for just a second. "A rebreather for one."

"What's that?"

"It's a device that allows you to keep breathing the same air when you're underwater or surrounded by smoke or whatever."

"That's impossible."

"No it's not. When you see Batman or James Bond go underwater with, like, a tube in his mouth, long-ways, that's for rebreathing."

"Huh. I always though those things pulled the oxygen out of the water."

"*That's* impossible."

Trent shrugged. "Fish do it. Besides, Batman is a comic book character. It's okay if it's impossible. "

"I'm telling you, it's real. When you breathe in, you only use like 15% of the oxygen before you breathe out. You can breathe the same air a few times over. I've been reading up on you. Eventually you get lightheaded and other gases start building up in you, but it lets you stay under water quite a while."

Trenton was feeling very good about his chances here. He could leverage this natural delay, while she tried to acquire any number of James Bond gadgets, and use the time to redirect her to sleuthing of the historical variety. Just to get a ballpark figure, he asked, "So how long do you think until you've got all this stuff?"

"Oh, I don't know. I may cut some corners. I mean, the town needs me now. Did you know there was *another* break-in last night? The hardware store. Your dad was telling me all about it."

Nice work, Dad. "Come on, Judith. A few break-ins do not mean we're all in horrible danger. And we have a police force. There's now seven cops instead of five. You think my dad can't handle a few break-ins?"

"I know Adam can handle it. But he's retiring soon. I wouldn't trust Dan Barton's dad to solve a crossword puzzle."

"You don't want to jump in without the right equipment, though, right? Do you have one of those spring-loaded guns that shoots grappling hooks?"

She scowled. "Are you making fun of me?"

"I'm not. I swear."

"Well, if you must know, I'm absolutely not going to use a grapple gun. Downtown Clinch Rock is full of historic buildings. Just think of the damage it would do every time I blasted the grappling hook through a wall in order to climb or swing or whatever. Besides, I don't need that."

Trenton did not feel like he'd poked many holes in the superhero idea, but this was the best segue he was likely to get. Time to close the deal.

"Speaking of old buildings, remember when I said I had something to show you?"

She perked up. "Yeah."

"You have to promise not to tell anyone.

Judith nodded. "I promise."

"Come here." He led her over to the enormous cut of bare wood, which he had pushed back into position as best he could. "This is gonna blow your mind."

He hooked the short end of the pry bar behind the wood and pulled with all his might. It came even further away from the wall than it had the night before, creating an opening almost a foot wide, by which they could easily enter the black space. He looked back to Judith, to read her reaction. Her mouth hung open for a good ten seconds before it slowly climbed up into a wide smile.

"And no one else knows about this?" she asked.

"Nope."

"Not even Zoe?"

"Not even Zoe."

She poked her head in through the opening. "Do you have a shop light?"

91

"Yeah, it's in the work shop." Trenton ran into the next room and rifled through a few boxes before returning with an old trouble light in a metal cage at the end of a long orange extension cord. He plugged it in, clicked it on, and handed it to Judith. She led him into the unknown, holding the light high like a torch.

The first thing they noticed was the map, painted on thick old canvas and taking up almost the entire back wall of the room. It was clearly downtown Clinch Rock, as evidenced by crude likenesses of the church, the town hall, the Cassel House, and several other recognizable buildings. The walls of the room were constructed, not of field stone, but of red brick. And in the center of the room was a small antique desk.

Judith was ecstatic, her breath coming heavy like a runner's.

"I guess this belongs to the church," Trenton said. "I wonder what it's worth. You ever see that one *Antiques Road Show* where the table from the guy's basement was worth like a hundred grand?"

"Who cares about the desk?" Judith said. "Have you looked in the drawers?" She dropped to her knees and looped her fingers through one of the handles.

"No. This is my first time in here. Go ahead."

She looked up at him. "You saved it for me?" He nodded and she smiled, her freckles seeming to float off her cheeks. Carefully, she pulled open the bottom drawer. Empty. Not even a dust bunny. The second drawer did not contain anything either. Trenton's stomach was in freefall. He had hooked her so completely and now the whole adventure could end and not with a bang only ten minutes after it started.

She tried the top drawer. Locked. Her eyes darted to his.

"I don't suppose you found any old keys in this place?"

"'Fraid not."

Judith pulled her phone from the pocket of her camo pants and opened YouTube, punching in 'How to pick an antique desk drawer lock" with her thumbs. They watched the video twice before collecting the tools they would need. Judith was a quick study and it was only her third try when Trenton heard the lock turn and saw the drawer slide open.

And then they saw the money.

CHAPTER NINE
"BENEATH THE FIRE"

"Whatever you do, give it a thousand percent! Kill distractions like the devils they are. Let me put it this way: while I don't advocate adding to the Bible, if I were going to round the Fruit of the Spirit up to ten, I'd add Tunnel Vision to the list."

—*Insane Faith: A Guide to Extreme Christianity for the Truly Faithful*
by Stephen Branding, p. 323

Is that what I think it is?" Trenton wanted to grab for the contents of the drawer, but stopped himself. This was Judith's big moment and it had to collide with her with enough force to change her momentum.

Judith reached slowly into the drawer, hands shaking, and pulled out what looked like a stack of very old paper. She lay the items down in a row along the top of the desk. First, the money: just two bills, which Trenton didn't recognize, and which both bore a prominent numeral fifty in the corners. He felt a wave of disappointment. A couple of outdated fifties would not help the church meet its budget or save his father any stress. Next to that she placed a book, a bit larger in width than the bills, its blank leather cover fastened shut by a thin leather cord wrapped over itself several times. Finally, a sealed envelope with nothing written on the outside.

Judith looked up at him again, her eyes dancing, waiting for his reaction.

"Open it," he said, his voice coming out with a bit of an adolescent squeak. And then he laughed. The whole thing had him feeling giddy.

Without much care at all, Judith tore into the enveloped and pulled out a single page of paper, which she unfolded to reveal a handwritten letter. The first thing to jump out at him was the signature at the bottom: "Rev. Jeremiah Wolcott." He'd spent half the morning reading letters from the late minister and quickly recognized this as another

"So what's it say?" he demanded.

Judith squinted. "I can't really read it."

Trenton sighed. "You're fluent in Morse Code but you can't read cursive?"

"Shut up," she said, handing it over. "It just takes me longer."

The letter was addressed, in the now-familiar slant of Wolcott's handwriting, to "My Dear Friend in Christ." Trenton read it out loud.

I choose to believe, with a measure of faith, that, at such time as this letter is discovered and read, Clinch Rock Independent Church will still be going strong, this house still its parsonage, and the man reading these words, my successor. For I shudder at the thought of any of this falling into the hands of the unregenerate

Perhaps you know of the recent (at least, recent as I write this) controversy which has so buffeted our town these past few years—of my dear friend Benjamin Cassel murdered in avarice and spite, of his assassin also put to death in a gruesome display of vengeance, and—depending on how I am remembered—of my having been caught up in these affairs.

Before he was murdered, Mr. Cassel informed me of his plans to donate a large sum of money—indeed, beyond large—to the church, for the furthering of the Kingdom of God. The very morning of his untimely death, he had entrusted to me nearly one thousand dollars and implied that the rest of his treasure had been deposited somewhere for me to find at a later date—somewhere, in his words, "beneath the fire."

He had been planning soon to vacate his mansion and to live the remainder of his days far from here, and free of the crushing weight of wealth and power, which brought such great temptation as always threatens to entice and drag away even a servant of the Most High God. He told me that I was to watch the post after his departure, for a final piece of information that would arrive in a letter and clinch for me the location of the treasure. However, seemingly before he could write this final letter, Cassel went the way of all flesh, leaving me with a single clue: "beneath the fire."

I searched everywhere. Under actual fireplaces and boilers. Beneath metaphorical fires (for example, the altar of the church). In the ashes of buildings that burned down while Cassel still lived. Before long, I am ashamed to say, this quest became an obsession and I spent what little I had left—both in treasure and integrity—pursuing it. Over time, this pursuit changed my character greatly, for the worse, causing me to neglect the ministry and despise my fellow man.

And so, on this 4th day of August 1895, I give it all up to the Lord, asking him, by his mercy, to turn my heart of stone back into a heart of flesh. I desire, like Cassel before me, to move on and to live a quiet and ordinary life, honoring Christ.

To that end, I considered burning all evidence of my search, that it too might disappear beneath the fire. However, I cannot rule out that God, in his providence, may have a time in mind when someone (perhaps you?) will find this inheritance and use it to bring glory to his name. And so I am walling off this long-forgotten chamber, perhaps never to be opened again. With this letter, I leave you my diary, which contains among many other things the details of my search, a map of each place I scoured, and two fifty dollar bank notes—all that remains of the money given me by Mr. Cassel.

The love of money has surely been the root of bitterness and greed in my heart. I pray that you will be spared this fate. Perhaps you should do that thing for which I lacked the constitution to do: feed these items to the fire and forget you ever came upon them.

I do not know if the treasure has already been discovered. I do not know if my friend's wicked bookkeeper, Heinrich Wellick, discovered and moved the cash or gold (for I know not which form it takes) before he, having lived by the sword, died by a blow from a pike pole, in my very presence. I do not know how you can save your soul while seeking the treasure.

God will be your guide.

To His Eternal Glory,
The Rev. Jeremiah Wolcott

Trent set the letter down on the desk and took a deep breath.

Judith furrowed her brow. "Did you write that? Is this some kind of joke?"

"Yeah, right. And I made this old money with my printing press." He picked the two bills up. They were identical, featuring an iconic woodcut of Washington crossing the Delaware on the left and a portrait of a man—also Washington?—in prayer on the other. Floating between them, in ornate writing, were the words "National Bank of Elgin." He flipped one of the bills over. Official looking seals and the words "Fifty Dollars."

"Do you think this is still good?" he mused. "Like, is it still even money?"

He could feel Judith nodding from over his shoulder. "Yeah. It's a bank note. That's how money got started, right? Banks would issue these little certificates and you could bring them in and trade them for that much gold. I think, if this bank is still around, you could walk right in and demand a hundred dollars' worth tomorrow."

Trenton chuckled. "That'd be hilarious. But really, I mean, what do you think we could get for this? They belong to the church."

"I don't know." She was still behind him and he could feel her breath. It was nice. "My crazy uncle Denny spent years collecting all this confederate money. Yes, he was a total racist, so don't ask. Anyway, after he died, my dad tried to unload like three thousand dollars' worth and he could only get about two hundred bucks." She picked up the diary and asked, "Do you mind?"

"Go for it."

She unwound the leather cord and riffled through the book, maybe three or four hundred pages long, and about two thirds full. "Yikes. Can you read this?" she asked, flipping back to page full of writing.

Trenton accepted the book and squinted at the script. It was smaller than the writing on the letters by a good deal and both faded and smudged, like maybe the book was comprised of inferior paper. Or maybe the reverend had a habit of closing the diary before the ink had dried. Or perhaps he just saved his most careful penmanship for correspondence. At any rate, it took him three times longer to read through a single page of the diary than one of the letters, and it just seemed to be a log of all the minister had done that day. "Visited the Widow Doane. Prepared sermon for west lumber camp. Met with baptismal candidates." It went on and on.

Judith had grown bored and was examining the map, spread across most of the back wall. It was about six feet squared, representing downtown Clinch Rock and some of the surrounding land. Throughout, there were small red icons—little tongues of fire—here and there, apparently marking off places where Wolcott had searched for the money his church had coming.

They were both engrossed in the map, when Trent's cell phone bleeped. He opened the text.

"My Dad's ordering from TOPPIT. Wants to know if we're hungry."

"Sure," Judith said, her eyes still glued to the map. "He knows what I like."

"Barf. Pineapple." He texted back,

yeah, shoot me a text when it gets here.

She turned and looked Trenton in the eye. "Are we telling him about this stuff?"

"Hmmm." Trent had been keeping Dad in his back pocket in all this. He would be a good ally in talking some sense into Judith the Superhero, but it was looking like he may not need him. Judith was all in. He could see that. And it was probably best to keep it between the two of them.

"I mean, Batman has Commissioner Gordon and everything," Judith said, "but I wonder if Adam and I are too close already, you know?"

"Yeah. Let's not add this to his list of concerns." A familiar weight returned to Trent's spirit. She was still thinking in superhero terms. He had to hook her more completely and reel her in. And he knew exactly how. He leaned back against the desk and said, "So wait till you hear the story Zoe's dad told me the other night . . ."

Judith sat in total silence while Trenton related the events surr-ounding the murder of Benjamin Cassel, the Crown Fire Boys, and the missing money. Then she let loose with a barrage of questions before demanding that he re-read the letter. Right as they finished, Trent's dad called down to say the pizzas had arrived.

"So that's what they're looking for," she whispered as they climbed the steps. "I told you, it's a conspiracy." Trenton didn't answer.

TOPPIT (which stood for "The Only Pizza Place in Town") was known less for the quality of their pizza than for their being, well, the only pizza place in town. But it was hot and it was pizza and it offered a welcome opportunity to connect with his dad. And having the three of them together again after at least three months apart was like a family reunion. Sure, nothing would stop the two of them from tapping messages to each other throughout dinner, but the jealousy was gone now, overcome by a cloud of nostalgia.

On a scale of *total chaos* to *all's right with the world*, things were moving in the right direction. Dad was feeling like his old care-free self, king of corny jokes and bad impressions. And Judith, whether she knew it or not, was being expertly corralled away from a potentially dangerous and humiliating obsession into one that, quite frankly, had Trent just as excited. When his dad suggested a round of Scrabble, an old favorite in the Marsh home, they couldn't say no.

In keeping with their tradition, his dad played all sorts of proper nouns and iffy police terms, which Judith challenged endlessly, this time adding a number of Greek words to the mix. He had just added O-S to the end of the word "angel," explaining that this was the Greek form of the word and therefore acceptable, when the doorbell rang.

Trent's dad excused himself from the dining room table, covered in letters, and disappeared into the living room.

"Well, hello Lori," Trent heard him say. Lori Farmer, the church treasurer. She was a few years younger than the new pastor and very pretty and when she had come over once before, Trent had hoped it might be the beginning of something between the two of them. But no, it had been bad news about the church's finances, as it probably was again tonight. Trent held his breath and tried not to listen in on the conversation. If only the church treasurer knew where to find the church's treasure.

"I thought you should hear from me first," she was saying. "It's not good. I've got to decide whether to pay the water bill, the electric bill, or our missionaries in Kenya."

"God will provide," Adam said.

"Yes, I know. He always does. Between you and me, we've been squeaking by like this for a few years. But we've lost some big givers in the past few months. We're barely making ends meet with your current pay scale. I really don't see how we can start paying you a full salary and still stay afloat. And pastor, we're going to need to reroof the church soon. It will cost twenty-five thousand, at least. I'm kind of afraid we'll have to sell this place at that point."

Trenton clicked on the old FM radio on the kitchen counter. He shouldn't be hearing this. He didn't want to hear it. When he'd slumped back into his seat, Judith reached over and squeezed his hand.

"Don't worry. We're going to find that money," she said. "I promise." They sat there for a few minutes, not saying anything, listening to the Tigers game.

When his dad returned, his countenance had changed entirely. "Sorry, kids," he said, "I've got a lot of work I should be catching up on. But this has been fun. We should do it again some . . . " He trailed off as he walked out of the room, toward his home office.

Judith dug a Moleskin notebook out of her bag. "Let's go outside," she said. The two of them sat on Trenton's old tire swing well into the night, brainstorming possible fires beneath which the treasure might be hidden. Even after deciding to double-check where Wolcott had already looked, they still ran dry after fourteen and so decided to take the Iron Horse downtown, looking for historic buildings marked with a date of 1895 or earlier. They found eight.

"I think we could have saved ourselves a trip," Trenton said, surveying their list. "These are all on that map that Wolcott left us."

Judith nodded. "You know what else is on that map? Every single building that's been broken into."

* * *

Once again, sleep eluded Trenton Marsh. But tonight he wasted no time tossing and turning. Instead, he clicked on his reading lamp and began flipping through Wolcott's diary. He had meant to send it with Judith, but she dropped him off just before his curfew and took off in her usual way, spitting dirt out from behind her rear wheel. Ten pages in and Trenton fell under the grip of an enormous yawn. For a record of treachery and hidden treasure, this may have been the dullest document he'd ever laid eyes on. Desperate for some action he flipped to the very last entry. It was dated August 5, 1895 and consisted of just one line:

All the vain things that charm me most, I sacrifice them to Thy blood.

Trenton clicked off the light and closed his eyes. He felt a sense of peace at reading those words, and wondered what it was like for a man possessed by such a relentless pursuit to just give it up, all at once. He imagined it was a bit like the way his dad had felt tonight, when for just a couple hours he forgot that he was wearing a bunch of hats, stretched thin by each and every one of them. Then again, Wolcott had probably gone back to his crazy schedule of preaching to the lumberjacks and miners, in addition to his ordinary ministerial duties . . .

Wait! The old copper mine! Cassel had not owned the mine outright, but was a heavy investor in it. Brian Green had mentioned that the night before. Trent rushed into the secret room and clicked on the trouble light. All of the little flame indicators on Wolcott's map were within the town limits of Clinch Rock. The mine, however, was a good five miles east of the border. And as for "beneath the fire," didn't mines have huge smelting furnaces? Could the money be hidden beneath?

Suddenly very awake, he grabbed his laptop and looked up the Ashton Copper Mine on Wikipedia. A large notice announced that this article "needed help" and was "a stub," which apparently meant it wasn't a real article. He read the short paragraph:

The Ashton Copper Mine, a conglomerate mine in Lake County Michigan, is the only copper mine in the Lower Peninsula. It was active from 1881 through 1893, under the joint ownership of the Goodwin and Stiles Mining Company and several wealthy local prospectors. The mine was founded when several Michigan lumber barons, hoping to replicate the Keweenaw copper boom and diversify their holdings, hired a team of geologic surveyors to locate reserves of precious metals nearby. Their only find was a very sparse deposit, which became the Ashton mine. While Copper mining in the Upper Peninsula boomed from 1845 until 1887, the Ashton Mine was never profitable. In 2016, a brave young girl spent a weekend living in a tunnel of the mine, on a dare [citation needed]."

Trenton chuckled. Obviously, Judith had added that last line.

Not much help, though. On a whim, he did an image search for "ox-goad," which he had been meaning to look up since Judith had come out of left field with the term. Huh. It was a long-handled wooden spear with a blunted end and a second curved spike branching off the first. He clicked through a few more pictures, some of them looking incredibly deadly with metal spikes and blades.

Trenton could see how, in the hands of a biblical hero, it might rack up quite a body count. What he couldn't understand was how anyone in her right mind might consider carrying one out into the not-so-mean streets of Clinch Rock, to battle the forces of darkness. He put the laptop to sleep and flopped back down on his bed.

In the dark, his mind wandered here and there, as it was wont to do. He thought about dinner with dad, the desk and its contents, the money and its mystery, and he thought way back to that morning, reading through a stack of letters at the Cassel House. Somehow it felt like two weeks ago. As he drifted off to sleep, he pictured Zoe's face reflected in the glass as she leaned her head against his shoulder that morning.

Only it wasn't Zoe's face he saw. It was Judith's.

CHAPTER TEN
"A SUDDEN, HORRIBLE REALIZATION"

"Get out of your comfort zone! *Live* out of your comfort zone! You know where the devil dwells? In your comfort zone! I used to have a magnet on my fridge that said, 'Do one thing every day that scares you.' But I threw it in the trash can. Because one thing is not nearly enough."

—*An Extreme Devotional: 90 Days of Inspiration from Insane Faith* by Stephen Branding, page 44

Trent awoke to the alarm on his phone: "Archery with Dad," it read. He chided himself for not remembering to delete it, and tried to go back to sleep. But it was pointless. Thoughts of Dad led to thoughts of last night and the discoveries in the old desk. Then he thought about the list he and Judith had put together and how he had yet to tell her about the old mine. Sure, it was early, but he'd give her a call anyway.

After the third ring, she answered, her voice hoarse. "Hello."

"Oh, I'm sorry sir. I was calling for Judith."

"Hilarious. You woke me up. Gimme a break."

Trenton laughed. "I thought of another place for our list last night."

"The lumber camp? I thought of it too."

"No, but that's a good idea. I was thinking of the copper mine."

"Ah, my second home," she said. "Let's do it. You want to get together this morning?"

Trent looked at the time. 6:40. He had a couple hours before work. "For sure."

"Be there in half an hour."

* * *

Judith roared up exactly half an hour later, wearing her usual vintage motorcycle goggles (snagged from Rerun) and the blue cowboy boots. Dressed in jeans and a cotton shirt over a wife-beater, with her hair in two short braids, she looked the part of a treasure-hunting adventurer in some sort of steam punk cartoon. She killed the motor and hopped off the bike.

"Good morning," she called up to Trent, who was sitting on the porch. "You got my favorite K-cups?"

"Yeah, help yourself."

She emerged from the house a few minutes later and they sat together on the porch in the early morning sun, sipping syrupy cappuccino drinks and going over their list.

Judith said, "So we can probably check your house, both our places of work, and maybe the church this morning, if we don't take our sweet time."

Trent grunted. "I guess one good thing came out of Dad standing me up for archery."

"He feels bad, you know," Judith said. "Besides, he didn't stand you up, he just rescheduled. One whole day later. How incredibly rude."

"I guess."

When they'd finished their drinks, they set about searching the parsonage. The fireplace was the most obvious place to start, although it was also the place least likely to have been missed by Jeremiah Wolcott, who undoubtedly built fires there on a regular basis. There was nothing much to see. An ash shoot down to the basement, which they examined, getting filthy in the process. The upstairs fireplace in Adam's bedroom yielded the same result.

They checked beneath the oven, although they agreed that was stupid, since the oven was from the nineties, yes, but the wrong nineties. It took both of their strength and finesse to get it shoved back into the narrow gap in the counter, and even then they scuffed up the floor tiles a bit.

Next they inspected the old coal-burning boiler in the unfinished half of the basement. The monstrosity sat there, inches off the packed dirt floor. Shining a flashlight beneath it only revealed a metropolis of spiders and centipedes.

"Scary down there," Trenton.

"Yeah, Richard Scarry. Get it?"

"No."

"Your loss," Judith said. "I guess it's time to dig."

"What? Dig into the basement floor? We don't even own this house."

"I thought we were serious about this."

"We are, but . . . I mean, the more I think about it, why would it be hidden in the house of the guy who was looking for it? That makes no sense. What, do we think Cassel snuck in when the reverend wasn't home and buried it right under his nose?"

"Makes perfect sense to me. And remember the map: no little fire icon for this place, which means maybe he didn't look here."

"Can we at least put it off? It's already eight. I'm supposed to be to work in an hour. This would probably take at least an hour."

"Alright," Judith agreed. "Let's head downtown."

* * *

Adam sat at his desk in the pastor's study, flipping through a ring of Greek vocab cards and fuming a little. When he'd arrived, before seven, Chet Bushman had been waiting at the church, pretending to change a fluorescent light bulb he'd already changed the week before. He made uncomfortable small talk for a few minutes before replacing the light cover and saying goodbye.

That was an hour and a half ago and Adam had seen no one else. He thought of Trenton and their archery tradition and how he'd missed it in order to sit in an empty office to satisfy a curmudgeon who would never actually be satisfied with Adam as pastor. He tried not to think about how these office hours now meant that his workday would extend from 7AM until 1AM, when he finished his patrol of the businesses downtown. Between would be two classes, a study group, and an hour and a half driving to and from the seminary.

There was a knock at his door, which was already open. He looked up to see Brent Sayer, a college kid who was home for the summer.

"Well hi, Brent. Come on in. Have a seat."

The lanky young man awkwardly folded himself into one of the low chairs, across the massive wooden desk from the pastor.

"What can I do for you?"

"Well," Brent began, pulling one long leg over the other, "I don't know how to say this, but . . . I'm kind of not sure I still believe all this Jesus stuff anymore. I've been learning a lot at school about science and sociology and everything and it seems like we probably don't really need religion."

Adam nodded, trying to look calm but concerned, even while his heart had begun pounding for some reason.

"Anyway," Brent went on, "my mom said I should talk to you. She thought you could answer my questions." He reached into his pocket and pulled out a piece of paper, which he unfolded to reveal a long numbered list.

"Let's start with an easy one: if the Bible is divinely inspired, how come the creation account doesn't acknowledge microorganisms?"

"Oh. Um . . . let me think about that a minute," Adam said.

* * *

"Is there a fireplace hidden somewhere behind all this crap?" Trenton asked. Rerun Vintage was absolutely packed with boxes of comics, shelves of trinkets, racks of bizarre clothes, and limbless mannequins sporting various hats and scarves.

"I've never come across one," Judith said. "There's an apartment upstairs, where Brook lives. I've only been up there a couple times, but I'm pretty sure there's no fireplace."

"Right. I guess we'd see a chimney outside. What are we looking for, then? Another boiler?"

"This way ," Judith said. She led him through the back room, down a dark staircase, into a dank cellar, which she filled with a weak orange glow by the pull of a chain. It was creepy down here, but not much worse than upstairs, where, in the watery light of the morning sun, the lifeless eyes of the Kewpie dolls and vintage Halloween masks gave him the willies.

"I guess this is it," Judith said, pointing at a monstrous boiler, more than twice the size of the one at Trenton's house. It sat on a massive concrete slab.

"Well, that's a bust," he said. "No way you could hide something under *that*." He felt his spirit deflate a little. "Let's just face it, Judith. This is a waste of time. A guy devoted more than a year of his life to finding this money, just after it was hidden. And *he* knew the man who hid it! And now we think we're going to just happen upon it more than a century later?"

"Well, we're not the only ones who think so."

"That's the other thing! Whoever's ransacking these old buildings is using power tools and practically taking the places apart. If they didn't find it, what hope do we have?"

"But that's just it," Judith said. "They're ripping open walls and looking in the floor. They don't know what we know: the money is *beneath the fire*."

This took a moment to sink in. "You've got a point, I guess. But Wolcott knew that and he already looked here. And at the Home Store. They were both marked on his map."

"Okay, let's branch out," she said. "I like your idea. Let's check out the mine."

"I can't," Trenton said, checking the time. "I'm already going to be late for work as it is. Second day in a row."

"Just call in sick. Have you ever even done that?"

"Well, no. But . . . "

"Come on, Trent. I'm going either way. I know my way around and everything, but apparently it's 'not safe' to go alone."

"So you're leaving me no choice?"

She smiled, innocently, her short braids curling up a bit in the humidity and a smudge of ash on her nose.

"Oh, all right."

* * *

"And do you know what Wally said to me last night? He said I was a Negative Nelly! Can you believe that? If anything, I'm overly optimistic."

April Summers had been waiting in the church office when Brent left, forty-five minutes ago, his questions still unanswered. Rather than shoot from the hip, Adam had asked if he could hang on to the list and do some research, so as to offer a more informed response to each question. As if he had time for that.

And now April was here, unloading her own list—not of questions, of course, but of complaints. Adam couldn't shake the feeling that Wally himself may have sent his wife over, both to justify the requirement of office hours and so someone else would have to endure her for a while.

"And did you see how those girls were dressed?" she was saying. He realized he'd unintentionally tuned her out.

"Uh huh," Adam said.

"I mean, I'm glad they're coming to church, but when I was a girl, only streetwalkers wore short shorts like that. And I don't know if anyone else noticed this, but I saw some of the men looking at them. Not my Wally, of course, but some of them. Something should really be done about that."

"Uh huh."

* * *

It was embarrassing enough to ride on the back of Judith's Honda motorbike, arms around her waist. But that was nothing compared with how Judith practically vaulted over the fence, using the NO TRESPASSING and DANGER: KEEP OUT signs as toe holds, before waiting patiently for Trent to clumsily ascended, struggling to jam his size-twelve sneakers into the chain link with each step, and struggling even more to dislodge them. Finally reaching the top, he swung a leg over, just as his other foot twisted free. He came down hard on the crossbar.

"Ouughhh!" He squeezed his eyes shut and saw fireworks.

Judith laughed. "You're halfway there. Suck it up!"

"Shut up! I'm injured. It's my . . . you know!"

"Oh, I know." She laughed. "Do you need me to call 911?"

"No," he said. "And you're dead to me now if you think this is funny." Gingerly, he brought his other leg over the fence and dropped the six feet to the ground. He staggered for a minute, hunched over.

"No offense," Judith said, "But you can't be my sidekick."

"Oh no," he deadpanned. "My life's ambition. And don't say *fence*."

She laughed again. "See? Your sense of humor's coming back already. You want to sit down a minute?"

"Yeah." He collapsed against the hard metal, dreading the very particular type of stomach ache that was about to set in.

"Hey, watch this," Judith announced, grabbing a dirty beer bottle up off the ground and propping it on a rock. She counted thirty paces away and unfurled a leather sling from her bag—almost identical to the one Trent had shown her in his Bible.

Great, he thought. *Now I'm enabling her.*

Dropping what looked like a large black marble into the pouch, she narrowed her eyes in concentration, focusing on the bottle and swinging the sling in an arc, slowly at first.

"Judith, be careful. Someone could get hurt here. And, for the record, he's already hurt."

She ignored him, swinging it faster and faster until it was just a blur. Then she released one end with a flourish. In the same moment, the bottle disintegrated in a shower of glass shards.

Trenton sat upright. "Whoa! How did you do that?"

"I've been working on it for a couple weeks, off and on. But, like I said, I think I'm a natural. All part of my calling, I guess."

He felt a pang of jealousy. For Trenton, mastering the bow and arrow had been a long and arduous process of slowly improving technique and many hours in practice.

"You could kill someone with that thing!"

"I won't, though," she said.

"But, whoever heard of a superhero with a sling anyway? That's just weird."

"Robin had one."

"Like, Batman and Robin?"

"Yeah."

"I don't think so," Trenton said. "Robin just swung around on a rope with those little pixie boots, looking like a circus freak."

"No, I mean in the '90s. The best Robin, Tim Drake. He had a collapsible bo-staff and a sling. And a girl was Robin for a while too. I bet you didn't know that."

"But this isn't a comic book. And Clinch Rock isn't Gotham City. And there are no super-villains here—just the most boring group of people to ever form a town. Even our crime wave is dull."

She tightly re-rolled the sling and slipped it into her bag. "Well, I'm good at it, as you can see. And anyway, it fits with the Bible theme. Speaking of, I'm trying to decide if I should choose my own name or let the public choose it for me, like with Arrow or the Rocketeer. I mean, I definitely have some ideas, but it might be better to wait and see what the papers say."

"The 'papers?' You mean, *The Clinch Rock Observer?* That two-page deal that comes out every other week and is, like, ninety percent ads?"

"Even they couldn't ignore a masked hero working to stop the break-ins."

Trenton shook his head. "Sure, they'd probably write a story about the crazy person in blue boots running around with a deadly weapon."

She went suddenly silent, her expression hard and defensive.

"What? Judith, did I say something that—?"

"Don't call me crazy."

"No, I just meant—"

"My dad calls me crazy." She stared at the ground.

"I'm sorry, Judith. I didn't mean it."

She shook it off. "Anyway, I thought you were on-board now. Why else would you bring me my first case?"

Trenton had a sudden, horrible realization. Yes, Judith was very much *into* solving the mystery they'd uncovered in his basement. But it wasn't a distraction from the superhero thing; rather, it was fuel for the fire. If anything, he'd sped things along, cancelled the grace period provided by her slow and gradual accumulation of equipment. And now, here she was, blowing bottles out of existence at thirty paces, trying to beat the criminals to the punch. He should have just left the whole thing alone. He should have brought Zoe and Brian down to look at the hidden room. He she should be at work right now. Because, while he swore to himself that he'd never again say it out loud, maybe Judith *was* crazy. Jason thought so, and that was before any of this.

But now he was in it with her and the best thing he could was keep an eye on her and steer her gently in the direction of sanity. He pulled himself to his feet and said, "Let's go check out this mine."

"Okay, follow me." She took a few steps and then looked back at him, over her shoulder. "And I mean *follow me*. You don't want to find out what it's like to free-fall a quarter of a mile."

She led him through a thick grove of conifers. As they reemerged into the light, he saw the ruins of a brick edifice, two stories tall and just as wide. The windows were broken, the bricks crumbling, and the roof covered in saplings. The closer they got, the more dilapidated the structure seemed.

They walked in through the open doorway and were greeted by the smell of rot. Brightly colored graffiti covered the interior walls and piles of decaying wood covered the floor. They walked past a mound of garbage: bottles, wrappers, hypodermic needles. The whole thing was very Third-World and Trenton suddenly felt very unsafe.

"Maybe this isn't a great idea," he said.

She snickered. "You scared?"

"Not exactly. It's just . . . " He sighed. "So where were the big fires, like to melt the copper? I think that's our best shot."

"At the smelter," she said. "This is the mine. Hey, you want to see where I slept?"

"Probably not."

"Come on," she said, leading him into an arched tunnel. "And turn your phone light on." He obeyed and entered the passage, having to hunch over a little. "Careful not to touch the ceiling," she added

"Why not?"

"You don't want to wake anybody up."

He cranked his head and shined the beam from his phone upward, almost letting out a shriek. Dozens of little brown bats were hanging there, curled up, sleeping.

"I think I'm gonna go back," he said, even as he followed her deeper in.

"We're almost there," she called. He kept following, out of sheer obstinacy. Judith might not care what anyone thought of her, but Trent had humiliated himself enough for one day. They trudged along for three or four more minutes before she said, "Take a right here."

Leaving the brick-lined tunnel, they entered a much rougher channel. Trenton could see the chisel marks in the wall. "We're going to get lost down here," he warned.

"No we're not. Stop whining. It's like twenty more steps." Trenton started counting. When he got to eighteen, she held up her hand. "Okay, stop. Look at this."

He squeezed in beside her and felt his insides tighten up. They were at the mouth of a very deep vertical shaft—so deep that the beam from Judith's phone dissipated in the blackness before hitting the bottom. At their feet, large squared timbers seemed to be holding up the wall of the shaft nearest them.

"This is a little tricky," she said. "Do exactly what I do." She turned her back to the shaft, squatted down to grip the horizontal beam and swung down into the darkness.

Adrenaline charged through Trenton's system. "Judith!" he yelled.

"Ahhhh!" Her voice got quieter and quieter.

His breath caught in his chest. He tried to shout her name again, but nothing came out.

"Splat," she said, from somewhere beneath his feet, then laughed uproariously.

"That not funny!"

"Come on down," she said. "Some of my stuff is still in here."

"I don't know."

"It's cozy. You'll love it." Trenton took a step back from the ledge. He was feeling a little dizzy and didn't trust himself near a literal dead-fall. Besides, he was not exactly a fan of heights in the best of circumstances.

Judith's voice came echoing up again. "Oh my gosh, this totally has to be my lair. How did I not think of that before? I'm so glad you wanted to come here."

"Be quiet a minute," Trent whispered, loudly.

"What?"

"I said shut up a second. Do you hear that?" He grabbed onto the chiseled rock wall and tried to quiet his own breathing. Yes, he definitely heard voices.

"Should I come back up?" Judith asked.

"No, hold on a second." Trenton began retracing his steps, sure he was moving toward the sound. When he reached the juncture with the arched tunnel, he closed his eyes and listened. The voices were not coming from the direction of the brick ruins, but further down the tunnel. Was there someone else down here with them? Keeping a careful eye on the ground beneath his feet (and a safe distance from the slumbering bats above), he pushed forward, the shuffling hunchback. He passed two more narrow tunnels branching off in either direction. The voices got louder until he could almost make out what they were saying.

Was that daylight? Yes! Up ahead and to the left. He quickened his pace, chugging along until he felt his hair brushing up against something soft. Panicking a bit, he dropped to his hands and knees and crawled the last ten feet.

The daylight stream in through another passage, breaking off to the left and leading up at a steep incline, framed by more heavy timbers. He couldn't see the end of it, but it clearly led back up to ground level. The source of both the light and the voices. He thumbed off his flash-light app and began to climb. It was narrower than the other channel and he had to squeeze himself through a few spots, but that only gave his eyes some time to adjust to the sunlight. He could now determine that it was two people talking up there: a man and a woman.

The passage terminated with a narrow vertical shaft, covered over with a metal grate. He hoisted himself up until his face was just inches from it, feeling a bit like a prisoner, tasting fresh air for the first time in years.

"And over here should be the footprint of another building," the woman was saying, amid the sound of rustling paper. "This would have been one of the outbuildings for supplies and food storage."

Then the woman walked into Trenton's field of vision and he almost let go of his tenuous grip.

It was Zoe, holding a huge, half-rolled-up paper and gazing off into the distance. "Those were bunkhouses over there, I think," she said. She looked back and forth between the paper in her hands and something in the distance.

Trent's first instinct was to call out to her. How funny would that be? Not funny, actually, because he had no explanation for his suddenly appearing like a mole-man underground, shouting up to her from beneath a metal grate. And down here with Judith, no less. Her presence, on the other hand, was easily explained. The Green family had purchased Cassel's house to make it a museum and the lumber camp for the same reason. Why wouldn't they be out here looking at what was left of the copper mine? The land was certainly not usable for anything else and could probably be snatched up for next to nothing.

"What I want to know is, where was the main office?" Wait. That was definitely not Brian Green's voice. It was kind of the opposite: thick, gravelly, unrefined. The voice's owner ambled into view and looked over Zoe's shoulder, at the document in her hands. He was on the short side, and stocky—maybe even fat—with a crew cut. Trenton knew him, but he couldn't place quite how. Until the man turned, revealing the bulky handgun holstered on his right hip. Trent swallowed a gasp.

What was Officer Cash doing here with Zoe?

CHAPTER ELEVEN
"TWO FOR THE PRICE OF TWO"

"Jesus never said 'no' to anyone who asked for his help. When we say 'no' to an opportunity to exercise Insane Faith, we're refusing to be like Jesus."

—*Insane Faith: A Guide to Extreme Christianity for the Truly Faithful* by Stephen Branding, p. 281

Trenton!" It was Judith's voice, just barely audible, bouncing up through the twists and turns of the rock-hewn passage. He dropped back down from his perch and scrambled as quickly as he could, back down to the point where it met the main tunnel, scraping himself up in the process.

"Hey, where'd you go?" She was closer now. Trenton wondered if they could hear her aboveground.

"Shhhh! Quiet!" he chided, in a whisper. He could see the light from her cell phone in the distance and ran toward it, practically doubled over. They met halfway.

"What's going on?" Judith asked.

"We've got to get out of here. John Cash is up there."

"Johnny Cash?" She snickered. "Sorry to be the bearer of bad news, but he's dead."

"No, Officer Cash. The policeman."

Judith's face went sour. "Wait, is he that tubby guy with the buzz-cut?"

"Yes. Let's go."

"That jerk gave me a ticket because he said my motorbike was too loud. Fascist."

"Who cares about a ticket, Judith? Do you realize how dead we are if my dad finds out we were crawling around down here?"

"Good point," she said. "To the Iron Horse." She turned sharply on the balls of her feet and paused for just a moment, as if waiting for a cape to whip around behind her, before taking off down the tunnel.

In less than five minutes, they were again climbing the fence, something Trenton did not want to be doing in a hurry. They hopped on her bike and left a cloud of dust behind.

"Where to now?" she shouted back at him.

He felt a sudden urge to unload all of this on his dad. Things were getting way out of hand. Hiding secret antechambers, sneaking into condemned mines, running from the police. He wanted to come clean. He wanted his dad to run all this stuff through the proper channels and simplify everything. And, above all, he wanted him to talk some sense into Judith. If anyone could do it, Dad could.

"Well?" she asked.

"Let's go to the church."

"Good idea."

* * *

Pulling up to the church, they passed Wally Summers, adding the words OFFICE HRS THURS 7AM-1P to the movable type sign. He scowled for a moment at the two teenagers on the loud motorbike, and then returned to his task.

Upon entering the church, Judith made a beeline for the Fireside Room, which is what the congregation called their fellowship hall, on account of the fireplace and mantel centered on the outer wall, despite the fact that Trenton had never seen an actual fire there.

She pulled away a decorative hinged screen and removed the iron rack with its three old birch logs, covered in a fuzzy layer of dust. Just like the fireplace in the parsonage, there was a small door beneath, access to the ash shoot. She opened it with a flourish, but only found a dozen Legos, stuffed down there and forgotten long ago.

With little care, she pushed everything back into place and bounded out of the room, up the steps to the second floor. Trenton couldn't keep up with her. He found her in the preschool room examining the sheetrock that now covered over the old fireplace there. A chalkboard was mounted on it, covered in Sunday School graffiti.

"I bet it's behind this," she said.

"No it's not. I helped put it in. The elders afraid a kid would try and climb up the chimney, so they voted to block it off. It was like four or five years ago, tops. Trust me, there's nothing behind there but more cobwebs. Besides, this is probably the place where Wolcott looked the hardest. It was definitely marked on the map."

She slumped in defeat. "Then why did you want to come here?"

"I don't know. I thought it was worth a shot. Hey, my dad's here. Let's stop in and say hello."

"Sure."

The door to the pastor's study was only open a crack. A woman's voice, soft and tentative, was saying, "Pastor, I can tell he's into something illegal. Or at least something shady."

Judith froze and cocked her head, clearly listening in. Trent grabbed her hand and gave a little tug. They should not be hearing this. She was unmoved.

"But how do you know?" he heard his dad ask.

"Just the way he's sneaking around."

Trent got in Judith's face and whispered. "We need to go." She waved him off.

"He's meeting up with different men in our garage," the woman was saying. "He even snuck out in the middle of the night last week. I pretended I was asleep when he came back, but he was gone two hours."

Trent pulled as hard as he could on Judith's arm, intent on physically dragging her away. She didn't budge. He couldn't believe how strong she was.

"There may be a perfectly reasonable explanation, Marilyn," the pastor said. "Have you asked him about it?"

"I did. And that was the scariest part. He got this look in his eyes. So threatening. And he knows he intimidates me to begin with, because he's so big and has such a temper. " Judith's face hardened as she listened. There was something in her eyes that truly scared Trent.

He took a step back, abandoning the idea that she could be compelled to move.

The woman—Marilyn—continued, "He trapped me up against the wall and he said that, if I ever asked him about what he was doing again, or if I ever told anyone about it, I'd be sorry." She began to sob.

"And when did this happen, exactly?" Trenton immediately recognized the change in his dad's voice. He was in cop-mode now, sorting out the details so he could take the proper action and bring about justice.

"No," Marilyn said, "he can't know I was here. I'm not telling you this as the chief of police, but as my pastor. I need prayer and advice. I don't want trouble."

"Right."

Judith clenched her fists at her sides. She was obviously feeling the same impulse as the pastor in his study. Trenton was mostly feeling compassion for his father. He was so in-control and confident as a police officer, so in his element. It was horrible to hear him drowning like his. "Well, let's pray, shall we? Heavenly Father . . . "

Judith quietly backed away, heading down the hall and out the front door of the church. Once outside, she put her hands on her hips and set her jaw. "How many Marilyns do you know who go to our church?" she asked. "Because I only know one."

"This is none of our business, Judith."

"And that's her car," she said, pointing at a battered old Lumina with a CLINCH ROCK WRESTLING bumper sticker. She looked over to Trent. "Marilyn Fischer."

"Look, we shouldn't have been eavesdropping in there. Just let my dad deal with this, okay?"

"But he can't now. Don't you see? Confidentiality. The confessional and all that stuff. He can't go the cop route—he's stuck. But I'm not."

Trenton grabbed two fistfuls of his own hair and yanked. What a colossal failure this day had been. It was barely noon and yet, he'd already tried three different ways to get Judith back on a path of sanity, only to push her three times in the opposite direction.

"You got something on your mind, Trenton?" she asked. "Go ahead and tell me. I'd love to hear you defend that scum bag."

"I'm not defending anyone. But don't think I'm in the dark here about what's really going on. This is about Coach Fischer kicking you off the wrestling team. Now you've got a reason to go after him somehow, and you're grabbing on to it."

"Think what you want," Judith said. "You mind walking home from here?"

"No, that's fine."

She nodded and remounted her bike. "Good. I've got some stuff to do." She revved up the bike, the scary look still in her eyes, and left a patch of rubber in front of the church.

Trenton hovered there, near the door. Should he wait for Marilyn to leave and then bring this to his dad? No. It would break the poor guy. He could hear in his voice how on-edge he was, how incompetent he felt. He wouldn't be the one to lay down this flaming bail of straw that would break the camel's back and immolate it in the process.

Besides, with his dad now in full-cop mode in there, there's no telling how he'd respond to the news that Trent and Judith had been trespassing and exploring the dangerous depths of the copper mine. Trent didn't feel like hearing, for the ten thousandth time, the story of the little girl up north who fell into a mine shaft in the sixties, and died. He didn't want to accidentally instigate an internal investigation against Officer Cash and an interrogation of his own girlfriend (*was* Zoe his girlfriend?) over what was probably a misunderstanding. And, despite all his reservations and the growing disquiet he felt, he sure didn't want to hand over the letter, diary, and map. It wasn't his to hand over. At the end of the day, nothing had changed. This was still Judith's secret; he'd given it to her and he couldn't take it back.

Trenton bummed around downtown for a little while, grabbing a dog from Coney Heaven, then dropped in at Jason's house. They played a couple hours of *Call of Duty* until Mrs. Dufresne literally pulled the plug and insisted Jason attend to a growing number of unfinished chores. Figuring he may as well tackle some of his own overdue tasks, Trenton returned home and began unpacking. He was surprised how quickly it went. By the time he felt hungry for dinner, the entire first floor was done and a huge stack of broken down boxes sat, twined together, to be taken to the recycling center.

He rewarded himself with a few more pages of the diary. Starting at the end, he moved backwards. Reading in reverse about the crisis of faith that led Jeremiah Wolcott to abandon his quest for the missing money. He was slowly getting better at deciphering the tiny, faded writing, but it still took twenty minutes and two passes to read each page—one to sort of translate the barely-legible text into regular English and once for actual comprehension.

At about eight o' clock, Trenton was contemplating unpacking the boxes in the workshop and garage when his cell rang. His boss.

"Hello," he answered.

"Trenton. It's Todd. How are you feeling? Any better?"

"Yeah, yeah. Thanks for asking. I'm fine." Trent felt a pang of guilt at the reminder of his lie.

"Good to hear. Hey, I've got an opportunity that I thought you may want to jump on, since you called in sick today and showed up late yesterday." He paused, as if Trenton might commit right now, sight-unseen.

"Yeah? What is it?"

"I need someone to come in real early tomorrow morning. About five. I'm getting a new delivery of countertops at ten and I need all those air conditioners and ceiling fans, and all that other stuff moved off that wall in the showroom, and into the back. It'll take some time. You can make up for the income you lost today."

Trenton hesitated. He felt an unexplainable sense of obligation, probably based on having lied when he called in sick. But five in the morning?

"I'll even pay you overtime," Todd said. "How about that?"

"No, I'll do it."

"So you're saying yes?"

"Yes."

"Alright then. See you tomorrow."

The moment the call ended, Trenton remembered. He and Dad had rescheduled their early-morning archery for tomorrow. He felt sick to his stomach at the thought of putting it off yet again. But it hadn't been Trent's fault the first time. And of course they both had jobs and responsibilities. Anyway, they'd just have to push it off to the next week.

Yeah. No big deal.

But the thing was, Trent didn't believe any of that.

* * *

Trenton stared at his alarm clock. 4:30 AM? Was that even a real time? It looked like some sort of a novelty joke time one might buy at Spencer's Gifts. All the same, he was able to get up, showered, and on his way quickly, and found himself unlocking the door to the resale shop at about ten minutes to five. He yawned violently.

As far as he was concerned, this would make up for any time he showed up late, past or future. He cracked open a Wattage energy drink and took a sip. Ugh. Tasted like perfume. How could Jason drink this swill?

Before he commenced lugging and dollying all this junk around, Trent wanted to get a feel for the space he had to work with. The stack of window A/C units was comically tall and he had no idea how he would begin to dismantle it. There was a HiLo in the storage room, but Trent was not allowed to use it. He went back there to see how much space he had to work with, hoping a plan might just occur to him. He scowled. It would be just like Todd to send him in here unprepared and then blame him for not being able to do the impossible.

Trenton froze. He was not alone back here. He could hear someone moving around. Was it Todd, here to help him? That would be nice. But something in his gut told him it was no one here to help. It was men—several men—speaking in hushed tones.

"You were gonna just leave your hammer," one of them said. "You trying to get us caught? I ought to bash your head in with it."

"I'm sorry."

"Choke on your apology. Just go get it. We need to be out here like ten minutes ago."

Footsteps. Coming this way. Trenton darted into the shadows and crouched down behind a gas stove. He heard someone walk past him and through the double doors to the store proper. A minute later, another man followed, pausing in the doorway to call out, "Hey, I almost forgot. Take something. Doesn't matter what. Just something they'll notice."

"Yeah, okay. How about this?"

"Fine. Let's just go. No excuses, no delays."

"But we didn't even look in the—"

"We're just getting it started. We'll have plenty of time to look later. All the time in the world."

The two men were walking back through the store room when one of them dropped something. It rolled, slowly, toward Trenton, crouched there in the shadows behind the stove. Right toward him. He willed it to change course, for someone to grab it before it reached its destination, but no one did and it kept coming. Trenton pressed himself as far back into the darkness as he could, trying to flatten his body against the chest freezer that blocked him in. The little round item bounced off the back wall, rolled up to Trenton, bumped against his leg, and toppled over.

A tin of tobacco. Blue Wolf Chewin' Tobacco.

Trenton pushed his hand up against his mouth. Footsteps were now approaching his hiding place. He offered up a frantic prayer as he saw a hand reach around the stove, searching. He pushed the tin into its path. A moment later, the hand was gone along with the tin.

He heard the two men rejoining at least two others and leaving out the back door, into the alley.

After another thirty seconds, he finally took a breath and emerged from behind the stove. For some reason, his first thought was of Judith. What would she have done? Fought four men? Tailed them back to their hideout? For sure, she wouldn't have hidden like a child and let them get away?

Then again, maybe they hadn't made a clean getaway just yet. If Trenton could spot their vehicle—maybe get the license plate number—his dad could arrest them, relieving the pressure, freeing him up to finally retire, toppling Judith's whole case for why she had to become a masked hero. This was the silver bullet.

Trenton gathered his nerves and slipped out the door, into the dark alley. He had no way of knowing which way they went, but his gut told him away from the street, toward Unity Park, which was itself just a glorified alley. He moved quickly through the darkness.

Yes! There. Four big guys in heavy work coats, moving quickly, avoiding the street lights. He only saw them in silhouette and from behind, but he was analyzing each of them in turn: their gait, their build. Was one of these men Ed Piper? Or was there actually someone else walking around Clinch Rock with a tin of Blue Wolf?

On Water Street, they all made for an old red pickup with a busted headlight cover. He thought about letting it drive by, so he could write down the plate. But what if they turned down Holmes? He'd never get a chance to see it. No, he had to get around the back of that truck. The men were moving a little slower now; maybe he could run around the block fast enough to come up from behind and catch the plate before they drove away.

Trenton took off with everything he had, down Front Street, left on Charlevoix. His lungs were on fire. He pushed through it. He hadn't sprinted any real distance in at least a year and his side began to ache. Then he saw an opening, a narrow alley that cut through between the antique mall and Sweet Tooth Candy Shop, and he turned down it. His legs ached as he commanded them to keep on chugging. He was so close. He heard the truck's engine come to life with a sick rattle. It wasn't far.

A discarded roll of carpet, jutting out from behind a dumpster, snagged his shoe and Trenton went down, hard, his hands clapping against the concrete just before his chest made contact. No time to lick his wounds, though. He bounced up, feeling it in every joint and muscle. Ten more feet. Lurching ahead, he cleared the alley and poked his head out on to Water Street. He was indeed behind the truck, which was just pulling away.

There was only one problem: no license plate.

* * *

"Okay, *think*, son. Did you see anything else at all?"

Trent had called 911 the moment the truck left his sight. Dispatch had contacted the station, where Jessie Finn called the chief at home. Within ten minutes, he was at the scene of the crime, hugging his son—a hug that went on a little longer than was comfortable for Trenton. Then, the moment he broke the embrace, he'd launched into a witness interview that was all-business.

"That's it," Trent said, emphatically. "I can tell you three more times, but it won't change anything. It was a beat-up old red truck. The headlight was broken. No license plate."

"And you didn't get a good look at any of the men? Just this tin of chewing tobacco." Trenton had described everything in detail, but hadn't mentioned Ed Piper by name. He didn't know why, but it seemed silly to assume his dad would even want to know the name of a random local man who chewed that brand. Besides, whenever he conjured an image of Ed, he always saw him leaning against the wall at the soup kitchen. Not skulking, not suspicious. Just sad. Like he was there, not for the food, but just to be around *someone*.

Trenton felt a lump of emotion trying to claw its way up his throat. "Sorry I cancelled with you this morning, Dad. I shouldn't have even been here."

"Hey, don't worry about that. I'm just glad you're okay. I love you, son."

"Love you too."

"Okay. I've told Todd he's not to have anyone working alone before sunup until we catch these guys. And that you're getting the rest of the day off with full pay. He agreed."

"Dad, that's stupid. I can—"

125

"No discussion," his father said. "You're shook up. You need some down time. Go waste the day, alright? Be a kid. Play the X-Station300 or whatever it is. Just relax. Officer Cash will give you a ride home."

Trenton felt his skin crawl. "At least let me walk home, okay?"

His dad shook his head. "Nope. Don't make me cuff you, buddy." He winked and smiled. "Think of your old man. Scared the hell out of me to get that call—my son was in the building when they broke in?" He shuddered a bit. "Let me have this one."

"Okay, dad."

Officer Cash drove exactly the speed limit back to the parsonage. Trent wanted to mine him for information about why he'd been with Zoe that afternoon, how he knew her, what interest the two of them shared in a long-abandoned, never-successful copper mine. But there was no way to do it without tipping his hand. So instead, he made small talk.

"So you're from Detroit?" he asked.

"Rochester Hills, actually. I grew up there. Not much more exciting than this place."

"You and Tango—or Officer Tyrell—are both from there, right?"

The cop laughed. It was a very friendly and disarming laugh. "Do me a favor, kid. Call him Tango. That's hilarious. He needs a good dose of humility once in a while." The smile stayed on his face for a few seconds, fading gradually, pleasantly, like the orange light after the sun disappears below the horizon.

"You guys known each other long?"

"Yeah, he's my brother in law. Before that, my best buddy. Barton offered me a job up here in May. Turns out our families were already thinking about moving up North, going a little more rural. So I said, 'Tell you what—you can get two for the price of two.'" He laughed again. "This your place up here?"

"Yeah." They pulled into the driveway and Trenton offered, "Thanks for the ride" as he exited the car.

"Don't mention it kid. Take it easy. Sorry you had such a rough morning."

He put the cruiser in reverse, waving as he backed out. Somehow, Trenton knew he meant it. The cop really was sorry about what had happened. And that was fitting. Because Trenton was also sure—absolutely sure—that one of those four men who broke into the Home Store that morning had been Officer Cash.

CHAPTER TWELVE
"OX GOAD"

"Forget this ball of rock! Forget your bank account! Forget the big game on Sunday! Forget your stupid lawn! Forget it all! That's what Insane Faith looks like."

—From the *Insane Faith Day-by-Day Calendar 2018*, August 18th

Trenton tried to follow his dad's instructions. He watched a few shows on Netflix and scrolled through his Twitter feed. But he was restless. By ten in the morning, he was back in the secret room, wheeling his desk chair behind him. He studied the big map for a while, then took a picture and printed it out, crossing out each of the buildings that no longer stood and realizing there was a decent chance the money had been hidden in one of them. But probably not. More than three quarters of them still stood and he would search each and every one.

As ready as he had been to give this all up the day before, at the moment he wanted nothing more than to *get back out there*. He called Judith for the second time that morning, but it went straight to voicemail. Was she ducking his calls? They hadn't parted on the best of terms. Part of him wanted to call Zoe, but he didn't know what to say. The more he thought about it, the more convinced he became that Officer Cash was one of the men who had piled into that red truck. So what was Zoe doing with him out at the Ashton mine? Could he trust her? Maybe Judith's paranoia was just rubbing off on him.

He sat at Wolcott's old desk and fired up his laptop, opening tab after tab in an attempt to establish the present value of those two fifty dollar bank notes. More than an hour later, all he knew was that they were called "brown backs" and that their value could vary significantly. Just about every site urged him to consult an expert.

Trenton searched for "antique money expert" within twenty miles of his zip code. The closest one was Eagle Coin in the nearby town of Baldwin, about a twenty-minute drive away. Should he go? Dad had been pretty clear. Still, he told himself, a pleasant trip to a rare coin shop was pretty much a lateral move from TV and video games, excitement-wise. He texted Jason,

> Hey, man. U up for a little road trip?

The answer came almost immediately:

> Where to?

> Baldwin. If you can get the minivan, I will show you something awesome.

Five minutes later, Jason replied:

> Turns out my mom is happy to get rid of me. Who knew? B over in a few

* * *

"A coin store?" Jason demanded. "What?! I thought you said I was going to see something awesome." They were zipping down US-10 in Mrs. Dufresne's minivan.

"You drive me to this coin shop and you will."

Jason shot him a skeptical look. "It's not a coin, is it?"

"Nope."

"Well, what then?"

"Just wait. In the meantime, let me tell you what went down today." Trent related the events of that morning, leaving out nothing.

When he got to the tin of tobacco, Jason practically swerved off the road.

"You're making this up!" he accused.

"I swear, it's true. Every word."

"I knew that guy was off! But *he's* the one breaking into all these building and ripping them apart? What a nut job! Has your dad arrested him yet?"

"You can't arrest someone for using the same chew as the criminals."

Jason pounded the steering wheel. "Oh, come *awwn!* That's solid evidence, man. That's the smoking gun! Or, like, the smokeless gun. See what I did there?"

"Don't kid yourself. Brian Green may think Clinch Rock is going to be the Cape Cod of the Great Lakes or whatever, but it's actually just a little town out in the sticks. Lots of people chew."

"But *Blue Wolf?*"

Trenton shrugged. "It's circumstantial. If it's even that. Turn here."

Jason took a left and they saw the store immediately. "We're not done talking about this," he promised.

The shop was small and old-looking. A faded old sign bore the words "Eagle Coin and Collectibles." A much newer sign, mounted just beneath it, announced "WE BUY GOLD."

The first thing Trenton noticed inside was the security cameras—three of them. The place was packed with glass display cases, most of them filled with coins, but a few exhibiting pocket watches or various medals and amulets. The man behind the counter—in his late thirties with an enormous hipster beard—narrowed his eyes at them.

"Can I help you?" he asked.

"I hope so." Trenton reached into a manila envelope and withdrew the two bank notes, setting them on the counter. "Are these worth anything?"

The man gaped for a moment and then, very carefully, examined every square inch of both bills, both sides. He then consulted two enormous reference volumes before again inspecting the notes, this time with a magnifying glass.

Finally, he set the bills on a black velvet pad and said, "The answer is yes."

"Yes, what?" Jason asked.

"Yes, they're worth something."

Trenton laughed, nervously. "But how much, though?"

The man pursed his lips for a moment. "If I offered you $500 for the pair, would you take it?"

"Heck yes!"

"Well, that's just stupid. You need to do some real research before you sell these. I don't know what they're worth exactly. I specialize in coins, not paper currency. However, I can tell you a few things. These are obsolete notes, so they have no value as legal tender. They're worth whatever someone will pay for them. And, at auction, you'd probably get a lot more than five hundred."

Jason punched Trenton in the arm. "So when are these auctions?" he asked.

"Never. Not around here." He pointed at one of the notes. "This one is probably worth about $85. You could sell it on eBay. But this one—you see that serial number? One thousand. That's what collectors look for. I wouldn't be surprised if it brought thousands of dollars at a coin and currency show."

"Thanks for being honest," Trenton said.

The man drew himself up. "I would never cheat a customer. I love currency far more than I love money."

Jason scoffed. "Whatever that means. "

The man ignored him and said to Trenton, "I can't let you take these out of here, though. Not in *that*." He indicated the envelope. "I'll give you a couple acid-free sleeves, on the house. Just promise me you'll get these into the hands of someone who can really appreciate them."

"Will do," Trenton said. "Thanks again."

Back on the road, Jason demanded, "Where did you get those?"

"Found them. In our basement."

"You think there's any more?"

Trenton just shrugged. He was full of excitement at what he'd learned about the bills, but also frustrated that their value was only theoretical at this point. How far would he have to go to get the best price? Grand Rapids? Chicago? One thing he knew for sure though: if the rest of Cassel's stash was in the form of bank notes, it would be worth even more today than it had been back when the Crown Fire Boys were willing to torture and kill for it. Probably lots more. Still, he'd have taken $500 now, to put in the plate at church, over $5000 at some undefined future date.

"By the way," Jason said, "I meant to ask you: how's it going with our favorite twenty-two year old hottie?"

"She's not 22."

"Sure, whatever. You go out with her again?"

"Not yet."

He shoved Trenton, in his seat. "Why not? I thought you were in! Something you're not telling me?"

Only about a million things. "No, I'm just waiting for the right moment."

"You mean you're waiting for her to ask *you* out again. You're going to look like a wuss."

Jason had a point. The momentum he enjoyed with Zoe wouldn't last forever. "You're right. I'll see if she's free tomorrow night. Los Guys are playing the State Theater."

"So do it then."

"What — *now*?"

Jason nodded. "I'm here to hold you accountable as a non-wuss."

"Sure, whatever." Trenton dialed up "Zoe less than three." She answered on the third ring.

"Hi, Trent. I was wondering when you were going to call."

"Yeah, sorry," he said. "Just been super busy. Work and everything."

"Me too. We've got three more displays ready for the museum. You should come over and have a look. But don't worry, I'm saving you the letters from Jeremiah Wolcott."

"Thanks." An awkward pause followed. "So, I was kind of calling because tomorrow night is Friday and everything. And this band, Los Guys, is playing at the State Theater. Not exactly high art or anything, but—"

"Sorry, Trent. I already have plans. Dan Barton asked me out."

Trenton felt like he was having a stroke. " . . . *seriously?*"

"I know he's kind of a meathead, but he was sweet in his own way and he apologized for being a jerk at the skating rink. Besides, I didn't hear from you at all yesterday, so —"

"No. Yeah. No. It's fine. Some other time."

"How about tonight?" she asked. "Dinner and a movie? You do have a movie theater here, right?"

"Yeah. It only has three screens, but . . . What time?"

"How about you come by at five?"

"Absolutely. See you tonight." He hung up to great fanfare from Jason, who high-fived him and called him "the man" at least half a dozen times. Trenton beamed.

Maybe Jason was a decent wing-man after all.

* * *

Adam Marsh was mixing a packet of powdered creamer into his coffee when he noticed it, right beneath his feet. How long had he been stepping over it, completely unaware? Trying not to be obvious, he bent down to retie his shoe, and inspected the hardwood floor. No, he wasn't imagining it. Shiny new nail heads in five—no six—floorboards. He stood and took a sip of his coffee, eyeballing the other people in the office. Rich Barton. Tango and Cash. Jessie Finn. Dennis Reid. Sheila Nguyen.

"Adam, you have a call on line one," announced Sheila, their civilian administrator.

"I'll take it in my office," he said. Shutting the door behind him, he picked up the handset. "This is Chief Marsh."

"You don't call. You don't write. If I didn't know any better, I'd think you'd forgotten me!" It was a familiar voice, and it caused all the stress and worry to melt away.

"Dr. Pardee. Oh, it's good to hear your voice, sir."

"Don't call me sir. It's Jim."

Adam laughed. "Someday, maybe."

"So how's my protégé been?"

"Exhausted would be an understatement."

"Anything I can help you with? I've got just a little bit of experience with your congregation."

"Honestly, they're the least of my concerns right now. I mean, yeah, Chet's still a thorn in my side and the money's still tight, but if that were all I had to worry about . . . " He trailed off.

"Go on. Get it off your chest."

Adam dropped his voice and walked over to click his door shut. "I think something's going on here, Dr. Pardee. In the department. But I can't really look into it like I should. I'm spread way too thin."

"I imagine you are."

"And if I stop for even a second, I feel like I'm dropping the ball. Actually, I feel like that all the time. I'm not there enough as a cop or as a pastor. Or as a father. And not nearly enough as a student. I'm in danger of failing two of my four classes. I just . . . I don't know how long I can keep this up. " He was surprised by how good it felt to just admit all of this out loud.

"Well, my offer stands," the old preacher said. "I'd gladly come back for a while as an interim. Give you a break and get them ready to fully support you. I bet I could even turn Bushman in your favor."

"I won't hear of it. You stay up at the lake house. You deserve it."

Dr. Pardee seemed to think for a moment before saying, "So what you're telling me is that I deserve rest and enjoyment, but you can't even have a moment of downtime or you feel guilty? Where do you suppose this is this coming from?"

"It's different with you," Adam said. "You've earned it. You're retired."

"Adam, you don't earn rest. Jesus earned it for us. It's over; it's done. *Come to me all who labor and are heavy-laden and I will . . . ?*"

"I know."

"Then say it."

"I will give you rest."

"Those are the words you need to follow, son." He paused, as if waiting for Adam to say something. When he didn't, Dr. Pardee added, "I know how much you love *that book*. I thought it was challenging too, and profitable. And I'm glad it made you revisit your priorities. But maybe you should give all this *Insane Faith* stuff a rest. You're going overboard."

"Overboard is the whole point."

"Is it? Even the Lord Jesus stopped to rest. Are you taking a Sabbath day?"

"No," he admitted.

"Something to think about. Look, it sounds like you're pushed for time, so I'll let you go. I just wanted to tell you I'm headed your way in a couple weeks. Why don't we get together?"

"I'd really like that, Dr. Pardee."

"Alright, then. I don't want to find you burned out. Take some time for rest, alright?"

"I'll try."

"There is no try. Do," he said in a bad impression of Yoda.

Adam laughed. "I'll *try*."

"Alright then. See you soon."

"Goodbye." Adam hung up the phone, realizing that he'd just lied to his mentor.

* * *

Trenton felt almost at ease walking up to Zoe's door that night. It was his third time there this week and it was beginning to feel familiar, in a good way. Of course, he was mildly aware of the quarantined zone in the back of his brain, where he'd isolated thoughts of John Cash, the silver mine, and Zoe's impending date with Dan Barton. But that was a necessity.

135

Brian answered the door, greeting him with a smile and a warm handshake.

"Come on in. Zoe's almost ready."

Trenton entered the parlor and immediately noticed the three new displays, standing next to the picture of Wolcott and Cassel.

"What do you think?" Brian asked. They were all photos of lumberjacks—felling trees, smoking pipes, sharing a meal—with lots of text.

"They look great!"

"Glad you approve." They both surveyed the displays for a moment before Brian added, "Zoe tells me you're going to see a film tonight."

"Yeah, that new Johnny Depp one where he's a spy but he doesn't know it."

"Mm. I guess I missed that one."

Trenton shrugged.

"Let me get your opinion on something else," Brian said, walking over to the card table in the corner, now covered with even more photos and papers. He picked up a page and handed it to Trenton. It contained two hand-written columns of text: *Cassel Heights, Cassel Springs, Mill Creek, Mill Run, Mill Valley, Oak Valley, Pine Meadow* . . . It went on and on.

"What's this?"

"Trenton, as we've been working with the town council to re-brand Clinch Rock, we've come to believe that the town's name is standing in our way. Not only do people associate the it with obscurity, rather than desirability, the name itself is kind of . . . *ugly*. Both of the words, *clinch* and *rock*, sound harsh. At first, we thought maybe just a new logo for the town, to kind of soften the name. But now we're toying with the idea of changing it all together."

"Can you do that?"

"Well, *I* can't. But I can recommend a simple vote of the town council, which would put it on the ballot. This great state is full of beautiful-sounding Indian names like Mackinaw and Petoskey, or descriptive, evocative names like Harbor Springs or Birch Run. They make people want to visit. Even some of the now-defunct lumber towns, like Seney—best known for a bloody tavern fight and that Hemingway poem about a deadly fire—have a pleasant ring to them. *Scenic Seney*. I picture a quaint bed and breakfast."

Trenton had no idea what to say. His gut reaction was to leave the town name alone. But what did he know about this stuff?

"Sorry to keep you waiting, Trenton," Zoe said, descending the stairs. She stole Trenton's breath, wearing the red dress she'd worn at camp and looking glamorous. Trent suddenly felt under-dressed, not only in his khakis and T-shirt, but in his own skin.

"No problem," he managed to say.

"You kids have fun," Brian called, turning his attention back to the stack of pictures on the coffee table.

At the car, Trenton opened Zoe's door for her, even though she was driving, because it seemed the thing to do. She laughed at the gesture, but said thank you all the same.

As they pulled out of the driveway, she asked, "Mind if I show you something before dinner?"

"Sure."

She smiled, broadly. "I love how you're game for anything, Trenton," and kissed him on the cheek, adding, "You're going to love this."

They headed away from downtown, then turned onto a county road, leading east.

A few minutes later, Trenton said, "I think I know where you're taking me."

"You've been here before?"

"Yeah, they brought our class out to the lumber camp in third grade."

She laughed quietly. "I think you'll be surprised at home much it's changed." They turned onto a long, unpaved drive, which cut through dense forest, curving this way and that for half a mile. When they emerged from the trees, Zoe gestured grandly. "What do you think?"

"Wow! Did you guys build all of this?"

"We oversaw it. Come on, let me show you around."

Trenton got out of the car and approached four newly recon-structed buildings. They were rustic, made of unfinished pine.

"This is amazing," he said. On an impulse, he added, "Total opp-osite of that bombed-out copper mine. You ever been there?"

She shook her head. "Nope." Trent felt his mood dive-bomb. How could she lie to him so easily?

Like an excited child, she led him over to a building labeled "Bunk House 1." "So we're going to have a whole presentation put together, taking visitors through an average day at a lumber camp." She straightened her back and adopted a tour guide tone. "The men would sleep in tight quarters, filed into these small bunkhouses. At three in the morning, the camp cook would rise and begin preparing breakfast, which would be on the table by five."

Trenton couldn't imagine starting work at five each morning. Once had almost killed him.

Zoe continued, "Most lumberjacks led rather sad lives, working twelve-hour days, wrecking their bodies, slowly getting behind to the company store. And even though the lumber companies were incredibly wealthy, they squeezed these men, pinched every penny, and stretched every resource. I think a good metaphor is the saw mill, where the lumber was taken, by river. They burned the scraps and sawdust from one board to create the steam to cut the next one. Of course, once in a while the whole thing might explode."

Trenton thought of his dad, also working insane hours, getting behind in every way, feeding the fire with scraps, and in danger of blowing up or flaming out.

"Speaking of which," Zoe went on, "the lumberjacks had to eat in absolute silence. No talking at meals, no drinking in the camp, no fighting in the camp. And so, whenever they had leave, they got a reputation for raising hell. But if they didn't cut loose once in a while, *they'd* probably explode." She let out a practiced laugh.

Trenton realized she was definitely reciting a memorized script and resisted the urge to ask how often they had such a leave.

"Oh, wait," she said, giving her head a little shake. "I was supposed to take you into the mess hall, to show you where they ate." They entered a narrow building, which was empty, save for a few informative placards, piled against one wall and a long-handled implement mounted on another.

Trenton gawked. "Why do you have an ox goad in here?" He studied the item, which looked almost exactly like one of the pictures he'd seen online.

She laughed. "That's actually called a Peavey. It was used for floating logs down the river. Any other questions?" She giggled. "This is fun."

"Yeah. Was there, like, a central fire where they all gathered?" he asked. After all, this place was on their list and not on Wolcott's map.

Zoe thought for a moment. "Not really. There would have been wood-burning cast iron stoves in the bunk houses and the cook's range here in the mess hall. He have reproductions being made. We're expecting them later this week."

They continued the impromptu tour for a good half hour, Zoe walking him through a day in a lumberjack's life, while Trenton eyed each and every possible "fire," beneath which he planned to search for the money, compiling a mental list.

Finally, she said, "I guess that's about it." She sighed, contentedly. "You know, there's something special about Clinch Rock. A lot of these old lumber towns have long-since become ghost towns. Dead and gone. This one's just sleeping."

"What do you mean, sleeping?" Trent asked.

"I mean, we just need to wake it up."

"But isn't the sleepiness part of the charm?"

She half-shrugged. "I suppose. But, really, what's the point of a town like this? I mean, the way it's been lately? My father and I have a vision for a vibrant business district, tourism industry, maybe some vineyards in the area, a revitalized downtown full of galleries, upscale shops. Trust me, you won't even recognize it."

Somehow, it sounded like a threat to Trenton

* * *

Back in Clinch Rock, they were walking hand-in-hand down Main Street toward the movie theater, when they came face-to-face with Dan Barton and his motley crew of lesser jocks.

"Hey, Zoe," he said, flashing his stupid, perfect white teeth.

"Hello." She was polite, but not flirty. Trenton picked up the pace.

As they passed through the sea of muscle-heads, Barton said, "I've got a great night lined up for us tomorrow. You'll probably forget all about whatever lame thing you guys are doing right now."

Without thinking, Trent released Zoe's hand, and stepped right up into Dan's face. He felt oddly courageous, invincible even. Maybe it was what he'd been through that morning—Barton might be tough, but was nothing compared to four grown men, breaking into buildings, threatening to bash each other's heads in. At any rate, before he knew it, Trent was looking up about an inch into the eyes of his nemesis, saying, "I am so sick of you and your crap."

Barton smirked. "You trying to show off for the lady, Marsh? Because you're not going to impress her by getting your head knocked off."

Zoe grabbed Trenton by the hand and pulled. "Neither of you is going to impress me by acting like little boys. Come on, Trenton. I want to look at this vintage dress in here. It's cute. What do you think?"

Trenton allowed himself to be led away. "You're right, Zoe. He's not worth it. How about I buy you the dress?" He threw a contemptuous look back at Dan as they walked away. Only as he followed her through the entrance to Rerun did he realize his miscalculation.

"Actually, Zoe, we might want to get our tickets now so we don't miss the previews."

Zoe looked at the stylish watch on her wrist. "Nonsense. We've got all sorts of time." She moved from the dress in the window to flipping through various clothes on a garment rack. "How have I never been in here?" she said absently, taking in the old tin ceilings and exposed brick. "It's a fabulous building. Just needs some work."

Trenton glanced at the counter, where a large cardboard sign, propped against the antique cash register, read, "Please Don't Steal

Anything. Karma's Watching and She's Kind of a . . . " beneath which was a drawing of an angry-looking cartoon pit bull, wearing a too-too. Trent knew this meant whoever was working that night—either Brook Yanich or Judith—had stepped out to the bathroom or for a smoke or a bite to eat. He was on borrowed time and he did not want his date with Zoe to collide with Judith, especially not if she was still mad at him.

"You want that dress?" he asked, practically assaulting the mannequin wearing it. "I'll get it for you. We'll have them set it aside so—"

"No, it's too big. And it'a little dingy—not worth having it altered."

"Okay, but let's—"

"*You!*" It was Judith's voice, from the back of the store, and it was full of righteous anger.

Trenton closed his eyes and cursed his luck.

"Excuse me?" Zoe said.

Judith stormed up to her, a folded paper in her hand. "You had a hand in this, right?" she demanded. "It says 'Town of Clinch Rock' on the letterhead, but you and your father are the 'consultants' it keeps mentioning. Tell me I'm wrong!"

"What is that?" Trenton asked.

"Oh, you mean you don't know what your little girlfriend's up to?" Judith said, her voice rising. "Well, let's see." She flicked the paper open and read, "'Guidelines for Downtown Businesses in a Rebooted Clinch Rock. Remove all hand-lettered signage and replace with professional, stylish, and tasteful signage. Businesses must keep consistent hours, rather than being open by appointment.' Oh, and my favorite: 'Businesses must present themselves in keeping with the sort of tourist destination that Clinch Rock strives to be.'"

Trenton tried for a consoling tone. "Judith, they're just suggestions."

"Actually," Zoe said, "that's not entirely true. These requirements will soon be reflected in zoning regulations and city ordinances. It's for the good of the town."

"That seems sort of messed up," Trenton said.

"Oh, that's not even the worst part!" Judith wailed. "They want to rename the town! It says the current name sounds, 'unpleasant and uncomfortable.' There's a whole list of possibilities here." She waited for Trent's reaction. "Wait, you *knew*?"

He shrugged. "I don't think it's necessary, but why not let the people vote on it?"

Zoe sighed, annoyed. "Judith, it's an ugly sound. Clinch Rock? It makes me feel like I'm squeezing a jagged stone in my fist. We can do better."

"*We?*" Judith laughed, mirthlessly. "How long have you lived here, two weeks? There's no *we*." She stalked over to a shelf full of used books and grabbed an old dictionary. "You're not even thinking of the right word. It's not 'clench.' It's *Clinch* Rock. She flipped through the Cs, settling on the right page. "*Definition 1. To settle a matter decisively.* As in, this stupid list clinches it for me: you should move back where you came from."

Trenton grimaced. "Judith, let's not say things we—"

"*Definition 2,*" she continued. "*To fasten by beating down a protruding end.*"

"Yes, yes," Zoe said, unamused. "I'm sure you want to clinch my—"

"*Definition 3! To hold fast, as in a passionate lover's embrace.* Maybe that sounds 'unpleasant and uncomfortable' to a robot like you. But we like it just fine."

"Are you quite done?" Zoe asked.

"No, they missed one. Definition 4. It's also a wrestling term."

Zoe rolled her eyes. "Well, Judith, most *ladies* don't know anything about wrestling."

"Well, let me show you then." For a moment, Trenton thought she was going to tackle Zoe, which brought on a flood of confusing and conflicting feelings. But instead, she gripped Trent around the neck with her left hand and grabbed his bicep with the other. "Do the same thing to me," she said.

For some reason, he complied, entering a wrestling position, their foreheads pressing together. She smelled like grapefruit. Some kind of lotion or hair product.

"This is how you start a wrestling match, grappling. In a clinch. Like you Greens and our town. Right now, you feel like you're about to take us to the mat, but you're not." He knew it was wildly inappropriate, but Trenton couldn't focus on anything but the citrus smell and how close their faces were. This more like Definition Three than Four.

"But watch this," she said. Suddenly, Trenton was upside-down, his legs flying in an arc through the air. He collided roughly with the hardwood floor, then felt Judith's upper body land on his, pinning him. "You see? I just clinched the situation. Decisively." The bell above the door jingled, as if to confirm the pin, and Trenton realized he was lying beneath his best friend in a public place while who-knew-who just walked in.

"Let me up," he said.

Judith rolled off him. "I guess I scared her away." Trenton looked around. Zoe was gone. "I tried to warn you about her. She's no good for you."

"Shut up, Judith!" He pulled himself off the floor and blasted out the door after Zoe, just in time to see her disappearing into her car.

"Zoe! Just wait!" he shouted. She turned down Nebobish and disappeared.

"Doesn't look good!" Barton called from outside Coney Heaven, across the street. "Stick with the Bag Lady, Marsh. She's more your style!"

Trenton ignored him and started the walk home. On the way, he tried calling Zoe three times, only to have it go right to voicemail each time. Stupid Barton. And Judith. What was she thinking with that stunt? And what was *he* thinking, playing along, letting her pull him into her crazy world yet again? Actually, what *had he* been thinking? Whatever it was, it had to be laid to rest. She was nuts, after all. The opposite of Zoe in so many ways.

Which meant Zoe was the opposite of Judith. The opposite of his best friend.

* * *

There were only three vehicles parked behind Mac's Road House. One of them was Coach Fischer's 2017 Silverado truck. Judith hung back , beneath the canopy of a white pine.

Actually, it wasn't Judith. It was the Angelus, the guardian angel of Clinch Rock.

She had decided the night before to assume the name Angelos, when Trent's dad lay that Greek word on the Scrabble board. After all, Angel and Archangel had both been claimed (by the same Marvel Comics character actually), and Guardian Angel by an obscure DC hero. So Angelos it was. But then she'd decided Latin was better than Greek in this case—more hardcore—leading her to the word Angelus, also the name of a prayer, which she found on YouTube, being chanted in haunting Latin with church bells behind it. Very Noir.

She was not in full costume, but close enough. She had the wings on her upper arms, of course, plus the mask, boots, leggings, and an armored leather vest she'd made from a biking shirt and this weird bondage corset thing that came into Rerun (now spray-painted blue) . She'd put them together while listening to Depeche Mode, seeing herself in some Molly Ringwald movie montage.

In lieu of a wig, she wore her hair up in a blue knit cap. This would be something of a test-run, she'd decided. Everyone knew where to find Coach Fischer. Friday nights, he'd be at the skating rink, keeping an eye on his wrestlers and, creepily, on many of the cheerleaders. All other nights, it was a safe bet he'd be here at Clinch Rock's only sports bar. Or, as she now knew, maybe home, getting rough with his wife.

The Angelus swung her weapon back and forth beneath the broad pine branches savoring the roar it made as it cut through the air. If Fischer came out with someone else, she'd follow behind on the Iron Horse, stashed nearby.

But if he was alone . . .

CHAPTER THIRTEEN
"SERVANTS' QUARTERS"

"I remember singing a song called 'Turn Your Eyes Upon Jesus' when I was a boy. It was a lovely song, and the climax was, *The things of earth will grow strangely dim in the light of his glory and grace.* You know what that tells me? If I love Jesus, the things of earth had better be dimming. We love to sing that, but we don't like to think about it. Because that includes good food, friends, wine, and sunsets. These things should be dimming. When Jesus returns, do you want to be looking full in his face, or distracted by the things of this world? How humiliating it would, when he returns, to be caught playing secular music, reading a novel, listening to a podcast, or watching television. Let it all dim. Let it fade to black."

—*Insane Faith: A Guide to Extreme Christianity for the Truly Faithful*
by Stephen Branding, p. 162

Trent was beyond distracted Friday morning. After trying Zoe two more times, with no answer, he'd gone to the White Tail Diner for breakfast. Only when his food was on the table did it occur to him that he and his dad would have had plenty of time for archery and eggs that morning. Dad had even taken the day off, which was a small miracle in itself. After two cancellations, they'd missed the best opportunity they were likely to get. Soon Trent would be off on the YLBC retreat and then back at school and such opportunities would be extinct. Combined with last night's date fiasco, this had Trent low-grade fuming all morning, nursing his regrets like a loving mother.

At work, Todd had already reprimanded him three times for slowness and sloppiness, and it was only 10:15. For the life of him, Trenton couldn't remember why he'd taken this job, which paid practically nothing, instead of taking driver's ed and at least getting a license, even if he lacked a car. The electronic door chime sounded, bringing a semi-audible groan from Trenton. He looked up and saw the mayor enter the store.

Mayor Groebel was a retired school administrator, who always wore a suit and tie. He seemed to be laboring under the idea that, even in towns the size of Clinch Rock where he was paid a stipend of $5,000 per year, the mayor should get free haircuts, the best tables at every restaurant (all five of them), a blind eye from the police when running red lights, and immediate fawning upon entering any establishment.

None of this actually happened, of course, and Trent approached him with all the enthusiasm of a dead moth. "May I help you?" he asked.

"Why yes, young man. I'm looking for a nice headboard."

Trent sighed. Thanks to pensions or investments or something, Mayor Groebel was one of the richest men in Clinch Rock; why would he need to shop at Second Life Home Store?

"We only have a few," he said. "Follow me."

Behind a few stacks of interior doors were exactly three headboards. Mayor Groebel clucked his disappointment, bending over them, inspecting. As he examined the last one, Trent noticed something shiny inside the man's suit coat, hanging open. A gold lapel pin. On the inside? He squinted at it.

C.F.B. And the same image tattooed on Sean's arm, if more refined.

"What's that?" Trenton demanded, pointing at the pin, knowing he was just making trouble to blow off steam. It was really a Jason move.

The mayor looked down, saw the pin, and fastened both buttons. "None of your concern," he said.

"It stands for Crown Fire Boys, right?"

The mayor stood, straightened his coat, and walked right out of the store without another word. Only when he'd left did the full weight of this development register. If the mayor really had been part of this group, how far did it go back? Certainly not all the way to the 1890s. Right? And was it just as Sean had described, a few teenagers killing time, or was Judith on to something with her theories of high-level conspiracy? The thought of Judith reminded him of the previous night, dragging him even lower.

As if he'd been waiting for that particular cue, Dan Barton walked into the store, wearing a bright orange T-shirt, emblazoned with the words "NO EXCUSES NO DELAYS—Clinch Rock Wrestling." He gave Trenton the once-over and smirked. "Hey Marsh, I need some speakers. What do you have here?"

"Nothing. Get lost."

The jock smiled wide. "Oh I get it. You're pissed at me because you couldn't keep the lady interested last night. Not my fault."

Trenton just glared at him.

Dan pushed further. "Or are you mad because, deep down, you know I'm at least gonna get a base hit tonight?"

"Just shut up. We don't have any speakers. Go to Best Buy."

Barton rolled his head around on his enormous neck, drawing a couple loud cracks. "Anyway, I like you better with the Bag Lady. Maybe the four of us could double date some time."

Trent stepped toward him, feeling the familiar anger coursing through him again. "I'm warning you . . . "

"I mean, she'd have to take a flea bath first, but, ya know . . . "

Trenton shoved him.

"Easy there, Nancy," Dan said, shoving him back, a little harder. "Zoe's not here to rescue you this time."

Trent wanted nothing more than to hit this jerk. To knock his block off. But really didn't know what the protocol was here. He'd never been in a fight in his life. So he pushed Dan again and immediately felt an explosion of pain in his abdomen. The punch had come so fast he couldn't even remember seeing it, nor going down to one knee. Yet here he was, trying to catch his breath.

The thought formed in his mind without his permission: *What would Judith do?* She wouldn't go down after one punch. Wouldn't stay down anyway. He forced himself back to his feet, exaggerating his pains for a moment before springing into action, slamming his fist into Barton's jaw with all the strength he could muster. The punch connected, bringing a satisfying thud he felt down to his toes and a sting he hadn't expected in his knuckles and wrist.

Dan put a hand to his stubbled jaw and rubbed, a malicious smile growing across his face. Trenton saw it all unfold with near-clairvoyance just before it actually did. He felt the blow to his right eye, the freefall, and his spine connecting with the hard floor.

Then he heard Todd's voice, somehow all around him. "That's it!" He grabbed Trenton by the shoulder and hauled him bodily to his feet as if he weighed nothing. "You're both too old for this crap. Now shake hands!" Dan reached out, smiling that fake toothy grin of his. Trenton pushed past him and made for the door.

"Yeah, both of you hooligans get out of here!" Todd chided. "You're lucky I don't call your fathers and report this." As Trent left— his palm pressed up against his screaming eye—he heard Todd call, "And don't bother coming back, Trent. You're fired!"

"You okay?" Barton asked, out on the sidewalk.

"Yeah."

"Well don't get used to it. Cause this isn't over." He turned and walked away.

Trenton collapsed on a bench a block from the store. His eye ached like fury and he had no place to be and no idea what to do. On TV, they always pushed a thick steak up against swelling eyes after a fight, but that seemed a bit cartoonish. Besides, the only steaks they had at home were frozen solid in the chest freezer.

He felt an urge to call his dad. That's how he'd always kept Barton at bay in the past. But no, that wouldn't work. Because Trent had started the fight. And his dad had taken the day off, meaning the only chief of police he would find at the station was Dan Barton's father. And here he'd begun the day thinking he couldn't descend any lower.

Intent on fixing something in his life, Trent stood, dramatically and a bit too quickly, causing his eye to complain. He began the ten-minute walk to Zoe's house, stopping at the Gas 'n' Sip on the way, for some ice. As he approached the Cassel house, he decided to try and leverage this turn of events, to use it to convince Zoe that Dan Barton was the meathead bully after all. There was no way to hide his pathetic appearance, shuffling along, icing an inevitable shiner. He may as well play it up.

Zoe answered the door, her phone pressed to her ear and her body language anything but welcoming.

"He's here now," she said into the phone. "Looks like you really hurt him." She listened for a few seconds. "I find that kind of hard to believe, Dan." She shook her head violently. "No, you won't be seeing me tonight. This little episode just proves that neither of you is mature enough to date me. Why don't you call me when you've grown up." She ended the call and crossed her arms, giving Trent an apprising look.

"He's a bully," Trent said, shrugging. "He just hit me. Can I come in?"

"A bully?" she repeated, with disgust. "You sound like a little boy. Can't you stand up for yourself?"

"I got a decent shot at his chin. I bet it left a mark."

Her disgust turned to pity, but not the kind he was hoping for. "I thought you said he just punched you and that was it?"

"Look, the whole thing was stupid. I'm sorry it happened. But I was thinking maybe we could go through the rest of the letters from Jeremiah Wolcott?"

She shook her head. "My father and I already did it." Her eyes softened just a bit. "Look, Trenton, I'm not saying I don't want to be friends. We're going to spend almost a week together at Picture Falls, but this did not help you. Understand?"

Trenton tried a nobler tack. "He insulted your honor. I was fighting for you!"

"Were you? Or were you fighting for Judith? Because that's what Dan said."

He shook his head. "I'm sorry about last night. That was weird, but it wasn't my fault."

"Of course not," she said, coldly. "Nothing ever is."

"That's not fair, Zoe," he complained, realizing he was just digging himself deeper into the very same pit.

She studied him for another moment before saying, "You need to decide if you're a little boy, like Dan Barton, or a man. Because I'm not a kid, Trent, and I have no time for little boys. A man doesn't complain about bullies or pal around with a mentally deranged female wrestler who dresses like she's in some kind of Japanese cartoon." The edge returned to her voice as she said, "Why don't you go back to the *servants' quarters* and think about that?" and shut the door in his face.

As he wandered away, feeling thoroughly savaged, he dialed up Jason's cell. He needed propping up and Jason would do it expertly, with a combination of encouragement and mocking Barton through any number of creative epithets.

"Hello?" Trenton recoiled. It was Mrs. Dufresne, perhaps the last voice he wanted to hear.

"Is Jason around?" he asked.

"Yes, he's around, but he won't be leaving the house or talking on the phone anytime soon. He's grounded until school starts isn't that right?"

Trenton was unsure if she was asking him for validation or, more likely, talking to Jason himself.

"Oh. Can I just talk to him for a minute? It's important."

"No, you can't. And maybe you should have thought of that before you took my van to Baldwin when I very clearly told him no."

His eye was throbbing. What an idiot Jason could be. "I'm sorry, Mrs. Dufresne. He said he had your permission."

"Well, he didn't. I almost reported it stolen. Don't bother calling this number again until the twenty-eighth. The battery is almost dead and I won't be plugging it in. Goodbye."

The line went dead. Of all the crappy luck. Just when he needed to unload, his dad was off getting a day-long dose of Insane Faith, his girlfriend had shut him out and was probably not even his girlfriend, Jason was grounded, and calling Judith was out of the question. Things were just weird between them and, by all rights, he really should be mad at her for tanking his date last night.

Defeated, he walked home and tried to get back into Wolcott's diary, continuing backwards from where he'd left off, the reverend nearing the end of his quest, cataloging a series of searches in what seemed to Trent like very unlikely possible locations. On the plus side, he found it easier to read the diary with just one eye, but after half an hour, his headache and wandering thoughts convinced him to give up.

Slipping back into the secret room, he again studied the map. A sudden Hail-Mary idea formed. Perhaps he wasn't out of the game completely. As far as he was concerned, Judith had given up exclusive rights to this secret. And there was a chance Zoe might forgive him if it meant an inside look inside Jeremiah Wolcott's desperate search and a diary that gave her access to his innermost thoughts.

Not wanting to overthink it, he called her up. Not surprisingly, the call went to voicemail after one ring.

"Hey, Zoe. I know you probably don't want to hear from me right now, but I had to call you. I've discovered the most amazing thing, just off my bedroom." Trent paused a moment. He hadn't decided how much to tell her over the phone. Probably better to err on the side of more information, try and really hook her. "It's a secret room. No joke. Built right into the foundation of the house. Some wild stuff in there too. Looks like Jeremiah Wolcott's diary or something. You'll want to see it. Give me a call."

No sooner had he hung up than he began to feel a crushing guilt. What would Judith say when she found out? How would he justify this? Trying to distract himself, he turned his attention back to the print-out of Wolcott's map, where he had marked all the break-ins in red. He added the two newest. He shivered, involuntarily. It was almost as if someone else had been in this room and seen this map. Or he was just feeling paranoid, which made sense, considering.

As he looked from the actual map down to the printout, it jumped out at him that there were only five buildings remaining that were both still standing and had not been broken into. Whoever the four intruders had been, Trenton now realized that he likely had the rest of their checklist in his possession. A glance at the remaining targets sent a shiver down his spine. It would be stupid to just sit on this information. Stupider still to give it to Judith. But he couldn't tell his dad. Not today anyway.

He grabbed his phone, dialing the station's non-emergency number by heart.

"Clinch Rock Police Department," a pleasant voice answered.

"Sheila! Hey, it's Trenton. How are you doing?"

"Oh, hi. We're . . . okay. Kind of crazy around here today. I'm afraid your dad is not . . . available."

"I know. Does Jessie Finn happen to be there? Or Kendra Brooks?"

"I'm afraid Jessie's on patrol. And Kendra works nights now."

"Who is there, cop-wise?"

"Chief Barton just walked in," Sheila said. "You want to talk to him?"

Trenton waffled. "Yeah, sure. Thanks." Whatever his beef with Dan Barton, it wasn't fair to pin it on the guy's dad.

"This is Chief Barton." He sounded frazzled.

"Hey it's Trenton Marsh. How you doing?"

"Honestly, Trent, I've had better days. What can I do for you?"

"This is going to sound kind of weird, but I've been looking at some old maps of the town, and I noticed that all the buildings where the break-ins happened were built before 1900."

"Yeah . . . ?" The chief was not masking his impatience well.

"Anyway, I've got this old map in front of me and it looks to me like there's only five possible buildings left these guys might hit: the Masonic Hall, the police station, that building on the corner of Grand and Center that's been like ten different restaurants . . . you know the one? It was a Chinese place until last year."

"Yeah, I know the one you mean."

"Right." Trenton cleared his throat. "Then there's the Cassel House and, uh . . . our house."

Chief Barton was silent.

"So, anyway, I figured you guys were spread so thin, it might be helpful to narrow it down, just focus on the likely targets. Really, it's just four possibilities, since I doubt anyone would try and break into the police station."

"You came up with this on your own?" Barton asked.

"Yeah."

"That's great kid," he said, his voice reflecting true gratitude. "What was the first one again?"

"The Masonic Hall." He could hear the chief writing.

"You got a bit of detective in you. Must have inherited that from your old man. Thanks for the call. This is gonna help. Seriously."

"Happy to do it. See ya." He hung up, feeling somewhat unburdened, but also a little uneasy, having identified his own home as a target for the first time, out loud. Obviously, it was on the map, but it hadn't previously occurred to him that anyone else might want a look inside. He went up to the garage and grabbed a baseball bat, which he wedged between his bed and the wall.

He jumped at the sensation of his phone ringing in his pocket. *Calm down, Marsh.* He fished it out. DAD, the display read.

"Hey Dad." he answered. "How's the conference?"

"I'm afraid I'm still here at the station."

"What? Why? You were taking the day off. You promised!"

"Trent, something serious has happened. It involves Judith. I need you to come down to the station right now."

CHAPTER FOURTEEN
"NOTHING BUT TROUBLE"

For the first time since returning from camp, Trenton grabbed his bike. He was way beyond caring if Zoe saw him on this juvenile mode of transport; Judith was more important. He stopped peddling for a second while he processed that thought. Judith was more important to him than Zoe. Of course she was.

He pushed it faster and pulled up to the police station in under five minutes. He dumped his bike onto the rack and was halfway up the steps when he heard the brief, halted squawk of a siren. It was Dad, sitting in his cruiser, beckoning Trent to join him.

He slid into the passenger seat and shut the door. It was freezing in here. Trent shifted sideways in his seat, facing toward his dad to try and mask the shiner. Somehow in the rush to leave, he'd thought to grab a pair of aviator shades which he hoped would kick the can of that uncomfortable conversation down the road a ways. Dad looked tired. And old. Like he'd aged ten years just this morning.

"Is she okay?" Trenton asked.

His dad nodded. "A little banged up, but physically, she'll be fine. Not sure about her mental state."

"What happened?"

"I got a call this morning from Grant MacDowell—owns the sport bar up there on ten. He said that last night, he saw someone attack Mr. Fischer, from school, out behind the bar. He said it was a woman and they were fighting—pretty intense stuff—so he went to get his gun and, by the time he got back out to the parking lot, Fischer was all alone, lying on the ground. Mac helped him get cleaned up and called Marilyn to come get him."

Trenton felt like he was sinking into the leather seat of the cruiser. This could not be happening. He thought about how big Coach Fischer was, compared to Judith. And then he thought about the voice he'd heard from one of the men in the Home Store. "No excuses, no delays," it had said. Was it possible he'd been one of the broad-shouldered burglars?

"This morning," his dad continued, "Mac called me and asked me to make sure he was alright, just check in on him. At first, Fischer didn't want to talk about it, until I mentioned Mac said it was a woman. Then he broke out with a stream of profanity and the name Morgan." He turned and looked at Trent. "Son, Judith attacked him. She lay in wait and attacked Mr. Fischer."

Trenton nodded.

"You don't seem all that surprised. Did you know she was thinking of doing this?"

"No! I mean, I knew she wanted to, but I didn't think she'd . . ." No, that wasn't true. He hoped she wouldn't. He wished she wouldn't. But deep down, he knew she would.

The chief rubbed his eyes, hard, for a minute and then said, "She mentioned Marilyn Fischer in her own rant. Do you know what this is about?"

Trenton nodded. "I do, and I'm really sorry, Dad. We stopped by the church to say Hi on Wednesday and your door was open a little. We overheard Marilyn talking about . . . ya know."

"I see. I assume you realize how inappropriate that is. Listening in, I mean. Your whole life I've been a police officer and you've had to respect that some things are confidential. It's no different with the pastorate."

"I know. We didn't mean to hear it. We just did." No one said anything for a minute. Finally, Trent asked, "So what happens to her now?"

"Well, Fischer's not pressing charges. I think he's humiliated that a girl beat him up. Mentioned about five times that she ambushed him and hit him with some kind of wooden spear or something. At first, he said his reflexes were dulled from all the beers he'd downed. Then I reminded him he'd been about to get behind the wheel and that might not be the smartest thing to tell the chief of police. Anyway, I brought Judith in regardless, just to talk to her, and saw her face like that. Can't get ahold of her parents—no surprise there. So I told her I was holding her until she admitted it was completely stupid and promised never to do anything like it again. That's why I called you."

"What? Why?" Trent asked.

"She won't promise."

Trenton shook his head. "Dad, if you can't get through to her . . "

Dad smiled, weakly. "I know, but I have to leave. I'm already late for this conference and it's an hour drive."

"So, she's inside?"

"Yeah, in my office. I'd really appreciate it, son, if you'd just give it a shot. I'll wait out here a few minutes while you give her the good cop routine, then I'm going to roar in and try to scare her straight." He gazed out the windshield. "She's always been a little weird. It was cute when she was younger."

Trenton laughed and reached for the door handle.

"Wait, Trent. One more thing." He pulled the sunglasses off his son's face. "Todd called this morning too. Talked to both me and Rich, said you and Dan Barton got in a fight? Looks like you might have lost."

"I got a good shot in," Trent said, defensively.

His dad frowned. "You've never behaved this way before. And now this craziness with Judith as well? What, do you kids have one of those fight clubs going? Is there something in the water?"

Trent shrugged.

"Todd said he'll give you another shot if you want your job back."

"I don't."

Trenton's father turned the A/C temp down one more tick. "I know we've been drifting apart a little lately, but this is completely insane."

"I don't know what to say, Dad."

"Tell me it won't happen again—that would be a good start. I really don't need this weighing on my mind right now. You *or* Judith."

"Hey, we thought you liked it *insane*, right?" Trent wished he could pull the words back into his mouth. He truly hated the thought of causing his father any sort of distress. "I'm sorry, Dad. I didn't mean that."

"No, I'm sorry. Boys fight. It's just that . . . can I talk to you man to man a minute?"

"Sure."

"I really feel like I'm being shut out of the investigation of the break-ins. I know I'm not around a lot because of class and pastoral stuff. And, yeah, I know Rich is just trying to stand on his own two feet, but . . . I don't know. And then this today and Rich is trying to push me out the door, saying he'll handle it. Go to my conference, blah, blah, blah.

"Of course, Jay Fischer's his friend. They came up together, so he wants to protect him, but I was their friend too. I just hate the way I'm losing control. I know I'm supposed to let go, but I hate it." He hesitated. "I shouldn't be telling you any of this. I've always had a great sense of boundaries, but . . . " He grappled for the words. "All the lines are blurring now, you know? Anyway, it's not fair to burden you with this stuff."

"It's okay," Trenton said. "But can you back up a second? *You* were friends with Coach Fischer?"

His dad smiled, sheepishly. "Yeah, he was two year ahead of me and I thought he was cool. Rich was in the class between us. We had our own little gang of buddies—maybe seven or eight guys. Not what you'd call a good influence on me. That's why I've always hammered into your head just how important it is to choose your friends well. Which I thought you'd done pretty safely with Judith, but . . . We got into a lot of trouble. I could have gone down a really bad road."

"You?" Trent couldn't help but laugh. "Reverend Police Chief? What kind of trouble?"

"Let's just say the first time I saw the inside of the holding cell was not as a cop. Our little group, we had this stupid initiation. I think Jay's older brother made it up a few years earlier."

Trenton felt the blood draining from his face. "Wait, you don't mean the Crown Fire Boys?"

His dad was taken back. "So it's still around. Huh." He ran a hand through his hair. "Do me a favor and those guys a wide berth. Nothing but trouble there."

"What was it like back then? Was it, like, serious?"

"For a couple guys, it was almost like a street gang." He laughed out loud. "In Clinch Rock. That's pretty lame when I say it out loud. But you know how it is." He gestured at Trenton's eye. "Getting in fights, getting into trouble. But you live in such a tiny little town, you try to make life feel bigger. Which is stupid, because what you realize when you grow up that, even if you stay in the little little town, before long, life is going to feel way, way too big." He checked his watch and said, "Why don't you give Judith a try, there, slugger? I really do need to leave."

"Alright. Good cop on his way." He re-donned his sunglasses and stepped out of the car.

"Hey, look who it is!" Officer Cash called from behind the desk. "How you doing there, Trent?" He was all smiles, the polar opposite of Officer Tyrell. When Trent began signing his name, the cop pulled back the clipboard and said, "No need for that. We know you." He dropped his voice and added, "Another weird day, huh?"

"You have no idea," Trenton said, heading back to his dad's office.

"You're rockin' those shades, by the way," Cash called out after him.

He opened the door to the office and saw Judith sitting there, legs crossed, totally at ease. A long, angry bruise stretched from her right eye, down to the apple of her cheek.

"Check it out, " she said, indicating her skirt. "I made it out of the ugliest, like, 1990s ties I could find. Isn't that hilarious?"

Trent kept a straight face and walked over to his dad's chair, where he sat with as much authority as he could muster. This was apparently hilarious to Judith.

"Your eye," he said. "That looks terrible."

She shrugged. "You should see the other guy. Hey, what's with the shades? Are you trying to look like a cop?"

He pulled them off.

"Whoa," she said. "We're twins. How'd that happen?"

"Dan Barton." Her face darkened. "Judith, don't even think about doing anything crazy. I started the fight, okay? Anyway, I'm here to talk about you, not me. What were you thinking?"

"I was thinking it was time for a test-run. And I'm thinking it went well."

"Seriously."

"Well, you know. I could have done without the black eye, but I got home in one piece. And now Fischer knows what will happen to him if he threatens his wife again."

"Which is what?"

"I'll take off the kid gloves."

"He says you ambushed him. Hit him with a pole or something."

Judith was offended. "Yeah, right! I walked right up to him while he was fumbling with his keys and you know what I did to get his attention? I knocked the side mirror off that stupid truck. You should have seen his face."

"And what did he do?" Despite wanting to thoroughly condemn the attack, Trent could not deny that he was intensely curious about how the whole thing went down.

"He just punched me. I fell back against the truck and then I kicked him, right in the chest. A couple blows to the head later and he was done. Not unconscious exactly, but definitely down for the count. I could have done anything I wanted to him after that. And he knows it."

"You've got to stop this, Judith," Trent said. "What if he had a gun?"

She shrugged. "I would have knocked it out of his hands."

"Are you delusional?"

Before she could answer, the door opened and the chief walked in. He sat on the corner of his desk and asked, "You make any progress with her?"

"Not really," Trent answered.

Adam fumbled with his badge for a moment, removing it from his shirt and placing it on the table. "Judith, I want to talk to you a minute, not as a policeman, but as your pastor." He paused for a moment, reconsidering. "No, forget that. I want to talk to you as a friend. Judy-bug, I've known you since you were six years old. I love you like a daughter. And the thought that you would put yourself into such a dangerous position, just . . . " he choked on his words and bit back some tears. One still managed to escape his right eye and trickle down his cheek.

Judith got up from her chair and hugged him around the neck. "I'm sorry," she said. "Please don't cry."

She sniffed and wiped away some of her own tears. They stood there, silently for a good twenty seconds before Trenton realized she was tapping a message onto his back. Almost another minute of tapping went by before Trent's dad nodded and said, "That's all I ask." He gave her one more squeeze and let her go. "I've got to go, kids."

"Am I free to go too?" she asked.

"Under one condition: whatever that thing was you hit Fischer with —he said it was some kind of wooden pitch fork or—"

"It was an ox goad," she said.

"Whatever it was, you chop it up into kindling. Okay?"

She nodded. "I promise. I don't need it anymore."

"Good to hear." He put his hat on. "Trent, I'll be home late tonight. See you tomorrow."

"Have a good day off," Trenton called after him, feeling stupid for it. After all, it was nearing noon already and he and Judith had filled the chief's morning with nothing but grief.

All the same, he was feeling great as he escorted Judith through the building, trying to shield her from the looks and whispers. It seemed as though his dad had pulled it off. Why hadn't he brought this to him a week ago? As they walked out into the heat of the day, someone called out, "Hey, Trent!" Looking up, he saw Rich Barton, standing against the wall of the station, having a cigarette. "Come here a minute," he said.

"Oh boy," Trenton mumbled. "I'll be right back," he said to Judith. "I hope." He jogged over to Barton, who was stomping out the cigarette amid a graveyard of extinguished butts and smeared tar.

"What's up, Mr. Barton?"

"Chief Barton."

"Right. Sorry."

Barton smiled. "It's fine. Let me get a look at that face." He gestured at Trent's glasses, and whistled low at the sight of the swollen eye behind them. "My Danny did that?"

Trenton nodded.

"He can be a bit of a Neanderthal. I know. I was just like him at that age. He start the fight?"

"No. It was me."

Barton looked impressed. "Still, though. He's a lot bigger than you. He should have walked away. I'll talk to him."

"That's not necessary, sir."

The chief nodded, approvingly. "Anyway, I just wanted to say again, thanks for that tip this morning. I've got my best guys on it. You ever think about joining the force when you graduate?"

"I kind of doubt it."

"Our loss, I guess. You'd be a real asset. Unlike your friend over there. If I had my way, she'd be doing five years."

Trent had no idea what to say to that.

"Well," Barton said, patting the circumference of his belt, as if to make sure nothing had fallen off, "I better get back to it." He ambled back into the station.

"Diner?" Judith prompted. "My treat."

"That sounds good." They began to walk, lazily, down the sidewalk. "I gotta tell you, Judith. I am so relieved you're putting this crazy stuff behind you. I don't think I've ever been so scared in my life as when I got that call."

"I know," she said. "I'll be more careful next time."

Trenton came to a stop. "What do you mean, *next time*? I thought you and my dad, like—"

"We reached an understanding," she said.

"What does that mean? What understanding?"

"That you should learn Morse Code." She started walking again. Trenton didn't.

"Judith, you can't save everybody. Heck, my dad had to save *you* this morning, or you'd be headed to juvie. Or jail! Did you think of that?"

She laughed and shook her head dismissively. "I knew going in that there was no possible world in which Fischer agrees to get up on a witness stand and publicly admit he got beat down by a girl. I'm untouchable."

Trenton tried to gather his thoughts together. For some reason, he felt like this moment was his best chance to make a real case against all this, to show Judith the absurdity of what she was doing. Reaching back into his mind, he tried to assemble the best argument of all the potential arguments—the one that would put an end to all of this. But he had nothing; he was tapped out. So he just threw up his hands and joined his friend for lunch at the White Tail Diner.

CHAPTER FIFTEEN
"PINKY SWEAR"

"You've heard that God will never give you more than you can handle, right? I challenge you to test him on that! Go nuts, try to *take* more than you can handle and see if God won't pump you up so you can shoulder the burden. You hear that still small voice? You know what it's saying? 'You've got this.'"

—*Insane Faith: Superhero Edition*
by Stephen Branding, page 188

INCOMING CALL: CHET BUSHMAN.

Adam tapped "Decline Call," feeling a rush of endorphins from the mere flick of his finger. What a sense of freedom. He had recorded a temporary voicemail greeting, declaring his absence for the day-long conference, and was determined that nothing would draw him back to Clinch Rock. He needed this: a day with no policework, no classwork, and most of all, no Bushman.

Then again, it wouldn't be a full day, would it? According to the clock in his dash, it was 12:10. The conference ran from ten to six. He stepped on the gas. Using the badge to skirt traffic laws was not something Adam made a habit of doing. But today was different. A bag in the back held civilian clothes, into which he planned to change when he got there. He probably wouldn't have time for that, though. It was vital he arrive before lunch was over.

Adam dug through the stack of documents on his passenger seat, searching for the conference schedule. He'd shelled out the extra two hundred bucks for the VIP pass, which meant lunch with Stephen Branding himself. And that was important, because he had many questions to ask the guru. Like, what do you do when your Insane Faith lifestyle begins to chip away at your very soul, burying you under broken commitments and constant guilt over not doing enough? He realized that he'd been putting off dealing with this present and growing danger to his soul and psyche by deferring to this day, this lunch, this face-to-face meeting with the man who'd changed his life. There it was: a whole packet of conference materials.

The schedule indicated that lunch went from 12:30-1:30 and the conference itself would resume at two. Just a hint of the familiar panic tinged the tips of his fingers and the bottoms of his lungs, where it always seemed to start. There was no way he'd make it—park in the ramp, trek to the entrance, register, find his way to this VIP lunch, and get a seat anywhere near the man himself. Besides, the conversation would already be waning. This was not going to happen. Unless, maybe if he used the uniform to get close, under pretense of some important news . . . No. Adam pulled over to the side of the road. His breaths were coming shallow and his vision swimming. Driving in this state would be foolish.

Then he noticed the little orange card paperclipped to the top. VIP BACKSTAGE PASS. A flicker of hope returned. Perhaps he could catch Branding for a few minutes during a break or after the event. The pass itself bore no further information and flipping through the packet, he found no answers. However, there was a 1-800 number to call with questions about the event.

As he began to dial, his phone again rang. Bushman. He declined the incoming call and finished punching in the number.

"Mega Events Management, this is Nina speaking. How may I help you?"

He took a slow breath. "Hi, there. I'm running a little late for the Insane Faith Live event in Grand Rapids, Michigan and I was really hoping to have a chance to speak with Stephen Branding. I've got the VIP package and I'm wondering if there might be an opportunity to speak with him after the event?"

Silence on the other end. And then, "Um, you didn't receive an e-mail last night?"

"I don't know. I have a few e-mail addresses; I don't always get to all of them."

"Well, I'm very sorry to be the bearer of sad news, but Mr. Branding was rushed to the hospital from the Denver airport last night. I'm afraid he passed away this morning."

Adam felt the air sucked from his chest.

"So," the woman went on, "there's no event. You'll receive a refund for your registration fee in the mail. I'm very sorry for this inconvenience."

"What . . . what was it?"

"I'm sorry?"

"How did he die?"

"The press release says 'a cardiac event.' That's all I know."

"Okay. Thank you." He ended the call. The car was spinning and shrinking around him and an unexplainable anxiety was growing within. Gripping the steering wheel and breathing like his doctor had taught him, he willed the episode to pass. But it didn't. The tightness in his chest was suffocating. He tried not to think about the ramifications of this. For most of a year, he'd been pinning everything on the writings of Stephen Branding and, as the pressure increased, he'd been looking to Branding for inspiration. He'd been trying to emulate the man's attitude and diet and sleep preferences. And now the guy was dead at the age of 51, and that changed everything.

Adam thought about calling 9-1-1. An ambulance would bring him to Fremont or maybe Big Rapids. He was out of Lake County now. With any luck, he could keep it from Barton.

No, he thought. *This is my day off. I will not waste it in a hospital bed.* He'd spend it on something that mattered. He'd surprise Trent with an afternoon just for the two of them. A couple hours of archery and maybe burgers at their favorite dive in Scottville. The thought calmed him. He was breathing easier. A few minutes later, he was fine, pulling back onto M-37, looking for a turn-around.

* * *

"You hated that job anyway," Judith said, gesticulating with a freakishly long fry. "If you want, I can ask Brook about bringing you on at Rerun."

"No thanks." Trenton looked down at his plate, where the wreckage of a grinder sat, mostly uneaten. His appetite had never materialized.

"Good thinking. More time for our search."

"Look, Judith. Let's make a pact."

"This sounds interesting," she said. "Go on."

"I'll quit nagging you and I'll even help you if you promise me we're focusing on this case, on finding the money. You won't go after Fischer again, you won't go after Dan. I need you to promise me you won't get distracted by anything else until we've recovered Cassel's lost treasure."

Judith thought for just a moment and nodded. "Deal," she said, extending her pinky finger. Trenton wrapped his own around it and tugged. They'd sealed every agreement with a pinky swear since they were little kids and it remained an unbreakable commitment in their eyes. "So where should we look after lunch?" she asked.

"I don't know. I really think our best bet is either the Cassel House or the lumber camp."

"Lumber camp," she said. "I don't want to step foot on Zoe Green's property."

"Well, then we better not go to the lumber camp."

Judith dropped her sandwich onto her plate. "Seriously? What are they, buying up the whole town?"

"Sort of, yeah. Maybe we need some fresh inspiration," Trenton said. "Let's go back to my house and read some more of the diary, try and get inside the head of the man who was closest to all this."

Judith waffled. "That's kind of a one-man job."

"No, we can read it together."

"How about this? Your dad left me stranded here without the Iron Horse. You go get the book and type up as much of that diary as you can. I'll walk home, get my bike, and meet you at your place. Then we can decide what's next."

"Sounds like a solid plan," Trenton said. He looked down at his plate again. Empty. Apparently his appetite had returned.

* * *

Adam had just passed the WELCOME TO CLINCH ROCK sign when he saw it: a battered old red pickup truck, zipping by on the cross street, maybe an eighth of a mile ahead. He felt a spike of energy. The only solid lead they had so far had come from Trent—the old red truck with no plate. What if this was it? If he could get a license to go with the men who broke in, that could very well break the case.

Thankful to be in his LeBaron, rather than the squad car, Adam turned onto Wilder. He could see the truck, way up ahead. He squinted and chided himself for not wearing his glasses. He had figured his VIP seats would be close enough to Stephen Branding that they would be unnecessary. Man, had this day taken a turn. More like three hard lefts in a row.

Adam slowed a bit and let the truck disappear over the horizon. When tailing someone, it was best to give them a sense that you didn't care whether you kept them in view or not. A few seconds later, he picked up the pace again. Wait, where had the truck gone? It was no longer on the road ahead of him. He craned his neck this way and that, searching for the old rust bucket.

Only as he passed it, did he see the thing disappearing down a half-overgrown two-track to the right. He consciously maintained his speed as he blew past and went another few hundred yards before pulling to a stop on the shoulder of the road and climbing out of the car. He touched the radio mounted on his left shoulder, but didn't depress the transmit button.

Should he wait for backup? It was the smart thing to do, but something was holding him back. He thought about the shiny new nail heads in the station floor. He thought about the chain of unsuccessful night watches and the fact that no break-in had been attempted during his own watch two nights earlier. And now this. He knew where that little trail led. It was the back way in to the old saw mill.

Years earlier, kids used to sneak in late at night to make out or smoke pot; tired of constantly patrolling this lonely backroad, the chief at the time had convinced the city to secure the building and install a padlock. Either the men in the truck were living in a crumbling, termite-infested sawmill, or there was another break-in happening. A daytime break-in. On the one day Chief Marsh was out of town and incommunicado, not expected back until late.

He realized that, while thinking he'd been walking in the direction of the mill. He'd call for backup, but only when he was right on top of the place. That way, if there was an inside man in his department, there'd be no time to warn the suspects.

As he made his way up the narrow path, Adam popped open the retention snap on his holster and drew his Glock 23. He'd only pulled it while on duty twice before in all his years on the job. Surprisingly, he felt no hint of the earlier panic. He was focused, ready for whatever he should find inside.

When the sagging old structure came into view, the dead beech trees partly obscuring it like vertical blinds, he finally made the call. "Dispatch, this is Chief Marsh. I'm at the old sawmill, pursuing possible suspects in the chain of B and Es. Requesting backup." He clicked the radio off and moved cautiously forward, entering the woods and moving parallel to the drive.

It took him a few minutes to reach the clearing and he was rewarded with a clear view of the red truck. He saw the license plate immediately: 4781DZL. He pulled out his notepad and jotted it down.

Now what? Now he'd wait for backup. He had the missing piece of information and the location of the suspects. It was less than a ten minute drive out here from the station. All he had to do was wait and they'd have the place surrounded. Then he could finally put this behind him. Retire from the force. Go truly full-time at the church. He felt the tightness return to his chest.

Then he heard a rustling in the brush behind him. Before he could turn to see who it was, an explosion of pain enveloped the back of his skull. He saw golden fireworks and then pure white. And then black.

* * *

Trenton was sitting on the living room couch with his laptop, well into his third page of the diary, when Zoe called. He was surprised at the drop he felt in his spirit upon seeing her name on the display. Just yesterday he would have given anything to reconcile. And, of course, that was the problem. He'd given too much.

"Hello," he answered.

"Hi, it's me! I've been trying to call you all morning." She had? "Are you home right now? I really want to see this room you're talking about."

Trenton couldn't help but note the stark contrast between her condescending tone when she'd slammed the door in his face that morning and her current chirpiness. He desperately wished he could retroactively take back that phone call. This secret was supposed to be for him and Judith alone. There was a pinky swear on the line.

"It's not really a secret room," he said. "I may have kind of embellished. More like a corner of the basement."

"But what about this diary? I'd give anything to see it." She sounded semi-desperate. It was a weird dynamic between the two of them — moving in this direction anyway.

Trent made a rash decision. He'd have to give Zoe up to protect Judith. If Judith had any inkling that Trenton had violated her trust like this, all bets were off. There was no telling who she'd be swooping down on, ox goad in hand.

"I lied," he said, lying. "I'm sorry. I just wanted to get you to call me. I missed you."

"You . . . *lied*," she repeated.

"Yeah, sorry."

"Lied about all of it? The room, the diary, the whole thing." She sounded less than convinced.

"Yeah. I just asked myself, what's the one thing that would get Zoe to call me back and that popped into my head."

There was a long, pregnant pause on the line, and then Zoe said, "Trenton?"

"Yeah?"

"Never call me again."

Just as the line went dead, the doorbell rang. He staggered over to answer it, feeling a bit woozy. He opened the door to reveal Officer Tyrell standing there in uniform, holding his hat in his hand and avoiding eye contact.

"Something's happened to your dad, Trent. I'm supposed to take to the hospital in Big Rapids."

* * *

Adam's skull ached. Every beat of his heart brought a new tidal wave of pain over the back half of his head. And just before each wave would recede, another crashed down on top of it. He experimentally lifted his head to look around the room and was surprised to find himself still staring at the ceiling. His head hadn't moved.

A flood of fear joined the pain at the base of skull for a moment. He wiggled his fingers, then his toes. They worked okay. Then he lifted his arms and legs. No paralysis. But his head refused to budge more than an inch off the pillow, as if it weighed five hundred pounds. So instead, he turned it to the right, where he saw a calendar hanging on the wall.

It was definitely a hospital room; that was the *where*. But the calendar raised the question, "What's the *when*?" How long had he been here, unconscious? He barely remembered the sound behind him and the blow to his head. He had a patchwork of half-memories, fading in and out. Officer Cash crouched down, concern all over his face, offering a steady stream of encouragement. Rich Barton in the ambulance with him.

A note, scrawled on a whiteboard next to the calendar, read, "Getting breakfast. Back soon. -T." Adam turned his head the other way and saw that he wasn't alone in the room.

A broad-shouldered older man with yellow-white hair stood with his back to Adam. He was shutting the door to the hospital room and lingered there, making sure it was clicked shut. He was dressed in a flannel shirt and dirty old jeans. In his half-conscious, medicated state, Adam felt a wave of warm nostalgia at the sight of this man. He was reminded of his long-dead great grandfather, who had always carried in his back pocket a little round tin of chewing tobacco.

CHAPTER SIXTEEN
"ORDINARY"

"Attention to humble duties is a better sign of grace than ambition
for lofty and elevated works."

—Charles Haddon Spurgeon

Judith pulled into Trent's driveway and killed the motor. The house looked deserted, which didn't surprise her. She'd been nearly home when the cryptic text had come through:

> Something happened to dad. Going to hospital.
> Please pray.

She had run the rest of the way home, texting back on the way. There was no reply. She'd tried calling Trenton twice, but it went right to voicemail. And now, a dull dread sapped her spirit as she banged on the door yet again. No answer. Adam's car was not in the driveway. Neither was his police cruiser.

Maybe Trent was home, though. He might be down in his room, unable to hear the doorbell, greatly in need of comfort from a friend. She circled around the back of the house, immediately spotting the fake-looking plastic rock that had housed the Marshes' spare key for as long as she could remember. Judith smiled despite herself at the long-running joke about how bad the police chief's home security was.

The smile disappeared. The plastic rock was empty. Judith approached the back door to the garage slowly, carefully, wishing she had her ox goad with her. But no, at Adam's insistence, she'd turned that into kindling. She tried the doorknob. It turned easily. Stepping into the dim light of the garage, she froze, the fight-or-flight reflex

172

rising up through her lungs, ever leaning hard toward *fight*. Someone was moving slowly down the stairs toward Trent's bedroom.

Judith scanned the walls for a weapon of some kind—a rake, a bat, a tennis racket, anything—but only saw the light switch. She flipped it, bringing the slow flicker of fluorescent tubes to bear on the two-stall garage. The figure on the stairs froze.

"Zoe?" Judith took an unconscious step forward, blocking the top of the staircase. "What are you doing here?"

Turning to face Judith, Zoe began a slow re-ascent "What do you think? I came to see if Trent was okay. His father got hurt today."

"How did you know that?"

Zoe stopped a step below Judith. A few inches taller and wearing heels, she met her gaze eye-to-eye. "We tell each other everything." She smiled, malevolently.

Judith was a little surprised that her instinct to find a weapon had not subsided one bit. "Like where he hides the key to his house? Trent tell you that? Or did you just find it?"

Zoe pushed some strands of hair behind her ear. "What Trent and I talk about is none of your business," she said. "Besides, he's not home. You have no business here. Let's go, shall we?"

"I've known Adam and Trent for more than ten years," Judith said. "You don't get to tell me my business with them."

Zoe rolled her eyes. "Whatever. I'm bored with this. Move aside, please."

Judith didn't budge. She eyed the rather large purse hanging over Zoe's shoulder. "If I were a cynic," she said, "I might think you knew Trent wasn't home and you were here to help yourself to something of his. Something priceless, maybe?"

Scoffing and looking around the bare garage, Zoe said, "What could I possibly want from this place?"

"If you don't know, then I guess he doesn't tell you everything after all." Judith took a step back, allowing Zoe to clear the stairs and exit the garage. She was a few steps out into the yard when Judith called out, "Don't forget to put the key back."

Zoe stopped in her tracks and turned to face her again. "Trenton told me to hang on to it."

"No he didn't. Put it back or I'll do it for you." Judith studied the eyes of the prim and proper young woman, surprised to find no trace of fear or intimidation.

Zoe reached into her purse and took out the key, tossing it at Judith's feet. "I know it must be hard for you," she said, with mock empathy, "daughter of a couple drunks. Grinding through an utterly inconsequential existence in a trailer park, knowing your life will never amount to anything. Did Daddy do that to your face? Hmm?"

Judith clenched her fists, said nothing.

"When I'm through with Clinch Rock," Zoe continued, "people like you won't be able to afford a lot for your sad little double-wides." She took a step toward Judith. "Tell me, are you afraid you peaked with that stint on the wrestling team? Because Trenton is. It keeps him up at night, poor guy."

Judith set her jaw. "You're lucky I follow Jesus," she said. "Because if I didn't, I'd knock that smug little smile down your throat."

Zoe emitted a tasteful country club laugh. "Very lady-like," she said. "Just see that you don't follow Jesus in my direction again. You probably think your life can't get worse. But trust me—it can." Her eyes narrowed and she added, "I suppose it's only fair to warn you that, while I've never been on a wrestling team, I did study Krav Maga in Tel Aviv and Kuntao in Indonesia." She spun on her heels and walked off, around the side of the house.

* * *

Trenton had scarcely left his dad's side since arriving at the hospital. He'd subsisted on gross, soggy sandwiches from a vending machine and slept in a faux-leather love seat designed by a sadist. Dad was still out of it, although the doctors said it was mostly the medication.

When Saturday morning arrived, Trenton finally took a lap around the hospital to stretch his legs and choked down some powdered eggs and greasy sausage in the cafeteria. And of course, that's when his dad woke up.

The first thing Trent saw when he returned to the hospital room was Ed Piper, standing by the bedside, an ID badge bearing his image clipped to the breast pocket of the same old flannel shirt. He was so out of place that it took a moment to register: Dad was sitting up! Well, not sitting up per se, but the bed was inclined, his eyes were open, and he was talking to Ed.

"Dad!" Trenton shouted, rushing to his father's side.

"Easy. Easy, son," the chief warned, laughing faintly.

"Are you okay? How do you feel?"

"Well, my head feels like a thirty-pound bowling ball. And if I move it too quickly, I feel like I'm going to puke. Other than that, never better." He seemed to remember his other guest and said, "Son, I'd like you to meet Ed Piper. He's a volunteer chaplain here."

Ed smiled and held out a massive paw. "Oh, we already know each other. Spent a whole week in the same cabin."

Trenton smiled and gave the rough hand a shake. "Good to see you again, Ed. I didn't know you worked here."

"Not full time or anything," he said. "I was a lifer in the air force—chaplain—and ever since I retired I've stayed plenty busy. I'm the night director at the Clinch Rock Soup Kitchen as well."

"That's how I know you!" Trent's dad exclaimed. "I took your statement on Monday." He looked up at Ed's smirk and said, "Hey, I've got a head injury over here. Cut me a break."

Ed chuckled and said, "I'll give you two some time." He squeezed Trenton's shoulder on his way out.

"It's so good to see you awake, Dad," Trent said. "And to hear your voice. I was so scared."

"Yeah, sorry I put you through that."

"What happened?"

His dad closed his eyes a minute, the gears of memory clearly turning. "It was the truck. The old red pickup."

"The one I saw? The one with no plate?"

"It had a plate, though." His eyes flew open and he tried to sit up for a moment. "Where are my pants?" he asked. "I wrote the plate number in my notepad.

Trenton rifled through a plastic bag marked "Personal Effects" hanging at the foot of the bed. He found the pants and pulled a wallet, car keys, and a small folding knife from the pockets. "I don't see your notepad. You sure you had it?"

His dad fell limply back against the pillow, wincing at the pain it caused. "They took it. They took my pad."

"Can you remember the plate? Even part of it?"

"No chance. I barely remember anything leading up to the thump on the head." He moaned. "I was so close . . . "

"Why were you even out there?" Trenton asked. "You were supposed to be in Grand Rapids."

Another hazy cloud of memories seemed to envelop him. "He's dead, Trent. Stephen Branding died a couple days ago."

"Oh, man. How?"

"They said it was a 'cardiac event.'"

"So . . . a heart attack."

"Yeah."

The door swung open and Chief Barton walked in, a massive Styrofoam cup of coffee in one hand and his hat in the other. "Hey! He's awake," he said, a little too loudly.

"Hi, Rich."

"Just so you know, I got your gun from security. It's locked up back at the station. They letting you go home any time soon?" he asked.

"I don't think so. A nurse popped in about twenty minutes ago. Seemed to think they were planning to keep me for observation a few more days."

"Good," Trent blurted out. He was struggling to process the news of Branding's heart attack and trying not to connect it with the memory of his dad crumpled and wheezing against the wall.

"You okay, kid?" Barton asked.

"Uh, yeah. I'm fine. Just worried about my dad."

"Don't," Barton said. "He's as tough as they come." To his fellow cop, he added, "But take your time, chief. We've got everything under control. Got some decent physical evidence from the mill; we're following up on that. We're gonna find whoever conked you on the melon and take them down. In the meantime, anything we can do for you—don't hesitate to ask. In fact, I've got an extra bunk in Danny's room. If you want, Trent can come and stay with us until you're back on your feet."

Trent felt a jolt of panic. "What? No! No way."

"I don't know," his dad said. "It's probably a good idea. You're old enough to stay by yourself for a night or two, but—"

"Dad," Trent gritted through his teeth, "look at my face. You want me to sleep in the same room as the guy who did this?"

Barton cleared his throat, but said nothing.

"I suppose not. But you have to promise me, you'll be home by your regular curfew, and you won't have anybody over. Agreed?"

"Yeah, sure. Jason's grounded until forever anyway."

"Okay," his dad said, "I guess it's only two more nights and then you're back up to Picture Falls. Are you riding with the mysterious Zoe?"

"I don't know, Dad. Maybe I shouldn't go."

"Nonsense. We'll both get a chance to relax and recharge. We deserve it, don't we?" He winked.

"Yeah, I guess we do."

"I'll swing by and check on him from time to time," Barton offered.

"Thanks, Rich."

Barton set down the coffee and massaged his hat with both hands. "Hey, uh, Trent, you mind if I talk to your old man for a few minutes? Police stuff."

"Sure." Trent squeezed his dad's hand, which he noticed for the first time was now a little smaller than his own, and headed out into the hall.

Near the elevators, he found Ed Piper sitting on a bench, flipping through a worn leather Bible. At the sight of Trenton, he flipped it closed and stood.

"You on your way out?" he asked.

"Not just yet. They're talking confidential police stuff, I guess." He re-centered the bill of his ball cap. "Told me to take a walk."

Ed seemed to notice that Trent's hands were shaking a half second before he did. "Are you okay?"

Trent shook his head *no* and felt a wall of grief threatening to crash through. Like the Dutch boy with his finger in the dyke, he held the tears back, knowing he would fail, and soon.

"Come with me," Ed said.

Trent managed to keep it together until he and Ed were safely in the hospital's All-Faiths Chapel. In a series of niches on the wall were a cross, a Menorah, a Koran, and some sort of bust of an Asian man Trent didn't recognize. He plopped down in a half-pew in front of the cross and began to weep.

Ed sat next to him and intermittently rubbed his back, waiting patiently for it to pass—all that had been bottled up through the months of mounting pressure, the craziness from Judith, the blow-up with Zoe, and now his Dad's hospitalization and the death of Stephen Branding which, weirdly, seemed almost on-par with all the rest as far as directly effecting Trenton's life. Through the tears, he tried to explain all that had been going on to Ed, but he feared he was making little sense.

"I feel like I've heard all this before," Ed finally said.

Trenton wiped the tears onto his sleeve. "Huh?"

"Your father. I got to talk with him for a good half hour and he said a lot of the same things. I'll tell you what I told him: you are living by the wrong book."

"I don't know what that means."

"They gave me a copy of that *Insane Faith* at Picture Falls. There was some good stuff in it, I guess, but over-all it was dangerous. That kind of thing tells people they're never doing enough, never spiritual enough, never measuring up. People are gluttons for punishment; they'll pay through the nose for that kind of message."

"Huh," Trenton said. "I totally feel that way. I mean, I've been doing a ton of stuff all summer—busier than ever—but it's all *ordinary* stuff. Trying to earn money for college, help Dad around the house, filling out scholarship applications." He decided not to mention his recent foray into treasure hunting and his efforts to keep a local super-hero at bay.

Ed chuckled in that way that only grizzled old men can. "Ordinary," he said. "That's become a dirty word, hasn't it? It's not just the one book. There's a hundred of them out there. And speakers and songs and video clips on the Facebooks. Real Christians do amazing things for Jesus, they all say. If you have a family, pay your mortgage, work hard, love your neighbor, go to school, well . . . you're just wasting your life. If it's not extreme and daring it's not worth doing. Everything's got to be 'radical' these days."

"Radical," Trenton snickered. "Kind of reminds me of my Bible. The *Radical Teenz* version. The church bought like a gross of them in the Nineties and they still give them to sixth graders every year. The thing's covered in pictures of people rock climbing and skydiving. Doing rollerblade tricks in a half-pipe."

Ed blanked on why this might be funny, but said, "That all comes from a backwards way of reading Scripture. You're encouraged to find yourself in every story, for you to be the hero. So we even tell little children when they read Daniel in the lion's den that the point is for them to be strong and fearless like Daniel. We read David and Goliath and tell them they're supposed to be the David and vanquish everything that stands in their path. Only we're not David. We're not supposed to be."

Trenton looked up at the man sitting next to him. "Who are we then?"

"We're not the point at all! It's about Jesus! He's the greater David who came to defeat the enemy. He didn't use five stones, but the five wounds he suffered on our behalf. If *we're* anyone in that story, we're David's brothers who scoffed at him and jeered when he came to save them."

"I've never heard that before," Trenton said.

179

"Well, you need to. When the focus is on me: am I doing enough? am I strong enough? am I brave enough?—the burden of that will crush us. And it's unbiblical! It's human religion, which demands, *Do! Do this! Do that!* But Jesus says, *It's done!* Jesus said, *Take my yoke upon you. My yoke is easy and my burden is light.*"

"But Stephen Branding quoted the Bible, like, a lot," Trent said.

"Let me tell you a little secret: if you ignore the context, you can use the Bible to justify anything. That's why we've got to study carefully. The first part of the New Testament is all about what Jesus did for us, right? The Gospels lay it all out.

"And then the rest is pretty much letters from the Apostles, and almost all of them start out by again laying out what Jesus has accomplished for us—the *done* part—and then they transition into, *Therefore, do . . .* here's what we should do in response. You got the *done* and the *therefore, do...* And you know which is extreme and insane and radical? It's the first part."

"I don't get it," Trent said.

"Think of it like this: what has Jesus done for us? By his blood, he's redeemed us—brought us from spiritual death to life. He's crushed the serpent's head, sealed us with his Holy Spirit, raised us up with him, grafted us into God's people, opened the way so we have access to our creator. That stuff is pretty extreme, pretty insane: making sinners into saints, resurrecting the dead. But then when he gets to what we should *do* in response, it's not quite the crazy adrenaline rush we've been led to believe.

"It's stuff like, *therefore* . . . love one another, teach and embrace sound doctrine, work with your hands to the glory of God, deal honestly with others, forgive each other, care for the poor and needy, tame your tongue. Avoid pride and sexual immorality. Honor your parents, love your spouse, raise up godly children. None of that will sell a million books or land you on the six o'clock news, but it's how God describes the Christian life.

"Don't get me wrong; it *is* extreme. You're killing the old self that still lives inside of you. But it's an internal war. And when we miss that we'll wind up putting on a heavy yoke to try to earn what God has already accomplished. That's when you see men leaving the jobs for which they're gifted to enter the ministry, for which they're not. We see ministers who tell us that Word and sacrament aren't enough. Books that tell us we're not doing enough to help the poor unless we go live under a bridge with them."

"So, what are you saying?" Trent asked. "My dad shouldn't be a pastor?"

"If he's called to it, he absolutely should. But it's no higher a calling than being a policeman. Or a shoe salesman. Or a janitor. All callings are high callings if we do them to the Glory of God. I'm just saying that it's not sinful to live an ordinary life. And if someone says otherwise, that's a mark of spiritual immaturity. After all, St. Paul told the Thessalonians, *Make it your ambition to lead a quiet life; mind your own business and work with your hands.* Don't let anyone tell you that's not 'living out your faith.'"

Trent thought of Judith, who of everyone he knew was most content to live a quiet life and mind her own business . . . right up until she decided God wanted her to become a superhero and was calling her to rescue someone. He said, "We can't all always live quiet lives though, right? Sometimes the right thing *is* the extreme thing."

"Sure. There are seasons when Christians are called upon to put their lives on the line and stand up to power, even to lay down their lives and die for their faith. But when Jesus told us to take up our cross daily and follow him, he was primarily describing not one grand gesture, but a life of obedience, one little step after another, slowly putting to death the old self and becoming more and more like Him. That kind of faithfulness isn't an exciting thrill-ride, it doesn't look sexy to the world, doesn't make us feel like a hero. But that's okay, We're not the hero.

"And when the time comes to lay it all on the line and do something huge for Christ, you know who actually follows through with it? People who *know* they're not the hero, who've plodded along faithfully day after day with no thought of glory or adventure or turning their spiritual life into skydiving and rock climbing. You want to be like Jesus? You need to learn to rest in Him, rather than trying to prove that your faith is 'insane enough' to earn God's love. Yes, Jesus toiled for the Kingdom, but he was also able to sleep in the belly of the ship during a horrible storm. That's my prayer for you. And for your dad."

Trenton nodded. "I get it. Thanks, Ed" He stood and chuckled. "You know, before today, I think I'd heard you say about two dozen words total."

Ed smiled, sheepishly. "I don't do well with groups, especially groups of kids. Always been more of a one-on-one guy. But they were a man short and I had the week free." He reached into his back pocket and pulled out a round plastic container, which he popped open and held out to Trent. "Would you like a mint?"

CHAPTER SEVENTEEN
"INTRUDER"

"At least once a week, I offer up what I call 'prayers for disruption.' If things are getting too routine, too vanilla, I ask God to throw a wrench into my gears and knock me off-balance. That's the sweet spot. When I'm off-balance, that's where God's work flourishes."

—*Insane Faith: A Guide to Extreme Christianity for the Truly Faithful* by Stephen Branding, p. 222

Trent had been ducking Judith's calls for almost twenty-four hours now, although he had been texting her updates—or non-updates, as it were—about his dad's condition. For whatever reason, he just felt he lacked the emotional energy required for a conversation with Judith.

Now that Dad was awake, though, Trent owed her a call.

"How is he?" she answered.

"Hello to you, too."

"Sorry. Hi. How is he?"

Trent chuckled. "Awake. He doesn't feel great, but he's alert and talking and like his old self. Like his *old* old self. He even said both he and I deserve to take a little time to unwind."

"Are you going to stay the night again?"

"I'm not sure. Chief Barton is heading back in about half an hour, so if I'm riding with him, I have to decide soon. Leaning toward sleeping in my own bed."

"Good," Judith said. "We've got work to do."

This. This right here is why Trent had been ducking her calls. This would not be a fun conversation. "No, Judith. That stuff's over. I think I'm just going to give the diary to Chief Barton."

"Barton? You must be joking."

"Think about it, Judith. Wouldn't it feel good to have that off our minds? No more secrets, get it out in the open . . . "

"You pinky swore," she said. "You told me this was our secret, that you saved it for me."

"I was trying to distract you from your superhero fixation. Obviously, it didn't work."

"You were trying to manipulate me?" Judith's voice hung heavy with a sense of betrayal.

"For your own good. Stephen Branding's dead. Did you know that?"

She was quiet for a minute, then asked, "How?"

"Heart attack. Apparently you can only go 110%, squeaking by on power-naps and protein bars so long before your ticker just gives up."

"He probably had a congenital defect."

"*What*? What does his heart have to do with his . . . ?"

"*Con*-genital, genius. Like inherited. I'm not basing any life decisions on this until I see an autopsy report."

A flash of frustration burst up through the layers of worry and fatigue, exploding like fireworks into, "Judith, get in touch with reality. You don't want people to think you're crazy? Stop acting crazy! There's no such thing as superheroes. That's only in comic books and cartoons and movies. You can't be one, because you don't live in a comic book or a cartoon or a movie. Okay? You live in the real world. Or at least you could if you chose to. In fact, this is me inviting you to come back to us!"

Silence from the other end of the phone call. The debris from the fireworks began to rain down in the form of guilt. "Look, I'm sorry Judith. I'm really tired and my nerves are shot. I just had a long talk with Ed Piper and he put everything into perspective. He was like, you don't have to be a superhero to follow Jesus faithfully. All that *Insane Faith* stuff is just a distraction from working hard every day, being a student or a police chief or whatever. Volunteering at the soup kitchen. You know? Following Jesus while doing ordinary stuff."

Judith's answer came loud and crisp, but somehow miles distant. "What if someone had said that to the apostles? Or Rachel Saint? Or Sojourner Truth?"

Trenton had no answer. He wished Ed was still here, so he could relay the question to him. "Look, Judith, I almost lost my dad today. The doctor said his brain was bleeding. I almost lost him. I can't lose you, too."

"There's more than one way to lose someone," she said. "Look, I have to go."

"Okay. Bye," Trenton said. But she'd already hung up.

Just then, the door opened and Chief Barton came out, stuffing his notepad into his pocket. "If you're coming with me, you better say goodbye to your dad. I've got to be back in Clinch Rock in an hour." He winked. "We'll light up the sirens."

Trent's dad worried over him a bit and reiterated several times: in by curfew and no visitors. As he and Chief Barton headed out into the parking lot, Trent was completely lost in thought: indecision about what to do with the diary, anxiety over staying by himself in one of the few remaining buildings to fit the profile, guilt over not having warned Zoe that her house was on the same exclusive list, regret for his harsh words to Judith.

Then something brought him back to the moment. To this place. What had it been? It was important. He stopped a moment and let Barton power-walk on, toward his police cruiser, illegally parked in the fire lane. Trenton felt a rush as his eyes landed on it. The old red truck with the busted headlight cover. He filled his lungs, ready to call out to Barton. But then he locked eyes with Officer Tyrell, sitting behind the wheel of the idling truck and the breath seemed to disappear.

"You coming, kid?" Barton shouted over his shoulder.

"Yeah." Trenton answered, jogging to catch up.

The hour drive home seemed to take five times that, as Trent's mind played ping pong with the question of whether he could trust Barton with the diary, the old bank notes, with Tyrell's connection to the old red truck and his certainty that Cash had been one of the men who climbed into the same truck earlier that week. Obviously he couldn't tell Dad while he recovered from a head injury, just as he was finally about to get some real rest. It was Barton or nothing. Or should he maybe tell Jessie Finn?

The ping pong match was a draw, tied at about five-thousand-up when Barton pulled into the driveway of the parsonage.

"Alright, kid," he said, "I'll be checking in on you. So remember what your old man said: no parties, no staying out late, got it?"

Trenton nodded weakly and stepped out of the car. "Thanks for the ride," he said. His stomach growled loudly. There was a Tombstone pizza in the freezer with his name on it. By the time he reached the front door, Barton had peeled away, sirens blaring once again.

Trenton paused at the storm door, where a note had been taped. The stationary read, "From the Desk of Zoe Green." It smelled like her perfume and the very scent reawakened something in Trenton—a familiar braiding of excitement, anxiety, and something more primal. He'd thrown away his last chance with the most beautiful, graceful, sophisticated woman he'd ever had a prayer of dating. And for what? So that Judith could just keep right on following Stephen Branding off the cliff?

Pulling the handwritten note off the window, he read the words of her beautiful cursive penmanship: "Trenton, I was so very sorry to hear what happened to your father. I did not want to bother you while you had so much on your mind, but please know that I've been praying for you both. I'm sorry about how we left things. If you can forgive me, call me when you get a chance. Love, Zoe." He read it through again and then read the "Love, Zoe" part about ten more times. Glancing up at the door, he saw his reflection in the glass and realized his ear-to-ear grin was threatening to permanently split his face. He may have blown it with this girl more than once, but this time would be different.

Trent dug the phone from his pocket as he unlocked the front door and was about to hit the button to dial Zoe when the handset clattered to the ground.

The Marsh home had been ransacked. Every drawer seemed to have been emptied onto the floor. Every book, finally shelved after months in boxes, had been fanned and dumped in a pile.

Picking up his phone, Trent considered calling 911, bringing Barton back to the house. Or better, Jessie Finn. Or worse, Officer Cash. No, that wouldn't do. There was a better than average chance that Tango and Cash had taken part in the ransacking.

"Hello?" he called out, taking a few tentative steps into the house. Everything was out of place, but nothing seemed to be missing. His dad's 60" flat screen was still mounted on the wall. It was clear that whoever did this was looking for something. And yet it was different from all the other break-ins—no holes in the walls. No floorboards pried up.

The diary. Any reservations gone, Trent flew out the side door to the garage and down the basement stairs to his bedroom. He breathed a sigh of deep relief. Everything seemed to be intact down here. His dresser drawers were in place and the long pine board was snugged up to the opening of the secret room, blocking the view of Jeremiah Wolcott's old desk.

Slipping into the hidden chamber, Trenton pulled out the bottom drawer and reached into the void, where he'd balanced the diary on a small ledge at the very back. His hand closed around the antique book and the rest of the tension left his body, but only for a moment.

There were so many questions. Was the chaos above his head the work of the same men who had broken in so many places? If so, why had they changed their methods? Did they know about the diary? And, most troubling, if they did know, how? Besides Judith, the only person he'd told was Zoe.

Then again, if Zoe was behind this, she would certainly have included his bedroom in the search. Right? It couldn't be her. Trent had known this was likely coming, as the list of potential targets dwindled. He'd even told Barton.

Oh, yeah. He'd told Barton.

Whatever the case, it made sense to call Zoe. If she was involved, he could feel her out. If not, he could warn her. Either way, he felt a pressing, growing need to hear her voice.

Her face and number still graced his contact list. It rang only once before she answered, her voice tender and compassionate. "How are you, Trenton?"

"I'm okay, considering. My dad woke up this morning. They want to keep him a couple days, but it looks like he should make a full recovery before too long."

"You must be so glad that he's leaving policework," she said. "I can't imagine how worried you would be if he went back out there."

"Yeah, I don't know." Trenton was a little confused by his own lack of apprehension regarding his father's work in law enforcement. Lately, it was his other occupation that had him in knots.

"So you're all alone?" Zoe asked.

"Yeah." Trent looked around. *I hope so.*

"Maybe I should come over," she said, coquettishly, "keep you company."

Trenton thought of the disaster upstairs. It would take hours to clean. And, of course, his dad had forbidden visitors while he was laid up.

"Why don't we get together in the morning?" Trent said. "I'm pretty tired. I just want to veg for a while and hit the hay early." It wasn't a lie.

"Okay," she said. "I'll call you. And, Trent, I really am sorry about the things I said the last time we talked."

"It's alright. I guess we just had our first fight."

"That wasn't a fight, Trenton." Zoe giggled. "When we've had our first fight, you'll know."

It took Trent just as long to restore order to the main floor of the house as it had to unpack the lion's share of their belongings. In his dad's room upstairs, he was surprised to find only a few drawers of clothes and the closet shelf disturbed. His home office, the next door over, was a little worse, but not horrible. The other two upstairs bedrooms were empty.

It was dark out by then and Trent was beginning to feel a bit cagey. On an intellectual level, it should have been a relief that their house had finally been hit. As far as he knew, no building had been broken into more than once. And yet, the thought of lying down and closing his eyes, with any hope of falling asleep was almost laughable. He needed to take precautions.

The basement would be his fortress, Trent decided. Not only had it not been violated, and thus seemed safer, there were more door locks between it and the outside world. To access it, one had to first get into the garage, either from the house or the outside. Trenton intended to make that impossible.

Feeling a bit like a cartoon coyote, he zipped off a dozen four-foot long 2 x 4s and screwed them into the doorframes. Yeah, Chet Bushman would freak if he saw the damage to the house's precious original woodwork, but at the moment, who really cared? The old electric garage door was easier to close off. A single pull on the orange string hanging from the ceiling deactivated the motor. A hard twist of the old half-rusted handle on the door itself and the garage was secured.

Once in the basement, Trent threw the deadbolt and pushed a huge rolling tool chest in front of the door. He was in for the night and anyone else who wanted to join him down here would be out of luck. He then shut and locked his bedroom door.

It was not even eight, but Trenton's eyes were getting heavy. A couple episodes of *Stranger Things* and he'd be out.

* * *

Officer Cash pulled his cruiser up next to his old truck in the parking lot. Tyrell was sitting behind the wheel, staring blankly at the hospital, in half a trance. Cash squawked the siren to get his attention and rolled the window down. The cool night air felt great.

"Hey, Ben. Anything to report?"

"Nothing. He's still in there."

"Well, did you at least pop in and see how he's doing?"

"Nope," Tyrell said. "Don't care."

"You're a real sweetheart, you know that?" Cash got out of the car and Tyrell followed suit. "You can shut the door," Cash said, "I'm gonna give my best to the chief." He disappeared into the hospital.

Officer Tyrell stretched, bringing a series of cracks from his spine. The last thing he wanted to do was get in the squad car and drive an hour plus back to Clinch Rock. Oh, well. This was the job.

"You still here?" Tyrell looked up to see an old man in a flannel shirt, carrying a Bible under his arm.

"Our police chief is a patient here," Tyrell said. "Just checking in. Maybe throw up a prayer for him, preacher."

"It's a sin," the old man said. "Lying."

"Excuse me?"

"You were sitting in this truck all day. I saw you a few times. Funny thing, I heard your chief say the guy who knocked him out was driving an old red truck."

"Obviously not this one, though. He sees me drive this truck into work every morning. Why don't you leave the policework to us, hey old-timer?"

The old man nodded easily and walked off toward a battered old Buick.

Tyrell pulled out his phone and took down the license plate.

* * *

Trenton had been in the deepest of sleeps when something dragged him back into the world of the waking. The glowing red numbers of his alarm clock came harshly into focus—2:21 AM. He sat up slowly, feeling a tilting inside that he couldn't quite explain. Something was off here. He could hear movement, like rats crawling through the walls.

Reaching down between his bed and the wall, he grabbed the aluminum bat he'd stashed there. Holding it at the ready, he got up and moved into the middle of the dark room. Only it wasn't totally dark. A faint glow spilled up from beneath the board blocking off the secret room, moving back and forth like the sliver of light bleeding out from a Xerox machine.

His first instinct was to get out of there as quickly as possible. But that was easier said than done. By barring everyone else out, he'd effectively locked himself in. Even opening the garage door would take an extra minute. The thought made him angry more than anything else. How had this person gained access to the basement? The windows were blocked in with metal mesh—a fire marshal's nightmare but good for security.

Trent made a decision. He would bring all this shady nonsense out of the shadows and expose the people involved to the harsh and unforgiving light. Or at least however many were now in his bedroom. The angry ferret clawed and snarled in his belly, but Trent didn't care. The man who'd knocked his father unconscious might be behind that board. Trent would return the favor if given have a chance.

He flipped on the overhead light. "Come out!" he growled, his best impression of menacing. "Nice and slow." The movement in the hidden room stopped. "I've got my dad's gun," he bluffed. "Don't try anything." Still no movement.

Peering in through the slim opening, Trent found the hidden room still aglow in warm light. His heart went double-speed at the sight of a man dressed head-to-toe in black, face obscured with a mask. But this was not one of the four broad-shouldered hulks from the Home Store—this intruder was slight, wiry.

And fast. With a sudden lurch the black clad figure slammed into the pine board, bringing the sharp corner into the bridge of Trent's nose and sending stumbling back. The man came rushed out from the secret room, colliding with Trent's dazed form, knocking him to the ground.

From his vantage point on the concrete floor, Trenton saw the intruder, upside down, heading for the door. No way. He wound up and threw the bat with all his might at the man's ankles, hoping to trip him up. It went wide, hitting the base of a six-foot tower of moving boxes. They toppled onto the intruder, knocking him momentarily to his knees.

Trent scrambled past him, grabbing the bat on the way, and planted himself between his bedroom door and the black-clad figure. "You're going nowhere," he said, squaring off in a batter's stance.

The intruder stood up straight and wavered for a moment, seemingly deciding between attacking and relenting, before pulling the mask off.

Shiny brown hair came cascading down. It was Zoe.

"*Now* we've had our first fight," she said.

CHAPTER EIGHTEEN
"BIRTHRIGHT"

"Let your defenses fall away. Embrace anything God drops in your path. Never push any challenge away from you. There's no comfort in living this way, but God didn't create you so he could comfort you. He created you to serve him with reckless intensity."

—*Insane Faith: A Guide to Extreme Christianity for the Truly Faithful* by Stephen Branding, p. 79

Trent gaped in silence for a minute, until he realized he was still holding the bat up as if to bash Zoe's head in. He dropped it to the floor and quietly asked, "Zoe?" It was a stupid question, but still one that occupied his mind at the moment.

"Let me explain," she said.

Trent wandered over to his bed and flopped down, dejected. He knew things weren't going great with Zoe, but this . . . his nose still hurt from where she'd used Cassel's gold pine to knock him down, trying to cover her escape. And if she'd succeeded, what then? Undoubtedly she'd have continued acting like everything was okay, cozying up to him.

Yes, it was acting. All of it.

Zoe sat on the bed next to him. "Trenton, please listen," she said.

"Listen?" He looked her full in the face, ready to let her have it, but found himself immediately tongue-tied. Her eyes were red and moist, her chin quivering—not the affected Half-Pint prelude to phony tears, but the involuntary spasms that precede the real thing. She covered her face before the dam broke and Trenton instinctively enveloped her in his arms, letting her soak his T-shirt.

"I'm so sorry," she said. "I had no choice. He'd kill me. He would. Please. You have to forgive me."

"What? Slow down. Who would kill you?"

She broke away from him and met his gaze once again. "Brian Green," she said, as if it were the most obvious thing in the world.

"Your dad would kill you?"

"He's not my father. He's a criminal."

"What . . . kind of criminal?"

"Art forgery. Insurance fraud. Grand larceny. He had a few of us girls separating older men from their savings in Vermont. He recruited me into his cons years ago and now I have no choice. If I try to leave, he'll pin everything we've so far done on me and I'll go to prison. Or worse, he'll just make me disappear. I've seen him do it."

"This doesn't make any sense, Zoe. Why would some big-time criminal be here, in Clinch Rock, starting a museum?"

"Don't you see? It's all a smokescreen. Brian Green is a direct descendent of Benjamin Cassel. He's been obsessed with the stories of the lost lumber treasure for years, collecting every letter, every artifact he could get his hands on. The museum is just an excuse to search Cassel's house and collect anything that might help him find the money, all under one roof."

It all began to line up for Trent. "Right. And he bought the lumber camp for the same reason. But why all this stuff about rebranding the town, renaming it even? Was that just to get the mayor and the town council on his side while he searched for the treasure?"

"Partially, maybe," she said. "But he does plan on staying. He intends to use his newfound wealth to buy up half the real estate here. He sees it as his birthright. Brian really does have a vision. It's very contagious. That's how he got us all to follow him in the first place"

"Who's *us*? Tango and Cash are working with for him too, right? I saw you and John Cash at the silver mine together."

"Were you spying on me?" she asked, incredulous.

"I don't think you're in any position to judge, Zoe. From the first moment we met, you pretended to be interested in me so you could get in here and search this house. And the church too. And maybe keep tabs on my dad. Tell me I'm wrong."

She looked down at her hands, folded on her lap. "At first, yes. But I swear to you, somewhere along the way, I really fell for you. I'm so sorry if I've hurt you."

Trenton didn't believe her; not even a little. Not even when she leaned in and kissed him on the lips, soft and warm. On paper, it was everything he dreamed it would be when it finally happened again, albeit with slightly different circumstances.

She seemed to think she was initiating something else entirely, but Trent broke off the kiss.

"I guess I should go," Zoe said.

Trent was in a bit of a daze as he walked her up to the garage. There, he asked, "So what happens now?" as he unlocked the garage door and reengaged the electric motor.

"I'm not going back there," she said. "I'll go to my aunt's house in Ontario for a time, while I decide what's next for me."

Trent nodded. "Well, best of luck." It was perhaps the lamest thing he'd ever said.

Zoe smiled, sadly, and walked out into the night. She was several yards away when her remote brought a *blurp* and a flash from the headlights of her Volvo, parked down the street. As he watched her disappear for what he assumed was the last time, it almost felt like this had been the inevitable outcome from day 1. Maybe not this exactly, but something like this.

He thought about the kiss, how it had lacked something he assumed would be there—the most important element of any kiss. And he thought about his demonstration clinch with Judith. Whatever *it* was, it had definitely been present then, in great supply. What did that mean?

As he closed and locked the garage door, a far more pressing question pushed out all others: how had Zoe gotten into his room? A chill grabbed him around the spine. It was as if Zoe's presence had pressed pause on the growing panic in his gut and now that she was gone, it was back with a vengeance. He double-checked the door to the house and the one to the backyard. Both were still secured.

With nowhere else to look for answers, Trenton went back down the stairs to his room and with a grunt pushed aside the giant cut of old growth pine, revealing the hidden room. For the first time, he saw it, not glowing warmly with a single incandescent bulb, but bathed in the unpleasant fluorescent buzz of his bedroom overheads.

There was something about the back wall, where the enormous old map of town hung. The map was no longer lying flat against the brick wall. Trent grabbed the bat once again and entered the room, on edge. He pulled the canvas back from the wall and felt his legs go weak at the sight of a dozen missing bricks, creating an opening to more empty, dark space beyond the secret room. Cool musty air moved in along a micro-jetstream.

Trent raced back to his dresser for a flashlight and shined it into the void, illuminating a long, brick-lined tunnel. Of course. The secret room wasn't a room at all. It had never made sense to Trent that the otherwise square footprint of the old house should have a little five by five underground chamber appended to it—one which seemed to have been walled off only as an afterthought. But a tunnel, that made more sense. Especially when he remembered what Zoe told him about Cassel's obsession with privacy and how he'd built separate servants' quarters on the opposite end of his property. Perhaps the tunnel was a compromise, allowing the staff to avoid trudging through snow or mud or rain. Or maybe it didn't go to the Cassel House at all.

Whatever the case, Trenton had to know. Gripping the flashlight in this left hand and the bat in his right, he forced himself through the opening in the brick wall. While it was more than big enough for Zoe, the corners of the brick and the ragged edge of the mortar scraped at his ribs as he wiggled through.

A natural sense of direction had never been his strong suit, but Trent was almost certain as he began following the brick-lined passage: this straight shot of a tunnel cut beneath the two blocks of houses between the servants' quarters and the lumber mansion, connecting the two.

Trent's dad had told him at least a dozen times over the years that courage was not the absence of fear, but the act of pushing through fear. He'd never really understood what that meant until now. The feeble stream of the flashlight disappeared into the darkness maybe ten feet ahead of him, but still it cut through, a little further with every step, like his resolve cutting through his own dense fear.

As he walked, nothing changed around him—the dirt floor, the brick walls and ceiling—it was like a poorly designed video game, leaving Trent no real sense of how far he'd travelled. He should have turned on his phone's GPS mapping feature, he thought. Then again, he almost certainly had no signal down here. After a couple minutes of putting one foot in front of the other, Trent began to second-guess where he was headed. As the crow flies, he ought to have reached Zoe's place by now. Just as his resolve began to ebb, a faint glow appeared in the distance—a literal light at the end of the tunnel.

Turning off his own light, he slowed his approach, moving as quietly as possible. The distant sound of voices echoed into the tunnel from somewhere just beyond and a new realization dawned on Trent. Brian Green had not been rewiring his house. The cycle of holes and plaster repairs was all about looking for the money.

And the one spot they'd left untouched was in the dining room—not because of the historical significance, but because the Crown Fire Boys had already looked there. It was likely in the process of this methodical search that they had stumbled upon the mansion-side tunnel entrance, long ago walled over by Cassel when he deeded the parsonage over to the church. Or perhaps Trent's voicemail to Zoe had clued them in to the tunnel's existence. Trenton came to a stop. The voices were just barely intelligible here.

"She should be back already." Officer Cash. Oddly, the image that popped into Trent's mind upon hearing his voice was the cop's easy, winsome smile. "I say we go check on her."

"What were you told?" Brian Green, his overly refined tone a bit reproachful, maybe even threatening. "Wait here for her to return. She can handle it."

Nausea and rage filled Trenton. This man was almost certainly responsible for the blow to the head that could have ended Adam Marsh's life. Maybe he hadn't struck him personally, but he was calling the shots. And this same man had been holding Zoe against her will, using fear to force her continued service to his cause. A little voice in Trenton's mind was urging him to rush through the uneven opening in the wall, taking Green and company by surprise with the aluminum bat.

But no. That was stupid. Brian Green had the law in his pocket. Especially with Trent's dad on the sidelines. Tango and Cash were clearly his puppets. And what about Chief Barton? He'd hired the two new officers, making him suspect at best. Trent realized he was now moving quickly back toward his bedroom, although he couldn't remember deciding to do so. When the light from the Cassel house was no longer visible, he broke into a sprint.

Spilling out into basement of the parsonage a minute later, Trenton hefted the unwieldy board back into place, knowing it would do nothing to keep these men out. No matter how he blocked off the doors above, Brian Green and his henchmen would have direct access to Trent's bedroom whenever they wanted, via this tunnel. He had to get out of here.

Trent grabbed a battered backpack from his closet and began stuffing clothes into it. Not knowing when he'd be back, he added a toothbrush, some Colgate, his deodorant. Oh, and of course, the diary, which he had zipped into his pillow earlier than afternoon. He blew some down feathers off the cover and slid it into the front pocket of the pack.

Heading up to the garage, he considered his options of where to go. The hospital in Big Rapids would be ideal, next to his dad, which always felt like the safest place on earth to Trent. But how could he get there at this hour? Uber had yet to enter the thriving metropolitan market of Clinch Rock. Maybe Judith's place? He punched up her number and it rang though to voice mail.

There really was only one viable option: Trent jumped on his bike and pedaled as hard as he could toward downtown. An old church building in the dead of night was not exactly the most inviting place to bed down after one had been attacked and discovered a secret tunnel into one's bedroom, but it was close and Trent had the key, snagged from his dad's backup set, so it had to do. Three minutes later, he was wheeling his bike in the front door of the church—so as not to broadcast his location to passing cops—and into the pastor's study.

The first thing he did was stash the diary behind a shelf full of commentaries and theology tomes. Then he went down to the makeshift stage in the church basement, where he'd been part of at least a dozen little musicals, plays, and pageants over the years. There he collected an armload of corny biblical costumes, to serve as his bed and a particularly soft-looking prop sheep that would have to suffice for a pillow.

Trent locked himself in the study and arranged something of a nest on the floor. As he settled in, he was surprised to find himself drifting off toward la-la land, despite his swirling thoughts. He was right at the gates when a troubling realization snatched him back: assuming Tango and Cash had searched the police station, Trent had literally chosen the last building on the list—the only pre-1895 structure in Clinch Rock to have not yet been ransacked and torn apart by the men at Brian Green's disposal—to serve as his home for the night. What an idiot.

* * *

Ed Piper was watching *El Dorado*. Well, sort of watching it. He'd awakened a little after three AM, fully alert—a normal occurrence for him at about that time. After reading a few chapters from the Scriptures, Ed had plopped down in his favorite old recliner and fed the VHS tape into the front of his tube TV. Now he found himself going in and out, dozing. Which was fine; he'd seen the film about three hundred times. It's not like he was missing important plot points.

But something was off as he came to yet again. A crash had awakened him. And yet, on screen, John Wayne was just talking in that perfect, macho drawl of his with James Caan. Where'd that noise come from? Ed cranked the lever on the recliner, launching him up to his feet. Another noise—definitely from the back of his trailer, by the washer-dryer. He grabbed a pipe wrench off the sideboard and hefted it in his calloused hands.

"Someone in here?" he called. "If you need help, I'll help ya. But if you surprise me, I can't promise I won't take your head off." He trudged around the wall that blocked off his utility area and found himself looking at the wrong end of a semiautomatic pistol. "Oh, it's you," he said. That dead-eyed cop from the hospital. "What're you doin' in my house?"

"Drop the weapon," the officer said.

"Am I under arrest?"

The cop smiled. "Not exactly."

That's when Ed felt the surgical steel of the knife slide up into his back, between two ribs. It didn't even hurt as much as it surprised him. It was the first thing to surprise him in years. He opened his mouth to cry out, but all his breath had gone out the back. The knife slid out and Ed collapsed onto legs that could no longer bear his weight. Breathing was no longer an option. It would be just a minute now.

Ed felt no fear, though. Only excitement and anticipation.

CHAPTER NINETEEN
"A KISS GOODBYE"

"Early to bed and early to rise might make a man healthy, wealthy, and wise, but it doesn't honor God. Jesus stayed up all night healing the sick. Paul preached until one of his listeners fell asleep and right out window. Embracing Insane Faith means burning the midnight oil and getting up early no matter what. Spring out of bed with a purpose, gather your visions and dreams like smooth stones, and attack the day as if you were David and it was Goliath."

—*Insane Faith: A Guide to Extreme Christianity for the Truly Faithful* by Stephen Branding, p. 66

Trenton's eyes flew open. He'd been in and out of a shallow sleep—mostly out—since lying down in his father's study. Each time he'd awakened, his heart had been racing and his skin cold and clammy, although he had no idea why. This time, though, it was no mystery. He heard voices outside the door. Multiple people Light leaked in through the translucent blinds.

The loudest voice—it was familiar. "Now that's what I call a preacher!" it said. Oh. Chet Bushman. Sounded like he was just outside the door. Trent looked at his watch. 9:15 AM, Sunday morning. The early service had just getting out. Chet's voice dropped considerably and he said, "You know, I hear he's looking for a church." Someone answered him, a thinner voice, the words failing to penetrate the door. "Well, yes of course," Chet said, "I pray Pastor Adam has a speedy recovery, but we do need to look at all our options and think about what's best for the church."

Trenton smacked his mouth slowly, feeling like the foul taste of morning breath had not been there a moment earlier, or at least not as bad. His father was in the hospital, having been injured while protecting and serving this community and, not only had the de facto leader of the elder board not visited him or even called, now he was actively laying groundwork to replace him.

Trent stood quickly, grabbed his backpack, and opened the door. Bushman and Scot Galt started as Trenton came striding out, giving the older man a welding torch glare and a taste of his shoulder as he shoved past him without a word. The older man's solid frame didn't give and Trent found himself staggering a bit down the hall.

Cutting through the exiting worshipers, Trent craned his neck, looking for Judith. She usually showed up just as the old folks service ended and helped set up the coffee and donuts for fellowship time. But he didn't see her coming in the door, nor in the fellowship hall.

Walking out into the morning sun, Trent was attacked by a sudden, almost violent, hunger. The smell from the White Tail Diner called to him and he answered, sliding into his and Judith's booth and ordering up a breakfast skillet. As he ate, he finally began to process all the things he'd tied off in the dead of night, the thoughts he'd squelched as he'd tried to sleep. Zoe, doing Brian Green's will, had sneaked into his hidden room, before attacking him. Was that *real?* Everything was different today. Upside-down. It all looked a little more like Judith's take on things in Clinch Rock. Maybe more than a little.

And where was Judith? He tried calling again, but got her voicemail. Trenton had a sense that she would know what to do next. And he had so much to tell her. If he couldn't relay the information now, though, he may as well try to gather some more. Going back home was not an option anyway, so he may as well try and dig a little deeper.. But where to start? The library? No, it was closed on Sundays.

A very obvious, albeit very bad, idea grabbed hold of Trent. He knew exactly where to go.

* * *

Jessie Finn was alone in the police station when Trenton arrived. "How you holding up, bud?" he asked.

"Hanging in there," Trent answered, because that's how you answer when someone asks, "How you holding up?" They shook hands and Jessie pulled him in for a brief, manly hug.

Jessie had been a close friend to the Marsh family, especially in the wake of their tragic loss, years earlier—always there to help, to listen, to try and take their mind off it all for a little while.. They were so close, in fact, that Trent had begun calling him "Uncle Jessie," until the officer put the kibosh on that—"because of the whole Stamos thing," he'd explained. The rift that had been growing between the two cops was probably harder on Trent than on either of them. And now, it was nice 'to see a friendly face, to be reminded that there were some people you could still trust, even when everything else was up for grabs.

"I haven't been up to see him," Jessie said. "I really do need to go."

"He'd love that," Trent said. "If you go later today, maybe you'd bring me?"

Jessie smiled. "You still can't drive?"

"Shut up," Trent laughed. "I can drive I just don't have a license."

"Well I can't allow that. Speaking of which, I'm supposed to make you sign in, I guess," Jessie said, nodding toward the clipboard.

"I'm just here for a second. Left some stuff in dad's office."

"We'll let protocol slide this time, but be quick about it."

"Thanks, Uncle Jessie."

"I told you no to—"

Trent was already through the swinging gate in the low wall that separated off the holding cells, evidence room, and chief's office, and pulling out his dad's spare key, with which he opened the office door. Once inside he tried to casually swing it shut, just enough to hide himself from anyone in the station proper, but not enough to raise suspicion. He slid into his dad's leather chair and wiggled the computer's mouse, bringing up the login prompt. "Lelanee1998" was the password. His mother's name and the year they were married. It was Dad's password for everything.

Once in, he ran a query for Zoe Green. Out of ten million residents, it returned only one record: a 51-year-old woman in Sault Sainte Marie who had been arrested for meth at least a dozen times.

Of course, if Brian Green wasn't her father, then Green wasn't really her name. In a flash, he remembered the fake ID in her wallet, and how she'd displayed it side-by-side with the real deal. Only the fake had been Zoe Green. What was the other name? It was Zoe something. Fromeyer? No. Frobisher! Or something like that. But how to spell it? On his third try, he hit pay dirt. All the particulars filled the screen, along with a mugshot. The woman staring back at him from the monitor was unmistakably Zoe, but looked older by a few years, despite the picture being dated 18 months earlier. Date of Birth: November 11, 1995.

So she really was twenty-two! He thought of their kiss and had a sudden urge to call Jason and brag. But no, that was ridiculous. Besides, Jason's phone was dead and locked away somewhere in the hall of mirrors and tacky knickknacks that Mrs. Dufresne called a bedroom.

Anyway. Back to the matter at hand. Zoe's current address was listed in Rochester Hills, hometown of both Tango and Cash. A short bullet list of misdemeanors included minor in possession and petty check fraud. A resonant voice filled the bullpen outside the office, reminding Trent that he was on borrowed time. He quickly hit "print record" and minimized the window, just as the door to the office whipped open.

"What are you doing?" Chief Barton demanded.

"Just checking my e-mail," Trent said.

"I mean where have you been? Stopped by your house three times this morning. You trying to give me a heart attack?"

"Oh, sorry. I—"

"Kid, I told your dad I'd keep an eye on you. And I meant it. You can't just disappear in the wee hours of the morning without telling me where you're going."

"I went to church," Trent said, shrugging. "I was there for the early service." Technically true. "It's Sunday morning; I thought you'd just assume."

The annoyance faded a bit from the chief's face. "Okay. Sorry to yell at you, but things have changed. It's not safe for you to stay there by yourself anymore."

Trent, who couldn't agree more, asked, "What do you mean, changed?"

Barton pulled up a chair, his hand practically grazing the fresh printout of Zoe's mugshot in the process. He sat down and took off his hat. "There was a murder last night." Trent's hand went to his mouth. "It wasn't in town," Barton continued, "out at the trailer park off 37."

Trent felt dizzy. He thought of Judith, not answering his calls. She always answered, even when she was mad.

"Who was it?" Trent managed to ask.

"No one you'd know. He wasn't from around here, kind of a drifter. Name was Edward something. Parker, I think."

The room was spinning now.

"We're pretty sure it wasn't random," Barton said, oblivious to Trent's distress. "Frankly, most of Clinch Rock's crime is out there. Lots of unsavory characters. Still, I have to insist you stay with us tonight. Candy's already made up the extra bunk in Danny's room. And don't worry; I had a talk with him. He'll behave."

This brought Trent back to himself. Mourn Ed Piper later. Think about who would want to kill him later. Form a plan now or sleep five feet away from Dan Barton. His best bet, he decided, was to acquiesce in the short term and then get back to the hospital before nightfall. He could crash there; he had clothes and everything else he might need in his backpack.

"Okay, Mr. Barton. But first, Jessie was going to take me to visit my dad."

Barton shook his head. "I don't think so. Officer Finn's shift doesn't end until 6 tonight. We have dinner at 6:30 and I expect you there. And it's Chief Barton."

Trent didn't have to dig deep to find the beginning of some tears.

"I really want to see him, Chief Barton. I miss him and I'm worried about him."

Barton squirmed in his chair. "I'll see if Officer Tyrell is willing to drive you a little later, but in return you've got to stay right here for the time being, so I can keep an eye on you. Deal?"

"Yes, sir." Trent said. Yeah, he'd stay here. And first chance he got he'd be pulling up Brian Green's record and printing it out too. An hour in the car with Tango wasn't appealing, especially after that awkward moment in the hospital parking lot, but he'd been there before and if it got him to dad's bedside, it was the lesser of two evils.

As it turned out, Trent was not able to get back on his dad's computer. Barton put him to work, filing paperwork, emptying trash cans, and helping Sheila with any number of administrative duties. He threw himself into the tasks, trying to block out thoughts of Ed Piper's death, keeping his eyes peeled the whole time, searching for any bit of useful information amongst the police reports. Nothing jumped out. A little after one, the chief sent Jessie to Zach's Delicatessen for sandwiches.

Just as they finished lunch, Officer Tyrell entered the station and told Trenton, "Get in the car. I'm taking you to Big Rapids."

A chill hung between them as they drove, to the point where Trent half expected the cop to turn on the window defogger. For more than an hour, neither of them said anything. As he pulled up to the hospital entrance, Tyrell simply spat, "You're welcome," barely waiting for Trent to clear the vehicle before squealing away and heading back the way they'd come.

Trent waited forever for the elevator and walked to the very end of a long hall, where the door to his dad's room was closed. He knocked softly twice before entering. The room was rather dark, but he could see that his dad was asleep. And that Judith was sitting in the chair next to the bed, holding his father's hand. She looked up at Trent and waved, vaguely. In the low light, it was hard to tell if it was a greeting or an invitation to get lost.

Grabbing a folding chair from the corner, Trent sat down next to her, close. He'd made up his mind not to mention the murder of Ed

Piper to his dad, but Judith lived in the same small trailer park. If she'd been here all day, she probably didn't know the potential danger lurking in her own back yard. Unzipping the front pocket of his backpack, Trent grabbed a pen and the first piece of paper he found. Only as he unfolded it did he remember what it was: Zoe Frobisher's mugshot. Judith snatched it from his hands and studied the page, reading the text slack jawed. Her eyes met his and Trent was annoyed at the hint of an "I-told-you-so" smile she was working to squelch.

But the smile died instantly as Trent grabbed the page, flipped it over, and wrote, "Ed Piper murdered last night" on the back. She stood and practically ran out into the hall. Trent followed, shutting the door behind them.

"Tell me everything," Judith hissed.

"That is everything. That's all I know. He was found murdered at his place. Barton says they don't have much to go on."

Judith scoffed. "Oh, Barton says...." She shifted her weight nervously between the balls of her feet. "So what now?"

"What now? Nothing now! This isn't a fun little adventure anymore. Someone is dead. I can't go home; they broke into our house while I was here yesterday, tore the place apart." Trent decided not to tell her about the tunnel. He'd already accidentally disclosed too much with the printout of Zoe's record.

"What about Zoe?' she asked. "How'd you find that?"

"How do you think? I logged into Dad's computer."

"But why were you even looking?"

"A hunch." He hated telling half-truths, but if Judith knew Zoe had broken into his bedroom and attacked him in the night, there would be no holding her back from exacting revenge.

Judith tightened her ponytail. "If you don't want to do anything about it, why even tell me?"

"Because you need to be careful too. Ed lived right near you. And if they know we were looking into this stuff."

"You're right." Judith nodded. "I need to take the fight to them."

"No. You don't even know who *they* are. Judith, just run home in the morning, grab some clothes, and hang with us here until Dad's back on his feet. We can play Scrabble. You can teach me Morse Code. It'll be fun, like old times."

"Hiding out's not my style," she said. "I told your Dad I'd get us some Jimmy John's for dinner. After that, I'm out." She stalked back into the room, Trent right on her heels.

"Dad, you're up," he said.

"Not up, but awake." He gestured at Trent's backpack. "Oh good, you remembered to packed."

"What do you mean, packed?"

"The retreat."

"Oh, Dad, no. I can't go. Not with you like this."

"You're going. I even got a ride lined up for you. But for now, Judy-bug's buying sandwiches. I've had it with this mush they're feeding me. And look what the chaplain gave me." He held up a sealed deck of cards. "Who's up for some Cribbage?"

The three of them played cards on a hand-drawn Cribbage board until it was dark out. Then they flipped on the TV, settling on an endless string of *I Love Lucy* reruns. Zoe squeezed into the pleather armchair with Trent, comfortable and comforting—almost enough to make him forget the danger looming back in Clinch Rock and her vow to throw herself right back into it. Sometime after ten, she began to snore and a slowly growing patch of drool appeared on Trent's shirt. He smiled as his own eyes grew heavy.

* * *

The sun was streaming in when Trent awoke to the sound of his dad sawing logs. The clock on the wall said 8:45. Judith was nowhere to be seen, but Trent's shirt was still damp where she'd been resting her head, meaning she couldn't have left too long ago. Ignoring the "Patient Use Only" sign, Trenton entered the bathroom and splashed some water on his face, patting it dry with a paper towel. He frowned at his reflection in the mirror. Right in the middle of his forehead, Judith's lipstick bore witness—she'd kissed him on her way out. For some reason, it seemed like a kiss goodbye. He said a quick prayer for her: for safety, for discernment, for sanity.

Coming back out of the bathroom, he stopped short. Jason's mom stood at the foot of the bed, chomping gum like a cow chewing cud.

"Mrs. Dufresne, what are you doing here?" he asked.

"Didn't your dad tell you?" she said. "I'm your ride to camp."

CHAPTER TWENTY
"THE DEVIL'S TAIL"

"Our perception determines our reality. How do you start each day? What's your mindset? What are your expectations? Will it be a great adventure worthy of retelling or just another slow leak of 24 precious hours? You decide."

—*(God Wants You to) Live Well Now* by Joshua Holton,
from the Foreword by Stephen Branding

Trenton desperately wished he had brought Wolcott's diary with him, not because he was still in treasure-hunting mode, but because the kind of concentration required to read it would discourage Mrs. Dufresne's constant yammering. Or at least drown it out. For more than five hours, she droned on and on about Jason's recent behavior, all the smart comments and back-talk, sneaking out and using her van without permission. Through all of this, she continued circling, but never quite touched the notion on, that Trent was the bad influence to blame for the corruption of her little angel Jason. Trent just fiddled with his phone and occasionally grunted.

When they finally arrived, he vacated the van as quickly as humanly possible, offering a halfhearted "thanks" over his shoulder. However, as he strode onto the grounds of the camp, backpack slung over his shoulder, he wished he could return to the familiarity of the Dufresne family vehicle and even to Mrs. Dufresne's nasal chatter.

Factoring in all the weekends and youth retreats he'd attended, this was probably the twentieth time he'd been to Picture Falls. But only the second time he'd been here without Judith. He missed her like crazy. Looking around, he saw five other teens milling awkwardly in bright orange INSANE FAITH T-shirts along with two middle aged women in same. He recognized the students from camp over the years, but none had really been his friends. In fact, the triumvirate of he,

Jason, and Judith had usually kept to themselves up here. Trent suddenly felt very alone.

Still, he was glad for this group of people, each of whom was a potential witness to keep Brian Green and his men at bay. Brian knew about this retreat, Trent reminded himself. They'd talked about it more than once. Even out here in the woods, Trent was not out of the woods, danger-wise.

Exchanging greetings and handshakes with the two other boys, Trent realized that he was very much underpacked. The others had suitcases, pillows, and sleeping bags. Trent had three changes of clothes and a few toiletries stuffed into a backpack. And, now, a fluorescent orange INSANE FAITH T-shirt, which he had been ordered to don. He couldn't, though—not with his dad in the hospital, Zoe on the run, Judith probably hunting her down, and Stephen Branding dead in a box.

The sight of Sean Taylor's cocky grin set him at ease a bit. The young man sauntered up to him and gave him a playful punch to the arm.

"Hey, camper!" he bellowed. "Good to see ya! You ready for this stuff? It's going to be intense!"

Trent deflated a bit. He'd had more than enough intensity of late. "Yeah, should be fun," he said, trying to generate some enthusiasm of his own. "Can't wait."

"That all you brought?" Sean asked, indicating the backpack.

"Yeah. I like to travel light."

"My man," Sean said.

"Okay, circle up, people!" Mike Van Buren called, gesturing broadly for the small group to converge around him. When they had, he said, "Welcome to Youth Leadership Boot Camp. This is how we'll be doing things, okay?" He gestured at the loose huddle around him. "On the go, not in the program center in folding chairs. You won't be listening; you'll be *doing*." This was only the second time Trent had seen Mike up close and it struck him just how young Van Buren looked. Still, his confidence commanded attention and projected competence.

"You six are it. The few, the proud." Mike laughed. "We were supposed to have seven—the perfect number—but one recruit had to drop out at the last minute." His eyes seemed to linger on Trent's for just a moment, bringing a high tide of nerves.

Mike clapped once, loudly, and waited for the echo to bounce back from the dining hall. "We're kicking things off right now with no ice-breakers and no nonsense. You'll be working on a team-building activity with Jen down by the fire pit and, throughout the morning we'll be taking each of you, one at a time, on a unique personal challenge. Gonna be a lot of growth this week and throughout the year! All right, follow Jen and get ready to grow!"

Trent turned to follow the crowd, but Mike snagged his arm. "You're first, Marsh," he said. "Time to step up."

"Okay," Trent said. He was annoyed, but not really. Whatever this was, best to get it out of the way. "Where should I put my stuff?" he asked.

"Bring it with you." Mike led him back toward the nurse's cabin, Sean following a few feet behind. He had a red vinyl drawstring backpack over one shoulder, bearing the words "Clinch Rock High 2012. Trenton wondered what it contained.

"I assume you've been up the Devil's Tail before," Mike said without looking back at him.

"Oh yeah. Lots of times."

Mike snickered. "Well, this time may be a little different."

They ascended the familiar trail at a pace Trent could barely maintain. Every time he stopped to catch his breath, Van Buren goaded him to immediately resume the climb, with such helpful chants as "Insane Faith! Insane Faith!" and "You got this! You're an animal, Marsh! Animals don't rest."

"Yes, they do, you idiot," he wanted to say, but he didn't have the wind for it. When they finally reached the high point of the trail, Trenton practically collapsed, trying to force himself to breathe deeply. The crash of the falls above, just barely visible through the conifers, helped to relax him.

"You like history, Trent?" Mike asked, smiling. He wasn't the least bit short of breath.

Trent just nodded.

"Did you know that all the land for this camp was donated by a millionaire named Benjamin Cassel? Guy was giving away practically everything he owned in the last year of his life and he gave this to the Michigan Christian Convention. He said it should be 'a site for family retreat.' You know, I've been thinking, if Cassel was going to hide something, this is where he would have hidden it. Lots of land, no one's likely to venture too far out from the main buildings. What do you think, Marsh?"

In that moment, Trent knew what Spiderman's sixth sense felt like. There was no visible threat. Everyone was smiling, the topic of conversation benign, maybe boring. But there was a very real danger. He stood and unconsciously clocked possible exit routes. There was the way they'd come up, the incredibly steep and sandy path down, and the thick woods all around them. "I'm not sure what you mean," Trent said, his voice quavering.

"Oh, you know more than you let on." Mike took a step closer to Trent, looking him right in the eye. The smile was gone, now replaced by unmasked malice. His breath was hot on Trent's face, hanging with the remnants of some fruity sports drink. "Where's the diary, Marsh?" he asked.

Trent tried to answer, but couldn't, not while his brain was grinding against this new development. Sean was here. Sean was part of this. Trent thought of the CFB tattoo, of Sean's minor brushes with the law through the years. That made sense. But who was Mike Van Buren and how did this relate to an official activity of the—

A burst of pain in Trent's solar plexus, spreading out like ripples through a pond, sent him down to his hands and knees.

"It's rude not to answer people, Marsh," Mike said. "Check his pack."

Trent felt his backpack zip open and Sean rifling through it.

"I'll take this," Sean said, removing Trent's cell phone and sliding it into his drawstring bag. Trent couldn't help but think about Dan

Barton and his wrestling friends lumbering through the halls with almost identical bags, loudly making jokes about their "sackpacks." Sean was just another Barton, only older and more dangerous.

"It's not here," he announced. Trent was able to breathe again, but not without pain.

"I'm going to ask you this one more time," Mike said, reaching under his shirt and pulling a handgun from his waistband at the small of his back. "Where's the diary, Trent?"

Sean too was holding a gun now—a snub-nosed revolver.

"I— I don't—" Everything was swirling around Trent. Nothing was clear, except this: if he told them where to find the diary, they would kill him. Why else would they be so transparent about all this? They'd drag him up to the falls and drown him or shove him down a steep embankment, where he'd break his neck. An extreme physical challenge during a quote/unquote "boot camp" was the perfect explanation for his death.

Sure, the camp's insurance premiums would go through the roof and they might get sued, but no criminal charges would stick to Mike and Sean. Besides, they obviously knew something he did not about the treasure's whereabouts. If the diary gave them the last piece of the puzzle, they'd be instantly rich beyond their wildest dreams, even if they only got a cut from Brian Green. They'd disappear, held accountable for nothing. No, he couldn't tell them what they wanted to know.

"Are you stupid, kid?" Mike shouted. "I told you, I'm not asking again. What I *will* do is count. To three." He jerked Trent up to his knees. "You don't tell me what I want to know, I'll blow your head off. *One.*"

"Hey, slow down," Sean said. "He's just scared. Let him—"

"Shut up, Sean. Turn around. You're not going to want to see this. *Two.*"

Sean turned his back. For some reason, this brought the swirling to a stop. This was real. This was happening. And Trent was almost hyperaware. He could feel the gun behind him, see his camp counselor, looking away, down the steep trail. Then, in a flash, he saw

Jason. Saw them running down the Devil's Tail, five, maybe six years ago. Trent was out of control. He connected with Jason and the two of them went sailing down, pinballing their way down the trail Trent clinging to his friend like a sled flying down an icy hill.

Mike's tongue was chambered against his teeth, the last number forming in his mouth. Trent was aware of this too. Then he saw his hands, both closed around fistfuls of sandy soil. With one motion, he threw them both back over his shoulders, in the direction of Mike's face, and burst to his feet, tackling Sean from behind.

The two of them hit the sand and immediately began picking up speed. They bounced against rocks and trees and banked around corners. They caught some air and, as they landed, Trent saw the revolver bounce out of Sean's hand and out into the thick scrub. As with poor Jason years earlier, Sean was taking the worst of the beating, his eyes and nose filling with sand and his body raking against stones and sticks buried shallowly beneath them.

This, of course, was why the Devil's Tail was now off-limits to campers.

The trail bent sharply ahead of them, but their momentum carried them straight-ahead, up out of the rut and directly into a beech tree. Sean's head collided with the solid trunk, crunching back against his neck. Trent launched from the man's back, but was able to bring his hands up in time to avoid the same fate. He pushed himself off the tree and landed in the dirt, sliding a few feet.

Trent gathered himself and slowly approached Sean's still form, almost certain that he was dead. No, he was breathing, shallow but steady. They needed help. Both of them. His one-time counselor needed to be strapped to a backboard and airlifted to a hospital. Trent just needed a way out of here without getting shot.

The drawstring of the red vinyl bag was still wrapped over Sean's shoulder. It was tight, tangled up with the sleeve of his T-shirt, but Trent managed to loosen the drawstring and reach in. Where was his phone? He thought he'd find it near the top, but during their ride everything had moved around. There was a hoodie sweatshirt, a bunch of power bars, a magazine. Sean was stirring now and Trent made the hardest choice of his life: forget the phone and get out of there.

Pointing himself in the general direction of the camp proper, he ran into the woods, off the path. He prayed for God's protection and for guidance; but first, he thanked God that he was wearing khaki shorts and a forest green T-shirt, blending in to his surroundings, while his pursuers were both decked out in bright orange Insane Faith.

CHAPTER TWENTY-ONE
"DOUBLE-BACK"

Trent's legs were a great representation of Jackson Pollock's Red Period, if he had a Red Period—the result of hundreds of thorns, thistles, and vines, snagging and scraping the flesh between his shorts and his shoes. He'd been through some poison oak too, he was sure, as they were also swelling and itchy. He tried to use the discomfort to push him forward, but it wasn't really working. He'd been slowing now for ten minutes as he cut through the woods, stopping every so often to listen for footfalls or snapping branches behind him.

So far, so good.

This was south, he thought, based on the position of the sun. Then again, it was early afternoon and the ground was slanted down significantly, leaving Trent less than sure. If he was headed south, he should eventually emerge from the woods behind the boys' cabins. Of this, he was only slightly more sure. He stopped again, hunched over a felled tree, trying to catch his breath. Clarity of thought was slowly returning, but with it came the sharp memory of Mike Van Buren's gun an inch from Trent's head, which did nothing to calm his nerves.

Trent resumed his descent, picking each step carefully. He chastised himself for not taking the extra second to find his phone in Sean's red bag, or to just get the whole bag. Sure, the guy had been coming around, but Trent had every advantage. What he should have done, he was now realizing in an exercise of perfect futility, was pull off Sean's belt and use it to bind his hands tightly behind his back. Maybe use the new T-shirt in his own backpack as a gag. Then he could have taken his time working through the red knapsack's contents.

While he was re-writing history, perhaps he should have marked the very spot where Sean's gun had bounced off into the woods, so he could go get it himself and even the playing field a bit. No, that was stupid. It was all stupid. Trent was lucky to be alive and he knew it. There hadn't been room for anything more than bare survival in the moment. Besides, he was a terrible marksman with a gun. His dad had taken him to the shooting range a few times and let him burn through a few magazines with his service weapon. Trent consistently shredded the lower-right corner of the paper target, without ever breaching even the outer circle, even once.

No, stick to what you're good at, Marsh. With a gun, he was useless. But with a bow . . . Trent came to a stop. He could just barely see the stone chimney of one of the cabins, perhaps a quarter mile more down the hill. His original plan, which he had no memory of even making, was to return to camp, get back in the midst of as many people as possible. But now he was rethinking that. The other campers were, as far as he knew, still off on a team-building activity with Jen. Meaning, Mike and Sean would be just as free to kill him on the dining hall porch as they were off the secluded trail by the falls.

A new plan formed—a better one. He pushed forward, following the tree line, about fifty yards back, rerouting as he went. He felt a second wind come upon him. Obviously, the winding, half-mile-long dirt drive into camp was not an option; someone was sure to be watching it. But just beyond, he saw the Rec Building. With the exception of the old Camp Mukwa ruins, it was the furthest removed of all the buildings on the property. It was also the newest.

Trent's bearings were back now and he closed in on the building without so much as a wasted step. He hesitated before leaving the cover of the woods, but sheer necessity gave him the last burst of courage needed to rush out into the clearing, over thirty feet of flat, open gravel, and into the screened off porch. He tried the main door into the structure. Locked. Trent grabbed a cheap plastic lacrosse stick from a pile of half-broken sports equipment and punched it through the window. He carefully reached in and disengaged the deadbolt.

As the door opened, Trent's spirits soared. He'd come here to arm himself, but now he remembered something even better. One of the camp's two phones was in this building. A ten-pound rotary job far older than the structure itself. Trent could call for help here! He'd dial 911 and summon the local sheriff. Then he'd call his dad's cell. And Judith; for some reason, that made perfect sense in the moment.

Rushing down the hall to the small office, he grabbed the handset off the cradle and grinned at the sound of the dial tone. He shoved his finger into the 9 and spun the wheel around to the stop. It seemed to take five seconds for the number to register, as the rotor spun, creating nine individual clicks inside the antiquated device. It was actually making sparks in there, he thought, his finger poised ready over the one, impatiently. Still, he couldn't help but love this old device that would bring help—probably save his life. But the love disappeared as the dial tone persisted. That wasn't right. Trent tried dialing the nine again. Nothing. Just more dial tone.

It was a crushing realization: these old rotary phones apparently didn't work anymore with modern phone lines. Trent slammed the handset down as hard as he could, trying to push the rage and fear aside to free up some mental space. There had to be a way. He had a phone and a working phoneline. All he needed was to dial 0 somehow, get an operator on the line, anything. *Think, Marsh.!*

His thoughts were derailed by the loud, almost violent, ringing of the phone, mere inches from his face. He snatched it up. "Hello! Who is this?" he shouted. "I need help!"

A low chuckle creeped out of the earpiece. "It's Mike. I was just going to give the boss an update. But now we know where you are."

Trent froze. Anyone who knew the camp in the least knew that there were only two phones. One in the kitchen, one here in the recreation office. Campers weren't allowed in the kitchen, so anyone homesick or actually sick or surreptitiously calling a girlfriend back home had to do so in here. Of course, that was back when this phone could actually dial out.

"Hello, Trent. This is Brian," another voice said. "Why don't you just stay there, okay? I'm sorry about the misunderstanding up on the trail. That's what I get for hiring local punks instead of professionals. You and I, though, we can work this out without threats or intimidation. I just want to know what you found in your home and what you did with it. You're a perfectly reasonable young man, aren't you?" For a moment, Trent was tempted. Brian was incredibly approachable, after all, even friendly, and he was coming across as calm and rational, especially compared with his gun-toting henchmen.

But then he remembered Ed Piper. And the attack on his father. And the fear in Zoe's eyes and voice. Trent could hear Mike's heavy breathing on the line. He was running from wherever he'd been—probably somewhere up the hill—down toward the Rec Building. Trent glanced up at the crude map of the camp framed on the wall. He guessed where Mike probably was, placing a mental dot, moving slowly, and another dot at the kitchen, where Brian Green must be. The rec building was a third point and connecting them resulted in a long isosceles triangle, which looked to Trent like an arrow, telling him to get out of there.

He dropped the handset, letting it swing, and rushed over to the equipment cabinet, where he grabbed a black compound bow and shoved two handfuls of arrows into the zipper pouch at the front of his backpack. He pulled the pack over both shoulders and rushed out the back door, his senses on high alert.

Trent began to climb once again, still seeing the map in his mind, his two pursuers converging behind him. He'd already taken one of them out, and that was before he had a weapon. One more and he might not be outnumbered. Of course, that raised the question: would he be able to fire an arrow into a human being? No, that wasn't the question. He'd be *able*, of course—even under the pressure of competition, Trent couldn't seem to miss—but was he willing? He didn't know the answer.

Shoving the thought away, he instead focused on the stupid irony that he was now again pushing his body to the limit, climbing the very same hill he'd just descended, albeit the other side of the hill. Somehow, though, it seemed easier going up than coming down. The ground here was covered in coarse moss rather than thorny ground-cover and he made quick progress. He was taking fewer rest stops and, in the midst of all this, another new plan was forming.

As he climbed, he would cut in toward the river. When he reached it, he would double back, following the river down, through the old camp, to where it emptied into the lake. Yeah, the lake would be his ticket out.

Trent had swum the lake four summers in a row and had no doubt he could do it again. The thought of pulling himself out into that vast body of water, of disappearing from view and then coming to shore at some random point a mile away appealed to him greatly. There were quite a few vacation homes on the other side. Someone was bound to be home. Someone who had a phone from this century, who could call for help.

Turning even more sharply toward the river, Trent continued his quick ascent. A glance at his watch told him he'd been at it for twenty-five minutes now, which was hard to believe. He should see the river any moment. Right? It's not like he could miss it.

There! The sun sparkled off the surface of the water as it rolled lazily downward. He begin to run, closing in on it, sliding a bit down into the bank. Downstream, the river twisted and turned, not exactly the shortest distance between two points but who cared? As long as he hugged the edge of the familiar waterway, he'd eventually hit the lake. And then disappear.

An angry roar, like a two-hundred pound bee, filled the air behind him. Trent ducked behind a massive cedar and looked out toward the source of the noise. Oh no. Trent punched the trunk of the tree in frustration and immediately regretted it. In the distance he saw the camp's blue and yellow drone, affectionately named Dory. It was outfitted with a GoPro camera and had been used to create some downright impressive promotional videos for the camp the past couple of summers. Now Dory was being forced to hunt down one of her own—a camper, running for his life.

Trent ducked down further and tried to strategize. As far as he remembered, the drone could only "see" what was directly beneath it. Still, it was moving fast and being piloted methodically back and forth. It was only a matter of time before Trent was spotted. And if Brian and Mike followed him out into the lake, he'd be a sitting duck. And then, in short order, a dead duck.

Reaching behind him Trent snatched an arrow from his pack and knocked it into the bowstring. He drew it back and took aim at poor Dory. He'd hit moving targets before, but never moving this fast. The first shot sailed right past, at least ten feet shy. Trent corrected, mentally. He needed to lead it more. The next shoot embedded itself in the drone's side, but had no effect on its flight. He waited for it to complete a pass over the hill and head back, now fifteen feet closer to his position, Trent that much closer to being discovered.

Trenton took a deep breath and let it out. He felt the target approaching, anticipating its arrival, and released another arrow. One of the drone's four rotors exploded from its mount, flitting down into the treetops beneath. The drone itself spun widely, out of control for a moment. It almost seemed like it might right itself when it too tipped and plummeted to the earth. Trent couldn't help but smile, smugly, although he did feel a pang of guilt for taking down Dory .

Pulling the bow over his torso, he returned to the river bank, right where the water met the mud. He sloshed quickly ahead, following the flow toward the lake, toward freedom. It led him left around one bend and then right around another. Then he came to a sudden halt, his feet stuck in the muck beneath. Trent looked on in disbelief. Why did this keep happening? For every little victory, he was met with another crashing defeat. This one in the form of a crashing waterfall.

Apparently, in his zeal, Trent had climbed quite a bit further than he intended, intersecting the river above the falls. Now that he was staring down at them, he clearly remembered hearing the growing white noise as he approached In his tunnel-vision, though, it hadn't registered just how fatal a flaw this was.

Slowly, carefully, Trent waded into the midst of the river and shuffled toward the edge. He peered down. It was a thirty-foot drop; at least that's what he'd always been told. The rocky outcropping on either side was too steep and too irregular to try climbing down. Should he just jump? It didn't look much higher than the high dive at the community college in Big Rapids and that had been downright fun. Then again, the water there had been eighteen feet deep. Looking down at the bubbling basin below, Trent had no idea how deep it was.

"Found ya!"

Trent turned to see Sean Tailor approaching along the west bank of the river, a nasty looking hunting knife in his hand. His face was full of cuts, bruises, and dirt, and he walked with a slight limp. Still the sight of him paralyzed Trent for a moment.

"Sean! I was afraid you were, like . . . ya know . . . "

"Dead?" He laughed. "You wish."

"No. I don't," Trent insisted. "I'm glad you're alright"

"Never give up," Sean said, as he leapt onto a large, jagged rock cresting the water. "Unless you're giving up giving up." He launched himself form the rock onto a tree root, branching out into the river like a lightning bolt. It was slippery and, for half a second, Trent thought he might go down, but he righted himself, knife still clenched in his hand, eyes searching for the next stone or root.

Trent looked back. He couldn't take even one more step in that direction without going over. He pulled the bow free and drew another arrow. "Back off!" he yelled, leveling the weapon at Sean.

The young man sneered. "What are you gonna do, Trent? Shoot me? You gonna put an arrow in me and watch me bleed out?" His eyes lighted on a clump of small rocks, just beneath the surface, another four feet closer.

Trent drew back the arrow and released. It found its mark and drew a shriek from Sean, who crumpled to the ground.

"You shot me!" he yelled, followed by a club mix of obscenity. The red vinyl bag slipped from his arm and dumped half its contents into the river, before falling in itself.

Trent drew another arrow, but could see immediately that he wouldn't need it. Sean was balled up, whimpering, his hands wrapped around the shaft of the arrow, which had gone right through his foot and buried itself in the tree root, pinning him in place. A thin rivulet of blood flowed through the water, toward Trent, pulling with it the buoyant contents of Sean's backpack.

My phone! Trent's eyes frantically searched the floating debris, coming at him quickly and all at once. There! A small object was reflecting light up at him and Trent slammed his hand down on it, remembering the arrow too late. Whatever it was, he'd punched right through it. Despair circled overhead as Trent forced his eyes to open, expecting the worst. But no, he hadn't killed his cellphone. Rather, he'd punctured a can of Blue Wolf Chewin' Tobacco—stabbed the cartoon wolf right between the eyes.

The red bag floated down, wrapping itself around Trent's ankles. It wasn't empty, meaning some hope of finding his phone remained. Trent grabbed up the bag just as Mike emerged from the trees, opposite Sean. He leveled his gun at Trent and shouted, "Drop it!" Glancing over at Sean he spat, "Stand up, Tailor. For crying out loud."

"I can't," Sean gritted. "My foot."

Mike rolled his eyes and addressed Trent once again. "I'm serious, Marsh. Dump the bow and walk toward me. Slowly. Or this is where you die."

CHAPTER TWENTY-TWO
"A PLAN, AND NOT A BAD ONE"

"Insane Faith is a willingness to jump off any cliff, trusting that the wind of the Spirit will blow you back to safety. And if it doesn't, trusting that God will send his angels to your aid, to gently set your feet on the ground below."

—*Insane Faith: A Guide to Extreme Christianity for the Truly Faithful* by Stephen Branding, page 88

Trent rose to his feet, his eyes fixed on the gun in Mike's hand.

"I'm serious, kid," Mike shouted. "Step away from the edge and give me what I asked for! I won't tell you again!"

Trent cranked his head back and looked down at the thirty-foot drop waiting behind him, should he jump or catch a bullet. It suddenly looked much higher. Down below, the crashing water continually filled the large round basin. Were he to take the leap—even if he somehow avoided breaking both legs—he'd bob around down there for a while in the churning waters, trying to make his way to where the basin emptied into the river—an easy target for Mike.

He glanced down at the familiar weapon in his hands. It felt strangely heavy and clumsy, as did the arrow—which made sense, as it was currently tipped with a small round tin of chewing tobacco. Between his submerged feet, the continual rivulet of blood rolled down from Sean's own impaled foot.

For just an instant, uninvited and inconvenient, an image of Zoe's face flashed into Trenton's mind and he wondered if she was safe. Then it was gone, self-interest crowding it out. He looked back at the waterfall one more time, swallowing hard. There was no denying it: that was his only route of escape.

"Don't even think about it!" Mike warned, still approaching along the edge of the river. He was ten yards away now, and closing. "I've got a hair-trigger here. You jump and I'll put three bullets in you before gravity takes hold."

A thick scream of pain filled the air as Sean wrenched the arrow from his foot. There was more blood in the water now and Sean was rolling back in the rushing river, wailing like a wounded dog.

"Sean?" Mike glanced over at the bleeding man. "What the—?" The muzzle of his gun dipped an inch or two.

It was a momentary distraction and, Trent was certain, the only chance he would get. In one motion, he knocked the arrow onto the string, drew it back, and released. It was by far the trickiest shot of his life, what with the bow weighed down by the contents of Sean's bag, still clenched in his hand, and the arrow by two ounces of what claimed to be "premium old-timey chew." Trent had aimed for the gun, while trying to compensate for the extra weight. The arrow went high, though, and connected with Mike's face, crushing his nose and blasting him off his feet.

Trent dropped the bow, took a hard step toward the falls, and launched himself off the ledge. At first, he saw only sky, then Sean's bright red drawstring bag above him, full of air like a tiny parachute. For half a second, he had a cartoonish vision of Winnie the Pooh floating lazily down from the honey tree with the aid of a simple umbrella. Then he felt the drop in his stomach and the cold slap of the water's surface against his body. He was sinking fast now, the force of the falls pushing him under.

The basin was deeper than he had dared hope and by the time Trent's feet touched bottom, his descent had slowed considerably. Down here, beneath the violently churning surface, the depths were relatively peaceful—clean water filled with dirty light. Off to his left, he could see a network of gnarled tree roots, emerging from the packed mud and stone. With three powerful kicks, Trent was there, shoving his foot beneath a root and locking his ankles. Six feet away, he saw the bow slowly sink to the bottom of the basin as well, useless here beneath the surface—something of a metaphor for his current predicament.

He had no plan beyond the moment and his short-sightedness almost brought a desperate laugh gurgling from his lips. But no, laughing would use precious oxygen and that was the one thing he didn't have.

Or did he? Clenched in his left hand, Sean's vinyl bag was trying to float away, still ballooned full of air. A small trail of tiny bubbles continually leaked from one corner, but other than that it seemed water-tight. Trent's first thought was that, if his phone was in there, it might still be dry. Then the real implication struck him and his surroundings seemed to brighten, transforming from watery grave to hidden sanctuary.

Looking up at the roiling water above, he realized how easy it would be for Mike and Sean to presume him dead, dragged beneath the relentless crash of the falls and pinned there. They would no doubt be pleased. No bullet holes in him, no difficult questions. The perfect situation, really. But how long would they wait before they assumed he'd drowned and moved on? Two minutes? Five? Ten? He glanced at his diving watch, which he'd never before taken diving.

The need for oxygen was catching up with him. No more room for procrastination. If this would work it had to work now. Careful not to disturb the precious bag, Trent slowly pulled an arrow from his own backpack. There were only four left that he could feel. The rest must have slipped out and faded away as he sank. No matter; he only needed one. With a surgeon's precision, he carefully punctured the bag's leaky corner. The trail of air bubbles thickened, picking up speed. Trent jerked the shaft back and forth, widening the opening, then released the arrow, which floated up toward the surface. He wrapped his mouth around the corner of the bag, drawing in a deep breath, before pinching it off.

The bag looked a little smaller than it had before, by maybe ten percent. Or maybe more. Trent tried to do the math. If there were ten breaths left, how long would that buy him down here, safely hidden away from the men who wanted to kill him? How long would each breath have to last him? His calculations were derailed by the sight of several trails cutting through the water, closer and closer to Trent's defenseless body. Bullets. The last one passed by so closely that he felt the fizz of the tiny bubbles against his arm.

Trent thanked God that neither his person nor his air supply had been perforated. Still, it was not looking good. His watch told him he'd been down here for less than a minute and already he needed more of his precious and very limited oxygen. He thought about forcing himself to wait longer, but the risk of blacking out and floating to the surface was too great. He struggled to plan, to strategize—how best to ration the air he had left?

What had Judith told him about conserving air underwater? She'd said you only use a fraction of the oxygen in each breath. If only he had one of those high-tech gadgets she'd been talking about. A *rebreather*. What he wouldn't give for a rebreather right now.

A smile spread across his face as he looked at the air-filled bag clenched in his hands and realized that it may not be high-tech, but if he used it right, it *was* a rebreather. Wrapping his lips around the punctured corner once again, he forced the air from his lungs back into the bag, watching it reinflate. He waited just a moment for the old air to mix with the new, knowing that was probably stupid, before taking another tug.

This breath he'd make last thirty seconds, he vowed. In the meantime, Trent ran through his inventory. Assuming he could get out of this giant death-bowl, he'd be in decent shape. Among his assets he counted the contents of Sean's bag, including a supply of breathable air, some energy bars for fuel, hopefully his phone. In addition, he had the bow and a few more arrows, and, with any luck, the fact that his enemies would assume him dead.

This time, he was able to wait thirty-eight seconds before exchanging the air in his lungs for another deep breath from the bag. The opposite corner was now leaking a thin trail of bubbles, but Trent was out of hands and could only sit by and watch it happen. How long could he keep this up? Eventually the air would get thinner; he'd get woozy. He had to get out of here before that happened.

Another exchange of breath, this one after only twenty-two seconds, but his head was still clear. He'd been under for three minutes now, and decided he'd wait three more and then then make his way out to the river. That should be enough time. At least he prayed it would. In the movies, the villain would indulge only the most cursory of looks off the bridge or cliff before jetting off to continue his evil plans, just as the hero bobbed to the surface, sucking precious air. In reality, how long would someone gaze down into the water, ready to pick off survivors? Surely not more than six minutes. With any luck, Mike was as impulsive and impatient as Sean and the two were already limping back toward camp, synchronizing their story of how exactly they'd lost a camper to the picturesque falls.

Whatever the case, Trent's plan hadn't changed. Follow the river through the old camp, down to the lake. *Ugh.* The thought of swimming across was far less appealing than it had been ten minutes ago. Still, what choice did he have? He had to summon help. This was far too big for him to handle on his own. It always had been. That's what he'd been trying to tell Judith all along.

Judith. How he wished she was here! He could almost see her at his side, sharing their limited oxygen reserves the way they'd shared everything since they were little kids. If Judith were here, three to one odds against him would be three to two. And surely Judith counted for more than one. Then again, who knew how many of Brian Green's conspirators were lurking in these woods?

The six minutes were up far more quickly than Trent would have liked. But he had to move. He was quite sure the grogginess setting in was not his imagination running wild. Besides, the bag was smaller now, consistently losing air one bubble at a time. Drawing another deep breath, Trent pushed off from the network of roots and swam toward the point where the water flowed out and the river resumed, slipping his left hand inside the bowstring as he went, like threading a needle.

He struggled to hug the bottom of the basin, holding the bag beneath his torso to block it from any eyes above. Once again, he thanked God he hadn't donned the bright orange T-shirt, which undoubtedly would have been visible, even through the white foam of the waterfall. Instead, his skin and clothes were all within a few shades of the sandstone beneath him. It took nearly a minute to find the mouth of the river, following the natural suction, during which Trent took two more breaths from his rapidly depleting air supply, no longer bothering to recycle it.

The current grabbed him and pulled his body out of the basin and downstream. This was the most exposed he had been since jumping from the falls, but soon he'd be hidden amongst thick trees. The river was narrower down here, and deeper. Still it was hard to remain underwater. His natural buoyancy, as well as the incidental flotation device in his hands, kept dragging him to the surface as he kicked along.

While navigating a wide bend, Trent pulled the bag to his lips for one last underwater breath. The air tasted like rubber and was immediately replaced by a surge of water, filling his mouth, leeching down his throat. Trent burst up through the surface of the river, hacking and gagging. To his surprise, he could stand easily here, the water only up to his waist.

Trenton took in his surroundings. While he could still hear the crash of the waterfall beyond the trees, he could not see it And the sound was more distant than he expected. The river pulled along with a significant current all around him and it was all Trent could do to keep upright. He was suddenly exhausted, the adrenaline wearing off. He staggered to the river's edge and dragged himself onto dry land, where he crawled six feet on hands and knees. A wave of nausea overtook him and he regurgitated funky water and bile.

The ground was warm and covered in a bed of leaves and moss. Falling onto his side, Trent closed his eyes. It was tempting to catch a nap, but inadvisable, he decided. For all he knew, Mike was right on his tail. He had this momentary advantage and he had to make the most of it. Suddenly remembering Sean's bag, he sat up against a tree trunk and dumped its contents on the ground before him. A hoodie, soaked through. Energy bars. Several motocross magazines, all wet. A cheap pair of headphones. No phone. Trent felt tears welling up. After all that, it *had* to be here.

Trent grabbed the balled-up sweatshirt and gave it a desperate shake. It remained stubbornly balled. There might have been something in there, though. Or it was just really heavy, waterlogged as it was. He snapped it again, sending a small object sailing away from him. He scrambled through the dirt and almost shouted for joy at the sight of it. His phone.

The screen glowed pure white. No image, no text, but there was clearly power. The fake stamped-steel texture of his so-called water-resistant phone case seemed to be taunting him. Trapped between the cover and the phone's own touch screen was a good deal of water like a specimen on a microscope slide. Had the phone been working, Trent would have gladly gone online and left a one-star review.

He pulled on the little plastic tabs to pop the case open. His first instinct was to rub the phone dry against his shirt. But, of course, all of his clothes were soaked. Ideally, he'd have a big Ziploc bag of uncooked rice at his disposal.

Scratch that. Ideally, he wouldn't even be here. He had to deal with what he had. The sun—he had that. The warm rays were finding their way down through the leaves above. Yes, the sun would be his ally here. He'd withdraw a ways from the river, open the phone, take out the battery, and leave it all to dry in the warm rays for a few minutes.

That was a plan, and not a bad one. And with growing distance from the situation, Trent was more sure than ever that Brian Green's men now considered him dealt with. There was plenty of hope here. And yet, this was cold comfort. He needed more than to escape. He needed his phone to work. He needed to call the police to come rescue him. But more than that, he needed to call his dad, to warn him.

And he needed to call Judith.

CHAPTER TWENTY-THREE
"A DIFFERENT PRAYER ALTOGETHER"

Trenton worked his way deeper into the woods. He could still barely hear the sound of the river babbling behind him. Better stop here to rest and let his phone dry. Actually, he'd better press ahead just a little more. He needed rays of warm sunlight and the canopy of the forest above him was letting very little in. Up ahead, though, it looked like the sea of trunks ended, giving way to a clearing.

As he passed out of the shadows and into the light, Trenton immediately recognized the place. He was back at Camp Makeout. He felt a surge of relief. He had hope that his phone might yet work, but even if it didn't, the lake was 100 yards away. The relief fermented into fatigue and, with it, doubt that he could make it to the other side, exhausted as he was. Sure, he'd done it before, but this was different.

Between the floor of his dad's study and the chair in the hospital room, he'd done little more than doze in and out over the past three nights. And of course today had been full of running, climbing, swimming, fighting. Trent was no star athlete and his body was as ragged as his mind. He needed to recharge, just sit in the sun next to his phone and rest. And he knew just the spot.

Tromping past the bare foundations of three small buildings and over fifty feet of new growth, he came upon the old outdoor chapel. It was a beautiful sight: old cedar-plank pews arranged around a rustic pulpit in front of a large rough-hewn cross, the whole thing in the protracted process of being reclaimed by the forest.

Trent plopped down on the back pew and arranged his phone and battery next to him in the warm orange-yellow light. His mind was swimming, or maybe treading water, in that uncharted area between sleep and awake, and he dared not lay down on the soft earth. He needed to rest, but he couldn't afford to fall asleep here; not while his pursuers were still somewhere nearby.

232

From back here Trent could barely make out the moss-covered inscription on the front of the pulpit: "John 6:29 - Come to me all who are weary and heavy-laden and I will give you rest.' He thought about Ed Piper, who had quoted this very verse a few days earlier in the hospital chapel. Ed who was now resting in peace until the sounding of the trumpet. The words themselves were comforting, at least in theory, but could anyone really find rest from his troubles in the midst of all this?

It wasn't just the lack of sleep or the physical punishment or even the men bent on killing him. No, it had been months since the Marsh men had stopped seeking peace and started chasing the ever-moving target of *enough*. The rest of Jesus' promise played over in Trenton's mind: "Take my yoke upon you and learn from me, for I am gentle and lowly in heart, and you will find rest for your souls. For my yoke is easy and my burden is light."

Through his mental and spiritual fog, Trenton's eyes drifted from the pulpit, down to the front row, where a man was sitting, his back to Trent, slumping under a heavy, unseen burden, as well as the weight of a long clerical robe, a bullet proof vest, and a hospital gown hanging open in the back. Trent knew he wasn't really there, of course—his over-fatigued mind playing tricks on him—but he was intrigued all the same. He couldn't see the man's face, but he knew—it was his dad.

The words inscribed on the podium wee glowing now, no longer fading away, and his dad was standing. For a moment, Trent thought he would walk up to the pulpit and begin to preach as he had every Sunday morning for the past few months. Instead, he fell to his knees, arms upraised to the heavens.

And then it happened. One by one, Trenton saw all the roles that had defined his father lifted away by unseen hands. Pastor came first, the heaviest of them all for Adam, and the most ill-fitting, lifted from his form, up into the air, where it simply disappeared. Then came student in a swirling of Greek verbs and dense footnotes. With these weights gone, his father looked like his old self, his back unhunched and his frame lighter, seemingly ten years younger.

Next was his calling as a peace officer. It came easily and hovered in the air above him, joined by the role of father. Trenton became aware of his own burdens being lifted one by one as well—the job he'd lost, the girl he'd lost, the treasure he hadn't found, his self-imposed responsibility to keep Jason out of Juvie and Judith from a life as a vigilante. They weren't gone per se, but they weren't his to bear anymore—at least not alone. He caught a glimpse of his father walking off into the woods, wearing the deep blue uniform and badge of the chief of police. His step was lighter.

And Trenton felt lighter too. A glance at his watch told him he'd been sitting here twenty minutes. It was time to move on. He could swim the lake if he needed to. Of that he was sure. First, though, he reassembled his phone. It was as dry as it would get, he decided, as the sun was now hidden behind a wall of dark clouds, rolling in from the west. As the device booted up, he shouldered Sean's bag and headed down toward the beach. No need to back-track to the river. From the old camp, Trent could make the trip blindfolded.

* * *

Adam Marsh pulled on his pants. He was checking out today. His doctor had pushed for another 48 hours of observation, but hadn't been seen since. In fact, it had been almost a full day since any medical personnel had spent more than ninety seconds in Adam's presence. After lunch, he'd taken a short nap and awakened feeling great, albeit increasingly restless about the piles of policework, classwork, and pastoral tasks building up in his absence.

He was certain: it was time to head back.

Of course, Adam had been taken here via ambulance and therefore had no car in the parking lot. Barton had been by a couple times, as had John Cash, but now that he needed a ride, they were nowhere to be found. Adam waited patiently until dinner arrived—greenish-gray Salisbury steak and cold mashed potatoes. Just then, Chet Bushman rang in to check on his pastor's condition and rehearse the health problems of each and every senior citizen in the congregation. Without thinking it through, Adam said, "I'm ready to head back, Chet, if you'll come and pick me up."

So, yeah. He was now looking forward to an hour in the car with Bushman. An hour of passive-aggressive questions and comments—the social equivalent of gray hospital steak. Oh well. The old grump should be here in about twenty minutes, meaning Adam would be home in an hour and a half. Real food. A real shower. A real bed. Real life.

He buttoned up his uniform shirt and checked his appearance in the mirror. But for his missing gun, he looked to be ready and fit for duty. The pain in the back of his skull came back whenever he stood, but it was manageable.

Adam stopped at the nurse's desk to announce his departure. He expected an argument, but received none—only a question about his copay. He rode the elevator down to the ground floor and stepped out into the cool night to wait for his ride.

"Hey, Chief," someone called form out in the parking lot. "Over here!"

Officer Cash was waving from beside his squad car. Great. If only he'd been just a little more patient, Adam could have avoided the Bushman Hour. Too late now. He began jogging over to the black and white, but slowed when his head complained. Upon reaching his employee, he shook his hand, heartily.

"They let you out?" Cash asked.

"Executive decision," Adam answered. "I need to get back."

"Hop in," Cash said, opening the back door of the squad car.

"Yeah, right."

"No, it'll be funny—chief being chauffeured around in the cage." The cop's voice was friendly, but his eyes had darkened.

Adam took a step back. His sixth sense was warning him of impending danger, although he could see none. "Thanks for the offer," he said, "but I've got a ride lined up." As he turned back toward the hospital, he stopped in his tracks. One row back from the squad car and a few spaces down—the red pickup, the same one, busted headlight cover and all. And a man was behind the wheel. The chief's hand went instinctively for his gun, but found only an empty holster. Then he felt the muzzle of Cash's pistol against his spine.

"Hand's behind your back, Chief," he said. "Don't make me do something we'll both regret."

Adam's heartrate kicked up and his head began to pound with each beat. He wanted to make a move, but he knew it was useless in his current state. He complied and felt the cuffs click shut around his wrists.

"Sorry chief. Your timing's bad. Shoulda stayed in the hospital. Watch your head on your way in." Cash's meaty hand brought a new explosion of pain.

As the car pulled out of the lot, lights flashing, Adam almost laughed out loud. Partly because of the absurdity of the situation, but mostly because the first clear thought to emerge when the pain subsided was about Chet Bushman and how angry he'd be when Adam was nowhere to be found.

* * *

The terrain began to decline and Trent could see the blue expanse of the lake in the breaks between the trees. He quickened his step and seemed to run face-first into the main flaw in his plan. Swimming the lake meant submerging himself and everything he had with him. Including his phone. His phone, which had been rebooting continually ever few seconds before he could dial a number or start a text. It still wasn't fully dry. He whispered a silent prayer for the stupid thing to work. Not for good, just for two minutes.

Then he cleared the tree line and looked down to the beach. A different prayer altogether had been answered. There, anchored maybe eight feet from shore, was a rather large jet boat, the kind that dragged campers around the lake on a long sled.

Trent had been at the controls of that boat more than once. And this one was almost identical. He splashed down into the water, threw the red bag and his phone on board, and launched himself over the side.

Scrambling to the ignition, he felt his hopes sink into the clear water below. There were no keys. Of course there weren't.

The echo of voices like waves crashing in from the wrong direction. Trent ducked down instinctively. The voices got louder. One of them was calling to the others, and they were answering. Three in all, he thought. And they were definitely getting closer to the boat. A small canvas cover was snapped over a storage compartment at the rear of the boat. Trent thought about squeezing in down there. Or he could go over the side and hope to swim far enough fast enough to avoid being spotted. No. The voices were too close for that. He'd rock the boat. He'd make a splash. Pulling just half a dozen snaps away, he squirmed down into the hold, which was bigger than he'd estimated, incredibly dark, and mostly empty. Reaching out, he was able to re-fasten two of the snaps before he hear the men boarding.

"I'm going to kill that kid," one of them was saying. Sean. "My foot is killing me."

"Your face doesn't look so hot either." That had to be Mike.

"Yeah, neither does yours."

"Tell me about it. Little twerp shot me. When we find him, you'll have to get in line behind me."

"Both of you, quiet." It was Brian Green. The two younger men immediately obeyed. No one said anything for a few seconds while Trent imagined Brian noticing something amiss about the canvas cover and pulling it back to investigate. Then the engine started up and they began to move through the water.

Trent powered up his phone and again tried to open a text, this one to Judith—#1 in his contact list. "Leaving camp by boat. Prisoner. Call for help." He hit the send button and a small status bar appeared for just a moment before the screen went black. The phone was dead.

Leaning his head back against a life jacket, Trenton saw a flash of lighting, even through the thick canvas, and heard a furious crash of thunder. The wind began to howl and the men above were shouting.

But Trent closed his eyes and felt himself drifting off to sleep, below deck in the midst of the storm.

TWENTY-FOUR
"OLD GROWTH"

"Believe me: power naps are your friend [SIC]. After a full day's work, you might be tempted to call it a day, to turn in early. Resist this temptation. A twenty-minute [power nap] can renew you entirely. People keep telling me to slow down, to sleep more. And I always answer the very same way: I can sleep when I'm dead."

—Transcript of "Q&A with Stephen Branding" at the "Breaking Barriers" Ministry Conference, June 6, 2015

Trent awoke gently, feeling the lazy sway of the boat. It took a minute to remember where he was and why. Another minute to realize that the boat's motor was no longer running. And that he was lying in several inches of water, down here in the boat's hold. He had no idea where he might be. His watch told him he'd been out for a little more than ninety minutes, which just happened to be how long it used to take to cut through Lake Michigan to Point Fournier in the Lower Peninsula. From there it was about a 45-minute drive to Clinch Rock.

But for all Trent knew, they were on the shores of Wisconsin or that Island off Ontario. Anything was possible. And what was the deal with the water. Thankfully, his phone was in his backpack, which he was hugging like a teddy bear, keeping it out of the water for now. But it was getting deeper—slowly, but steadily. He could hear voices above. No rain or wind. The storm must be past. What were they saying up there?

"I lost her, Mr. Green. I'm sorry." Sean.

"Well, find her, you pathetic plebe. She can't have gotten far in the past five minutes." Brian, no doubt about it.

"But, do we really. . . ya know. . . need her?"

Five seconds of silence and then, "Are you questioning me?"

"No, sir. I just thought—"

"No you didn't. And I'll overlook it this once. Find her and bring her to me. She's done enough damage and I want her stopped. Besides, we need that diary. If we have his little girlfriend, Marsh will come to us and lead us right to it."

"You got it. Sorry." The boat rocked as Sean jumped off into the water and splashed away.

A spike of anxiety pushed up through Trent's psyche. Zoe hadn't made it after all. Or at least they were on the verge of finding her. What were they willing to do to her? Should he just tell them where to find the diary? If it meant trading the treasure for Zoe's life, it was a no-brainer. But there was a quiet voice telling Trent that if he made himself known, they'd never let him go.

"You go with him," came another voice. This one was Mike Van Buren. That was odd. Was Mike calling the shots or was Brian?

The answer came in the form of another slosh back and forth while Brian de-boarded. Before sloshing away, he called up, "You'd better get off that boat. You're quickly taking on water."

"Yeah," Mike answered. "I'll gather everything and meet you at the truck."

Not for the first time in his life, Trent was feeling claustrophobic as the water level rose. Could he wait until Mike too had abandoned ship and then slip away into the woods? Would that even make sense with Sean and Brian combing those same woods looking for Zoe? The water was coming in faster now and the boat had tipped at least thirty degrees to his right. He could hear Mike moving around on the other side of the tarp.

Trent was still deciding when the tarp disappeared, replaced with a vicious wall of blinding sunlight. Before his eyes could fully adjust, Mike's head popped down into the storage space and his blackened eyes locked with Trenton's.

"What the—?"

The heel of Trent's shoe connected hard with Mike's already-broken nose, launching him back out onto the deck of the boat, clanging his skull against an aluminum handrail. Scrambling to his feet and clearing the opening, Trent swung his backpack hard, bringing it down against Mike's face. The young man looked dazed, his eyes struggling to focus, as his muscular arms bicycled, grasping for a hand hold by which to right himself on the tilting boat.

Then the gun came out, once again, from beneath the folds of fluorescent cotton. Desperately swinging the backpack like a Louisville Slugger, Trent knocked the gun from Mike's hand and out of the boat. It *blooped* down in to the lake and disappeared from sight. As he landed another blow with the admittedly light and limp pack, intent on keeping his opponent down, Trent noticed an orange life vest tangled up in its straps. A plan clicked together in his mind.

Trent balled up a fist and brought it down hard against Mike's jaw. It was only the second real punch he'd ever thrown and it was far more effective than the first. Mike went limp for a moment, which was all Trent needed to yank the life vest free, pull it backwards around Mike's neck, and tie the canvas straps, as tightly as he could, to the handrail. He used a nautical knot he'd learned in Boy Scouts, the name of which escaped him now. Giving the straps an extra pull, he noticed Mike's iPhone, sitting on the deck of the boat, under three inches of water. That too was good news.

Trent flinched as Mike, suddenly all fight again, grabbed wildly for his throat. But he was at an awkward angle now, secured to the boat and unable to really see. Trent sidestepped the desperate attack, re-hefted his backpack onto his shoulders, and jumped down into the thigh-deep water.

"Hey!" Mike shouted. "Down here!"

"Before you say another word," Trent all-but-whispered, from just a few inches behind the man's ear, "I can either push you and your sinking boat out into the deep blue, or I can pull you to shore. The choice is yours. So . . . can you be quiet?"

"I'm going to kill you," came Mike's response, calm and cool. "I'll find you and I'll kill you, And your girl too. Go ahead and run. In fact, I prefer it that way."

Trent was shocked and more than a little troubled at just how badly he wanted to push the boat out into the lake. The waves would prob-ably bring it back to shore before the handrail went under. He just wanted Mike to feel the same sense of dread and fear he'd inspired. Instead, Trent forced a laugh and said, "Tough words for a guy tied to a sinking ship." He grabbed a cleat near the bow and dragged the vessel to shore, giving it one last hard yank onto the wet sand of the beach.

"You may want to put a little ice on that nose," he quipped before sprinting off into the woods. It was supposed to be a carefree one-liner, like John McLane or Spiderman taunting their foes, but instead it sounded oddly conciliatory, serving only to remind Trent how unprepared he was for all of this. No sooner had he cleared the tree line, embedding himself in dense forest, than Mike began shouting from the top of his lungs.

"Sean! Brian! Down here!"

Trent went deeper as fast as his feet would carry him, which wasn't very fast. The mud was thick, as were the trees. And their trunks were enormous. Bigger than any he'd seen. For a moment, he stopped and looked around. He knew exactly where he was. He'd been here before. Lakeshore Pines—one of three preserves of old growth Michigan white pine that had somehow escaped the axes and saws hired by Benjamin Cassel and his competitors. This one was a state park, just off the lake shore and less than an hour's drive from his front door.

Trent felt a boost in his legs, like a video game power-up, and he began moving more quickly. The park was only about half an acre and a major highway passed right by. Sure, there was only one of him and three of his pursuers, but Mike was drawing them back to the beach, effectively giving Trent a head start. He'd make it to the highway, throw himself in front of a car, and demand a ride to the nearest state police outpost.

He thought of nothing but the ground beneath his feet for five minutes or more, until he came upon a small, groomed trail. There he cashed in a moment of progress while he weighed the pros and cons of following the trail out. The *yeas* carried the vote and Trent was able to more than double his speed along the muddy but level terrain.

For another ten minutes Trent slogged on, ignoring the burning in his calves. He was sure the highway was near. At least, he prayed it was. It dawned on him that Lakeshore Pines butted up against the Huron Manistee National Forest, which was literal a million acres of land, extending from the lake all the way to Clinch Rock. If he somehow wandered off into those woods, he could be lost for days.

But no, these trees were still old-growth, hundreds of years old, like the ones pictured in Brian Green's museum. He estimated the biggest ones to be four feet in diameter at eye level. He must still be in the state park. Trent's thoughts were interrupted by the sight of Chief Barton casually walking around a corner in full police uniform, and spotting Trenton.

At first, Trent felt a rush of relief. Judith had gotten his text after all and called the police. Trent ran as fast at the mud would allow and threw his arms around the chief's neck like a little kid.

"Mr. Barton—Chief Barton! Thank God! They're trying to—" All at once it hit him. Even if his text had gone through, how would Barton have found him? His cell phone was dead—untraceable—and his message had been light on details to say the least.

He dropped the embrace and took a step back, finding his miscalculation confirmed by the look in the man's eyes—the same look his son had given Trent, along with a beating, the week before.

"Turn around and place your hands behind your back," Barton said, his voice devoid of emotion. Trent complied and felt the hard metal cuffs closing around his wrists. Barton spun him back around and looked him right in the eye, hand on his gun.

"Where's the diary, kid?" he asked. "I don't want to hurt you. This can all go away if you just tell me."

Trent tried to form the words, but managed only a series of *uhhhs*.

"On your knees," Barton commanded, kicking Trent's feet out from under him. He pulled his sidearm and leveled it at Trent, whose eyes crossed as he looked right down the barrel of a gun for the second time today.

"It's at the church," he managed to croak. "In my dad's study. Behind some books."

"If you're lying to me . . . "

"I'm not! Why would I lie? I don't want to die!"

The chief bobbed his head side to side while maintaining eye contact, as if he could get just the right angle to see down into the teenager's brain. "You're telling the truth," he said. "Sorry about this kid. We can't have any witnesses. You understand." He pulled back the hammer of the pistol. "For what it's worth, your dad will be joining you soon."

Trent squeezed his eyes shut. "No! Please don't! Help!"

Barton scoffed. "Go out like a man, Marsh. Danny was right about you."

Trenton tried to pray, but his mind was locked up. Then he heard the unbelievably loud report of the gun and felt warm blood on his face. He thought about his mom and, for just a second, felt a sense of joy about seeing her again. But no, he was still on his knees in the mud.

Forcing his eyes open, Trent found himself looking up at Chief Barton, who was gawking silently down at his right hand, which looked more like a piece of raw roast beef. And then, in Trent's periphery: movement.

Bright blue.

From between two massive white pines emerged a woman with shiny blue hair, blue boots, a blue mask. White porcelain wings emerging from her arms. She was stepping quickly toward the peace officer, although Trent would later remember it in slow motion. She dropped another metal ball into her sling and closed the space between herself and the policeman with two more long strides, during which she swung the sling around three times, and slammed it down on Barton's head. He crumped to the ground.

But the Angelus wasn't done with him. She kicked his gun hard and it bounced twice off the surface of the mud, landing some fifteen feet away. She then reached down to Barton's belt and plucked up the Taser. He swiped at her awkwardly with his uninjured hand, trying twice to rise to his feet, but finding no traction.

The masked woman studied the device. "How does this thing—?" Two probes shot out the front and embedded themselves in Barton's back. A series of clicks brought spasms as he lurched back to the muddy ground. A few dozen brightly colored little paper circles flittered through the air.

"Oh look," she deadpanned. "Confetti. It's like a little party." She hit the Taser again, bringing another series of clicks and Barton grunted against the pain. Reaching again to his belt, she pulled off a retractable key holder. "Let's see. This looks like a handcuff key. She disappeared behind Trent for a moment and then he felt the metal grip loosen on his right wrist, followed by his left.

Trent stood, experimentally.

"You okay?" Judith asked, a hand on his shoulder. He pulled her in around the waist and pushed his mouth against hers, smudging the bright blue sparkly lipstick. The moment their lips touched, an insane thought popped up in his mind, fully formed: *it was worth it*. Getting chased, beaten, shot at, shipwrecked, it was all worth it because it led to this kiss. He brought his hand, shaking slightly, up to her cheek, softer than anything he'd ever felt, and renewed the kiss with even more passion.

Judith went along for a minute, then broke it off. A smile played at the corner of her lips. "So you're saying I need to make the suit more modest," she said.

Trenton laughed. He was feeling giddy. "How did you find me?"

"I just followed this guy." She pushed at Barton's inert form with the toe of her boot. "Thirty seconds after I got your text, he came roaring by, sirens blaring. I just hopped on my bike and followed." She leaned down and stuffed her slingshot, rolled up tightly, into her right boot. "You know, Barton, for a cop, you kind of suck at spotting a tail. Now, where's that phone?" She reached into his pants pocket and pulled out a wicked-looking folding knife. "I better take this," she said, moving on to the opposite pocket. "Ah yes, here we go. She slipped his phone into her other boot. "Trent, help me get this guy up."

They hoisted Barton's dead weight and carried him like a blackout drunk a good forty feet into the woods, until Judith deemed they'd come far enough.

"Okay," she said, "let's wrap his arms around this trunk here." The pine was enormous and the chief's arms barely made it around. "Perfect," Judith said, cuffing his wrist together. She flicked his ear. "I never figured you for a tree-hugger, Rich."

"What are you doing?" Barton slurred. He was coming around again. "You're assaulting a police officer. Think this through."

"We can't leave him like this," Trent said. "His hand is bleeding."

"Oh, boohoo. He was going to execute you, Trenton."

"But we're not like him, right?"

Judith thought for a moment and nodded, solemnly. "You're lucky I follow Jesus," she said to Barton. She pulled a roll of gauze from a blue pleather pouch on her belt and began wrapping it around the chief's hand. "That should hold you," she said, using Barton's own knife to cut the bandage off.

She held his phone up, looking for a signal. "You got a GPS on this thing? Let's find our coordinates here."

"Trent," Barton said. "Listen to me. If you ever want to see your girlfriend again—"

"Who, Zoe?" Trent forced another laugh, no more convincing than the last. "She's not my girlfriend; I know she's working for you."

"Okay," Judith said. "Got your location. I'll send help. Eventually."

Barton glared at her. "I swear, you'll regret this, you little—"

"Do I need to zap you again?" she asked, sort of sing-songy.

He spat in her face. Judith wiped it onto her glove and said, "That is super gross. I think it's time to shut you up." She looped the remainder of the gauze over the chief's face and pulled it into his mouth, wrapping it around tightly four times before she ran out and tied it off.

"Come on Trent," she said. "Let's get out of here."

Trent began to follow her toward the trail, then turned back. He reached under Barton's left arm and found the badge, which he ripped from his shirt. "You don't deserve to wear this," he said.

Barton tried to answer, but gagged against the gauze.

As they neared the trail, Trenton spotted Barton's gun. He grabbed it up and began wiping the mud off on his shorts. "Okay, now. Let's get out of here."

Judith stared at him. "Not with that thing."

"Are you kidding? There's more of these guys out there! We need the protection!"

She shook her head slowly, pityingly. "Superheroes don't use guns."

His response was almost a reflex. "There's no such thi—" The words caught up in his throat. That was one argument he'd lost decisively. Judith's lips screwed up into a little, crooked smile.

"Okay," Trent said. "No guns."

CHAPTER TWENTY-FIVE
"THE GIRLFRIEND SEAT"

Trent ejected the magazine from the 9mm and threw it off into the distance. He then removed the slide and chucked it in the opposite direction. The rest of the gun he tossed into a patch of poison ivy a few feet away.

"I still think this is stupid," he said. "Brian Green is out there, along with Sean Tailor and this other guy—Mike from camp. They all have guns."

"I know," Judith said. "I sunk their boat."

"You *what*?"

She beamed "All it took was one shot from the old sling."

"I was *on that boat*."

"Oh, you're fine." She waved a hand. "And you're welcome, by the way. We better get going. I stashed the Iron Horse about a quarter mile from here."

Trent followed her into the woods. A series of strategically snapped twigs and branches marked the way back. As he trudged, he found himself turning the same question over and over in his mind: was Zoe really in danger? When Brian had referred to Trent's "girlfriend," saying she "couldn't have gotten far," he was talking about the masked girl who had just sunk his boat, right? He meant Judith was his girlfriend. He felt the flapping of myriad butterfly wings where the ferret had once called home—wonky timing, but undeniable. His girlfriend. Jason had known. Even Brian had somehow known. Funny how Trent was the last one to the party.

But Barton had used the word too. "If you want to see your girlfriend alive . . . " And he must have meant Zoe. Was it just an idle threat? Or had they found her?

"So what I think we should do next," Judith said, jerking him back to the moment, "is work our way to the center of the conspiracy. Maybe start with Fischer. Then those two new cops. All the way up to the mayor if we have to." She planted a hand on a massive fallen log and swung her legs over, effortlessly.

"What? No," Trent said. "We know what they want. The diary. And now Barton knows where to find it. We need to get there first."

"The guy's chained to a tree, though."

"For now. But who's to say Sean or one of the others won't stumble upon him and cut him loose? We need to go grab the diary while we can. It's our only bargaining chip."

Judith stopped hiking and turned to face him. "Bargaining? What are you talking about?"

"They've got Zoe. We get the diary and offer to trade her for it."

Judith smiled. "I like where your head's at, Marsh. We lure them in with a trade and then we—"

"I'm serious. I know you don't like Zoe. I'm not crazy about her either. She lied to all of us. But she's a victim in this."

"I'm not so sure about that," Judith mumbled.

"Either way, we want leverage, right?"

"I guess."

"So we get the diary and we figure out why they want it so bad they're willing to kill me for it. Then we stash it somewhere and we've got the upper hand."

"What about your dad? Is it time to loop him in?"

Trent leaned against a smaller pine and scratched a bunch of new mosquito bites on his leg. If he was honest, he'd been avoiding this very question with his endless analyses of his little love triangle. "I'm not sure," he said. "He's in no condition to rush back into the fight. Then again, they're supposed to discharge him tomorrow. Barton's guys will probably be waiting for him. I wouldn't be surprised if he was counting on Barton driving him home."

"Oh, this will be over by then." Judith pulled her cell phone from a compartment on her belt. "I'll send him a text. Warn him to watch his back." Her thumbs flew over the screen for a few seconds before she snapped the phone back into its pouch. "Okay, my bike's just up here."

"Hold up," Trent said. "You know my dad. After all the crap we've pulled in the last few days, you really think he's going to just stay put because you told him to?" He decided not to add, *He thinks you're a few tacos short of a combo plate.*

Judith twisted her lips up in thought for a moment and Trent commanded the butterflies to stand down. "I've got it," she said, pulling Barton's phone from her boot. "Watch . . . your . . . back . . . Chief." she said as she typed. "We're coming for you." She punched SEND. "That should keep him on guard."

* * *

Chief Marsh's phone buzzed on Cash's desk, where it sat a few inches from the cop's feet. He was leaning back in his desk chair, watching an old Charles Bronson movie on an ancient tube TV. Behind him, Jessie Finn busied himself with paperwork at his own desk. The phone buzzed again.

"Can you please see who that is?" Adam asked. He'd been pacing in the holding cell for more than an hour without a peep.

"I'm not givin' you your phone," Cash grunted, eyes glued to the TV. "You think I'm stupid?"

"I didn't ask you to. I'm worried about my son, okay? Can you just tell me if the messages are from him? Jessie, help me out here."

Cash leaned forward and grabbed the device with his sausage fingers. "What's your unlock code?"

Adam hesitated.

"You want to hear the messages or not?"

"It's 1998," Jessie said. "Everyone knows that."

Adam gave the bars an angry shake. "Jessie, what are you doing?"

"Calm down, Marsh," Cash said, punching in the PIN. "Let's see here. We got a message from 'Judy Bug.' That the little brat who went all Barry Bonds on Fischer the other day?"

Adam collapsed onto the long wooden bench at the back of the cell and studied the floor.

"*Don't trust Barton,*" Cash read, "*he's not who you think he is.*" He raised his eyebrows. "*Or Tango and Cash.*" He laughed, amused. "Smart kid. A little late, though. Oh, and you got a message from the new chief too." He thumbed it open. "*Watch your back, Chief,*" he read. "*We're coming for—* What the heck? Barton didn't write this." He stood and approached the holding cell. "How'd this get kid get a hold of the chief's phone?"

Adam smirked, but said nothing. He thought of the many wrestling meets he'd gone to the year before and how each and every opponent had underestimated Judith, sauntering up all cocky before slinking away, humiliated, having been pinned by a girl.

"Forget it," Cash said. "I'll find her and ask her myself. You like that idea?"

"How long have you known me, Jessie?" Adam asked, quietly.

"Years," came the response.

"That's right. Years. Now let me out of here. That's an order."

Jessie dropped his pen, but didn't look in the chief's direction. "I've already got my orders, Adam. You're the one who tagged Barton as the next police chief. You're the one who told us to call him Chief Barton, treat him *as* chief, follow his orders. And now he claims to have evidence you killed Ed Piper. So it's on you when there's protocol I have to follow."

"But you know me, Jessie. Do you really believe I would kill someone?"

"Just following the chain of command," Jessie answered, resuming his paperwork. "Maybe if I'd been promoted to chief, I could come to my own conclusions."

* * *

Judith pulled the pile of brush away from her motorbike. "Hope you don't mind the girlfriend seat." She threw her leg over the bike. "Hop on."

"Judith, wait. . . " Trent knew this was laughably bad timing for what he had to say, but his urgency to get out of here was more than matched by his urgency to clear the air, for the two of them to ride back into Clinch Rock with nothing hanging between them.

"What?" she asked, her foot hovering over the kickstart.

"Just . . . I never really apologized about the other day. The stuff I said."

She narrowed her eyes. "No. You didn't."

"We", I'm sorr—"

"Later" She patted the seat behind her. "Let's go."

"Fine." Trent mounted the bike and wrapped his arms around her stomach.

"Just don't try to kiss me again until you've groveled a little." She looked back and winked at him, her glittery blue eye shadow sparking in the sunlight.

"Okay." Trent chuckled. "You look really pretty by the way."

Her response was lost in the roar of the engine. They off-roaded their way to the pavement, where Judith opened it up.

They made good time on the mostly deserted state highway, passing exactly six fellow motorists, all of whom gawked and stared at the Iron Horse and its riders. Trent couldn't blame them. They must have been a sight to behold. At one point, as they passed the trailer of a fuel transport, he caught their reflection. It was surreal: a masked woman with blue hair and her trusty sidekick packing a bow and arrows. For a minute, he envisioned the generic cartoon superhero from the cover of Judith's book flying alongside them.

A block from the church, Judith killed the engine and coasted up beneath a broad old weeping willow in the church's north lawn. The light was just starting to go orange in the west as they dismounted and peeked out from behind the thick foliage.

"Nobody parked out front," Trent observed. "I think we're clear."

"Give it another minute," Judith said. "Something doesn't feel right." As they waited, Trent heard only the thudding of his heart, timed perfectly with Judith's even breaths. She seemed just about satisfied that the coast was clear when a man came lumbering around the corner from the rear of the building. He moved slowly, deliberately, his eyes darting this way and that.

"Fischer," Judith hissed.

The big bald coach pulled back his Hawaiian shirt just long enough to adjust the .38 stuffed into his pants, undoubtedly digging into his flab.

Judith cracked her knuckles. "Time for a rematch," she said, under her breath. Trenton grabbed her gloved hand around the wrist and pulled her back.

"Let me go."

"Quick and quiet should be our goal," Trent said. "I've got my dad's master key."

"You don't think I can take him?" Judith demanded.

"I'm sure you can. But why take the chance? I mean, is this about revenge? Is that what we're doing here?"

Judith mulled this over, watching Fischer approach the front of the building. "No. You're right." She locked her eyes onto the coach as he disappeared around the corner. "I forgive you," she said, quietly; then, to Trent, "By the way, just so you know, the only reason I've got this much eye makeup on is to cover up the shiner he gave me. It was a dead giveaway."

"Right," Trent laughed. "Let's move." He led the way to the church's side entrance, slid his dad's key into the lock, and held the door like a gentleman. They stayed low through the dark halls to the pastor's study. Once inside, Trent double-checked that the door was locked before reaching back behind the row of thick tomes where he'd stashed the antique book. His hand searched for a few uncertain seconds before closing around the leather cover.

He unwrapped the cord from the ancient book and flipped through it, as if he could visually confirm that every word was still there.

"How much of that thing have you read?" Judith asked.

"Maybe a quarter of it, starting from the back."

She was peering over his shoulder as he absentmindedly turned the old pages. "Obviously, there's something specific Brian needs here," he said. "Some kind of giveaway for the location of the cash hoard. But it would take forever to read the whole thing."

"Let me see it."

Trent handed the book to her and leaned back against his dad's desk. "Let's think through it backwards," he said. "Brian and his guys don't know what we know: that the treasure is beneath the fire. If they did, they wouldn't be looking in the walls and under the floorboards."

"Right," Judith said, "because we're the only ones who've seen Cassel's letter from the desk."

"But they have other letters. Dozens of them. Maybe a hundred. I read quite a few myself." Trent closed his eyes and tried to remember the specifics. It was no use. He hadn't been trying to build the scaffolding of a vast mystery that morning; he'd just been looking for a fascinating paragraph or two to showcase in the display.

"Wait!" he shouted, in a whisper. "The display. We were looking for three letters to showcase, from Wolcott to Cassel. But there was already a letter mounted there *to Wolcott*—still in the envelope, but not sealed, sort of peeking out."

"Yeah, I got no idea what you're talking about," Judith said.

"They found all those letters up in the attic. Why would Cassel have a letter that he wrote to someone else?"

"Guess he never sent it."

"Exactly. Cassel said that, after he left town, he'd follow up with the final piece of the puzzle. What if he wrote a letter to Wolcott, but was killed before he had a chance to send it? And what better place to hide something like that than right out in the open, locked in between two thick sheets of safety glass, in the form of an insanely boring museum display? No one would give it a second look."

Judith shook her head. "If team Brian had a note that told them right where to find the treasure, they'd just go get it."

"It wouldn't say the exact location. The guy was paranoid, remember? He was dropping a series of hints. The first one was 'Beneath the fire.' The final one was supposed to come 'by post, within a week.' It never got there. And who knows how many more hints are in there?" He pointed at the diary in her hands.

Judith pulled her long blue costume gloves back up to her elbows. "I guess we need to have a look at that letter. I don't suppose Zoe gave you a key to her place."

"No," Trent said. "But I've got something better."

* * *

They first scoped out the Cassel House, ditching the bike down the road and picking their way through the wooded property around the mansion. The place was dark inside, save for one light in the entryway. But out front, in the circle drive, Sean Tailor sat on the hood of his 1987 Firebird, a rifle in his hands.

"What happened to that guy?" Judith asked.

"I rode him down the Devil's Tail like a sled and then I shot him in the foot with an arrow."

Judith smiled. "I changed my mind; you can be my sidekick."

"Hard pass."

Sean eased himself off the car and began a pained, limping circuit of the house.

"This should be pretty easy," Trent breathed. "We stash your bike in my garage, come up from the tunnel, grab the letter, and disappear back to my place."

"I love it," Judith said. "But keep your guard up." They walked her bike the long way around toward Trent's house, not wanting to attract any more attention than necessary. The sun was just dipping below the horizon and the streetlights had not yet come on, allowing them to glide unnoticed through the twilight.

"You really think she's innocent in all this?" Judith asked as they turned onto Trenton's street.

"Huh? Who's innocent?"

"Zoe, duh."

Trent thought for a moment. "Not completely. But definitely in over her head. Anyway, superheroes have to rescue everyone, right? Not just people who are completely innocent."

Judith came to a stop, two houses short of the parsonage. "Whose car is that," she asked, "on the street?" A ridiculously detailed purple Escalade was parked right in front of the Marsh house, bearing the vanity plate SLVDUP.

"That's Connor What's-his-name. He owns the tattoo and piercing place by the old grain elevator. You've seen him—big, mean looking dude, all that hardware in his face."

All at once, Trent could see the four men walking away from the Home Store, but from the front, falling into place like the solution to a higher math problem, previously thought unsolvable. He saw them left-to-right: Officer Cash, Connor the Tattoo Guy, Coach Fischer, and Sean Tailor. Their combined strength overwhelmed him. He and Judith may have had some lucky breaks combined with some strategic victories, but enough thick-necked brutes would cancel that out. "What do you want to do?" he asked.

Judith dumped her bike against some hedges and creeped up into Trent's neighbor's yard, ducking down behind a yew bush. "I think he's up on your porch. Maybe. If I can spot him, I think I can knock him out." She retrieved the sling from her boot.

"Are nuts? You could kill him. And even if you don't, you could shoot his eye out."

"Really? I'll 'shoot his eye out?'"

"You know what I mean."

"Well, I'm open to suggestions," she said.

"Look, all we need is someone to draw him away from the house for a minute so we can slip in the back and go down to my room. Someone who would have a good reason to be there, wouldn't raise suspicion."

"No," Judith said. "Tell me you're not thinking what I think you're thinking."

"Yeah," Trenton said. "We need Jason."

CHAPTER TWENTY-SIX
"AMATEUR VIGILANTE SHENANIGANS"

Why can't we just call him?" Judith asked. They were crouched behind the filter of the Dufresne family's above-ground swimming pool, which was loudly chugging away, although Trent wondered to what end, as the pool's water always seemed to maintain an off-putting green tinge.

"He's grounded from his phone," Trent explained. "We kind of took his mom's van without permission—it's a whole thing. Anyway, they don't have a landline anymore, so we do it this way." He cocked back his arm and chucked a pebble at Jason's second-story bedroom window—the only light coming from the rear of the house. The pebble went low. He tried again, this time losing track of the projectile in the darkness, mid-flight.

"I can hit the window," Judith said.

"No sling. You'll shatter it."

"I can throw it."

"Yeah, right," Trent said. "You throw like—"

"You say like a girl and you'll regret it."

"No, that's not it. Not *enough* like a girl. You're like one of those crazy escaped service bots on *Wall-E*. Just give me a second. I've got this."

He chucked another pebble and heard the telltale sound of stone-on-glass. A moment later, Jason's face appeared in the window. Trent waved.

Throwing the window wide, Jason shouted, "T! Oh, thank God, man. I'm losing my mind over here. Come on up! I've been playing *Car Jack 8*."

"Shhhh! Your parents." Trent stage-whispered.

"It's their anniversary," he called. "So that's gross. They're out, like, wining and dining and dancing and stuff. I don't want to think about it. You wanna go for a swim? You still have a suit here."

"No thanks, man. We actually need your help with something. At my place."

"Who's *we*?"

"Me and Judith."

Jason nodded, thoughtfully, visibly weighing his options, then announced, "We can take my mom's van."

At Trent's instruction, Jason removed the seats from the minivan and pulled it around the corner, where Trent and Judith quickly loaded first the Iron Horse and then themselves into the back, before the whole party headed up to Charles Webis Park, a dilapidated municipal lot a couple miles past Trent's house, whose only park-like feature was a tetherball post with a chain but no ball.

"I hate this place," Jason said, looking out the window, shiftily. "You know a guy hung himself from that pole, right? During the seventies. People *see stuff* out here."

"That's an urban legend," Trent said.

"No it's not. His great-nephew was on my flag football team." Jason peered off into the darkness. "Seriously, why do we have to talk here?"

Judith clicked on the dome light in the back. "Because I know it scares you and I find that amusing," she said.

"Well, that's just rude." Jason crawled over the console to join them. "I mean, it's no laughing matter when—" He gaped at Judith, seeing her clearly for the first time. "What the heck are you supposed to—?"

"It's a long story," Trent interrupted. "For another time."

Judith nodded her agreement. "Just know that we're letting you in to the inner circle," she said. "It's a privilege. You tell anyone about this and I'll kill you."

"Yeah, totally," Jason agreed, his eyes darting down to Judith's boots and back up to the wig. "So what's this secret mission? We gonna egg Fischer's house? Nut-nock the place? Pig whistle him? Slip the fish? Oh wait, I got it! We could sneak into the school and upper-deck his office bathroom. Let it stew till Wednesday. Can you imagine?" He grinned from Trent to Judith and back. "Oh man, it feels so good to have human contact again. It's been too long."

"You've been grounded for like three days," Trent said.

"Ugh, I know. And I've felt every minute."

"Look, it's really quite simple," Judith explained. "There's a guy guarding Trent's house. He's looking for Trent and possibly Chief Marsh. We need you to approach him and—" She sighed. "Is there a problem, Jason?"

"What? What do you mean?"

"You keep looking at me like that."

Jason shrugged. "I'm sorry, it's just . . . I never noticed before."

"Noticed what?"

"You're *so hot!*"

Judith threw a sideline glance at Trenton. "Control your boy. Or I will."

Trent chuckled. "You don't want that, man. Trust me."

"Dude, I'm gonna be honest: I don't know *what* I want right now."

"Yeah, this was a bad idea," Judith said.

"No, wait," Jason practically shouted. "I'm good. I'm cool. I can't go back home. I will literally lose my mind. What do you want me to do to this guy at Trent's place? Knock him out? Rufie him?" He pointed in the direction of Trent's borrowed bow, hanging from the handlebars of the motorbike. "Poison tipped arrow maybe?"

"Just talk to him," Trent said.

"Just . . . talk to him."

"Yeah. Ask if I'm home. When I'll be back. That kind of stuff. Keep him busy while we slip into the back door to the basement."

"I can do that." He grinned. "And what are you two guys doing?"

"We're going through a secret tunnel to Zoe's house to find a clue that will lead us to Benjamin Cassel's treasure."

"If that's a euphemism," Jason said, "I've never heard of it."

"Shut up, Jason."

* * *

Trent and Judith bailed out a block from the parsonage and once again approached along the hedge of his neighbor's house. Jason pulled up the driveway slowly, loud rap music blaring from the open windows of the van. He pulled right up to the garage door, the van's bumper just about kissing it, killed the engine, and hopped out.

"This might actually work," Judith whispered. "I never thought Jason would actually serve a purpose."

"He's a good guy," Trent said.

"No, he's not."

"Yeah. I know."

Jason was three steps out from the van when Connor Dupree came lumbering down from the porch to meet him. He wore a tight wifebeater, revealing thick arms, torso, and neck, all covered with ink. Skulls, Harleys, tribal designs. On his sternum, spilling up onto his throat, a mermaid somehow straddled a Detroit Lions logo.

"Can I help you with somethin'?" he asked.

"I'm looking for Trent," Jason said. "Trenton Marsh. He lives here."

"Yeah, he's not home. I'll tell him you stopped by."

In the bushes, Trenton whispered, "Okay, let's go."

"Not yet," Judith cautioned.

"Do you even know who I am?" Jason asked.

"Am I supposed to?" The big guy cracked his neck, the sound of which actually echoed off the garage.

"No. But, I mean, how can you tell him I stopped by if you don't know who I am?"

"So who are you?"

"You know what? I'll just leave him a note," Jason said, making for the front door.

"Just one more second," Judith breathed.

"Whoa!" They heard Jason shout. "Hands off, there, Tiny. I don't know you. What are you even doing here?"

"Wait," Trent said, just as Judith seemed about to take off. "It's no good. We've got to abort."

"Why?"

"I just remembered: there's a motion-activated security light on the back of the house. It's super-bright. You can see it from the road. Cats and coyotes keep setting it off."

"That thing's not even real!" Jason protested from the front of the house. "You're telling me *you're* a cop? Trent's dad hired *you*? I mean, no offense, but you look like an ad for Hepatitis."

"We've got to get him out of there," Trent said. "That guy's gonna kill him"

"No. This is our one shot. Where's the bulb?"

"It's the flood light, right up under the gutter. *Why?*"

She pulled the sling from her boot and another small metal ball from the belt compartment.

"It's too risky," Trent protested. "If you miss, you'll trigger the light."

"I don't miss," she said.

"Well do you at least know when he'll be home?" Jason asked. He was practically shouting.

Judith began swinging the sling in tight circles, creating a dull roar as it cut through the air, drowning out the growl of Connor's reply.

"Yeah, fine," Jason was saying. "But let me ask you one more thing: does all that metal stuff in your face hurt? 'Cause it looks rough. Like you should be going, *Ahhhhhhhhhhh!* like, all the time."

The light bulb disintegrated with a tinkle of glass.

"Ow!" Jason cried. "Let go of me. My dad's a lawyer, you know!"

Judith dropped another steel ball into the sling and took a step toward the front yard, her face carved out of stone.

"Sheesh! I'm leaving!" Jason announced. A moment later, they heard the van door, the ignition, and the rap music, fading off into the night.

Trent silently unlocked the door and the two of them slipped down into his bedroom. They counted to three and hoisted the slab of pine away from the opening. For the first time, Judith peered down the inky black tunnel, disappearing into forever. She smiled.

"No, there's nothing weird going on in Clinch Rock," she said.

"Okay."

"You're just being paranoid, Judith."

"Yeah, point made. Loud and clear."

"Or maybe," she said, pulling a small, high-powered flashlight from her belt and clicking it on, "maybe you're all just really gullible."

"If you don't shut up, I'm gonna kiss you again."

"Don't you dare." She began moving down the tunnel, sling in hand.

At the mouth of the passage, Trenton noticed a large box marked "Archery," which he'd pulled out a week earlier in anticipation of a morning shoot with his dad. Dumping the camp's bow to the floor, he retrieved his own compound bow and a fistful of additional arrows, then rushed to catch up with Judith.

The tunnel seemed twice as long as it had the first time he traversed it, giving Trent plenty of time to second-guess all of this. Sure, Judith had been right about a few things, but that didn't mean their best course of action was amateur vigilante shenanigans. They could still call the sheriff's office. Or the state police. Or have Jason drive them to the hospital and lay it all out for Dad. Before he could reach a conclusion, though, Judith slowed to a stop in front of him. Her light shone on a rough-cut staircase, which led up to a plaster wall, a large chunk of which had been smashed away, revealing the backside of a tall bookshelf.

"You ready for this?" Judith asked, excitement in her eyes.

"Not a bit."

She flashed her slightly crooked teeth and said, "Just stay close to me."

They quietly pushed the bookshelf away from the opening and crawled into the dark house, staying low.

"Where's the letter?" Judith asked.

"Up here, in the parlor."

Judith scoffed. "Of course Zoe has a *parlor*."

Trent led the way to the six-foot display, now containing three open pages from letters to Cassel and the envelope bearing the name, "Rev. Jeremiah Wolcott."

"Philips or standard screws?" Judith asked, handing over the flashlight and digging through a pouch on her belt.

Trent examined the exhibit. "Neither. It's one of those star-shaped things."

She quit digging. "Crud. I guess we're going to have to break the glass."

"That might not be so easy. It's crazy-thick."

"I got it," she said. "Step back." Before Trent could object, she spun her sling three times over and released. The exhibit disintegrated and a shower of broken glass sloughed to the ground, releasing the antique letters from its grip.

"That was so loud," Trent said, sifting gingerly through the shards of glass.

"Yeah," Judith agreed. "Grab the letter. And be careful." She peeked out the front window. "Tailor's still sitting on his car. I think we're good. So what's it say?"

* * *

Sean had just finished another circuit of the house and pulled himself, with great difficulty, back onto the hood of his Firebird when he heard the *pop* from inside. Almost sounded like a small caliber gunshot. He looked at the .22 rifle in his hands and spat. Stupid Marsh had knocked his favorite gun off into the woods up at the camp. And stupid Mike wouldn't let him take ten minutes to find it. And now here he was with this glorified pea shooter.

The thought of Trenton Marsh made his foot ache all the more. It was getting worse with each passing hour, screaming with every step. Sean pulled his phone out and scrolled down to Officer Tyrell's number. If he was possibly going up against an armed intruder with nothing but a .22 and a gimpy foot, best to have some backup.

* * *

"You sure you don't want to head back to my place and read it?" Trent asked. "Or even wait until we're safe in Jason's van?"

"What if the treasure's here in the mansion? I don't want to have to come back here."

"Good point." Trent unfolded the letter, which filled half the page with penmanship that was much easier to decipher than Wolcott's.

He read:

Brother Wolcott, my friend and my guide, who led me from the darkness of avarice to the light of the Gospel,

Grace and peace to you. By the time you receive this letter, you will have laid eyes on me for the last time. I am leaving all of this behind in favor of a simple life, taking up my cross each morning and laying down my head each night with the knowledge that I have served my fellow man to the glory of my God. Please do not take offense that I leave no forwarding address. I think it best that no one from my old life should find me, not even you, though I hope to write to you again in due course.

The reason for this letter is twofold: first, to inform you of my decision to deed my house and everything in it to my book keeper and good friend Heinrich Wellick. He has been loyal to me for years and it would not be right to do away with my entire fortune and leave him nothing. But please, Jeremiah, know that, if Wellick is my Eleazar, you are my Isaac.

And this brings me to the primary design of this correspondence—to direct you to the moneys I have left for the benefit of the church and the men and women I have long exploited. Repentance requires not only a change of heart, but a change in direction. Restitution. And having lived by the passions of the flesh for so long, I am eager to be free of the fortune I wasted my life in amassing. If you will use it to minister to the lumbermen, cooks, log drivers, and laborers who

served in my camps and mines as well as their wives and children,
I will be forever in your debt.

I pray you still recall the hint I laid for you two weeks ago as
to the situation of this cache of worldly mammon—that detail
awaiting a locale. I will not repeat it here, out of fear that this
letter should fall into the hands of a weaker soul. Bearing in
mind the former clue, you will find what I have left you in the
place where we first met. I confess that on that day, I thought of
you as a superstitious fool, but now I see that you . . .

"Blah blah blah . . . *saved my soul* . . . blah blah. That's it, Judith! It's
beneath the fire, wherever Wolcott and Cassel first met!"

"So where's that?"

"No idea. But obviously that's why they want the diary so bad. For
sure, Wolcott would make a note of meeting one of the richest, most
powerful men in the state!"

Judith frowned. "You've been working on that thing for a week and
you've barely scratched the surface.

"Yeah, but now we can narrow it down." Trent folded the letter
into the diary, which he slipped into the waistband of his shorts, at the
small of his back, before getting down on his knees and sifting through
the broken glass, each piece silkscreened with a bit of text or photo like
the world's most dangerous jigsaw puzzle.

"What are you doing?" Judith asked.

"Before you broke the display into a billion little shards, it used to
say when they met. I think it was February. I don't know what
year. *Ow!* Dang it!" Trent felt the blood trickling down his knee,
pooling amongst the broken glass. "I'll be right back," he said, rising to
his feet and hobbling toward the kitchen. "You keep looking.
Carefully."

At the kitchen sink, he wet a dish towel and used it to wipe away
the blood and tiny grains of glass embedded in the wound.

"You okay?" Judith called from the front of the house, careful to
keep her voice down. Then, without waiting for an answer, she

announced. "I found one that says 'r-l-y F-e-b-r.' That's got to be early February. Just need a year."

Trent put pressure on the cut for a few more seconds and then had a look at. It was still bleeding a bit, but it wasn't deep. He rifled quietly through some drawers, looking for a First Aid kit or box of Band-Aids. Instead, he came upon a roll of duct tape, which he used to affix a damp sock from his backpack onto his knee.

Judith appeared in the doorway, a grin on her face. "Got it," she said. "Early February 1893."

As he reached for the diary, Trent smiled. But then he heard Sean Tailor's voice from behind Judith, saying, "Like a statue, Blue. Hands where I can see 'em."

* * *

"I'm not gonna tell you again," Officer Cash warned. "Shut. Up."

"I'm talking to Jessie," Adam said, "who happens to outrank you, by the way. As do I." Cash said nothing, just turned up the volume on the old TV. "Come on, Jessie," the chief continued, "There's been no due process here. Did a magistrate actually issue an arrest warrant? If so, when? I haven't been given a phone call. No one has notified my son what's going on. There's been zero talk of a lawyer or even what I'm being charged with. Has anyone even called Cooper's office? Think about it, Jessie." He could tell Jessie was thinking about it.

"Isn't it obvious what they were doing here?" he continued. "They bought into Brian Green's old buried treasure schtick and started tearing apart historical buildings, looking for the loot. And once a building became a crime scene, they could take their time, methodically searching the place without drawing suspicion. They even brought in that drain camera thing. And where was I? At the church. At class. I dropped the ball here. And I'm sorry. But that shouldn't mean they get away with it."

Jessie finally met Adam's gaze. "Cash is right," he said. "The prisoner is not to speak unless spoken to."

* * *

Judith gestured with her eyes for Trent to leave the kitchen out the other door. Clearly, the plan was to double back around, flank Sean. He nodded and grabbed up his backpack as Judith turned to face their enemy.

"What do you want?" she said.

Slipping out through the old servant's entrance, he heard Sean say, "Oh it's you. Tyrell's gonna be happy to get his hands on you, honey. That was his boat, you sunk."

Trent came out through Brian's office, silently moving into the parlor, praying he wouldn't hit a squeaky board. There: his bow, propped up in the corner. He plucked it up and knocked an arrow onto the string.

"Man, what happened to you?" Judith asked. "You look terrible."

"Don't worry about me," Sean said. "I never give up. Unless I'm giving up giving up."

"Wait," Judith said, "I know you. You're that guy in his twenties that still comes to high school parties. Right?"

"Just shut your mouth. You'll be in the back of a squad car in ten minutes."

Trent entered the dining room and found himself looking at Sean's back. He felt the breath sucked from his lungs, like he was jumping over the falls again. Sean had a cell phone in one hand, making a call, and a rifle in the other, pointed at Judith.

Trent lowered the bow. They were beat here. No way would he risk Judith getting shot. This whole thing had gone way too far, and now it was over.

"Oh, hi, Trent," Judith said, waving at him. Sean wheeled and Judith lunged at him, stomping on his injured foot.

Sean shrieked and dropped the gun to the floor. Judith went for it, but instead caught a backhand from Sean, spinning her 180 degrees. He fell to the floor, reaching for the gun.

Trent drew back the arrow and let it fly, putting it right through the faded, blurred crown in Sean's CFB tattoo. The young man ground his teeth, cursing and grunting at the shaft of the arrow protruding from his forearm. Trent popped another arrow into place and leveled the bow at Sean.

"Next one goes a little closer to home," he said. "Believe me?" Sean nodded. "Good. Now back away from the gun."

Sean scooted back on his butt. "You shot me," he said. "Twice!"

Trent shrugged. "You hit my girlfriend. You're lucky I didn't put it straight through. I could have."

Judith was back on her feet. "I'd say you hit like a girl," she said with a smirk, "But that would be an insult to girls everywhere, wouldn't it?" She reached into a compartment in her belt and pulled out a heavy-duty, bright-blue zip tie. "I'm afraid I'm going to have to restrain you," she said.

Two minutes later, Sean secured to a radiator and his gun in less than working order, they were rushing back down the tunnel, toward the parsonage.

Judith was silent until the end was in sight—the yellow glow of Trent's bedroom off in the distance. "I can't believe you said that," she muttered.

"Said what?"

"You hit my girlfriend."

Trent came to a stop. "Oh. Um. Sorry, I didn't mean to assume anything. I just thought—"

"Do you not know how secret identities work?" she demanded.

"Seriously? You don't think they can put it together?"

"Well, they can *now*."

A dozen objections formed in Trent's mind, but he ignored them all. "Sorry," he said. "Won't happen again."

"Good."

They covered the rest of the tunnel in a matter of seconds and spilled out into the bedroom. They were three steps in when they saw Officer Tyrell, sitting casually on the end of Trent's bed, gun drawn.

"Drop the bow, Marsh," he said, standing up and nearly hitting his head on the drop ceiling. "You two brats are coming with me."

CHAPTER TWENTY-SEVEN
"QUICKER THAN CIGARETTES"

Trent and Judith were up against the wall—literally—palms flat against it at Tyrell's orders.

"Feet shoulder width apart!" he barked, coming up behind Trent, gun looming just out of sight. Trenton felt a jerk to his backpack and then heard the clatter of a dozen arrows tossed across the room, rolling along the floor. "You know we got your old man in lockup?" he said. "Try anything dumb and he's gonna hang himself right in the cell." He laughed. "Silly me, I forgot to take his belt when I booked him."

Connor appeared in the doorway, apparently winded from descending the stairs. "You called?"

"Yeah," the cop said. "Draw your piece and stand by while I disarm these delinquents. Not taking any chances this time."

"You got it." The tattoo artist pulled out a fat revolver with a comically long barrel.

Tyrell stepped over to Judith, leering menacingly. "So you're the one who destroyed my boat," he said. "That's gonna cost you."

"You should have heard it," Judith deadpanned. "It begged for its life, right up until it went under. Then it was just like, *Glub glub glub.*"

"Real funny." He holstered his weapon. "Take off those gloves. One at a time."

Judith rolled her eyes. *"One at a time?* As opposed to . . . ?" She removed the long silky gloves and flung them in Tyrell's face.

"Now the belt," he said. "Drop it to the floor and kick it over to me." She complied.

"Good. Now grab wall again. I'm going to pat you down."

"You're not laying a finger on me," Judith declared. "I know my rights. I demand a female officer search me."

"You think I won't call one? We got two lady cops." He picked up the elaborate belt and turned it over twice.

Judith shrugged. "So get one of them over here."

"I give the orders," he said, popping open the widest compartment on her belt and pulling out her phone, which he examined for a moment and then pocketed. From the next pouch, he withdrew a large folding knife. He tapped it against her shoulder and said, "Carrying a concealed weapon. You're gonna be popular in juvie. I understand they're real nice to weirdos down there."

"That's not mine," Judith said.

"Doesn't matter."

"Oh, I think it does. Look at the initials."

"What the heck?" Tyrell grabbed her by the wig and rapped the knife—still closed—against her forehead. "This is Chief Barton's knife. Where'd you get it?"

She smiled. "You've got our chief. We've got yours. How about a trade?"

"Yeah, right. Look at you," Tyrell said. "You've lost touch with reality. What are you supposed to be?"

"I'm supposed to be the one who knows where we locked up Rich Barton. Haven't heard from him in a while, have you?"

Tyrell was silent for a moment, mulling it over. "I don't care," he said. "The chief's a big boy. He can handle himself." Then he pulled a flip phone from his back pocket and dialed a number.

"Who you calling?" she asked.

"Shut your mouth." He waited a few rings, cursed, and hung up. "Where is he?" he demanded.

"He's chained to a tree in the national forest!" Trent blurted. "Not too far from the lakeshore. I can show you!"

Judith glared at him. "What are you doing?"

"They've got my dad!"

Tyrell was dialing again. He pressed the phone to his ear and said, "John. It's me. You heard from Barton lately?" His brow slowly descended as he listened. "*Judy Bug*, you say? Mm hmmm. I've got her in custody. At Marsh's house. She's got the chief's pocket knife on her. Says they chained him to a tree." He listened again for a few seconds and answered, "Yeah, Tailor's not picking up either."

Judith laughed. "It's six o'clock. Do you know where your henchmen are?"

Without breaking off the conversation, Tyrell drove a fist into Judith's kidney. She went down to one knee, but didn't cry out.

Trent tried to shout in protest, but he was paralyzed. The hand canon pointed in his direction, the news that his dad was locked up, the fatigue he was feeling after 24 hours of running and fighting—they had him feeling docile, almost relieved to be caught. Tears were trying to find their way out the corners of his eyes but couldn't quite seemed to make it.

"I'll call you back," Tyrell said and flipped his phone shut.

Judith rose to her feet. "My grandpa used to have that phone," she said. "But then he got a Blackberry when I was like five."

"Where's Sean Tailor?" the cop asked.

Judith just smirked.

"What about you, lover boy? I got you at gunpoint in this basement. No bodycam. No witnesses but this guy," he poked a thumb at Connor, "and he's not about to blow any whistles. I've got both your little girlfriends and dear old dad. You really wanna play games with me? I got a game. It's called 'Guess whose finger this used to be.' You want I should tell you the rules?"

Trent finally found his voice again. "He's tied to a radiator at the Cassel House."

"Check it out," Tyrell said to Connor.

"You got it." The tattooist headed for the door.

"Take the tunnel, meat head."

"Oh," Connor said. "Right." Gun in hand, he disappeared into the darkness of the passageway.

"Now give me that backpack, kid," Tyrell instructed, again drawing his sidearm. Trent sloughed it off and kicked it back to him.

"Is the book in here?" Tyrell asked, snatching it up, unzipping pockets.

"No."

"So where is it?"

Judith caught Trent's eye and gave her head a little shake. She wanted to keep their leverage. Maybe she was right. If they gave up everything, they became loose ends—Dad, Judith, Zoe. All of them.

Tyrell turned the backpack upside down and shook the contents to the floor, pushing through them with the toe of his shoe.

"Don't want to talk?" he asked. "It's somewhere here in your room, isn't it? I used to keep cigarettes and girly magazine behind a loose panel in my closet when I was your age. You got something like that going on?"

Trent said nothing.

"Mom found them eventually. She said, *Cigarettes'll kill you*. And she was right. I'll kill you quicker, though. Not *quick*, mind you. But quicker than cigarettes." He began pulling drawers from the dresser, spilling their contents all around him. "When we tossed the place, we didn't know you had this little pad down here. Hadn't found the tunnel yet." He dumped the last drawer and commenced knocking archery trophies and model cars from a shelf. "Exercising the old Miranda rights, huh? That's fine. We got nothing but time here. In fact, you two are under arrest for impeding an investigation. Hands behind your backs."

He cuffed Judith first. Trent held his breath, expecting her to make a move, knock the lanky cop down and turn the tables on him. But she didn't. She just stood there, half-smiling while he locked her wrists together. Then he cuffed Trent as well and ordered them both to sit on the floor, against the wall while he ransacked the rest of the room.

Ten minutes later, the bedroom now a disaster, Connor reappeared from the tunnel, assisting Sean, who alternately hopped and limped his way into the room.

"You," he said, pointing at Trent. "Connor, do me a solid and bring me that little jerkwad."

Trent felt himself lifted roughly from the ground and shoved toward Sean, who buried a fist in his stomach. He coughed and fell to the concrete floor, going fetal.

"That's for shooting me!" he shouted. Another blow to the abdomen from Sean's good foot. "And that's for shooting me again!"

"Enough," Tyrell said. "These are my prisoners."

"Right," Judith said. "So only you get to beat on us."

"You find the book?" Sean asked.

"Nah, it's not here," Tyrell answered. "We're gonna to have to make them talk the fun way. Let's bring them to the boss."

Sean grinned. "Great idea."

The whole party ascended the stairs to the garage and proceeded out into the night, where a squad car was parked in the driveway.

"Watch your head," Tyrell said, loading Trent into the back seat. He shoved Judith in harder and she landed in a heap on Trent's lap. Sean's face appeared, hovering just outside the car.

"I told you, didn't I? I said you'd be in the back of a squad car in ten minutes. What was that, ten minutes ago?" He laughed.

"It was like half an hour," Judith said.

"Whatever." He slammed the door.

Judith leaned in to Trent's ear and whispered, "First chance I get, I'm bailing. I'll rescue your dad. You keep these guys busy until we can find you."

"You can't bail out," Trent said. "The back doors don't open from the inside."

"I know."

Both front doors opened. Tyrell slid in behind the wheel and Sean gingerly arranged himself in the passenger seat, grunting in pain as he fastened his seatbelt.

"See if you can find the location of the treasure before you get wherever they're taking us," Judith whispered. "But whatever you do, don't give them the diary."

"What are you two, necking back there?" Tyrell said. "Knock it off. It ain't that kind of back seat."

"Necking?" Judith laughed. "Who says *necking*?"

The car came to life and they headed out, away from downtown, past the park with the haunted tetherball pole and out toward the state highway.

"I thought you were taking us to jail," Judith said. "You're going the wrong way."

"This is more interesting," Sean offered.

Headlights appeared in the distance, coming toward them, high beams illuminating the back seat for a moment. Trent did a double-take. Judith's arms, locked behind her back a moment ago, where now in front of her, hands digging for something in her right boot.

For just a second Trent wondered if she might actually have superpowers. Then he remembered that she did. Sort of. Judith was double-jointed. Her secret weapon on the wrestling mat and, apparently, while escaping police custody. Another car approached and he saw her produce Chief Barton's keys. She quickly removed the handcuff key from the ring and dropped the rest back into her boot.

They took a right on Shiawassee and sped up. They were now way out in the woods, the national forest to their left and miles of cornfield to the right.

In the dim light from the dashboard, Trent watched Judith, now free of the handcuffs, slide them into her boot as well. She removed the decorative wing from her left arm, and said, "You two idiots really think you can hold me back here with nothing but cuffs and a metal grate?"

Tyrell laughed. "Yeah, I think we can."

"Then you don't know who I am."

"You're that Morgan kid. You jumped Jay Fischer last week. He's been itching for a rematch, by the way. Oh, and I threw your father in the drunk tank last month. Whole family full of losers and jailbirds."

"Wrong," Judith said. "I'm the Angelus." She dropped the porcelain wing to the floor of the car and stomped it with the heel of her boot, crushing it into a dozen pieces.

"What are you doing back there?" Tyrell said. "You don't want me to stop this car. Trust me."

"Go ahead," Judith taunted. "Your funeral."

"Don't test me, kid."

She scoffed. "You're all talk. 'Tango and Cash?' Yeah, right . . . You make Barney Fife look like that guy from *Training Day*."

"That so?"

Judith grabbed the cage separating them from the front of the car and rattled it hard. "Prove me wrong."

Tyrell wheeled and gawked. "How did you—?" The car began to slow. "That's it. You're in trouble now."

Trent felt the cold metal of the handcuff key pressed into his palm and heard Judith whisper. "Close your eyes, Trent. Tight." She scooped a handful of broken white wing from the floor and reared back.

Trent squeezed his eyes shut and heard the window explode next to his head, then felt the cool night air filling the car. Judith scrambled across his lap and launched herself out of the car, rolling as she landed.

Tyrell slammed on the brakes and the tires squealed on the wet pavement. They fishtailed and recovered, coming to a stop. The cop threw his door open and took three steps out into the road, drawing his gun. But Judith was gone, disappeared into the woods beyond. He clicked on the mounted spotlight and directed it toward the trees, but there was no sign of her.

"Stay with Marsh," Sean said. "I'll bring her back. In pieces if I have to."

Tyrell slid back in the car. "Yeah, right. With that foot?"

"Well then you go and I'll stay. We can't just leave her behind!"

"Forget her," Tyrell said, shifting back into drive. "She's got no idea where we're headed and she's got no place to go. Besides, she's a kid alone in the woods, in the dark. She's got no car and I've got her phone. And even if she makes it back to town, who's she gonna go to? The cops?" He flipped on the flashing lights and punched the gas.

"You stay where you are, kid," he threw over his shoulder. "You try anything like that, I'll gut your old man. I promise."

Judith darted into the woods, moving as fast as she could for a couple minutes, swinging around tree trunks, ducking under limbs, before coming across a thick stand of white pines. Crawling beneath the branches of the largest one, she pulled Barton's cell phone from her boot and powered it up.

Using the backlight from the screen, she searched the ground for ammunition. The steel balls were the preferable to stones. More accurate from a distance. But she'd trained with both. Pawing through the dirt with her fingernails, she found just what she was looking for. A smooth, flat stone, two inches long. Then another. And another. Five of them, all told, like God had put them here just for her. She still had her sling, rolled up in her other boot, and the darkness, covering her escape. Now she just needed transportation.

Barton's phone was at the home screen now. No passcode needed. Another bit of providence. Her first instinct was to call Jason, who was waiting in that stupid van with the Iron Horse. But he didn't have a phone—grounded. How stupid. In hindsight, they should have left Trent's phone with him.

Oh well. She'd improvise. Opening the contacts screen, her eyes fell on #2: Danny. She grinned and began composing a text.

> Bring the car to the main entrance of the H-M National Forest, a couple miles west of Coit Road. Now.

A reply came almost immediately:

> ???? I'm with the guys at TOPPIT

> I said NOW. No excuses. No delays.

CHAPTER TWENTY-EIGHT
"BE GENTLE WITH ME"

Dan Barton eased on the brake and squinted at the sign. There were no street lights out here and, even with his high-beams on, he was practically on top of the intersection before he could make out the street name. Technically, he was supposed to be wearing glasses, but he never did. As he passed the cross street he could finally make out the words: Trowbridge Road. Not what he was looking for.

He swore and hit the gas again. He didn't know this area. Why would he? The Barton family lived in the new subdivision on the east side, not some Podunk farm house or boondock trailer park. When the text from Dad arrived, he'd been hanging with his boys at the pizza parlor and making some progress with Sadie Dewitt. Now he was out here, undoubtedly getting mud all over his freshly-detailed car. It had only rained for about half an hour earlier in the night, but it came down hard. Like, biblical flood type stuff.

Oh, well. The mud would wash off. Sadie would be there tomorrow night. And it wasn't like he could say no anyway. His 2008 Ford Flex wasn't really his and Dad never let him forget it. Sure, he'd been allowed to get the spoiler installed and he covered the insurance payments from his own pocket, but that didn't change the fact that it was still Dad's car. And Dad was more than ready to take it back at any time, for any reason.

There. Coit Road. Dan slowed down, missed the entrance, and had to drive more than half a mile before he found another drive where he could turn around. This was so stupid. Weren't there actual cops who got paid to drive all over town at the chief's orders? Come to think of it, this wasn't even in town; he'd passed the "Now Leaving Clinch Rock—Visit Again Soon" sign nearly ten minutes ago. Maybe Dad was out of his jurisdiction. Maybe he needed someone he could really trust. Someone like his only son.

Turning onto the dark access road, he felt a tinge of fear and excitement. He dropped down into a rain-filled pothole and, as the car bounced back out, his lights glinted off the heavy chain spanning the dirt drive and the "PARK CLOSED" sign suspended from it. Slamming on the brakes, he felt the car slide in the mud and connect with the heavy steel links. The chain stretched back, but didn't break. Dan cursed again and shifted into reverse.

It took a moment for the tires to win traction and as he slowly backed up the chain came with him, now connected with the grill somehow. A triple knot formed in his stomach. Dad was going to kill him. Dad, who was allegedly somewhere nearby. Finally the car and the chain separated and the metal sign dropped to the ground.

Maybe there was no damage, he thought. Maybe Dad hadn't seen it happen. Things usually worked out for Dan Barton, he reminded himself, as he opened the car door and stepped out into another mudpuddle, drenching his shoe and sock. "Dad?" he called out. "You here?"

His phone buzzed.

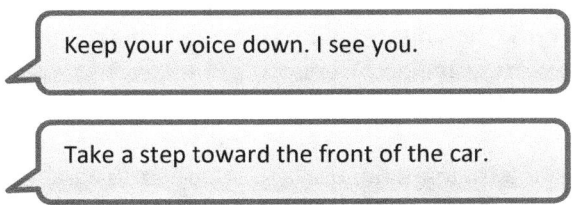

Keep your voice down. I see you.

Take a step toward the front of the car.

Dan obeyed, stopping just short of the high-beams, which shone out to illuminate the black space between trees. No one out there. Another message buzzed in.

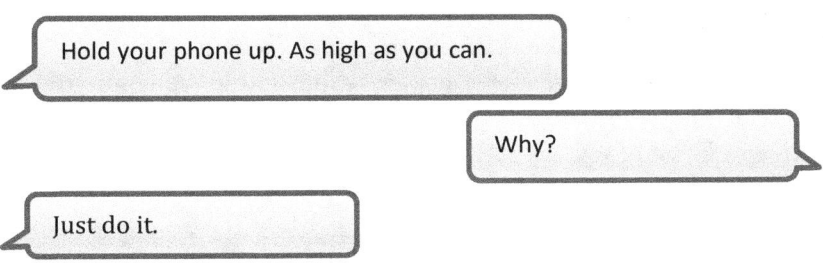

Hold your phone up. As high as you can.

Why?

Just do it.

Dan complied, rising up onto his toes and extending his arm up high, bringing the top his phone nine feet off the ground. The glow of the screen barely illuminated the roof of the car and Dan was thinking about turning on the flashlight when the device exploded in his hand. Just . . . gone! One moment it was there and the next it was blasted out of existence, as though a sniper had shot it from his hand.

Before he could begin to process this, he saw a flash of blue cut through the outer rim of the far headlight and someone slid over the hood of the car, Dukes of Hazzard style. The sharp edge of a boot heel dug into his hip and Barton slipped down into the mud. He rolled twice before coming to rest on his elbows, covered in muck.

Looking up, he saw his assailant, a woman in a blue skirt and leggings with . . . blue hair? She slid in behind the wheel of the Flex and pulled the door shut.

"Hey!" Dan shouted, rising frantically and lunging toward the car, only to feel his feet slip out from under him once again. The car backed up ten feet, spraying muddy water all over him, and came to a stop halfway to where the dirt drive met the highway. Barton stood again, slower this time, and took a successful step. Then another. The car was idling now and through the headlights Dan could barely make out the driver under the feeble glow of the dome lamp.

She was going through his gym bag. What was going on? And where was Dad? Dan was just a few steps shy of the car, when the woman leaned out the open window and asked, "Do you have a pen in here?" nonchalantly, as though she'd stopped him on the street.

"Uh, yeah," Dan said. "In the glove box." Where did he know this chick from? Her voice was younger than he expected. And she was hot, which he realized was a weird thing to think about someone who'd just kicked him into the mud and seemed to be stealing his car. But still, he loved the blue hair and the heavy makeup.

She was tossing maps and napkins from the glove compartment, then came out with a small spray bottle in a vinyl case. "Pepper spray? Seriously? You're such a pansy."

Barton took another step toward the car. "That's my mom's. It's not—"

"Oh, here we go. Perfect." She bit the cap off a Sharpee and started writing a string of numbers on the back of his practice shirt. He smiled. Whoever she was, she was into him. Of course. Sadie was alright, but this was different. Exciting. Crazy chick literally coming out of the woodwork to give him her number. They'd have a great story about how they met.

"Hand me those sweats," he said. "Let me get out of these muddy clothes?"

The blue-haired girl tossed the T-shirt at him. Wait, this wasn't right. She'd written way too many digits. "What is this?" he asked.

"GPS coordinates. That's where you'll find your dad. I chained him to a tree."

"You chained my dad . . . ? *What?*"

"It's a long story, but trust me—he had it coming. Anyway, you should probably get there ASAP. It's starting to get cold out. Oh, and you'll need some bolt cutters. Ya know, for the chain."

Barton grabbed the door handle and yanked. Locked. The blue-haired chick smirked at him and shifted into reverse. A flash of rage crackled up his spine, filling his temporal lobes—the same rage that had flattened countless linebackers on the turf and pinned champions on the mat. He grabbed for a handful of blue hair, but the car was backing up again, faster this time.

She laughed. It was so familiar. How did he know her?

"Oh, come on, Danny," she called. "You can do better than that."

He growled and began running alongside the car as it picked up speed. The window was closing now—literally and figuratively. Dan dug deep and picked up the pace. He'd break the window, drag her out by that stupid blue hair. No one made a fool of Dan Barton.

The car pulled out onto the road. As the chick with the blue hair shifted into drive, she caught his eye and winked, coyly. Something clicked in Barton's head—recognition—just as he lost his footing. He landed back in the mud with a *slap*, and slid two feet. The car disappeared into the distance.

Dan lay there in the mud and said, "Bag Lady?"

* * *

Trent felt the cuff loosen its grip on his left wrist and then slip off. Finally. The maneuver was much harder than it seemed and he'd dropped the key twice in the process, losing in the seat cushion the second time. Fishing it out had been so gross he'd momentarily forgotten the imminent danger they were facing.

Looking out the window, he recognized the road, long and bare, lined with drainage ditches on both sides. He was certain; they were headed to the old lumber camp. And they'd be there soon.

Sean and Tyrell were in the midst of a heated debate, although it was hard to tell about what over the sound of the wind whipping in through the broken window. Trent carefully pulled the diary from his waistband, under his T-shirt, and opened it on the seat next to him. The greenish backlight of his watch was enough to help him navigate to the right month: February 1893, not twenty pages from the beginning of the diary.

If only he'd started from the front of the book, he'd have found this entry a week ago. Still, he'd become rather skilled at reading Wolcott's wild penmanship and was surprised to find himself able to skim through the slanted cursive text.

February 1 detailed a revival meeting, attended by only three men, one of whom was very drunk, followed by a prayer of lament regarding the minister's lack of converts thus far. There was no entry on the second, and the third was quite short—just a catalog of tasks he'd accomplished that day. The fourth, however, was several pages long. Trenton glanced up at the front seat. He hadn't been noticed. Yet.

His heart bucking against his ribcage, he began reading about what Wolcott called "a most encouraging and providential day." The preacher had been visiting the lumber camp, offering Bibles to the camp workers, when the lumbermen returned for the evening meal. The camp cook had asked Wolcott to stay and say grace for the men. "Little did I know," Trenton read, "who would be in attendance, inspecting the enterprise that had made him wealthier than any man I have ever met."

A harsh beam of light suddenly blinded Trent. "Whatcha got there, Marsh?" Sean asked. He let out a deep, cruel laugh. "Hey Tango, you're gonna want to pull over. I think I found what we been looking for."

* * *

Judith parked at the curb in front of the police station. A hand-lettered sign on the front door read "Sorry, We're Closed. Call 911 for Emergency."

Of course they were keeping the place locked down. With the chief in the holding cell, they couldn't afford drop-ins or lookyloos. She surveyed the outside of the small building. The windows were reinforced with wire mesh, none of them lower than eight feet off the ground. There was an emergency exit next to the cornerstone—ERECTED 1898—but no handle on the outside.

No, there was only one way in. Right up the steps to the front door. She reached into her right boot and withdrew the handcuffs. This was going to be tricky. One wrong move and she'd find herself cellmates with Adam.

No, that couldn't happen. She whispered the words of the Angelus prayer, "Pour forth your grace into my heart, that as I have known the incarnation of Christ, your Son by the message of an angel, so by His passion and cross I may be brought to the glory of his resurrection..." She could hear the church bells from YouTube clanging in her head and the hardcore Latin chanting. It was working. She added, "Lord, keep Adam safe. Give me strength and speed. And send your angels to help me. Amen."

Judith opened the door and was halfway out of the car when she remembered Barton's pepper spray. "Expires February 2006," the bottle said. A dozen years ago. "One more thing Lord," she said. "I really need this little can of mace to work. Bet you don't hear that very often."

* * *

The squad car squealed to a stop on the empty road and Tyrell stepped out. Trenton panicked and chucked the diary out the open window. He heard the cop shout in protest and then the *sploosh* of the old book landing in the ditch.

Tyrell reached into the car, grabbed two fistfuls of Trent's shirt, dragged him out through the window, and dumped him to the ground. "Go get it," he ordered. "And don't even think of running if you want to see your old man again."

Trent crossed the street in the moonlight and walked along the side of the road, peering down into the ditch. He prayed that Judith was even now coming to her senses and calling the authorities. Any authorities. All of them. Sure, she'd done incredible things today, but even Judith had to see that breaking a man out of jail was beyond her abilities.

The squad car pulled up next to him and the spotlight came to life, shining down into the ditch, slowly sweeping back and forth.

"Wait!" Trent shouted. "Go back!" The leather-bound book was floating along in the murky water, caught up in the suction current.

"Well, what are you waiting for?" Tyrell demanded, opening the car door hard into Trent's back, propelling him down into the ditch. The water was pleasantly cool as Trent stood and waded along in it, easily catching up to the book and snatching it from amongst the other floating debris. Climbing back out of the ditch, however, was a lot more difficult. The steep incline was covered in slick, wet grass

"For crying out loud," Tyrell said, taking a step halfway down into the ditch and extending his long arm. "Grab on."

Trent knew immediately what Judith would do: grab that lanky cop by the wrist and jerk him down into the ditch. Use a knee to pin his head under water, while she relieved him of his gun. But Trent just took his captor's proffered hand and felt himself yanked up to street level, where he was rewarded with an open-hand to the face that nearly knocked him back down into the water.

Tyrell grabbed the waterlogged book, gave it one hard shake, and tried to flip through it. The pages were sticking and the ink was running, which Trenton supposed was both good news and bad. Good for leverage; bad for Tyrell's temper.

"You're making it worse, dude," Sean warned from the passenger seat. "Just set it up here by the heater to dry it off."

Tyrell fixed Trent with a look of pure hatred. For a moment, it felt like he was building up to another blow, then he took a deep breath and said, almost pleasantly, "One more trick and I'll kill you."

* * *

Adam sat on the bench at the rear of the cell and prayed. A half an hour earlier, he'd given up on winning Jessie over and turned to a higher source of help. He'd been praying for justice to be done, for God to confound the plans of the wicked, and mostly for Trent's safety. As far as Adam knew his son was still up at the camp in the U.P., pleasantly oblivious to all of this and insulated from it. And yet, he felt an enduring sense of disquiet.

But now, out of nowhere, it was replaced by an overwhelming need to pray for Judith. For her to have wisdom and a clear head. For her to remain tethered to reality, however this should all unfold. That's when the pounding on the station door began.

"People in this town can't read?" Cash grumbled, his feet still propped up on the desk, portly frame wedged in his chair, immersed in his movie.

Adam stood and approached the bars of his cell. The surveillance cameras — both inside and out — fed to a bank of monitors, which faced the chief's office and, as it happened, this particular holding cell. In fact, Adam was the only one who could see the black and white image of Judith standing outside, metrically banging the door with her fist. She had a wig on from the looks of it. He might not have even known it was her, but for the fact that she was wearing the same crazy getup Jay Fischer had described the week before. *Judith, what are you doing?*

"Hey Jessie, do me a solid and get rid of this illiterate hick." Cash called out. "My favorite part's coming up."

"You don't need to bother," Adam said. "You don't need to answer the door. You posted a sign right? They'll go away."

"I told you, Marsh" Cash said. "Shut up."

Adam held his breath and willed Judith to just accept that the place was closed and be on her way. Right. Because that sounded like Judith.

Bang! Bang! Bang! Judith pounded the door all the harder, rapping the metal of the cuffs against the solid oak. If they didn't answer soon, she might have to move on to Plan B, although she didn't really have a Plan B. Pull the door off its hinges somehow? Maybe try to smoke the dirty cops out?

Just then, the door opened a few inches and Jessie Finn's face appeared. "Sorry, we're clo—" The word folded in on itself. "What are you supposed to be?" His eyes drifted past her, to the street, and he called out, "Hey John, come here a minute. Isn't that Chief Barton's car?"

"Please, sir, let me in," Judith begged, hands clasped behind her back. "They're after me!"

"Who's *they*?" Jessie opened the door wider, giving Judith a clear view, past the front desk and the old-timey wooden rail, to the grid of officers' desks and the holding cells beyond. She avoided Adam's gaze and instead focused on Officer Cash, sitting slack-jawed, watching TV. He was the wild card here. She had to be quick. Brutal.

"Sorry about this," Judith said, raising the pepper spray and pushing her thumb against the trigger. A feeble red stream arced out, catching Jessie full in the face. He took an involuntary step back and brought his hands instinctively to his eyes, hacking and wheezing. Judith lunged at him, shoving him back into the front desk with her shoulder. She secured one of the handcuffs around his left wrist, then jumped the desk, yanking Jessie across, and locked the other end of the cuffs to a desk drawer.

Cash frantically kicked his stubby legs, scrambling to his feet, spilling a tower of files in Judith's direction. She approached quickly, steadily, kicking open the low, spring-loaded gate in the wooden rail that separated off the bull pen.

"Don't move!" Cash shouted before his gun had even cleared its holster.

Judith smirked. "Step aside, Johnny Cash. The chief is coming with me."

"Not happening. Hands on your head!" Cash warned. "I'll fire!"

From behind her, Jessie called out, "She's just a kid; put the gun away!" He was pouring the remains of a bottle of spring water onto his eyes.

"Listen to Sergeant Finn," Adam urged. "No one needs to get hurt here, John."

"Too late for that!" Jessie wheezed.

"Okay, no one *else* needs to get hurt."

"Shut up," Cash ordered.

Judith laughed in that sort of practiced, pretentious way that rich people laugh on TV. "Come on, Johnny. You really need a gun to deal with a teenage girl half your size? Or—I don't know—a third of your size?"

Jessie had his keys out, struggling with the handcuff lock. "What did you put in here—gum?"

"Yeah," Judith answered. "Hubba Bubba. Watermelon blast."

"Hands on your head," Cash repeated. "And get on your knees."

"Are you even listening to me?" Judith bent down and picked up the remote control from the top of the fallen tower of files at her feet. "I don't think I have your full attention." She raised the remote at the cop, mirroring his stance, and clicked off the TV. Dropping her hands to her sides, she pointed the remote at the security camera and pushed the volume button. *Dot dot dash. Dot dot dash.* She finally made eye contact with Adam. He nodded.

Invisible to the naked eye, the infrared light from the remote lit up the image on the security monitor like a three-pound Maglite. She began tapping out her message, dots and dashes coming automatically: G . . . U . . .

"Last chance," Cash practically whispered. "I've seen gunshot wounds. You want no part of that."

"Really? You're going to shoot me, an unarmed girl in a police station?" N . . . T . . .

"If I have to," Cash said.

"No you're not. Not in front of the chief of police. And what about Jessie?" H . . . R . . . U . . . "Actually Jessie probably can't see. But he's not stupid. That's two witnesses." In her peripheral, she could see Adam spelling in his head. B . . . A . . . "You think Jessie will lie for you? Because I don't think he wants any part of this." R . . . S.

Sudden recognition dawned on the chief's face. He shook his head vehemently and mouthed "No."

Cash holstered his gun. "Alright, how about I just Tase you instead? You can flop around on the floor, pee yourself. Maybe you'll bite through your tongue."

Judith tossed the remote aside. "Okay, officer. You win." She dropped to her knees, her weight balanced on the balls of her feet. Looking up at the cop with doe eyes she said, "Be gentle with me. I'm just a girl in the world."

Cash snapped his cuffs from his belt and took a step toward the gate. "You have the right to shut your stupid mouth. Anything you say can and will—"

Judith launched herself into his frame, connecting with his stomach and driving his ample mass three feet off the ground. She'd done it a hundred times before. Only instead of dropping him to the mat, she slammed his shoulder blades against the metal cage behind him and, reaching out as wide as she could, grabbed a bar in each hand, pulling inward, crushing the cop against the hard iron.

Jesse pulled his own Taser. "I'm gonna zap her," he announced. "My vision's coming back! Sort of."

"No, don't," Cash managed through clenched teeth. "It'll Tase me too, dummy!" He slammed his forehead down against Judith's, bringing stars into her field of vision. She loosened her grip and Cash pressed the advantage, bringing a knee up to her stomach, then landing a solid kick to her chest, blasting her to the floor, where she slid six feet along the worn hardwood.

"Bad move, brat," Officer Cash said, taking a step toward her. He reached for his sidearm. It wasn't there.

"Not a twitch, John," Adam said, gun trained on his captor's back.

Jessie drew his own gun, squinting hard toward the action. "Come on, Chief, keep your head here. You don't want any more trouble than you've already got. Put it down!"

"I don't answer to you, Jessie. You answer to me. Remember? I swore you in when you practically a kid. We've had each other's backs for years. These things they say I did? I didn't do them. And for what it's worth, I'm sorry I didn't recommend you for chief. Believe me, I wish I had. But this ends tonight. I'm locking Cash up in here and I'm bringing in Barton and Tyrell too. So tell me, Jessie: are you with me or not?"

CHAPTER TWENTY-NINE
"SHOTS FIRED"

Trenton was right about their destination, as it turned out.

Tyrell guided the squad car up the rutted dirt drive to the historic lumber camp at 35 miles per hour, heedless to the complaints of the car's suspension. Trent bounced in the back seat, once again cuffed, but no longer secured by a seatbelt. His face made contact with the metal cage more than a few times.

The undefined shapes in the darkness just outside the missing window were calling to him, but he dared not answer. Restrained as he was, he'd probably break his neck trying to exit the vehicle. And even if he made it, he could see Tyrell following him out toward the woods with that giant spotlight and picking him off like a buck from a deer blind.

As they pulled up to the renovated bunk house, the cruiser's headlights illuminated first the old red truck he'd seen the morning of the robbery, and then Brian Green, standing just outside the door, face hard and cold. His features were unmistakably Brian's but to Trent he looked like someone else entirely. He wasn't even wearing a vest.

Tyrell killed the engine and unwedged himself from the driver's seat, this time kind enough to open the door for Trent. "Out," he ordered.

The sole of Trent's shoe sunk a quarter inch into the spongy ground as he stepped out and it occurred to him that this was pretty much how he felt on the inside as well—his thoughts heavy, wavering somewhere between complete resignation and concocting a long and elaborate escape plan that he knew he'd never execute.

"Hello, Trenton," Brian said. "Zoe will be so happy to see you." He gestured at the door, as if inviting a friend in for a chat, and Tyrell shoved his prisoner into the long, wooden building and down the aisle between the rows of bunks. He could hear Sean limping behind them, taking up the rear.

The first thing Trent noticed, other than the smell of fresh cut pine, was that out of maybe fifty bunks, only one was made up. As he passed it he recognized Zoe's sleeping bag—the one he'd carried to her car for her a week and a half earlier. He felt his spirits fall further. So they *had* caught up to her before she could leave town. And if they weren't bluffing about holding her captive, they probably weren't bluffing about dad either.

Tyrell shoved him again. "Keep moving."

"It's like the Green Mile, right?" Sean laughed.

"How so?" Brian asked.

"I don't know. I never saw it."

A moment later, they emerged from the bunks, into a small sitting area, containing a few benches, a rough-cut table, and a single chair, where Zoe sat, gagged and bound, tears streaking her cheeks.

"Zoe!" Trent rushed toward her instinctively, but Tyrell's long leg shot out and Trent spilled onto the hardwood floor, where he found himself looking at Zoe's ankles, duct taped to the legs of the chair. He guessed her wrists must be taped as well, wedged in behind her slender frame. They locked eyes for a second, hers full of abject terror and in that moment, Trenton knew one thing: these men had no intention of letting either of them go.

Someone jerked Trent to his knees and only then did he see Mike Van Buren holding a handgun to Zoe's head.

"You find the diary?" he asked Tyrell.

"Yeah," the cop answered, "but this little twerp threw it in a ditch. Doubt you'll be able to read it."

Sean set the old book down on the table and shrugged an apology. "Maybe once it dries out. But the good news is our little junior detective here has read the whole thing. Haven't you?"

Trent could only shake his head no, his eyes never leaving the gun at Zoe's temple.

"Well," Mike said, "I hope for her sake—and yours—that you learned something useful."

* * *

Adam killed the headlights and slowed to a crawl.

"What are we doing here?" Jessie asked. "Officer Cash said we'd find them at the old sawmill. At this point he's got no reason to lie."

"Ex-officer Cash," Adam corrected. "And he lies because he's a liar. He doesn't need a reason. Anyway, I pinged the GPS locator in Tyrell's cruiser. It's just up ahead here. In fact, this is probably close enough." He pulled off the drive, between some trees, and back into the woods about twenty feet. There he parked and turned off the ignition.

"You ready?" he asked, drawing his sidearm.

"I don't know, chief." Jessie studied his lap. "I don't know about this."

Adam sighed impatiently. "I thought you said you were with me, Jessie."

"I am, it's just . . . Don't you think we should wait for backup?"

"*Who?*"

"I dunno. Staties? Sheriff's department? Kendra at least. I bet you a case of Pabst she's right down the road at Eastwood Lanes!"

"Yeah, and I bet she's had more than a few. You can wait if you want. I'm going after my son."

"You know I can hear you guys, right?" Judith said from the back seat. "This is totally hurting my feelings."

"Guess I'll have to live with that," Adam said.

"Well then what did you bring me for?"

"Honestly, I didn't trust you not to do something foolish and get yourself killed. And I couldn't leave you locked up next to John Cash with no one standing guard."

"I already saved Trent's life at least once today," Judith said. "I can help you."

"Look, I'm grateful for what you've done. I am. But you're staying in here. I thought we had an understanding."

"That I'd let you do your job. And now I want to help you do your job. There's no conflict there."

The chief opened the door and swung a leg out. "Just stay there, okay? For me?"

"Not like I have a choice." She poked at the metal cage separating her from the front seat.

"If you want to help," Adam said, "pray for Trent."

Judith stared out the window and nodded.

"I Love you, Judy-Bug."

"Love you too," she murmured.

Adam met Jessie around the back of the car and opened the trunk. "You've always been the better shot with these things," he said, indicating the 12 gauge pump. "You want it?"

"You know it." Jessie chambered a slug and the two of them began slowly working their way through the darkness of the woods.

* * *

"So this is simple," Mike said. "I have some simple, straightforward questions for you. You give me simple answers and the girl's head stays a nice simple round shape—with the shiny hair and those pretty brown eyes. You screw with me, things get . . . complicated."

The room was silent, the four men and two captives all poised in the moment, barely daring to breathe.

"First question: where'd you find the book?" Mike asked.

"In a secret room. In our basement. It was in an old desk with a letter from Wolcott."

"And when did you find it?"

"A week ago. About that."

Mike's eyes skipped to Zoe and back to Trent. "And you expect me to believe that in a week's time you didn't read the whole thing, knowing it contained clues to the whereabouts of millions of dollars? How dumb do you think I am?"

"I don't—not dumb. Not dumb! I read a lot of it. And I think I know where the—"

All at once, Trenton had no one's attention. The men were all looking past him, back toward the door, toward some movement. It was only after the fact that he remember hearing his dad shout, "Police! Drop your weapons! Now!"

Then everything went fast-forward and slow-mo at the same time. He saw Sean raise the rifle at his side and heard the crack of a gunshot echoing off every surface. Sean dropped the weapon and stumbled back into the unfinished wood of the wall, leaving a crimson trail as he slid down to the floor.

Mike hesitated, then dropped his pistol and raised his hands. Tyrell and Brian raised theirs as well.

"Put 'em on your heads, fingers interlocked," Jessie barked, walking into view, shotgun up and at the ready. They all complied.

Trenton felt himself lifted gently to his feet by his dad's strong hands and then embraced for just a moment. "You okay, son?" he asked.

"Yeah. I think." Trent was in a bit of a fog of course. But that was okay. It was over. Finally.

"Okay then. I'll tend to the injured man," his dad said. "Trent, you free the young lady. Jessie, head on a swivel. Anybody makes a move, put 'em down."

"Yes, sir."

Adam had already rolled Sean onto his back and was applying pressure to the wound in his shoulder by the time Trent shook off the daze and took a step toward Zoe. He'd lost track of how many guns had been pointed at him and fired near him in the past twenty-four hours, but he was certainly not getting used to it. If anything, the opposite.

He pulled the gag from Zoe's mouth and asked, "Are you alright?"

"I think so," she rasped, gazing up at him, her eyes sad and scared, her beautiful face streaked with mascara. Trent felt sorry for her, but nothing more. What was that song—*You're Just Somebody that I Used to Know*? Zoe wasn't even that. Everything he thought he knew about her had been a lie.

"We okay to call this in?" Jessie asked.

"Yeah," the chief said. "Just the ambulance for Tailor. Between my car and Tyrell's we can bring the rest into custody. Not taking any more chances tonight."

Jessie hit the transmit button on his shoulder-mount and said "Central, Two Charlie Six. Shots fired. Shots fired. I have a man down with a GSW to the shoulder. We are Signal One. Need a rig at our current location . . . " He released the button. "Anyone know the address out here?"

Trent chuckled and turned his attention to Zoe's ankles—wrapped several times over in duct tape and yet not taped to the chair. Well, that was easy.

"Turn around," he said, guiding her out of the chair by her shoulders. "I'll get your wrists."

Zoe stood, brought a compact pistol from behind her back, and fired two shots into Jessie's chest.

More shots.

Judith dropped the other porcelain wing to the filthy floormat and stomped it with her heel. After the first gunshot, she'd almost busted out to get a look at things. Now she wished she had.

The window shattered on contact with the shards of aluminum oxide and Judith was out of the car and into the night in a moment. She moved quickly through the trees, the same direction she'd watched Adam and Jessie disappear.

Zoe buried the muzzle of the gun in Trenton's back and dragged him backwards to where Jessie lay wheezing on the floor. With a solid kick, she sent the shotgun sliding over to Mike, who grabbed it up and turned it on Adam.

"Trent, would you be a dear and get his sidearm?" Zoe said. "And don't try anything stupid or you'll end up just like him."

Trent obeyed, pulling the handgun from Jessie's paddle holster. He was surprised at how calm he felt. Was this shock? Resignation to his fate? Or was it just that this whole thing seemed unreal?

"Now drop it," Zoe ordered. "And kick it over to Brian."

Tyrell had now drawn his own gun and relieved Adam of his. In the course of ten seconds the tables had completely turned.

"Officer Tyrell," Brian said, "where does Marsh keep his backup piece?"

"How should I know?"

Brian swung his gun toward the chief. "Where is it?"

"Backup piece?" Adam chuckled, mirthlessly. "In Clinch Rock?" He pulled up both pant legs, to his knees, revealing nothing but black socks. "Sometimes I don't carry a gun at all." He went back to applying pressure to Sean's wound.

"Ugh, is he going to die?" Zoe demanded.

"If he doesn't get some medical attention soon," Adam answered. "So will Jessie. You want to spend the rest of your life in prison? Cop-killers tend to get the maximum."

"I'll chance it," Zoe said.

"Do really want two more deaths on your conscience?"

"Not two," Sean insisted. "I'm fine. Takes more than a slug in the shoulder to keep me down. I'm Wile E. Coyote meets the friggin' Energizer Bunny." He tried to sit up, cried out in pain, and flopped back to the ground.

"What a mess," Zoe said, her eyes drifting from Jessie to Sean to the chief and his son. "I blame you for this," she said, her gaze finally landing on Brian. "This is on you."

"You must be joking. How is this my fault? I told you to wait until Marsh was out of the picture! A couple more months and we would have *owned* the police department."

"You said that two months ago."

"It's not my fault he kept putting off retirement. And it's not my fault you've got no patience! If you want someone to blame, have a look in the mirror!"

Zoe shook her head and clucked her tongue. "Take some responsibility for once, Brian. You overpromised and underdelivered. Again. I'm afraid I'm going to have to let you go. Michael?"

Mike leveled the shotgun at the slender man and blasted him to the ground. The gears in Trenton's mind ground to a halt, unable to even begin processing what he had just seen. Sure, in the back of his mind he'd always known that he and Zoe never really connected at any deep level. And considering that their breakup had taken place while she was breaking into his house, they hadn't parted on the best of terms. But nothing could have prepared him for this: watching Zoe murder her father—casually, like she was swiping left on her cell phone. Then again, Brian Green wasn't really her father.

In fact, Trenton knew very little about this woman—just that her name was Zoe Frobisher, she was twenty-two years old, and came from Vermont. And add to that, of course, that she was a cold-blooded killer, who would not hesitate to take multiple lives if it meant finding the money.

Zoe was rubbing her temples, as if warding off a stress headache. "Such a waste," she said. "He was right about one thing, though. My patience has run out. I know you don't want to hear this, Trent, but unless you've got something huge for me, I think it's time to say goodbye to Daddy."

"I know where the money is!" Trent blurted. "It's here at the camp! I'll take you to it! Just don't hurt him!"

"You'll forgive me if I'm a tad skeptical," Zoe said. "So you know, if you're buying time, you can't afford much."

"No, I swear! It's where they first met, right? February 3, 1898. I found it in the diary. I can show you exactly where!"

Mike shrugged. "Worth a look; we've got nothing else to go on."

Zoe seemed to consider this for a moment before saying, "Here's what we'll do. Tyrell, you stay here with your brothers in blue. Everyone who's still breathing, try to keep them that way. For now. We're going on a little field trip with Trenton. Any of you tries anything cute, you all die. Understood?"

No one answered, but it was clear: they all understood.

Judith watched from just outside the building's lone window, as Trenton led Zoe and Mike back toward the door. This was good. She'd been helpless to intervene while the enemy was fortified and heavily armed. She had no smoke bombs, no flash-bangs. Any attempt to catch the enemy by surprise would likely end with at least one of the Marshes shot dead.

But now they were giving up their advantage. One of them lay dead on the floor and the rest were separating, two of them heading out into the darkness, unaware that they were about to become the prey. Adam could handle himself; she was willing to bet on that. But saving Trent was up to her. Deep down, she'd always known: this is why she became the Angelus in the first place.

Judith moved silently through the darkness, ready to pick up the trail.

CHAPTER THIRTY
"A REAL SIDE-SPLITTER"

During the past fifteen minutes, Trenton's world had been turned over and shaken like a toddler with a snow globe, and the pieces were just starting to settle—in a very unsettling way. Zoe was not a pawn in all this, but the mastermind. And a murderer. That much he'd managed to process. So much else had happened so quickly though—three men shot, one of them dead, his father held at gunpoint—that most if it was just lost in the noise. Trent filed it all away in a mental box labeled "To be dealt with if I survive this."

Instead, as they walked the fifty yards to the reconstructed mess hall, he chose to focus on perhaps the most bizarre development of all—the miniscule but undeniable kernel of jealousy lodged in the back of his mind, like a wood chip in a shoe. Mike and Zoe were obviously an item. Sure, she'd just shot a dear friend and threatened to kill Trent's whole family, but somehow that didn't quite negate the fact that she had been cheating on him during the entire span of their brief courtship. He glanced back at Mike, two steps behind them, an over-sized handgun stuck in his waistband and a wood-handled shovel in his hands, then back to Zoe. In this moment, he hated her far more than he'd ever liked her.

"Don't give me that pitiful look, Trenton," she said. "This is nothing personal. I'm just taking back what's rightfully mine. I don't expect you to understand. I do, however, expect you to show me exactly where the money is."

"Oh, I fully understand. Cassel was your ancestor, right? Like, your great-great-great-grandfather or something. Why else would you have all that stuff?"

"You're not serious," she said.

"No, why else would you even know—or care—about some local legend of buried treasure like a thousand miles from where you grew up?"

Zoe stopped walking. "Is that really what you think? I'm the descendent of that weak and sentimental old fool? Not likely. I come from a line of people who take what they want, using whatever means the situation requires."

"What, the book keeper? Wellick? "

She tapped her temple and resumed walking. Mike nudged Trent hard between the shoulder blades with the shovel handle and he began to move again as well.

"I wasted three years trying to find myself," Zoe said. "Travelling the world, burning through my inheritance, making and spending a few fortunes. And I came up empty. But ten dollars to that family tree website and I found my true calling. Now I have a purpose—a goal. I've got my house back, I'm getting this town back, and I am going to get the rest of my money, whatever it takes."

They entered the dark interior of the mess hall, the most finished of the renovated buildings, and were well inside before Mike flicked on the electric lights, tastefully disguised as gas lamps. It was as if the orange light came from a horrible epiphany in an old cartoon. Deep down, Trent had been holding onto a sliver of hope that Zoe was planning to just grab the money and disappear. But if she was planning on staying in town, putting down roots with her newly recovered fortune . . . she'd have to kill everyone who knew her secret.

Somehow the light made it seem all the darker.

Judith had followed parallel to the three of them, back among the trees. Now it was time to act. It would have to be a quick and vicious attack—like at the police station, but without the kid gloves. These weren't cops, after all, but criminals. Her prey. She'd use the sling to take one of them out, from out in the darkness, through the open door—the guy with the gun, she decided—and then rush Zoe before she knew what hit her. Judith smiled. Yes, this was first and foremost an act of necessity. But she had to admit: knocking Zoe on her dainty little butt was something she'd wanted to do for a while now.

Judith retrieved the sling from her boot, dropped the second smooth stone into the pouch, and stepped quickly into the clearing, her tunnel vision pulling her toward the glow of the doorway like a tractor beam. She was still thirty paces off when a sharp blast of pain enveloped her skull and she went down into the marshy sod. She felt warm blood oozing from a split in her scalp, beneath the wig. Then something cold and metallic pulled her up to her feet, closing off her airway. A rifle? No, bigger. A shotgun.

"Still trying to play hero, huh? What a joke." The whisper was soft and menacing, no more than an inch from her right ear. "How do you like it? How do you like to be blindsided? Sucker-punched?"

She tried to answer, but only managed to taste blood and intensify the pain in her throat. The blow from the gunstock flared as well, as if to keep pace.

"Shhhh," Coach Fischer said. "We can't let them know I'm out here. Ya see, if I'm right, then a whole lot of money is gonna come walking out that door in a few minutes. And I'm gonna take it. Those two punks'll be doing twenty years a piece for murder while I spend the rest of my days on the beach." He snorted derisively.

That cruel laugh brought Judith back to herself. She'd heard it a hundred times. Capping thinly-veiled sexist jokes at wrestling practice, while turning a blind-eye on the bus ride home from away meets. *It's just a friendly prank. You want to be a wrestler, you'd better toughen up.*

A deep rage began to grow in her chest, even as her vision dimmed around the edges. She'd break his face. Smooth stone #2 had Fischer's name on it and oh, did he have it coming. That's when she realized her hands were empty. The sling and the stone it contained were gone.

"Looks like your vest stopped both of them," Adam whispered.

"Doesn't feel like it," Jessie wheezed. "I'm looking at broken ribs at least." Adam was bent over him in the shadow of the last bunk, pretending to sop up blood with some of Zoe's clothes, which Tyrell had fished from a duffel bag and tossed in their direction. Eight feet away, a bunch of T-shirts were making a half-decent bandage for Sean's shoulder. Meaning Adam and Jessie had a moment to conspire. But just a moment. Tyrell still had one eye on them and one hand on his gun. And he was finishing up. Soon he'd be free to focus on their every move once again.

"You know they're going to kill us, right?" Jessie rasped. "Trent too."

"I know," Adam said. "What are you thinking?"

Jessie smiled. "I'm thinking they should have searched you for that backup piece."

Mike drummed his finger against the grip of his pistol and said, "Okay, Marsh. Where is it?"

Trent looked around the interior of the building. In the center was the reproduction of the cook's range, towering and shiny. The pine walls were adorned with blown-up photos of cooks and lumberjacks, none of them smiling. On the far wall hung a reproduction of a Peavey, the kind of cant hook particular to rivermen as they floated their precious timber to its destination. This couldn't all be a cover for Zoe's search. It was a trophy—a way for her to rub the town's face in what her ancestor had procured and somehow, against all odds, managed to keep in the family. Trent laughed.

"This is funny," Zoe observed. "I'm glad you're amused. I've got a real side-splitter for you." She dragged an antique chair to the middle of the room. "This is the captain's chair from the Cassel House—part of a dining set commissioned by Benjamin Cassel in 1887. You can still see where the ropes wore into the arms when the Crown Fire Boys tied Wellick down and tortured him. How do you feel about doing a little historical reenactment?"

Trent went white. "Nothing's funny. It's just . . . you were so close." He pointed at the shiny new cast iron stove, installed since his last visit here. "The money is under there."

Mike shook his head. "We looked before. Didn't find anything. This is stupid. The kid's just buying time, wasting ours."

Trent shrugged. "Maybe you didn't look deep enough. All I know is that's where Cassel hid it. Your letter said the first place they met, right? That was right here in the mess hall. And my letter said the money was 'beneath the fire.' If this is where the original stove was, then this is where the money's buried."

Mike inspected the feet of the cast iron stove, sitting freely on the packed earth of the dirt floor. "You better be telling the truth," he mumbled, before throwing his whole body into the broad kettle-shaped appliance. He struggled, grunting loudly for a few seconds before it slowly began moving, inch by inch, back a couple of feet.

He handed the shovel to Trent and said, "Dig."

Judith had been at least ten seconds without a breath. The pressure on her throat was steady, pulling her back into Fischer's ample gut and once-muscular chest. Somehow, she still couldn't imagine that her old coach intended to kill her, but she had no plans to find out. She needed a reversal. Two points for a takedown One for an escape. Two for a reversal. She needed to even the score.

But how? Her superpower was that everyone who looked at her saw some harmless little girl. Some weirdo. Trailer trash. Again and again in her life, this had been her secret weapon. No one saw her as a threat until she'd already struck and it was too late. But Fischer was wise to her. He knew what she was capable of, and he wasn't about to underestimate her again.

Then she remembered her other superpower: she was double jointed. It was stupid of course as superpowers go. But every hero had a secondary power. Really, how often does freeze breath or the ability to control insects come in handy, compared to flight or super-strength?

Judith opened her mouth and imagined taking in a deep breath, then slammed her right elbow into Fischer's temple with all of her might. The pressure on her throat lessened for half a second and she leaned into the gun, gaining six inches and cracking the coach in the nose with her other elbow, bringing an explosion of hot, viscous gunk onto her arm. Fischer cried out in pain. Judith pivoted on her hip and slammed the shotgun out of his hands with both fists, sending it tumbling off into the darkness.

Cool, crisp air filled her lungs as she ducked under Fischer's clumsy swinging fist and spun to face him. A certain glee filled her up along with the precious, delicious air. She'd wanted this for a year. One on one with this Neanderthal. No mat, no ref. She pounced at his knees, as she had with Cash, intent on taking him down.

But Fischer sprawled, shooting his legs back, incredibly spry for his size, pinning her to the ground with his massive frame. A second later, she was up off the ground, upside down, locked in the coach's python arms. Then airborne, the earth and sky switching places. The mud broke her fall a bit, but the impact was enough to dislodge her excitement about the confrontation. She lay there for two seconds, gathering her strength, expecting Fischer to close in on her any moment.

But he didn't. He was hanging back, waiting for her. Toying with her. She smiled to herself. The Kryptonite had worn off already. She was once again no threat to her nemesis and that was her greatest strength. She pulled herself to her feet and assumed a wrestling stance.

"Seriously?" Fischer laughed. "Why don't you just quit, like you quit the team."

"Round two," she said through ragged breath. "Let's go."

"You don't want this, little girl," he sneered.

Judith wiped a clod of mud from her cheek. "No excuses. No delays."

A whistle blast filled the air, inaudible to all but Judith and Fischer. They clinched.

The sandy soil came away easily, clearing a funnel of earth away and creating a matching pyramid next to it. Trent was almost three feet down when the shovel hit something solid. Zoe practically shoved

Mike down into the hole to help. Within five minutes, they'd cleared off a half-rotten set of wooden shutters, which Mike threw open with a flourish.

The dank stench of mold came wafting out. Mike grinned up at Zoe. "This is it," he said. She smiled back—not an evil grin, but the same cute and winsome smile she'd used to jerk Trent around by the heartstrings.

Mike was out of the hole now, kissing her, deep and gross, like he was trying to repo her uvula. The gun in his belt beckoned Trent. He knew he should grab it now while they were both distracted, just as sure as he knew that he wasn't going to try.

Zoe broke off their embrace and wiped tears of joy from her pale cheeks. "And you were so sure it was at Picture Falls," she said, playfully.

"You got me," Mike said. "You were right." He looked down at Trent, who realized he was gawking. "Sorry to steal your girl, Marsh. Although, to be fair, I met her three years ago." He tossed him a flashlight and said, "Don't lose that; it cost me a hundred and fifty bucks." Grinning wickedly, he added, "Moment of truth, Marsh. You and Dad can either go home together tonight and get a good night's sleep or you can both make your final resting place right here, under the stove."

Despite himself, Trent let out a halted sob, which he managed to half-swallow.

"Keep it together," Mike ordered. "You want to live? Go down there and get our money."

CHAPTER THIRTY-ONE
"THE HIGH GROUND"

Trent descended through the shutters and into the void. On either side, rotting timbers struggled to hold back the earth from swallowing the pit as if it had never been there. The old wood of the stairs felt soft like Nerf treads beneath his feet. From Mike's flashlight, the cone of luminescence trembled as it played across first the floor and then the walls of the hastily dug cellar. Stepping into the middle of the cramped room, he did a full three-sixty survey. Nothing really to see except that, behind the staircase, the wall had collapsed in, admitting an avalanche of dirt and worms that seemed to be reclaiming the space like a glacier, an inch at a time.

"What do you see?" Mike demanded from above.

Trent finally looked down at his feet and felt his pulse pounding in his temples. There it was, all at once, just sitting there: the object of their search. Two ornate wooden chests, both secured with old fashioned padlocks.

"Looks like treasure chests," he called up. "Hold on, I'll feed them up to you!"

Hefting the first box, Trent felt his vertebrae compress and complain. He knew paper was heavy, but this felt like a box of concrete, leading him to worry about the integrity of the rotting stairs under such a load. What was in here? Gold? The bottom of the chest was moist and crumbling against his fingers. Would it even hold?

As he ascended the creaking stairs, he prayed that the contents were still viable. If they weren't, he had no doubt about who would bear the brunt of Mike's rage and Zoe's cold vengeance.

When he was still a few steps from the top, Trent hoisted the trunk up onto the dirt floor at chest level. It shuttered against the floor, but did not come apart. Mike brought the blade of the shovel down hard against the padlock three times, producing a shower of sparks but failing to break the mechanism.

"What are you lookin' at, Marsh?" he spat. "This ain't a union gig. Go get the rest of them."

Trent went back down into the darkness and fumbled with the other box, managing to lift it first onto his hip and then up against his chest. As he re-emerged into the soft light of the mess hall, the padlock on the first trunk finally exploded under the force of the shovel. Trenton heaved the second chest up next to the first and waited, his breath caught in his lungs. Zoe gently opened the lid, her eyes full of avarice and anticipation. Just then, something deep in Trenton's spirit pulled him back down the stairs.

Sure, he was beyond curious about the contents, but he already knew what they'd find. The old bills in the antique desk—those had been a down payment of sorts. *More where this came from,* was the implication. And these boxes, which were meant to be found and removed within weeks of their deposit, not languish here for more than a century, could never have protected stacks of paper currency.

As if to confirm his fears, Mike shouted a stream of curses, intermingled with words like "worthless" and "garbage." Trent stood frozen in the darkness while he listened to Mike savagely attack the top of the second chest. The sound of splintering wood was quickly replaced by another wave of rage and despair.

Trent knew there was nothing for him aboveground. He needed to make a stand down here. It was his only chance. Buy some time, lay a trap, and finally make his move. He was done being threatened and ordered around, wishing he had Judith's fearlessness.

First thing he needed was a weapon. Beneath the stairs, he found it, half covered by the cascading dirt: a board about eight inches wide and three feet long, broken off when the wall gave way. The end had cracked along a knothole, creating a nice, four-inch long handle of sorts. A little grip tape and it could have passed for a cricket bat.

He clicked off the flashlight and stuffed it in his pocked, retreating back to the rear of the chamber. This was his best bet for an ambush. That's when Trent saw the faint moonlight spilling in from the ruins of the back wall.

Another idea formed—admittedly a stupid one, but it was better than staying to fight.

"There's three more chests down here!" he shouted, "stacked up! Wait, no—six! And the top few are dry! Kind of hard to get to, though. Just a second . . . "

Trent climbed on his hands and knees, up the mini-rockslide of the collapsed retaining wall, holding the improvised club in front of him. Or rather, it was a digging tool now. At the top of the incline, a narrow tunnel branched left following a gnarled, brittle old tree root about ten feet, where it seemed to terminate with an opening at the surface—the source of the moonlight.

He didn't know if it was an intentionally dug air shaft or simply the result of the tree root dying, but it looked just a little too small to accommodate a full-grown man. Drips of water fell here and there from above, like underground rain. This long shot was looking longer by the second.

Using the end of the beam, he began widening the tunnel, knocking clumps of dirt from above, which he pulled back into the cellar.

"Let's go!" Mike called down. "You need help or what?"

"No. I got it," Trent answered as he tossed his club in ahead of him and wedged his body into the shaft, using the root to pull himself along. The earth around him was squeezing in and, with every foot of progress, he felt a little more trapped.

"Officer Tyrell, I need another set of hands here," Adam shouted, dusting his words with a bit of panic. Hunched over Jessie, back to his captor, he glance over his shoulder to see if the former cop would take the bait.

Tyrell approached two or three steps, then paused. "What is it." It was a challenge, not a question. His hand was wrapped around the grip of his pistol, still in its holster. Tyrell's 6'7" frame already gave him the high ground in any given situation, but this went well beyond. By any definition, he had the drop on them.

"I need you to hold his arms down while I pack this wound. We have to work fast."

Tyrell drew his gun and clasped it in front of himself, fig leaf. In this moment, the police uniform did nothing to hide the gangster lurking within. He shook his head. "I wouldn't bother, Marsh."

Adam rose to his knees and turned to face him. He held his arms up high, gesticulating wildly—misdirection—while he felt Jessie reach up, pull his shirt tail out, and slip the Kel Tec PF-9 from its concealed holster at the small of the chief's back. "This is getting out of control," Adam said. "You know what you need to do."

"Yeah," Tyrell agreed. "I do. Nothin' personal."

Adam swallowed hard. "You're overlooking something big, though."

"Yeah? What's that?"

He lunged for the pistol in Tyrell's hand and felt his fingers close around the metal slide. Tyrell resisted, slowly overpowering him with seemingly little effort, bringing the barrel of the gun back up toward the chief. Adam slid his left index finger into the guard, behind the trigger. Sure, his finger would be crushed, but at least Tyrell wouldn't be able to fire.

Throwing all his weight off to the side, Adam pulled him off balance and opened a clean shot for his ally.

"Drop it!" Jessie barked. He was on his back, the 9mm pistol sighted in right between Tyrell's eyes. "You've seen me at the range, Ben," he warned. "You know I don't miss."

Tyrell sneered. "You pull that trigger, Trenton's dead. She'll kill him without a second thought. You think I'm lying?"

Adam stomped the side of Tyrell's knee, filling the room with a *pop* and a scream of pain. Tyrell let go of his gun, which clacked to the ground and slid six feet along the wood floor.

Jessie was rising slowly to his feet and commanding Tyrell down to the floor. When he'd complied, Adam used Tyrell's own handcuffs to secure his wrists.

"Hey chief," Jessie called out, "watch your six."

Adam turned to see Sean, crawling with great pain and effort, a few inches at a time, toward the gun on the floor. With three quick strides Adam grabbed it up, Sean still six feet away.

"Come on Tailor," he said, "just give up already."

"Chief, I've got this under control," Jessie announced. "You go get your son."

Judith's body hit the ground again. She rolled and popped back to her feet, trying to look like she could do this all day. But she could feel fatigue taking hold. It was the third round. There wouldn't be a fourth. There never was. Fischer was still toying with her, but it was feeling less and less like an advantage.

She needed to fight dirty, to end this. Trent was in danger and every minute she wasted with this clown made it that much more likely that she'd be too late to save him. She scooped a handful of mud from the ground and launched it at his face. The clod pancaked against his eyes and Judith threw herself into his legs with everything she had. Her fastball had once been clocked at 84 mph. As she connected with Fischer's thighs, she chastised herself for throwing mud, rather than a stone.

Coach Fischer came a few inches off the ground. Then Judith felt four knuckles bury themselves into her spine. She went back down into the mud, whimpering despite herself. Fischer pulled her up by the wig, jerking at her scalp, and flung her six feet. As she landed, her skull connected with a rock, bringing a revived pain to her already bruised and lacerated head. She went limp and watched the coach walk right past her. Where was he going?

Like a poke from a cattle prod, she felt a surge of electricity and sprang to her feet. Fischer was going for the shotgun, which had bounced off in that direction. The wrestling match was over. This was life and death. Catlike and silent, she sprung onto his back, wrapping her right arm tight around his throat and clamping her left hand onto the back of his neck.

The sleeper hold.

Trenton was stuck now, without a doubt, and the seeds of claustrophobia sown at the silver mine were bearing fruit—a bumper crop of hysteria, almost ready for harvest. The moonlight taunting him a few feet away and yet utterly inaccessible, wasn't helping, nor was the sight of his digging implement, just out of reach and useless anyway with his arms basically pinned to his sides. Above him, the dirt was soft, wet, and smelly, while the rest was gritty and harsh. He'd been trying to push forward for two minutes and had succeeding only in wedging himself in good and tight, to the point where backing out was no longer an option.

He needed to further widen the tunnel somehow. To that end, he focused his efforts on arching his back up against the tree root and wiggling side to side. Perhaps he could use it to cut away some of the looser soil and kick it back down the shaft. Even if he couldn't escape, if he could just hide himself behind enough dirt, maybe Mike would waste time searching the grounds for him.

The root was moving more and more, coming loose from its former casement and encouraging Trent to push all the harder. This just might work. All at once, it snapped in two and Trent found his upper body rising up out of the earth, emerging through the dirt and grass like a zombie from the grave. He was no more than a foot from the wall of the mess hall, but he was outside and that's what mattered.

Clods of dirt rained down from his body as Trent stepped up and out into the night. He reached down into the earth and grabbed the board—a club once again—before circling around the back of the mess hall and padding down toward the bunkhouse and his dad.

When the sleeper hold had clamped down on him, Fischer seemed to waste precious seconds just trying to grasp what was going on. Then he went berserk, swatting at her with his beefy arms, which—single-jointed as they were—couldn't quite get a hold of her. She was counting silently. Fifteen seconds should knock him out. At least that's what the YouTube video had said. And she was at nine. Make that ten. Fischer's legs buckled beneath him for half a second, wobbled and then recovered.

Twelve seconds.

He and Judith spotted the shotgun at the same time, the metal glinting at them from six feet away. He lurched forward and, a moment later, had his hands on it, swinging the barrel back toward Judith's face. She tightened her grip on his throat and ducked her head as far back behind Fischer's monstrous frame as she could. Anyone in his right mind would know that a blast of buckshot at this range would be as disastrous to him as it would be to her, Judith thought. But Fischer was blinded by rage, his brain deprived of oxygen.

It had been sixteen seconds and he was still upright, still fighting. Maybe Fischer was right and the sleeper hold was the stuff of TV wrestling and schoolyard lore. Or maybe she wasn't strong enough to shut off the flow of blood and air under his flabby neck.

Just then, the coach collapsed hard under both their weight. Judith jumped off his back and tugged his arms out from under his torso. He was breathing deeply with a phlegm-rattling snore. Wasting no time, she went into her inside boot compartment and found two more zip ties. She was tempted to use them both on Fischer, but resisted the urge.

She'd need that last one.

For Zoe.

"Come on, Marsh," Mike shouted. "You don't want to play games with me right now. Trust me!"

"Go see what the problem is," Zoe ordered.

Mike drew his gun and clicked on another flashlight. "You try anything, I'll put six holes in you," he promised as he descended the stairs. This little pain in the butt had proven resourceful and beyond sneaky and Mike was ready for anything.

Anything except this. Trent had apparently disappeared into thin air. Mike swung the beam from his flashlight twice around the room before he noticed the only possible exit route.

Propping the light up under his pistol like a TV SWAT guy, he approached the deluge of dirt. Then he saw the tunnel, and the moonlight. He cursed and dashed up the stairs.

"He's gone!" he declared. "There's another way out down there."

"Well, go get him," Zoe countered. "There's only one place he can run: back to Daddy. When you find him, you know what to do."

Mike ran his fingers down his broken nose. "Gladly," he said.

He was halfway out the door when Zoe added, "And Michael? All of them." He nodded and disappeared into the night.

Left alone with the rotten fruits of all their effort and expense, Zoe realized that she didn't know if Trent had been telling truth about more money down below. Probably not. And that was okay. She had plenty of ideas how she could use this town to regain the inheritance that was rightfully hers. Of course, it couldn't hurt to check.

She descended the stairs hesitantly, her own compact pistol at the ready. It wasn't that she didn't trust Mike. He just wasn't that bright. She'd been cornered by Trenton once before and wasn't about to let it happen again.

But Trent was not down here. Neither was any more money. What a filthy, depressing place for this all to end. In a muddy pit. It wasn't a total disaster, though. The disappearance of several bedrock members of the community would be a great opportunity for her to step up—the heir to both the lumber mansion and the crusade to revive and reinvent the town. Not to mention the object of great sympathy at losing her "father." The mayor would throw in with her, as would the new chief of police.

And of course this particular muddy pit was the perfect place to bury four bodies. She remembered Sean's injury. Make that five. With a couple more to follow.

Adam made it all of fifteen feet toward the mess hall before a wave of nausea and vertigo seemed to spill down from his pounding head, bringing him to a standstill. He wavered for a moment, hunched over, hands on his knees, then puked up the two protein bars Jessie had given him. Two more dry heaves brought more pain to the back of his head, threatening to steal his balance altogether.

"God, give me strength and perseverance," he prayed. "Just five minutes. Then I'll collapse. I'll rest for a year. Just let me reach Trenton before it's too late."

He stood up straight. His head still ached. The world was still spinning. But Adam pushed on. This was his calling. He was a protector and no one was going to hurt his son.

Zoe mounted the steps up into the mess hall. She'd decided to leave the money in the pit with the rest of the loose ends—put this whole thing behind her. She was lost in thought as her head and shoulders emerged from the cellar, her ears perked for the inevitable sound of gunshots a stone's throw away. Instead, she noticed that the door to the mess hall was closed. Mike had left it open.

A flash of blue and something hard crushed her nose. The next thing she knew, she was lying on her back on the mud floor of the makeshift cellar, looking up at a bizarre sight. Backlit by orange light and framed by the open shutters was a masked woman with blue hair wearing a ridiculous outfit. There was something oddly familiar about her.

Wait. Could it be—? No way.

"I'm going to give you one chance to surrender quietly," Judith said, "because I'm the good guy. But if I'm honest, I really hope you don't take it."

CHAPTER THIRTY-TWO
"PEAVEY"

Trenton was closing in on the bunk house now, with no idea what he would do when he got there. Should he try and lure Tyrell out into the night and bash him over the head with the club? Or maybe sneak into the building all stealth-like to assess the situation first? Before he could make up his mind, he felt a burst of adrenaline chug through his body. Someone was running toward him, stumbling a bit, barely visible in the thin moonlight between the two buildings.

The man seemed to spot Trenton before coming to a stop and taking aim with a handgun.

Zoe came tearing up the stairs, sights set on Judith. She wasn't usually given to emotional outbursts, but the timing of all this made it pretty much inevitable: her least favorite yokel—the girl who stood for everything Zoe hated in Clinch Rock—would bear the blame and feel the pain for all of her wasted work. Judith was a perfect scapegoat and it would feel so good to break her. To kill her. One more loose end buried beneath the cook's range, never to be seen again.

As Zoe cleared the stairs, though, Judith stooped down, catching her abdomen at the shoulder, then stood, using her opponent's momentum to flip her onto her back.

The hard-packed earth stole the breath from Zoe. The landing had hurt, but more than that it enraged her. She stood quickly, dusting herself off. *Keep calm,* she thought. Judith was a simple brute, powered by angst, Mountain Dew, and whatever poor people ate. Zoe, however, would keep her head, approach this strategically.

Her gun was nowhere to be seen—probably down in the pit. But no matter. She assumed a turning stance and breathed deeply, remembering her training: slip her opponent's strikes, get in close and counter-attack with the heels of her palms, the knife-edge of her hands, her knees. Then a throw and a pin.

And a final blow.

"Well?" Zoe said. "What are you waiting for?"

Trent's momentum was too great for him to reverse course or even to come to a stop. Instead, he reared back with the club, gripping it in both hands.

"Trent?" the man with the gun called.

"Dad!" Trent abandoned the blow and went in for the hug instead, accidentally clapping the club down against his father's back.

"Get down!" his dad shouted, shoving him to the ground. The crack of a gunshot sounded from the direction of the mess hall. And then another, much closer, as his dad returned fire. "Go!" he shouted, shoving Trent toward a stand of trees just outside the clearing. Trent scrambled toward it, his father right behind him. Two more shots filled the night.

They took cover behind the broad, bare trunk of a white pine. Clearly the shooter had followed their path, as evidenced by an explosion of bark, nine inches from Trent's face.

The chief spoke into his radio. "Jessie, we got a shooter pinning us down here. If your prisoners are secure, I could use some backup."

"Way ahead of you," came the response, as Jessie charged out from the front of the bunk house, the chief's backup piece in one hand and the shotgun in the other. He fired a round from the pistol, then dove for cover as Mike returned fire. Two bullets missed him by inches, shattering the reproduction kerosene lamp on the front porch.

Grabbing the distraction, Trent's dad fired three more rounds up toward the shooter. Trent could see that he was still not 100%. Not even close. His arms wavered as he tried to steady the gun and the bullets buried themselves in the earth thirty feet short of their intended target, resulting in little explosions of mud like tiny landmines.

It was clear to Trent: the three of them were indeed pinned down. It was bad. And then there was the question of Zoe's whereabouts. She had a gun too. For all he knew, she was coming around behind even now to flank them.

Adam turned his attention back to Trent. He gripped him solidly around the back of the neck, and said, "Sherriff's less than twenty minutes out. Eight deputies with him. We just need to stay alive until then." He looked deep into his son's eyes and said, "Promise me you'll stay low, out in the darkness until it's all over." He didn't wait for a response. "I'll draw his fire away from you. I love you son."

Before Trenton could object, his dad stumbled out from behind the tree, toward the sound of the gunshots.

Judith flashed her hand up to Zoe's face, bringing a flinch from the slender woman. In that blink of an eye, she shot for Zoe's left leg, sweeping it up. Flawlessly, she went for the single-leg takedown. Two points.

A blow to the ear from Zoe's palm rocked her head and Judith dropped the leg, dazed. Another blow—this one catching the bridge of her nose, had her reeling. Disoriented. She looked up at the insufferable young woman before her and had a vision of her standing behind Trent's house, bragging about all her training in some obscure form of karate or something. Apparently that hadn't been all talk.

A kick to the abdomen, barely even a blur, doubled Judith over. She overrode the pain and stood again, hands up in a wrestling stance. With each blow she felt a little slower and a little weaker. This wasn't like fighting Fischer. Sure, he broke the rules, but at least they had the same rulebook to begin with.

Zoe was hanging back now, waiting for Judith to come to her. She'd come alright. Like a freight train. Kung Fu didn't work on freight trains. With a yell, Judith threw herself forward.

Calmly, Zoe stepped back from the blitz, snagging Judith's outstretched hand and bending it hard against her forearm, creating a flash of paralyzing pain. Judith fell backwards and gasped at the sharpness of it, her arm now bending backward, at its absolute limit. Struggling only made it worse, so she stopped fighting and went limp.

For the first time it occurred to her that she might be outmatched. At least here and now. The reality was that she'd been exhausted before this confrontation even started. If tapping out were an option, she'd gladly take it, no shame. But, of course, it wasn't an option.

The unmistakable *pop-pop* of two gunshots sounded outside.

"You hear that?" Zoe asked, grinning. "Sounds like your boy-friend's dead."

More gunshots. Seemingly from every direction.

Trent crouched at the base of the pine and willed his thoughts to come into focus—like they had at the waterfall and out in the wilderness of the camp. What would Judith do if she were here? That was the question that had brought such clarity in the woods that morning. He closed his eyes and breathed deeply. He could feel the gears turning and his pupils dilating.

His eyes opened and an epiphany formed. Make that two. First: he realized he could see Mike's position, hunkered down behind a woodpile a ways up the slope, choosing each shot carefully, taking his time. Trent's night vision seemed almost superhuman in that moment, to the point of making out the permanent bro-sneer on the guy's face, thirty yards away. Secondly: Trent realized he was still gripping the improvised club he'd found in the cellar.

A third insight followed. He knew exactly what Judith would do in this situation. She'd silently make her way over to Mike while the punk was singularly focused on the firefight, and knock his block off. That was the insane thing to do. And if ever there was a time for a little insanity, it was now.

Judith swept Zoe's legs out from under her and pounced, landing a solid punch to the jaw. She pulled her fist back for another blow, but her opponent was gone, rolling to her feet. Slippery.

Zoe was anything but unscathed, though. Her shoulders heaved up and down, her fists clenched in an apparent attempt to hold in her rage. Blood dribbled from her nose, and her hair had come loose, frizzing up all around her. She was no longer smiling, but the *crazy* in her eyes was all the scarier.

Then, all at once, her rage seemed to melt away. The *crazy* was still there, beneath the surface, but it wasn't the out-of-control kind. More like the earn-your-trust-and-kill-you-in-your-sleep variety.

More gunshots sounded outside. "That's a lot of shooting," Judith said. "Might not be my boyfriend who's in trouble."

Zoe shrugged. "It doesn't matter. Mike is a means to an end. And tonight's the end. For all of you."

Sean Tailor's words played over in Trenton's mind as he cut his way through the woods, toward Mike: *If either of you is signing up for YLBC, don't even think about sneaking out after curfew. Mike Van Buren will sniff you out, hunt you down.* He prayed it had been an empty threat, even as he prayed that the sound of the gunshots would drown out all the noise he was making, despite his efforts at stealth.

Trent went deeper into the woods, the details of his plan falling into place. Behind Mike was twenty feet of open ground. Too risky. But if Trent approached him from the side, he could see a path to victory. Just six feet from the cover of the trees to his target.

He was still a ways back in the woods when Mike ducked down to reload. This would be the perfect moment to strike: rush him and crush him before he could slide another magazine in. But Trent wasn't close enough. A moment later, Mike popped back up, looking down the sight of his gun for one of Clinch Rock's finest.

Trent was at the edge of the woods now, still wavering. He had to attack; his dad's life depended on it. But he couldn't ignore the fact that he'd brought an old, broken hunk of wood to a gunfight.

The blow had been to her throat, but it was really a matter of tripping over her own feet that brought Judith back to the hard ground. She commanded her body to once again roll with the momentum, bounce back up. But her body disobeyed and absorbed the impact. The noise that escaped her mouth sounded more like a whimper than Judith cared to acknowledge.

Lying there, one eye swelling shut beneath the mask, blood trickling from one nostril and one ear, she looked up at her arch-nemesis, now going in and out of focus like the image on a broken video camera: Zoe hovering overhead, waiting for the chance to knock her down yet again.

Judith thought about the weapon in her left boot. It would be easy enough to pull it out, surprise her enemy, end this. *No.* Superheroes didn't have that option. It would be better for her to go down fighting.

Maybe it didn't matter that Judith couldn't win. Her goal had been to save Trenton. And he wasn't here. Outside, the sound of gunfire persisted, meaning the fight wasn't over. And undoubtedly more cops were on the way. It would only be a matter of time before the bad guys were outnumbered and all was set right. In the meantime, perhaps she was meant to sacrifice herself. Was anything more Insane than that?

The image came back into focus again, but it wasn't Zoe in frame. It was something hanging from two pegs on the wall, next to the door by which she'd entered. Judith closed her eyes and gave her head a little shake, which answered with a roar of pain. But when she opened her eyes, the thing was still there. This made no sense. Was it possible she'd missed it coming in? And of all things why would there be an ox goad hanging on the wall of this rugged structure just outside Clinch Rock?

Then again, what did it matter? Whether a figment of her imagination or a divine appointment, Judith had nothing to lose by going for it. Reaching into the zipper compartment inside her right boot, she pulled out the last three smooth stones and hurled them at Zoe with all her might—the biggest one first, and then the other two at the same time. One of them connected with Zoe's forehead, throwing her back.

Powered by the last fleeting fumes in her tank, Judith rolled to her feet and stumbled forward, reaching out for the ox goad. She half expected her hands to pass right through it—an apparition. Instead, Zoe's dainty hands snatched it right out from her grasp.

The implement was tipped with six-inches of steel, which came to an abrupt point, with a nine-inch hooked spike protruding from it.

With some effort, Judith chuckled. She was on her feet again and figured she may as well fight on until there was truly no fight left in her. "Do you even know how to use an ox goad in combat?" she asked. "Not many people do."

"It's called a Peavey, you imbecile."

Judith pushed the blue hair from out of her eyes. "Well, whatever you call it, bad choice, Princess."

Trenton was still hesitating back in the brush when Mike casually glanced his way and the two of them locked eyes.

Now or never.

Bursting out from the trees, the club high above his head, Trent rushed his nemesis, screaming bloody murder, fully expecting to feel a bullet tear through his chest. But Mike just stared back in disbelief as Trent brought the club down against his wrists with all the might and momentum at his disposal. It broke off at the handle and the brunt of the thing bounced up against Mike's face, knocking him back two steps.

Trent dropped to his knees, frantically searching for the gun. It should be right here somewhere. His eyes and fingers desperately worked over the ground beneath him. But he saw nothing.

Then he saw Mike reach down to his ankle and pull out another pistol. He laughed. "Nice knowing you, kid."

"I'm so bored with this," Zoe said. "I mean, I think we both knew how it would end." She gripped the long handle of the Peavey with both hands, leveled it at Judith, and ran straight for her.

Judith sidestepped the attack and the spiked tip embedded itself between two pine panels. Pushing off from the wall, she slid along the shaft and slammed her shoulder into Zoe's, sending her sprawling to the ground like a hockey player checked off the boards. With a single tug, Judith freed the implement from the wall and gave it a tight spin, feeling it out. The bull-roar of the weapon cutting through the air filled the little building. It was a familiar sound to Judith, and a familiar feeling.

"Let me show you how it's done," she said.

"Freeze!" The command sounded almost comical to Trent, who had never been more frozen in his life. It was his dad's voice, coming from behind him, full of authority and strength. "Drop the weapon or I will fire."

Trent raised his head and saw Mike's right hand holding the pistol down at his side. Looking back, he saw his dad, gun clasped in two steady hands, leveled at the perpetrator.

Not feeling even a little silly about it, Trent scurried back on all fours until he was safely behind his father.

"I won't ask again," the chief warned.

Jessie rushed up beside him, shotgun at the ready. Mike looked from one cop to the other and dropped the pistol.

"Hand's on your head," Adam ordered. "Good. Now tell me: where's the girl?"

Zoe rose from the dirt floor, doing a poor job of masking her pain. She reassumed her fighting stance. "You don't get to win," she said. "You're a loser, Judith. A zero. You'll never be anything. Never *have* anything. Face it: you wouldn't even have Trent if I hadn't tossed him aside." She lunged at Judith, who popped her in the forehead with the handle of the Peavey, snagged her around the neck with the curved metal hook, and launched her into the wall. Zoe staggered a bit, like a drunk leaving a bar.

"I'm going to enjoy killing you," Zoe vowed, shaking it off. The conviction had left her voice, but she seemed unable to turn off the monologue "I doubt anyone will cry. I wonder how many will even notice."

Judith swung the handle of the Peavey down, catching Zoe behind the knees and dumping her to the ground. Zoe rolled to her stomach and was beginning to rise when Judith brought the side of the steel head down against her shoulder blades like a sledgehammer.

Zoe Frobisher, direct descendant of Heinrich Wellick, crumpled back to the ground. "I hate you," she wheezed. "White trash." A string of epithets followed, interwoven liberally with four-letter words.

Judith pushed the sharp tip of the Peavey firmly against Zoe's back and snickered.

"Now who's low-class?"

Adam rushed toward the mess hall. His head was still full of sand and pain, but the world was no longer spinning. And things were looking up. Trent was safe. Most of the perps were either dead or in handcuffs . . . But he would not let the ringleader slip away. This ended tonight. With a solid kick, he broke open the door of the mess hall, pistol at the ready.

He intended to shout, "Police!" but what he saw stole the breath from his lungs: a masked woman with blue hair securing Zoe's hands behind her back with a thick blue zip tie.

Looking up at Adam, she said, "All yours, Chief." She then reached into her left boot and pulled out a compact pistol, which she set carefully on the floor. "Here's her firearm."

Adam smiled for a moment, but went serious when Judith did not reciprocate. "Whoever you are," he said, "Clinch Rock owes you a great debt."

The masked woman nodded once, solemnly, and faded out into the night.

"You know that's Judith Morgan, right?" Zoe scoffed, face down on the ground.

"You and I haven't really met, have we?" Adam said. "I'm Chief Marsh. And you are under arrest for the murder of Brian Green, as well as attempted murder, conspiracy, breaking and entering, and about a dozen other things—including breaking my son's heart. You have the right to remain silent and I suggest you use it."

TEN DAYS LATER

"I can't believe Jason would miss this," Judith said.

She and Trent were sitting on his bed, waiting rather impatiently.

"Yeah," Trenton said, "he swore he was going to be the *Geraldo* of the appraisal, whatever that's supposed to mean. But he's grounded for like six more weeks now."

"Because of the van?"

"Uh huh."

Judith grimaced. "That's kind of our fault, isn't it?"

"I guess. But who cares?"

They could hear his dad coming down the stairs now, leading at least two others. Trent felt his stomach tighten up a little, mild nerves.

As it turned out, the money in the two chests was undeniably the property of the Clinch Rock Independent Church (now Clinch Rock Community Church), as evidence by a barely legible handwritten note from Cassel, placed in each trunk. But since the chests and their contents were now evidence in an open case, getting an appraisal done had proven rather complicated.

To that end, Chief Marsh had e-mailed half a dozen experts in antique currency, only one of whom offered to drive up from Detroit and have a look at the money in the evidence room of the Lake County Sheriff's Office. It had been Trent's idea to also invite an antique furniture appraiser from Traverse City to have a look at the desk, down here in its not-so-natural habitat.

Trent's father entered the bedroom, a man and a woman trailing behind him.

"Kids, this is Phil Kay and Erin Baldwin," he said. Then, pointing first at Kay, then at Baldwin, he added, "Money. Furniture. And speaking of which, here's the desk." He gestured into the mouth of the tunnel.

The appraiser gawked for a moment before entering the chamber and examining the antique, opening the rolltop and all the drawers.

325

"Have you already appraised the old bills?" Judith asked Mr. Kay.

"Yes," he answered, "and I'm afraid the water damage has rendered them quite worthless. It's a shame too. The lot of them would have gathered quite a sum in mint condition. Thousands."

"Oh," Trent said. His disappointment was deep, but not unexpected. It was surely a longshot that anything good would come out of the whole mess that had embroiled their town. Still, he had been unwilling to let go of hope altogether.

Mr. Kay smiled sympathetically. "Sorry to be the bearer of bad news. Quite a story, though. I actually tagged along here because I was curious about this tunnel and the old map. What a fascinating find."

Ms. Baldwin turned her attention from the desk to those gathered around it. "I'm sorry, but I've got more bad news. There's nothing remarkable here, except for the provenance. I'd recommend keeping it. Maybe put it on display in your church. It's worth more as a conversation piece than as a piece of furniture. On consignment, you might get twelve hundred for it. Probably less."

Adam nodded. "Well, I appreciate your time and expertise. Both of you"

"But wait," Judith said. "What was wrong with the first two bills? They weren't damaged."

Mr. Kay furrowed his brow. "*First two?* I'm not sure what you mean."

"The ones from the desk."

"Oh my gosh," Trent said. "I totally forgot." He rushed over to his bed, unzipped his pillow and withdrew the two fifty dollar bills, still in the acid-free sleeve. Scrambling back into the tunnel, he handed them to Mr. Kay.

The appraiser carefully slid the bank notes out and set them on the desk, turning the first one over twice. "Hmmm. Very good shape," he said. "At auction, you could probably get four or five hundred for it." He then turned his attention to the other note and froze, mouth agape.

"Well, this is something else," he finally managed. "Serial number one thousand. That's a collector's dream. These 1882 series fifty dollar brown backs are very scarce. And I've never seen one issued by this bank. Never even heard of one. Factor in that serial number and you'll get multiple collectors fighting over this item at auction. Bet on it."

"More than five hundred dollars, you think?" Trenton asked.

"I wouldn't be surprised if it brought more than fifty thousand."

Trent caught his dad's eye. "More than enough to reroof the church," he said. "The next pastor can come in without all that doom and gloom hanging over their head."

Adam smiled. It was the kind of easy smile Trent had been seeing more and more this past week and a half—Old Dad, who (ironically) looked quite a bit younger. It was as if all the stress and demands of *Insane Faith* had been packed up in the boxes all around them. Yes, father and son had begun repacking their things, just two weeks after finally getting settled into the parsonage. There was no hurry, but eventually the old house would be home to someone else, ideally someone whose call to ministry had come from the Spirit within, not guilt from without.

In his newly recovered spare time, Trent's dad—no longer a graduate student or a cleric—was interviewing officers to replace the three now awaiting trial. He'd also taken over the Youth Leadership Boot Camp program up at Picture Falls, enjoying the comradery and one-on-one mentoring of the position far more than he'd ever enjoyed preaching. Judith was signed up now too, taking Zoe's place, and the group had already met twice with big plans for mission trips and discipleship activities well into the school year.

A sense of peace enveloped the secret chamber.

In that moment, the two strangers seemed to fade away and the three of them—Adam, Judith, and Trent—huddled together. A family of sorts. They'd been through so much together and they'd learned even more: life was not about seeking out insanity to prove yourself worthy of God's love. It was about a willingness to be faithful through the dull days and the wild ones alike. To live a quiet life as far as they were able, all the while ready to endure whatever may come, for the sake of the Name.

And whatever came their way, one thing was sure: it wasn't on them to be the heroes of this story. That role was already filled.

ABOUT THE AUTHOR

Zachary Bartels is the author of critically acclaimed Christian suspense novels. An award-winning preacher and Bible teacher, Zachary has served as pastor of Judson Baptist Church since 2005. He holds degrees from Cornerstone University and Grand Rapids Theological Seminary.

Zachary lives with his wife and son in the capital city of a mitten-shaped state, where he enjoys film, fine cigars, stimulating conversation, gourmet coffee, reading, writing, and cycling. He also hosts *Clinch: A Podcast of Fiction and Not-Fiction* and co-hosts *These Go to 11* and *The Gut Check Podcast* (www.zacharybartels.com/podcasts).

You can find more information about Zachary (as well as follow his blog, Twitter, and Facebook) at www.zacharybartels.com.

www.ingramcontent.com/pod-product-compliance
Lightning Source LLC
Chambersburg PA
CBHW060357260626
47160CB00006B/2343